DEADLINE

BLOOD TRAILS, BOOK 1

JENNIFER BLACKSTREAM

SKELETON KEY PUBLISHING

DEADLINE
A Blood Trails Novel, Book 1

USA Today Bestselling Author
JENNIFER BLACKSTREAM

To join my mailing list, visit
www.jenniferblackstream.com

Deadline
©Copyright Jennifer Blackstream 2017, Skeleton Key Publishing
Edited by 720 Editing
Cover Art by Yocla Designs © Copyright 2017

Join my mailing list on my website www.jenniferblackstream.com to be alerted when new titles are released.

To my children, who are my own pixie familiars. I hope that, like Shade, you have the courage to live your dreams, no matter how scary they might seem...

ACKNOWLEDGMENTS

To Alexandra and Jes, whose enthusiasm gave me the boost I needed to get through edits. To my sib who read this more times, in more versions, than any sane person should have to. To the Dragon, who burned the first beloved manuscript. And to Capt. Flanigan, who provided invaluable technical advice.

"The eye sees only what the mind is prepared to comprehend."

— HENRI BERGSON

DEADLINE

JENNIFER BLACKSTREAM

"Mrs. Harvesty, I told you, I cannot call your cat Majesty. It sets a bad precedent for the relationship."

My knees screamed in protest from holding a crouching position for too long, and I winced. Squatting on the floor behind the driver's seat of a parked Ford Focus just wasn't something a person over the age of eight was built for. I kept my cell phone pressed to my ear, careful not to mash the red end call button as I shifted from foot to foot. The pain persisted.

"But that's his name!" Mrs. Harvesty insisted, her voice cruelly amplified by the phone. "And he's such a beautiful kitten, when you see him you'll understand why I call him that. If you could just come over now. Please?"

"I will not call him Majesty." I leaned my head against the back of the driver's seat, resisting the urge to use a healing spell to give my aching knees relief. My mentor, Mother Hazel, would burst into flames if she learned I'd used magic for something as ridiculous as personal comfort. "Mrs. Harvesty, I'm very sorry your cat isn't feeling well, but I can't come over just this second."

My familiar, Peasblossom, shot me an amused glance from her position on the dashboard. At six inches even, she was an average height for a pixie, though she could seem bigger when she was mad. Right now, she was playing lookout, the morning sunlight glinting off the gossamer wings humming behind her back. It was February, and since we were outside in a cold car, her wings vibrated constantly to keep her warm, filling the air with a low buzzing sound. I raised the slim dagger clutched in my right hand and jabbed it toward the windshield. Peasblossom scowled, but returned her attention to the river ten yards away from where we were parked at the edge of the tree line marking the southern border of Dresden Park.

"But I'm only a few blocks away!"

This is Dresden, Ohio. Everyone *is only a few blocks away.*

"I see it!" Peasblossom gave a little hop as she pointed out the windshield. "It's there!"

A trickle of adrenaline leaked into my bloodstream, chasing back the discomfort in my knees. I gripped the dagger, the hilt a familiar weight against my palm. "I'm sorry. I have to go. I can come over tomorrow." I unfolded myself from the floorboard to sit on the edge of the back seat.

"*First* thing tomorrow? The very first thing?"

I let my head fall forward, my long, dark hair cascading around me in a shroud, mourning the death of my resistance. "Yes, fine. First thing tomorrow."

"Oh, all right. Goodbye then, Mother Renard."

A tiny snort was all the warning I had before something snagged hold of my hair and used it like a climbing rope. I rolled my eyes to the side and glimpsed tiny pink hands. After the electronic beep in my ear assured me Mrs. Harvesty had hung up, I scowled and let the phone thud to the floor of the Focus. "It's not funny."

"It's a little funny." Peasblossom snickered, feet bracing against my skull as she shimmied the last few inches. She sat on my head with a light thump, sliding her fingers through my hair to hold on.

"I have asked her numerous times not to call me 'Mother' Renard. I told her, Shade is fine, Ms. Renard is fine."

"Mother Hazel won't like to hear you say that. 'Mother' is the proper title for a witch."

"A few centuries ago," I muttered. "Now it just makes people look at me funny."

"Well, Mother Hazel is old. Set in her ways." Peasblossom snickered again. "Too bad for you she took the time to introduce you before assigning you this village."

I gritted my teeth. Yes, she had. And unfortunately, when Mother Hazel told people to do something, they did it. Whether it was to take the "medicine" she'd given them, stop doing something she said they oughtn't do, or call someone by a seemingly ridiculous title. Of the one thousand or so people who made Dresden their home, only a handful truly believed I was a real witch, and understood the title. The rest just thought I was strange.

Mrs. Harvesty was the former.

"It needs to stop. I can be a proper witch without the antiquated title whether Mother Hazel thinks so or not." I peered out the windshield to assess my prey's progress out of the river. A shiver ran down my spine, and it had nothing to do with the car's cold interior.

The *eurypterid* dragged its body out of the freezing brown water of the Muskingham River, brittle legs scuttling over the hard-packed dirt of the riverbank. A cross between a lobster and a scorpion, the beast was four feet long from the base of its tail to the pincers curving from its jaw. It stabbed into the muddy riverbank with a spike-tipped, swollen claw big enough to take a child's head off—children being a favorite meal of the opportunistic aquatic predator. Beady black eyes glittered from an armored face, and small, arched legs pushed it forward. Morning sunlight reflected off its midnight-blue, segmented body, highlighting the long stinger tipping its knobby tail.

3

"What are you waiting for?" Peasblossom said. "Make with the magic and let's go home! I'm cold." Her wings vibrated harder for emphasis.

"One lobster dinner, coming up," I murmured.

Power warmed my insides as I called my magic, drawing it like water being pulled from the depths of a natural well. I pressed my lips together and hummed, the vibration twisting the energy into a cone. Pressure built in my lungs, up my windpipe. I inhaled slowly, deeply, making room for it to expand. I held the creature in my sight and jerked the car door open. Rising in one smooth movement, I held on to the edge of the car door and braced one foot on the frozen ground. The vortex struck my voice box and I screamed.

Sound waves spiraled outward in a piercing sound that only my target would hear, striking it in a whorl of red energy before it could register my presence. The hard shell of its body cracked under the force of the spell, the scream flowing past my lips vibrating its exoskeleton until it shattered. The force of it was more than I'd expected, and my control slipped. Pain sliced into my throat, filling my mouth with the taste of copper as the magic drew blood on its way out. I choked, the sound ending in a wet gurgle.

"Are you okay?" Peasblossom asked, worry pushing her voice higher.

"I'm fine," I rasped. I winced and swallowed more blood. It wasn't much, but even a few drops felt like a mouthful. For a few seconds, it was all I could do not to vomit.

"Serves you right for thinking you could do a spell like that without any gestures or the proper materials to focus. A little mint oil rubbed on your neck in a spiral would have saved you the sore throat."

I slammed the car door behind me, ignoring my heaving stomach. She wasn't wrong. Casting a spell meant harnessing my magic, bending it to my will. There were a variety of ways to focus that energy, words, gestures and materials. Casting the spell without said foci was akin to catching a wild horse by tackling it out in the open. It could be done, but the experience was often painful and significantly less dignified than the alternative.

"I need to practice controlling it with my will. I won't always have the luxury of time to get my materials ready, or draw out the proper gesture." I held the dagger ready as I crept closer to the broken corpse of the *eurypterid*. I didn't think it could have survived, not when I could see the damage even from several yards away, but better safe than sorry.

I needn't have worried. As I stood over the monster, I noted that shards of its own body had punctured its guts, turning its internal organs into so much putrid meat. Brackish blue blood seeped onto the frostbitten ground, giving the surrounding dirt a cerulean sheen in the morning sunlight.

"Ew, it smells like rotten eggs floating in rancid milk." Peasblossom shifted on top of my head. "Talk about an appetite killer. I should have eaten breakfast before we left."

I didn't bother pointing out I'd said as much before we'd got in the car this morning. I-told-you-sos rolled over a pixie like water off a mermaid's back. Instead, I tightened my grip on the blade and knelt to cut off the stinger.

"I thought these things were saltwater creatures?" Peasblossom said.

"They are." I gripped the tail, careful not to cut myself on the broken pieces of exoskeleton protruding inches from my knee. "Either this one made the impressive journey from the Gulf of Mexico, up the Mississippi River, across the Ohio River, and into the Muskingum River…" I sighed. "Or someone's pet grew too big and they tossed it in the river."

"Probably an ogre. Or a troll."

"Any species might have done it." I put the tip of the blade between the metasomal segments of its tail just below the stinger. "No one says no to children anymore."

"Is that really necessary?" Peasblossom asked.

"Waste not." I held my breath and shoved the blade through the plastic-like chitin of the *eurypterid's* armor. It tore with the dull cracking sound of a shrimp being shelled. I tried to block out the smell of the creature's bodily fluids as I severed the stinger from the end of the tail. It wasn't as bad as it might have been in warm weather, but even the winter air couldn't protect me from the putrescence when I was kneeling right beside it. A particularly stubborn piece of exoskeleton halted my dagger, and I put more weight into my efforts. My center of weight shifted, and I lost my balance, catching myself with a knee on the ground. Something wet soaked through my leggings. I cursed. Make that kneeling *in* putrescence.

I pulled hard on the stinger, cutting through the last of its tail with one final grunt of effort. Peasblossom wrinkled her nose at my leggings.

"You're going to have to— Look out!"

Pain erupted in my thigh and all the air left my lungs on a gasp. Peasblossom screamed. The stinger and my dagger fell from my fingers, and for a second all I could do was stare in shock at the six-inch stinger piercing my thigh.

The *eurypterid* hadn't been alone. Its mate crouched behind me, hissing as it reached for me with monstrous black claws, ready to tear off hunks of flesh in a mad rage. My heart lodged in my throat, blocking the scream bubbling up my windpipe. Venom burned my thigh, and already I couldn't move my leg. I lunged forward onto the ground, closing my mouth on a scream as the stinger pulled free of my leg with a wet sucking sound. I tried to roll, desperate to avoid the first grab of its claws, but something caught on my leg, keeping me from turning.

"Shade!" Peasblossom shrieked.

"Get back!" I clapped a hand over my thigh to staunch the flow of blood. I didn't have time to heal now, I had to stop it before it struck again. If it managed to inject its venom into my neck, or my chest…

I raised my free hand, magic tingling in my fingers and the words of a spell forming on my lips. The *eurypterid* jerked me back with enough force that my face hit the ground.

Pain radiated from my cheek and I grunted, my magic dispersing as my attention faltered. Panic turned the air in my lungs to shards of broken glass as I realized the *eurypterid* had snagged my ankle. It should have hurt, but it didn't. The venom had already rendered the entire limb numb.

I sucked in a startled breath just before the monster dragged me off the bank and into the river. The frigid water ripped a gasp from my lungs as it sucked the heat from my body. My heart pounded and my muscles tightened, violent shivers rolling over me. I flailed, but it was no use. I snapped my mouth shut a second before the water closed over my head.

A cold, dark death waited for me at the bottom of the river, rushing to meet me as the aquatic beast pulled me deeper. The icy water made it hard to move, my body already sluggish, not wanting to obey my commands. I shoved my hand down, desperation barely enough to force my fingers against the claw around my ankle. I concentrated on the feel of that limb, digging my fingers into the pockmarked exoskeleton. I centered myself as best I could with my instincts screaming at me that I needed air *now*.

Glatio.

My teeth chattered and I pressed my lips harder together to keep water from seeping into my mouth. I thought the word for the spell in my mind, imagined myself saying it, pictured my lips moving. I visualized green light flowing down the monster's body, freezing the water around it.

Energy pulsed from my hand, biting the tips of my fingers as ice formed over the *eurypterid*. Elation shot through me, fighting back the shock threatening to render me motionless. I kept my hand on the claw, my lungs burning, warning me that, victory or not, if I didn't get to the surface soon, I would drown. I poured more energy into the spell, thickening the magic. Triumph filled me as the buoyant ice rose to the surface—dragging me with it.

The first breath hurt, as if my lungs had already resigned themselves to death and were caught unprepared by this sudden demand for breathing. I gasped and maneuvered onto my back with my would-be assassin still attached to my ankle, floating until I could regain the strength to swim to shore.

"Shade!" Peasblossom stomped on my forehead.

"Hey!" I shouted, lifting my head to keep my face from being dunked underwater.

"You're alive!"

"Not for long if you keep pushing my head underwater." My teeth chattered violently. It should have hurt my jaw, but I felt no pain. That was bad. The ice-cold water had slowed the venom's progress and kept me from bleeding out from the wound in my leg, but now I had hypothermia *and* a neurotoxin working against me. I needed to get out of the water, and I needed an antidote. Now.

I opened my eyes to see Peasblossom's face pinched with worry. I forced a smile even as the shivers turned violent, making the world around me jerk up and down. "I-I'm ok-k-kay. T-t-told you I needed to p-p-practice without the w-words and m-m-m-m-materials."

With a grunt of effort, I lunged for the shore. Peasblossom stayed on top of my head, her calm a testament to her faith that I could make it out of the freezing river.

"Shouldn't have let your guard down." She sniffed. "Lazy witching, that's what that was."

It took me three tries to make my hand hold the edge of the river bank, and another two tries to hold myself out of the water enough to unzip the black nylon pouch around my waist. I held it out of the water as much as possible while I clung to the bank and dug around for a potion. "There sh-sh-shouldn't have been one in the r-r-river, let alone t-two."

"Live and learn," Peasblossom said, climbing up the wet tendrils of my hair. "If you're lucky."

A handful of mint leaves, two grocery store receipts, and a pack of gum met my shaking hand before my fingers brushed the potion bottle I needed. The glass warmed my palm, making the water around me even colder by comparison. I pulled it out and popped the cork to take a drink. The orange peels mixed with chamomile soothed my throat as I swallowed, the magic of the potion flowing through my body. The antidote would neutralize the venom, but I was still bleeding, still needed a healing potion. *First, get out of the river.*

"I'll get it. You just hold on." Peasblossom dove into the pouch in a zip of pink light, vanishing into the enchanted, bottomless depths.

"H-hand me a h-hammer, w-would you?" I called out.

After a few loud I-hope-you-appreciate-my-effort grunts, the handle of a hammer poked out of the pouch. I grabbed it, then set to work prying the claw open. It wasn't easy with my arms shaking worse by the second, but my efforts had the added benefit of warming my muscles and getting my blood flowing again. By the time my ankle was free, I had the energy I needed to haul myself onto the bank.

When I finally got the trunk of my body out of the water, an evil voice told me to rest, just lie on the bank and catch my breath. I'd killed not one, but two *eurypterids*, and survived neurotoxic venom, a vicious leg wound, and freezing to death in an icy river. Surely I deserved just a tiny rest. Just a little...

I didn't even realize I'd closed my eyes, until Peasblossom stepped on my throat.

The pressure hit the cut on my windpipe from earlier, and a few drops of blood oozed down my throat. I gagged and blinked, the bright morning sky stabbing at my eyeballs. "What—"

Peasblossom didn't wait for me to finish. The pop of a cork was the only warning I had before the potion hit the back of my tongue. I swallowed quickly, automatically. The flavor of cherry blossom and elm bark coated my taste buds, and I let out a relieved breath as the dull ache in my thigh eased away. The next time I swallowed, there was no blood.

"You'll need to make more potions. You've been using too many of them this past week."

"Goddess, you're feeling judgy today," I grumbled. "I've been working overtime this past week. I'm tired."

Peasblossom snorted. "Lazy. Witching."

I opened my mouth to argue, then closed it. The pixie was right. Drawing magic from inside myself as I needed it required concentration and effort. Casting spells wasn't unlike flexing a muscle, and like using a muscle, you had to keep working it to make it stronger. Of course, no matter how strong that muscle got, there came a point when exhaustion and exertion took their toll. I had enough magic to cast spells indefinitely, but casting after a certain point was like firing a gun while riding a Jet Ski through rough surf. Dangerous for everyone. Potions, on the other hand, could be made ahead of time and took only a few seconds to gulp down when the need arose. Easy peasy.

Before I could defend myself, a new voice came from the path weaving through the forest around the park.

"Mother Renard?"

"Blood and bones," I cursed. I shot to my feet, swaying with a brief bout of vertigo. I fumbled in the pouch for the wand I always kept there. Chewing gum, cough medicine, a single sock. "Come on, come *on*."

"You are so disorganized." Peasblossom sighed.

I ignored her, raising a slim wand of pale ash in triumph. With a so-there lift of my chin at the pixie, I flicked the wand toward my head.

"*Prestidigitation.*" The spell broke over me in a rainbow of colors, washing the bloodstains and the river water from my clothes and hair, and blessedly lifting the *eurypterid* blood and guts from my leggings. They were still torn in the thigh where the stinger had stabbed me, and punctured at the ankle where it'd grabbed me with its claw, but there was no time for a mending spell. I looked at the rank remains of the first *eurypterid* and the grisly ice cube I'd made of the second. "Bugger."

Leaves crunched a few yards away, and a surge of adrenaline spun me around. I pinned a smile to my face to greet the approaching young couple, both wearing vibrant blue and green running clothes. The man was a stranger to me, but I recognized the girl. "Good morning, Amy. Please, call me Shade."

"Shade," Amy said. The sun struck her brown hair, turning it almost blonde as it swung back and forth in its ponytail. "Are you all right? I—" Suddenly her gaze landed on the creature at my feet. Her eyes bugged out of her head and her jaw dropped. "Oh my God."

The brown-haired man at her side wrinkled his nose at the shattered *eurypterid*. "It's amazing what some people throw in the woods. Like nature is their own personal garbage can. Is that a vacuum cleaner?" His hair was cut short at the sides and back, but the bangs were left long so they swung forward as he angled his head to see over the bank, looking directly at the second *eurypterid*-turned-monster-cube. "Man, they really unloaded all their trash. Is that thing shrink-wrapped?"

"You're not from Dresden, are you?" I mused.

In my experience, humans fell into three categories. Those who believed in magic with all their hearts, those who were open to the idea, but hadn't witnessed anything to cement the belief, and those who rejected the idea of magic so completely that they could come face to face with a *eurypterid* and see...well, a discarded vacuum cleaner. Or shrink-wrapped garbage.

Amy had just moved from "magic is possible" to "oh, my God, magic is real." The way she looked at me now made me think we had an interesting conversation in our future. When my mentor, Mother Hazel, had assigned me to Dresden, she'd been upfront about telling everyone I was a witch. But it was one thing for Amy to think I was a witch as in a New Age practitioner of Wicca, and quite another for her to realize Mother Hazel might have meant something completely different.

"Amy, who's your friend?" I prompted.

"This is…Jeff. He's…my boyfriend." Amy gaped from one monster to the other. "What…?"

I gave her a sympathetic pat on the shoulder. "It's upsetting, I know. Perhaps you could come by later this week and we'll have a chat over a nice cup of tea?" I turned to Jeff. "It's a shame, isn't it? Terrible how some people treat the earth, just tossing their garbage wherever they please."

"Yes it is. I love your accent, by the way. Where are you from?"

If he couldn't see the mess before him for the dead monsters they were, then he certainly wasn't ready for the real answer to that question. I smiled. "London."

"I thought so."

Peasblossom snorted from her hiding place under my hair. I cleared my throat and planted my hands on my hips. "Well, I'll call someone and have this hauled away, I suppose. I don't want to keep you standing here in the cold. It's important to keep the blood pumping when you take a constitutional in February."

Jeff smiled at me again and clapped his gloved hands together. "An excellent point. We should keep moving. It was nice to meet you, Shade."

"The pleasure was mine. Amy, perhaps I'll see you later?"

Amy blinked, still staring at the dead *eurypterid* as Jeff pulled her to continue their walk. When they were out of sight, I braced my foot on the monster's remains and shoved it into the water. There were plenty of fish who would appreciate a free meal.

Waste not.

I scooped up my dagger and the stinger and tucked it into my pouch, already thinking of what I could use it for. A dagger, sure, but perhaps something more creative. A cup. If I removed the venom…

"You'll be late for your next appointment," Peasblossom reminded me.

I swore and ran to my car, creative thought process severed. "Bryan! I forgot."

"That's why you have me." Peasblossom grunted and tightened her grip on my hair. "Slow down, I'm falling off!"

"You *fly*!"

She sniffed at me as I climbed into the car and slammed the door behind me. "I know I can fly. But why expend unnecessary calories when you're right there?" She tucked herself into the neck of my shirt, cuddling close to my skin to get warm. "I swear, sometimes I don't think you appreciate my company."

I ignored her, all my attention on getting home as quickly as possible.

It was never a good idea to be late to a meeting with the FBI.

CHAPTER 2

Dresden was only one square mile total, so it took less than two minutes to get back to my house. I pulled into the garage and headed inside, making a beeline for the refrigerator.

"Didn't you say you weren't drinking soda anymore?"

I popped the top on the can of Coke and took a defiant swig, more than a little satisfied at the squeak of dismay that came from my judgmental familiar as she wavered on her perch atop my head. "I earned this. I killed a *eurypterid* before breakfast. Two *eurypterids*. And I almost died. Not to mention, Mrs. Harvesty kept me on the phone for ten minutes talking about that cat."

"I hate cats." Peasblossom clung to my head like a living barrette. "Nasty beasties, always try to eat me like I'm a flying snack. Barbaric."

"I love cats. I just don't want to drop everything because Mrs. Harvesty claims her furry little child is having an emotional crisis."

"Emotional crisis?"

"The kitten is refusing to come out of his mummy's boot." I held a sip of Coke in my mouth for a moment as if I were sampling fine wine.

Peasblossom snickered. "Puss in Boots."

I snorted, then swore as carbonated soda shot up my nose, burning like fire. Peasblossom careened off my head in a fit of mad giggles as I ran to the stove and the faded blue hand towel hanging there.

"Blood and bones, that burns," I wheezed, squeezing my eyes shut as I pressed the towel to my nose.

More laughter made me open my eyes in time to watch Peasblossom fly in a semi-drunken bobbing path to land on the counter beside the stove. Tears of mirth glittered in her pink eyes, matching the iridescent sparkles on her insect-like wings. "Serves you right for drinking a *second* soda."

I glared at her for a few minutes as I waited for the burning to stop. When I'd recovered, I replaced the wet towel with a clean one and deposited the soda-and-snot-spotted cloth in the hamper. "If you're quite finished, perhaps you could run me through today's to-do list? I want to make sure I didn't forget anything."

Still giggling, Peasblossom flew to the large desk in the dining room and picked up a sheet of notebook paper tucked beside the laptop. "Settle dispute between the hamadryads over who's the eldest," she read.

"Done. Once they realized the only way to age a tree is to lop off a piece of it, they were happy to call it a draw."

"Find out if a goblin ate the Roberts' dog."

"No. Sgt. Pepper was hiding under the neighbor's house *again.* Mrs. Barns just didn't want to admit it because she didn't want to hear Mr. Roberts accuse her of trying to steal his dog for the tenth time. Sgt. Pepper went home when he got hungry."

Peasblossom peered at me over the top of the list. "Find an office."

I took a long swig of the soda, avoiding eye contact. "Move it to tomorrow."

"Again," Peasblossom said under her breath. She put the paper down and hefted a miniature pen she'd taken from a child's art kit. Sticking out her tongue in concentration, she made a notation on the to-do list.

Aluminum groaned as I tightened my grip. "I *will* do it."

"Of course you will. Because you're going to be a real detective."

"Private investigator. And yes, I am."

"Mother Hazel won't like it."

I clenched my teeth. No, my mentor wouldn't like it. I could hear her voice now, telling me to leave the battling to the wizards—witches had more important things to do.

Like play psychiatrist to a cat.

I strode over to the desk, put the can of soda down with a determined thunk, then snatched up a stack of Post-its and a black fine-point marker. Peasblossom watched as I scrawled, "Find an office today," and underlined *today* three times. I stuck the reminder to the frame of my computer screen.

"You used a hot-pink Post-it. You must be serious now."

I ignored her sarcasm. I *would* find an office tomorrow. It was time.

I didn't know how long I'd been Mother Hazel's apprentice. Her house existed betwixt and between, both here and there. Time didn't know what to do with it. I'd never kept a calendar before moving here.

Dresden—current population one thousand and some change—had always been a favorite place for Mother Hazel to take us, a fact that, in retrospect, should have warned me of her intentions. We'd often left the odd sanctuary of her house to visit the village, and I'd been there when she gifted the first tomato seeds to the town's founder. I'd greeted the first of the Longabergers, who later made the village famous for their wicker baskets, and I'd watched Dresden along with the rest of the world say goodbye to horse and buggies and radios the size of furniture, and hello to automobiles and smart phones. I'd known this town long before I lived here. Long before I knew it would become my responsibility.

"I tried it her way. She wanted me to be the village witch, and for three years, I've been exactly that. I've assisted with child rearing. I've provided medical care. I've helped with crops, protected my people from Otherworldly threats. I've been everything and anything my people need me to be."

Peasblossom landed on my shoulder. "And you've done an incredible job. But you still need this, this private investigator dream. Why?"

To the best of my knowledge, there were no witches in my family. When whatever force had imbued me with my magic had done so—and they hadn't held back—they'd left me drunk on power I had no control over, or understanding of. For years I'd been "sick" or "crazy." I hadn't learned the truth of what I was until after I'd made some terrible choices.

"I have to balance the scales," I said quietly.

A tiny pink hand stroked my cheek. "The only person who hasn't forgiven you yet is you."

I studied the tab on my soda, plucking at it with my short fingernail. "Then I'm doing it for me. This is what I need to…to…"

Tears blurred my vision, catching me by surprise. I stared at the Post-it. "I've had such a late start."

"A very late start," the pixie agreed. "But you're a witch. You have centuries of life ahead of you." She paused. "And, maybe, behind you. I wonder if Mother Hazel knows how old you are."

"I'd rather not know," I muttered, heading to my bedroom for a change of clothes. "Bad enough she treats me like a teenager. If I find out I'm two hundred years old and still being treated like I'm sixteen, I'll need a hundred-year lie-down."

I found a clean pair of leggings and a fresh shirt, and was just putting on my boots when I heard a knock at the door. Peasblossom tucked herself under my hair, and I waited for her to get settled before going to greet my guest.

Bryan Foundling stood on my doorstep, his five-foot-eleven frame forcing me to crane my neck to peer up at him from my five foot three. He'd combed his brown hair, and his light beard and mustache were trimmed until they were little more than a pale shadow over his jaw line and around his mouth. He wore dark blue jeans and a midnight-blue shirt, both of which were neatly pressed. A black leather jacket offered protection from the stiff February wind.

"Hi, Bryan. Please, come in." I stepped back and gestured for him to enter.

"Your first real case," Peasblossom whispered.

I snuffed out the hint of excitement that rose at Peasblossom's comment. Bryan worked at the FBI, yes, but he wasn't an agent. His mom had mentioned something about working security, checking IDs at the door and such. Still…

I led Bryan to the center of the living room. Like everyone who came into my house, it took Bryan a while to examine his surroundings, the little furrow between his eyebrows deepening as he did so. He took in the small windows in my living room, the bare beige walls, the single gray couch with its little side table. Then he swept his gaze over the kitchen-dining room area that held a desk where the table should be. It was a violent contrast to my mentor's house, with its herb-covered walls and magic-item-strewn tables and chairs. There was scarcely room to breathe in Mother Hazel's house for all the things she kept around, and by comparison, my house was downright Spartan.

Exactly the way I wanted it.

"Doesn't look like a witch's house, does it?"

I'd meant to put him at ease, but he jerked like I'd smacked him. "No. I mean, yes." He scratched his head. "Er, I mean—"

"Bryan, please relax." I offered a reassuring smile. "It's not what the fairy tales led you to expect, but I promise, I'm a proper witch. And I can help you with...?"

His eye twitched at the words "proper witch," and I thought he would look down, stare at my magenta and black spattered leggings—the bane of my mentor's existence. I wasn't sure what bothered Mother Hazel more, the brightly colored leggings or the fuzzy, multi-hued, pink-faux-fur-lined slipper-boots. Bryan earned a lot of Brownie points when he nodded without commenting on either.

"It's my friend Andy, Mother Renard. An agent in my building. He's working a case, and I think... I think it's *Other.*"

"Other" and "Otherworld" was how most humans referred to the non-mundane world. "Other" was an adjective, and Otherworld was an umbrella term that encompassed all the magical people and creatures that lived both here in the "real world" and in places like the astral plane or the underground realms of the high-court fey. I nodded and gestured to the couch for him to sit. "You don't have to call me Mother Renard. Shade is just fine."

He slid his hands over his legs as he sat, clasping his knees as if to ground himself. "But I thought... I wouldn't want to be disrespectful."

"It is not disrespectful for you to call me Shade," I promised. As soon as the words were out of my mouth, I paused. My mentor wasn't the only witch who insisted on the title of "Mother" as a necessary sign of respect. Bryan wasn't likely to encounter many witches, let alone those who would stand on such old-world ceremony, but still... "Since I asked you to," I added. "It's always safest to address a witch with their title unless you're invited to do otherwise."

"All right...Shade." He waited as if expecting a sudden strike of lightning from the clear morning sky.

I cleared my throat. "You were saying about your friend Andy?"

"Andy, yeah. Well, a few weeks ago, he was assigned a missing person case. An architect's husband reported her missing. The FBI doesn't usually handle missing person cases without some evidence that the person's been transported over state lines, but this lady, Helen Miller, might have connections to organized crime."

"She worked for the mob?" I asked.

"Not exactly. There were two drug raids, one in 2011 and one in 2015. In both cases, the drugs were hidden in a secret room on the property. Secret rooms aren't unusual, but these two had traps set up to burn the evidence if someone tried to get into the room without disabling the device first. Weird traps like something you'd see in a Dungeons & Dragons game. The agents on the case were able to trace the work back to Helen Miller." He shrugged. "They watched her for a while, but they could never prove she had connections to the drugs beyond building the rooms."

"And building the rooms isn't illegal."

"Right. And it doesn't look like any of those people had a reason to want her dead, either. So far, she has no enemies, no criminal record." Bryan leaned forward, resting his forearms on his knees. "It's been three weeks, and no one's heard from her, no one's seen her. Not a single clue."

"But there's no body." I raised my hand to take a sip of my Coke, only to realize I'd left it on the desk. "You said you thought it was Other," I continued, resting my hands in my lap. "What makes you say that?"

"It's Andy. He's not a superstitious person, and he doesn't believe—" He stopped and swallowed hard.

I waved a hand. "You won't offend me, Bryan. I know most people don't believe." I grinned and glanced at his arm where I knew a scar lay under the shirt sleeve. "Not everyone is bitten by a *kobold* as a child."

Bryan put a hand over the scar, rubbing it through the the cotton. "Yeah, I guess." He shook his head. "You told me once that nonbelievers can't even see the Otherworld when it stares them in the face, even though they've always been around, always existed right alongside us."

I thought of Amy's boyfriend Jeff. "That's right. The brain is a powerful organ, and it's nothing for someone to reimagine something Other as mundane. It's how a lot of people keep their sanity."

"But it's possible for them to change, right?"

I shrugged, trying to keep my mind on the subject at hand instead of the myriad of questions swarming my thoughts. I wanted to ask Bryan what he knew about the case. What mob had they thought the victim was involved with? What did he know about her relationship with her husband? Was foul play ruled out?

I reminded myself that this was not Bryan's case. And it wasn't mine. He was here because he was worried about his friend, and he wanted me to determine if something Other could be involved. End of story.

For now.

"Anything is possible," I said. "Do you think Andy is on the brink of believing?"

Bryan sighed and leaned back. "Andy is the most analytical person I've ever met. Have you ever seen an old western? *Cheyenne* or anything like that?"

An image of James Garner in *Support Your Local Sheriff* popped into my head, and I nodded. "Yes."

"That's Andy. Always calm, always taking things in, processing. He's your archetypal lawman. But this case… Every time he visits the missing woman's husband, he gets back to the office and he's…different."

"Different how?"

This time Bryan's eyes met mine and held them. "He looks *shaken*. Mother Renard—Shade. Andy doesn't get shaken. And last time he came back, he shook my hand and his skin was ice cold. I can't help but think of a story my mom told me about my aunt right after my uncle died, and…" He shook his head. "I think Andy's seen a ghost."

A ghost. My brain came alive with everything I knew about the undeparted dead. Not every person who died became a ghost. Usually, a ghost came from an individual who'd suffered an injustice in life, something disturbing enough to keep them from resting in peace. The injustice could be real, or imagined, but either way, the spirit remained trapped on the physical plane, unable to put things right. I'd only dealt with ghosts a few times, and never without—

An older, feminine voice came from the doorway behind me. "A ghost, you say?"

Bryan shot to his feet like a child caught playing with his father's power tools. "Mother Hazel."

I swallowed a groan as I rose to face my mentor. Mother Hazel stood by the door leading into my kitchen from the garage, her spine ramrod straight so her brown robes fell in long, sloping lines from her five-foot-seven frame. Her hair hung down her back in a wind-tossed waterfall of gray, with a long lock on either side of her face brushing the edge of her skirt when she moved. She carried the scent of herbs and fresh earth, but if you stood closer to her, you'd pick up traces of other scents. Chicken feathers and iron shavings. There'd been a time she'd intimidated me, but living together, for however long it had been, had changed our relationship.

Now her interference was just annoying.

"Mother Renard." She held my gaze, making it clear she knew what I was up to and what her thoughts on it were.

"Mother Hazel." I picked an invisible piece of lint from my eye-melting leggings.

Her eye twitched, and she took her attention off me to focus on Bryan. Her mouth lifted into a bright smile, her blue eyes no longer piercing, but full of welcoming light.

"A pleasure to see you again, child. I've just come from a lovely visit with your mother. She tells me you're doing well, very successful at the FBI." She said the last line the way a grandmother might tell her grandson how proud she was that he'd learned all his colors.

Bryan bowed his head at the compliment. "I try."

"But you need help now, it seems. Help from our young Mother Renard?"

I gritted my teeth and walked around the couch to put myself between my mentor and Bryan. "He's here to talk about some difficulties his friend is having. A good idea for him to consult a witch, don't you think?"

Mother Hazel nodded, as I'd known she would. My mentor was of the opinion that a witch should be consulted about everything, from childbirth to what occupation best suited a person. Witches are experts in everything, that was her motto.

"Yes, always best to consult a witch," she agreed. "But have you considered a private investigator?"

Bryan went still. "I... I didn't realize..." He looked at me like a man who'd eaten the last cookie, only to find it belonged to someone else. "I thought *you* were a private investigator?"

"I am." I spoke with all the authority I could manage with Mother Hazel's stare boring into the back of my skull. "You know what, Bryan, why don't you write down the address of the missing woman's house? I'll pay Mr. Miller a visit now and see if I can't get a feel for what's rubbing Andy the wrong way, and I'll call you and let you know what I find out. Sound good?"

Even with the old witch hovering like a specter of death behind us, Bryan's shoulders sagged with relief. "Thank you, Moth— Shade. I would appreciate that."

I beamed at him in reward for using my name, my pulse quickening when he pulled a small notebook and pen from his breast pocket. I could feel Mother Hazel seething behind me, stewing over hearing someone use my first name. As soon as he finished writing the address down, I stepped forward and plucked it out of his extended hand.

"Thank you."

"Thank you." He inclined his head toward Mother Hazel. "And thank you. Have a wonderful evening."

After the door closed behind him, I locked my gaze on the soda still sitting on my desk and marched toward it.

The old crone's voice followed me. "I overheard Mrs. Harvesty talking about her cat. She says she called you and you refused to come."

My sip of Coke deepened to a gulp. The slip of paper crunched as I made a fist, pressing my knuckles to the desk.

"Will you be shirking all your duties to pursue this...detective dream of yours?"

Carbonation burned my throat, convincing me to abandon my wild soda consummation. The half-full aluminum can made a less-than-satisfactory thunk as I thumped it down and faced my fate.

"I told Mrs. Harvesty that I would see to her cat first thing in the morning. I couldn't leave immediately because I was waiting for Bryan." I stuck my chin out. "And I haven't shirked any of my responsibilities."

"The new mothers meeting?"

"Mrs. Smith has decided to let Thea eat oatmeal whenever she wants. I told her if Mrs. Roker tries to lecture her again about forcing a child to eat what they don't want, she should call me and I'll have a word with Mrs. Roker."

"And when you said 'have a word?'"

"I lowered my voice and give her a witchy look."

Mother Hazel cackled. "Good, good." She paused. "Let me see your witchy look."

I sighed, but did as she'd asked. The expression, in my mentor's opinion, was the number one weapon in a witch's arsenal. It ranged from mild disapproval to a full-on evil eye, and was best used to remind people that witches were not to be trifled with. Ever.

"Good. Your eyebrows are getting the hang of it. I don't think you're ready for a haunting."

The compliment-slash-insult was one of her favorite tactics, and I knew her well enough that it didn't faze me. "I am ready, and I am going."

I blinked and the old witch was standing at the desk, staring down at the ink-spattered paper and the runes I'd been attempting yesterday. My hands tingled with the urge to cover it, but there was no point. Runes were the magical equivalent of today's QR code. Only instead of a barcode pattern being read and translated by a camera or computer, the runes were careful inscriptions written by magic users that could be consciously or subconsciously read by the intended audience. Some runes were obvious, intended to be read by whomever saw them and could translate them. Mine were subtler, worked into what the untrained eye would see as a decorative design. Only the person's subconscious would get the message.

"You're using runes to advertise on The Web again."

As always, she made the words sound capitalized.

"I am."

She looked down her nose at me. "You sound like a wizard. Witches do not advertise for their services. We are sought when we are needed."

"I'm not putting out an ad for a witch's services. The ad is for private investigating—period. I put the runes in the logo."

"These runes are designed to speak to people without them realizing it." She squinted at the wriggly lines again. "People who've seen or sensed something Other will feel you're someone who will believe them, help them." She straightened. "I assume that's what coaxed our young Bryan to come to you with this missing person-ghost business?"

I only hesitated for a second. If she wanted to know, she'd

find out anyway. "I put the same runes in the card I sent him for winter solstice last year."

Something passed through the old witch's eyes, emotion I almost would have called pride. "Clever."

Tension seeped out of my shoulders. I didn't need my mentor's support, but having it would make things easier. "Thank you."

"It was my idea." Peasblossom leaned around my neck, emboldened by Mother Hazel's sudden approval.

"The runes or turning my apprentice into a wizard-ish crime fighter who will like as not get herself killed and leave her community witch-less?"

"Just the runes," Peasblossom squeaked.

So much for approval.

Mother Hazel stared at me, a penetrating but not unsympathetic gaze. "You still feel guilt for your past. You've chosen a very specific means of redeeming yourself, this private investigating business. Why?"

I'd asked myself the same question. More than once. "Do you remember Mary Jane? The dancer who lost all her money and committed suicide?"

"New York, 1943." Mother Hazel tilted her head. "What about her?"

"I met her mother a few years after that. The poor woman was still as devastated as if it had just happened. Couldn't believe her daughter had killed herself."

"The loss of a child is always sad," Mother Hazel said gently. "And no mother wants to believe her child would take her own life."

"I know. But something she said bothered me. She went on and on about how Mary had been so responsible with her money. Always saved, always sent money home. She'd taken care of seven brothers and sisters, sent them all to school."

Mother Hazel considered that. "You think someone stole her money."

"I know they did. I looked into it." I went to the computer and grabbed the mouse, quickly accessing the folder where I kept old cases. "Mary's neighbor, a man unfailingly described as mean and lazy, experienced a mysterious gain in wealth at the same time Mary lost all her money. I saw a picture of him in the local paper and he was holding a *toyol* statue." I found the picture I was looking for and clicked on it, making it as big as I could and zooming in on the statue held in the man's tight-fisted grip.

Mother Hazel frowned at the screen. The *toyol* had a childlike stature and the bald head of a newborn, though its head appeared too large for its body. The statue was a pale grayish-green, with red eyes, and small streaks over its surface gave the impression of fur not unlike a monkey's. "He summoned a *toyol* to steal her money?"

"Yes." I rubbed my arms to get rid of the sudden chill. *Toyol* were disturbing spirits, created by using a special embalming process on an aborted fetus. Their nature hovered somewhere between a child and an animal, and when one was summoned to be used as an Otherworldly thief, it had...needs. One such need was sucking blood from its master's breast or toe, and being provided a child's toys to amuse itself between thefts. Disturbing on so many levels.

"You never told me you discovered this crime."

I didn't bother pointing out that such an action would invariably have led to a lecture on abandoning my studies for frivolous sleuthing. "I reported it to the Vanguard. That's what they're there for, right? To keep the Otherworld from preying on humans?"

Mother Hazel crossed her arms, probably in response to the derision in my voice when I spoke of the Vanguard. She knew my thoughts on the Otherworld's version of INTERPOL. I wasn't a fan.

"What does this have to do with your need to redeem yourself this way?"

"Members of the Otherworld shouldn't be able to get away with murder just because humans don't believe in them enough to protect themselves." I lifted my chin. "I won't let them get away with it."

"As you said, that is what the Vanguard is for. It is left to them to deal with those who take advantage of humans, to mediate disputes between species."

"But most humans stopped believing in the Otherworld a long time ago," I argued, rubbing my chest to ease a sudden tightness around my heart. "They think people who call themselves witches are just people who practice a New Age religion. The vampires and werewolves pass as human, and if a monster does manage to kill someone, the death is attributed to a natural predator, a shark or a tiger. Humans are easy prey to any Otherworlder who cares enough to be subtle. And they get away with it."

"Like you did," Mother Hazel said softly.

I blinked, surprised to find tears in my eyes. I wiped them away. "Yes."

The harsh lines of the crone's face softened, making her look like a kindly grandmother instead of a stern witch. When she spoke, her voice was softer too, a gentle admonition. "There are other ways for you to find forgiveness. Have you given any more thought to calling your sister?"

"No." I took another sip of my soda, ignoring my shaking hand. Memories battered against the psychic wall I'd erected to protect myself, memories I'd promised myself I'd examine later, after I'd become the sort of person who could face them.

"All right." Mother Hazel nodded. "All right."

Somehow her kindness was harder to bear than her disapproval. I took another sip of soda, trying to drown the sob attempting to crawl out of my throat. When I thought I could speak without my voice breaking, I put the can on the desk. "I can do this."

Mother Hazel sighed. "I trust you remember how to prepare for encountering a ghost?"

I took a step toward my back room and all my supplies. "Yes."

"Shade?"

I paused, looked back over my shoulder. Mother Hazel's face grew serious, an unsettling intensity in her eyes pinning me in place like a physical weight.

"Your path is forking. Once you take this step, you can never go back."

It sounded like something you'd find in a fortune cookie, but Mother Hazel's voice gave the words power, drilling them down into my soul. I'd known this decision meant a fork in my path, every choice did. But the way Mother Hazel said it… It sounded more important. More final. No going back. A chill ran over my skin and I shivered, my eyes drifting closed.

When I opened them again, she was gone.

CHAPTER 3

"She's dead, isn't she?"

Peasblossom's voice was tinier than usual, even with her arms around my neck and her mouth a hair's breadth from my earlobe. I patted her between the wings with one finger, trying to ignore the chill coating my skin like the kiss of unnatural fog. I stood in the Millers' driveway with my feet planted on pristine white cement, but I hadn't quite managed to make myself close the car door. Instinct screamed at me to keep it open. Be ready for a quick escape.

"We don't know she's dead." I pried my hand off the door, forcing myself to step back so I could close it. My nerve endings tingled, aware that there was no longer anything standing between me and that house. I pulled a gem from my pocket, staring down at the multifaceted cerulean surface. A pulse of blue light flickered inside the stone, confirming what my fight-or-flight reflex had already told me. That *haunted* house.

It towered before me, the crown jewel of a neighborhood that looked like it would cost a hundred dollars just to drive through. White stone glowed in the high noon sunlight, a few spots of darker stone providing artistic contrast. A heavy mahogany door topped a small front porch squeezed between two massive white pillars that screamed decadence more than functionality.

But no beauty could hide the shadows. Darkness unrelated to a lack of sunlight teased the edges of my vision. I stood in full sunlight on a day that felt more like May than February, but even my bones felt the cold.

"She's dead," Peasblossom repeated.

I put the stone in the pocket of my shirt, squaring my shoulders as I faced the house. "It could be a different ghost tripping the spell." I gestured behind the house. "That's Lake Erie. We're not that far from the wreck of the Anthony Wayne."

"The Anthony Wayne," Peasblossom echoed. She stood a little taller, and for a second I thought she'd fly up to get a better look at the water. "I don't remember that one."

My brain seized the welcome distraction, and I nodded. "It happened at the end of the eighteenth century. The Anthony Wayne was carrying wine and whiskey along with almost a hundred passengers from Toledo, Ohio to Buffalo, New York. They were near this area when two starboard boilers exploded. Only thirty people survived."

"That's awful."

I looked out at the lake, the slate-gray water looking even more ominous in the light of the grisly images parading through my mind. I hadn't been there for the wreck, but I remembered reading about it in the paper the next day.

"You know, the strange thing is, both of the boilers that exploded were brand new," I murmured. "They shouldn't have malfunctioned, let alone exploded."

"You suspect foul play?"

"I wondered," I admitted. "At the time, Mother Hazel wasn't giving me much free rein. The wreck happened just after that unfortunate incident with the banshee."

Peasblossom shuddered. "Let's not talk about that. Lesson learned, don't anger the washerwoman."

"I should have looked into it. You know, there was a man on board with his two children. They were escorting his wife's coffin to Buffalo to be buried. When the ship sank, he put his children on her coffin to keep them afloat." Sadness swept over me and I looked away from the water. The waves had eventually swept the young boy off the coffin. Only the father and his daughter had survived. Peasblossom didn't need to know that part of the tragedy, though. Despite her bravado, the pixie had a soft heart.

"Maybe instead of this private investigator business, we can be salvagers? Eh?" Peasblossom suggested. "Modern-day treasure hunters. Much safer than hanging about with a dead woman."

"We don't know she's dead," I said again. I tore my thoughts from the past and faced the door to the Miller home. "We have to stay objective. Leaping to conclusions won't do anyone any good." I straightened my fleece wrap, making sure it was tucked securely over my shoulder. "Did you find anything else on Mr. Miller?"

"He has a few social media accounts, but he hasn't been very active. Some of his profiles are private, but from what I could see, it was mostly friends and family offering condolences on Helen. People stopped saying she'll be back about three days ago." She poked me in the neck with one tiny finger. "We'd know more about him if you'd asked Bryan for the file."

"First of all, we weren't hired to find Helen Miller," I said calmly. "We were asked to find out if Bryan's hunch is right, and there's a ghost haunting the Miller house. Second, Bryan doesn't have access to those files, so he'd have to ask the agent assigned to the case. We need more to bring to the table if we're going to earn a place in the investigation."

I'd parked in front of a massive, five-car garage, and I had to resist the urge to peek inside one of the small windows lining the brown doors just to distract myself from what I knew was coming. One foot in front of the other carried me to the front porch, and with grim determination, I climbed the four small steps and knocked on the door.

"She must have been a successful architect to have a beach-front home." Peasblossom cleared her throat. "Living at the edge of the water, they must have seen more than their fair share of the Otherworld. Think he'll see me?"

"Best not to find out. If he's living with a ghost, he'll be on edge. No need to push him over."

I'd half expected an argument, but Peasblossom edged around my neck and wormed under the fleece wrap to drop into the small decorative hood on the back of my shirt. "Taking his own time to answer, isn't he?"

"It's been half a second. The house is huge, it'll take him ten minutes to walk to the door."

It didn't. The door opened before I'd finished speaking, revealing a man in his mid-thirties or early forties. Brown eyes showed too much white, and a brown beard did nothing to hide the gauntness of his face. Product-tamed hair betrayed signs of having a hand run through it a few too many times, and dark circles under his eyes broadcast a lack of sleep. The black pants and collared white shirt hung on his frame as if he'd lost a lot of weight, and for a tense moment I feared he'd spill out of the door and collapse onto the front stoop.

Before I could offer him a juice box or a cookie—both of which I had in my waist pouch—he gave me a smile that didn't quite reach his haunted eyes. "Hi. Can I help you?"

"Hi, are you Mr. Miller?"

"Yes."

I raised my hand, simultaneously drawing on my power, threading it through my voice. "My name is Shade Renard. I'm here to talk to you about your wife's disappearance."

He swayed forward, swallowing hard. "Have you found her?"

"I'm sorry, no."

Suspicion narrowed his eyes and he tightened his grip on the door. "I don't recognize you. You work for the FBI?"

I poured a little more magic into my voice. Purple light glittered in the air between us, imperceptible to anyone but me and my familiar. "I'm consulting for the FBI. I'd like to speak with you inside for a moment, if that's all right? It won't take long."

The mention of going inside drew a flinch from my host, and for a moment I thought he'd refuse even with the charm softening his resistance. Now that I thought about it, he'd come out on the porch as soon as he'd answered the door, even though that meant leaving less-than-polite distance between us. Tension hummed in his body, and when I took a small step back, he followed, as if fighting the urge to run away from the house. *He's terrified.*

"I promise it really won't take long." I gave the magic another push to get past not only his natural suspicion, but his apparent desperation to flee, to get away from something inside the house. His wife's ghost, I guessed.

Finally, he nodded and stepped back. "I'm sorry, where are my manners? Yes, of course. Come in, please."

Cautiously, I crossed the threshold. A cold wind that had nothing to do with the February chill swept up my spine. Mr. Miller held out a hand, offering to take my wrap, but I shook my head, using the length of black fleece to hide my hand as I drew a few symbols in the air.

"*Revelare*," I whispered.

Power pulsed through the room in a wide silver net. It settled like a film over my surroundings, but there was no answering tingle of energy, no twinkling lights snared in the net. The wind wasn't magic, then, not a spell. There were no enchanted objects nearby, not beyond what I carried myself. I slid a hand into my pocket, opening it to glance down at the stone inside. The blue light glowed brighter. A warning the undead were near.

"Mr. Miller?"

"Yes?"

"Did your wife have a favorite room?"

He paused in the entryway to the living room, a cavernous area outlined with leather couches and dominated by a theater-worthy entertainment center. "She liked the porch. Said it helped her dream of new buildings when she wasn't trapped inside an existing one."

I pretended to scratch the back of my neck, trapping Peasblossom where she'd crawled out to have a look around. She strained against my hold, and I could almost see her reaching for the shiny buttons glittering from the media center. "Could I see it?"

Something passed through his brown eyes, deepening the crow's feet at each corner. One hand closed into a fist. For a moment I thought he would refuse my request. Perhaps being in her favorite room was too painful. Then he nodded.

"This way."

Everything in the Miller house screamed class and expense—all the furniture butter-soft leather, all the carpets so thick it was like walking on a cloud. There wasn't a single scratch on any of the polished wood, not a smudge on the stark white walls. Even with the ghost's presence pressing against me, the unmistakable dread filling every breath of air with the despair of the undead, I was acutely aware of the fact that just a few hours ago I'd been tromping about a muddy riverbank. My neck itched with the need to turn and see if my thick winter boots had left footprints in my wake.

"This is it. Her favorite spot. Please don't touch the sketchpad on the table. She doesn't like—" He stopped, then gritted his teeth. "She doesn't like people to touch her things."

Doesn't, not didn't. He wasn't ready to admit she was gone. My heart ached for him, and when he stopped a few yards from the patio door, I stopped with him.

"Mr. Miller, if I could trouble you for a cup of tea?" I asked, keeping my voice light. "It's chilly today, I could use the warmup."

He nodded too fast, a fine trembling starting in his hands and traveling down his body. He didn't run from the patio, but there was a definite lurch to his step, as if he had to fight not to break into a sprint. Peasblossom climbed out of my hood to look after him.

"She's been haunting him for a while. He needs to go somewhere else, a friend's, family's, somewhere."

I nodded. "I'll take him with me when we leave. He must have a friend nearby he can stay with."

"He's not sleeping, that's for sure. I'll bet he hasn't had a decent meal in forever, either." Peasblossom propped her chin on my shoulder. "We should send him some honey."

"You have a good heart, Peasblossom."

We were stalling again. The glass door of the patio offered an unrestricted view of a lavish, sheltered area crowned by a broad fireplace with a large television mounted in the stone above it. Pictures lined the mantel, and even from this distance I could see they were of the Millers. An eight-by-ten photo had them sitting on the beach, Mrs. Miller draped across her husband's lap. They were both laughing. Happy. I forced myself forward, grasped the handle, and slid the door open.

Air flowed over me like a gust from a walk-in freezer. Immediately I felt eyes on me. The unmistakable weight of someone's full and undivided attention. I turned, refocusing my gaze across the paved floor to the red-cushioned wicker furniture surrounding a squat stone coffee table. There, sitting on the couch facing the water, was Mrs. Miller.

What was left of her.

The ghost didn't move. She stared out over Lake Erie, flyaways from her long, straight blonde ponytail stirred by the breeze. A pair of thick-rimmed rectangular glasses perched on her nose, and she wore a broad-strapped black tank top and beige Capri pants. The translucent nature of her form gave me a good view of the cushions on the other side of the couch.

"Mrs. Miller?" I kept my voice calm, just loud enough to keep the breeze over the lake from stealing my voice. "My name is Shade Renard."

Peasblossom shouted a warning, a wordless shriek before she shot into the air and disappeared in a streak of pink light. My heart leapt into my throat. I shoved my hand into my left pocket, grabbing a handful of grave dust as I threw myself back.

Helen hurtled toward me like a sheet caught on a sharp gust of wind, her gauzy form fading away at mid-thigh. Her eyes bleached to pure white orbs rolling in their sockets, and her mouth opened impossibly wide, giving her a macabre look straight from a Hollywood horror film. My breath caught in my throat, frozen in my lungs by the frigid cold rolling off her. I hurled the grave dust.

Gray powder coated the ghost's incorporeal form. She shuddered and froze in midair, twitching like a fly pinned to a glue trap. Those empty eyes widened even further, and she fixed me with a look that shoved wicked shards of ice into my bloodstream.

I closed my hand into a fist until the ring on my finger dug into the fingers on either side, a comforting reminder of the enchanted object's presence. *"Armatura."* A flare of blue energy flowed out of the gold band, coating my body with a thin shield. My heart pounded as the shield closed just as the first sound trickled from the ghost's lips.

There's a reason people who encounter ghosts always mention the moaning. For a ghost, a moan isn't just a sound, isn't just a mournful cry. It's fear and desperation, fury and pain, all melted into a sound that drives itself into your body, poisons your mind. The warbling, chilling sound flowed from Helen's mouth, bored into my ears, and froze my insides one molecule of blood at a time. I folded, my spine bowing and my head falling so my dark hair almost brushed the ground. Tears filled my eyes and my breathing came faster and faster. I knew I had to calm down, knew I had to stop before I hyperventilated, but I couldn't catch my breath. I wrapped my arms around myself, closed my eyes, and reached for my magic.

Run, run, run, get away, flee.

I couldn't shut the sound out, couldn't stop that moan from reverberating louder and louder in my mind. Every nerve ending trembled, and the urge to run burned in the muscles of my legs.

Shattering ceramic behind me betrayed Mr. Miller's return. I had a second to realize I must have been standing here longer than I thought, frozen with fear long enough for my host to return with my tea. I wrenched my face up to look at him, to see what happened next. Another moan poured from the ghost, a wind heavy with despair and pain.

The effect on Mr. Miller was instantaneous. He screamed and fled, feet pounding the floor as he bolted though the house. The front door slammed. A second later, a shout of pain followed.

My heart skipped a beat. Was he hurt? What happened?

Pull yourself together. Do what you came here to do.

I gritted my teeth, picked a spot on the floor, and stared hard at it. I planted my feet shoulder width apart and forced myself to look at Helen.

She stood facing me with those empty white eyes, her mouth still open in that awful, skin-crawling moan. The sound made my legs tremble with the need to flee, but I locked my knees together and raised my chin. *She's not evil,* I reminded myself, grasping the fraying ends of my courage. *She's in pain. She needs help.*

"My name is Shade Renard," I said again, putting as much strength into my voice as I could. "I'm here to help you. Helen Miller, I'm here to help you."

The moaning stopped. Brown irises bobbed to the surface of those empty eyes, darkening her gaze. She blinked, and for just a second, she looked more human, more…present. Her head lolled forward and her shoulders shook as she cried.

My legs wobbled as though made of rubber, but I forced myself to take a step toward her. "Can you talk?" I lurched forward another step. "Can you tell me what happened to you?"

Asking who killed her would be pointless. The trauma of murder almost always wiped the experience clean from a ghost's mind. But she should recall something, some detail that might help. Some clue to start me on the right path.

"Can you tell me the last thing you remember?"

Helen's legs rematerialized. She wavered, tried to step back, but the grave dust held her in place.

"What's wrong with her?"

Peasblossom's voice drew my attention to her new location above the television. I said a small prayer of gratitude, thankful she'd avoided the brunt of the ghost's moan.

"I'm not sure. Even a murder victim's ghost can speak. Should speak." I steeled myself against any sudden moves or changes on behalf of the ghost. Despite her translucent state, the details of Mrs. Miller's body remained visible. I'd seen her from every angle but the back, but I'd seen no sign of how she'd died. "Her ghost form should reveal clues to her murder, at least in some small way, but I don't see anything. No slash marks on her flesh or clothing, no bullet wounds. No burns, no scars. Do you see anything?"

"Her mind is gone." Peasblossom's voice was soft, and she landed with care on my shoulder, her attention focused on the ghost. Helen had stopped fighting, and was sobbing now, still pinned in midair.

My stomach rolled. "If whoever killed her did that much damage to her mind then it had to be…" I shuddered. "A death like that would leave evidence on the ghost's body, a wound, something."

"Unless it was magic," Peasblossom pointed out. "Or poison."

"True." I sighed and ran a hand through my hair. "I wanted to believe she was just missing."

"Nothing like jumping into the deep end with your first case." Peasblossom's wings fanned against her back, stirring my hair. "Are you going to tell her husband?"

I shivered, remembering the moan that had driven Mr. Miller from the room in a blind panic. "He already knows. Somewhere deep inside, he already knows."

"If he's been living with her like this since she disappeared, then yes, I suppose he does." She scooted closer to my neck, pressing against me. "Whatever they did to her is driving her mad. I can't imagine what he's heard. What he feels."

I backed away from the ghost, not ready to give her my back despite my sympathy for her. The grave dirt wouldn't anchor her for long, not out here, where the wind would soon sweep it away. Helen stared out at the water, a ghostly statue. I didn't think she noticed when I left.

"I heard a shout," I said. "I think he hurt himself trying to get away."

I found Mr. Miller just in front of the porch. He'd fallen in his haste to escape, and from the way he was cradling his ankle, I was guessing he'd tripped down the steps and landed wrong. He sat there, staring back at the house, his face pale and sweat beading at his temples.

I knelt beside him and unzipped the pouch at my waist. "I'm sorry about your wife."

"She's not dead."

My chest tightened. "Let me see your ankle."

I didn't know if it was trust or shock, but he sat there silently and let me raise his pant leg. I pushed his sock down, noting the bulge around his ankle. I touched it gently, but he didn't make a sound. I pressed a little harder, noting the stiff ligaments. It didn't feel broken. "Just a sprain." I dug around in the pouch, searching for one of the healing potions I always kept on hand. The pouch was enchanted, capable of holding more than I'd ever need. But even if space were limited, I'd always keep a healing potion on hand. Never a bad choice, healing.

"It must have been hard for you these past months." I pulled a thin string of purple energy from the well inside me and tied it around my voice, once again using a charm to put him at ease, lower his defenses. "I'm going to help you. I *can* help you, and I *will* help you. In order for me to do that, you have to trust me. I will not laugh. I will not judge. You have nothing to fear from me. If you tell me what happened, if you share with me everything you know, everything you *feel*, I will do my best to find out what happened to your wife. I will help both of you move on. Here. Drink this."

Power pulsed into the air with every breath, every syllable. The deep creases around Mr. Miller's eyes lessened, but didn't disappear, and the hard line of his jaw eased as he bowed his head. I held out the small bottle with the potion inside and he stared at it for a moment before accepting it. I waited while he drank it, letting the charm and the healing potion sink in before I spoke again.

"Why don't we go somewhere else and talk?" I suggested.

The last of his resistance broke, and his shoulders drooped. He put the potion bottle on the ground and nodded. "Yes," he whispered. "All right."

He levered himself to his feet. The fact that his healed ankle didn't surprise him probably spoke more to his shock than any belief in the Otherworld, but I made a mental note regardless. Peasblossom remained tucked out of sight as I led him to my car.

"Do you have any friends that live nearby?"

I passed him the GPS, letting the blinking cursor urge him to enter an address. He stared at the screen for a full minute before punching in the information. With the destination set, I followed the machine's initial instructions, giving my passenger a moment to collect himself before I spoke.

"Tell me about your wife's disappearance."

Mr. Miller melted a little farther into his seat, his gaze locked on the horizon. "The week before she disappeared, Helen kept getting these phone calls. From a woman." He shrugged. "It was nothing unusual, she got a lot of business calls at home. But something felt off. When she called, she'd speak with Helen for less than a minute, and then Helen would leave."

"Did she tell you who was calling her or why?"

"She said it was a client, and I didn't ask for any more detail than that." He rubbed a hand over his face. "I know this might sound strange to you, but I tried to give Helen her privacy where work was concerned. She specialized in secret rooms and such, so a lot of her clients demanded confidentiality. It didn't bother me, though. I trusted her."

The way he said the last sentence made me tilt my head in his direction. The power I'd called still filled the air between us, and I spoke into that power. "We all want to trust the people we love. But sometimes we doubt, and that's all right."

His mouth tightened at the corners. "I answered several calls that week from the same woman. She was always formal, asked for Helen Miller. Usually after she starts a job, Helen makes a schedule with the person who hired her, sets out what days she'll come in and what time. With this job, they called as if they had to hire her for a different job every day. It didn't make sense. And when I mentioned it to her, she looked at me like I was crazy."

"Do you know where she was calling from?"

"A hotel called Suite Dreams. S-u-i-t-e. It's near Progressive Field."

"Do you remember anything else? Strange behavior, visitors who seemed out of place?"

"No." He rubbed the bridge of his nose. "Everything else was normal. Then one day, a car came to pick her up. It wasn't unusual, a lot of her clients provided transportation. She kissed me goodbye in the morning and left. That was the last time I saw her."

"The sketchbook on the table. You said that was hers and she didn't like people touching it. Did she always leave it out there?"

"No, she usually took it with her."

"Did she take it with her that day?"

"Yes." His jaw clenched. "I know what you're thinking. Yes, the police looked at me. They tore my place apart, looking for secret rooms, blood, anything to suggest I killed her." His eyes hardened and he stared at me. "I didn't kill her. I would never hurt Helen. I don't know how her sketchbook ended up on that table."

My magic still hung in the air, still entered his body with every breath he took. I would have been impressed if he could lie to me with that charm so thick around us. So either he was fighting my spell…or whoever had killed Helen had put that sketchbook on the table. Possibly to make it seem as if she'd come home? Was someone setting up Mr. Miller?

"Did your wife have any enemies?" I asked.

"You mean because she supposedly worked for the mob?" He laughed, a short, humorless sound. "Helen worked for whoever hired her. She didn't judge and she didn't ask for a fuckin' résumé. It was all about the challenge for her, the art." His face softened. "When she was a kid, she loved mysteries. Anything that involved something hidden, something secret. She said secret rooms gave buildings a layer of mystique. She loved looking around the city, seeing different houses and different buildings and knowing that there was more to them than met the eye. There was something about them only a handful of people knew about, and she was one of them." He stared at me. "If she built a secret room for someone and they used it for something bad, that doesn't make Helen bad. She's not responsible for what they use it for."

I held my tongue. The truth was that I did think Helen bore a little responsibility. I'd had people come to me over the years, wanting a love spell, or a curse. I could have made them, could have lost myself in the art of creating the magic objects, reveled in the challenge of it. But I didn't. I turned them away. She didn't just design secret rooms. She designed traps to protect them. Some of those traps had burned evidence, drugs. What had others done? Had it just been contraband that was destroyed?

"You have arrived."

His friend, as it turned out, only lived a few blocks from the Miller residence. I pulled into another massive driveway that could have doubled as a parking lot. The gold front door would have looked gaudy on any other house, but on the sprawling gray stone mansion, it fit. A man sat on the porch drinking a beer, his muscular body cradled by a chair that looked like it cost more than all my furniture put together. He stood when he noticed Mr. Miller in my passenger seat.

"All right." I put my hand on his and concentrated on feeding the magic between us. "Thank you for trusting me. You've been very helpful. I'm leaving now, but I'll be in touch." I reached into the tactical pouch fastened around my waist, groping in one of the side pockets for a card. My fingers found a nest of twisty ties, and I frowned. *That's not right.* I groped in the pocket next to it, then the next. Four pockets later, I found a card and made yet another mental note to reorganize the stupid bag.

"Take this." I put the card in his cold palm. "If you think of anything else"—I looked into his eyes, concentrating on the lingering magic—*"anything* else, call me, day or night."

He nodded. I watched him walk up the driveway, noting with satisfaction that the man holding the beer came to meet him. Beer man gave Mr. Miller a pat on the shoulder in the usual "there, there" motion most men seemed to associate with comfort. I got the impression that whoever the man was, he was a friend, and he'd noticed Mr. Miller's pain. The widower was in good hands.

Peasblossom crawled out from under my hair and sat on my

shoulder. "Well, that settles that. She's not missing, she's dead. Time to call Bryan and go home."

I grabbed the GPS and searched for nearby hotels, scrolling down the list until I spotted Suite Dreams. "Not yet."

Peasblossom groaned. "Bryan wanted to know if Andy's case was Other. He didn't say anything about poking our nose into a murder. This is your first case—let's call it a win and pass it on!"

"First of all, that's not a win. That's an assist. Second of all, I'm not comfortable passing on this information knowing the person I'm passing it on to isn't equipped to deal with it." The GPS considered my request, then reluctantly spat out the directions. "We're just going to take a quick peek and make sure we're not sending Agent Bradford into anything dangerous."

"You mean you want to get to the danger first. Sort of like stomping through a field you think is laced with land mines to keep your friend from getting blown up."

"This isn't just a missing person case, or even just a murder case. There's a ghost involved, and a mad ghost at that. Even if I wasn't a private investigator, this is solidly in witch territory. I need to lay Helen Miller to rest, for her sake and for the sake of her husband's sanity. And laying her to rest will be much easier if her killer is brought to justice." I bit my lip. "Her ghost is tied to the house. Either she was killed there, or something near her when she was killed was brought there afterward."

"You think it was the sketchbook."

I nodded. "It was a prized possession. If it was near her at the time of death, she could have bonded to it."

Peasblossom looked out the rear windshield. "So you think her husband killed her?"

I bit my lip. "He is the most obvious suspect. But..."

"But?"

"He's human. He shouldn't have been able to lie to me so easily under that charm. And he genuinely seemed to believe she was still alive. The way only a person who loves someone can."

"So either he's not human…"

"Or someone set him up," I said grimly. "Someone could have met Helen somewhere else, then returned her sketchbook to make it look like she came home."

"And you think they met her at the hotel? Suite Dreams?"

"Her husband said she acted strange while she was working there. I think it's worth taking a look around."

I paused before backing out of the driveway. "You know what would be helpful? If I had a spy. Someone fast enough—someone *clever* enough—to discover if anything strange is going on in that hotel."

Peasblossom sniffed. "I know you're manipulating me." She beamed. "But I don't care. It's been *ages* since I've been nosy."

That wasn't even a little true, as poor Mary Kate and her formerly secret lover Steven would attest to, but I didn't comment. If Peasblossom was excited at the prospect of doing what I'd asked her to do, I wouldn't question it.

With my GPS settled, and my seatbelt secure, I pulled out of the long driveway. The route took me past the Miller house, and even though I couldn't see it, I couldn't shake the eerie feeling that Helen watched me go.

CHAPTER 4

"More construction?"

I gaped out the windshield, not wanting to believe my eyes. Twenty minutes. Twenty minutes was how long my GPS had informed me it would take to get from the Millers' house to the Suite Dreams hotel.

It had been forty minutes. And we still weren't there.

Peasblossom mumbled against my shoulder, then flopped over and went back to sleep. The steering wheel groaned in my hands as I tightened my grip, resisting the urge to bang my head against it. Orange cones lined the road on one side, and temporary cement walls lined the other. The semitruck in front of me blocked my view, but it didn't matter. If the last forty minutes were anything to go by, up ahead was more of the same. Cars, cones, and cement.

"I can see the hotel," I said, swiping a hand toward the passenger window where the towering glass and white stone form of Suite Dreams stretched skyward. "I've been able to see it for the last ten minutes. And I'll probably watch it for another ten before I get there. I could *walk* anywhere in Dresden in less time than this." I leaned my head back against the headrest and closed my eyes. "I'm regretting the two cups of coffee."

"And the two Cokes," Peasblossom murmured sleepily.

"Thanks for that, Judgy MacJudgerson." My bladder tingled in a way that warned me this was not a drill. I should have used the bathroom at the Millers' house. I should have known better than to drive through a major metropolitan city with a full bladder.

"If you'd studied harder, perhaps you'd be able to teleport the car to the nearest gas station."

I opened my eyes, unsurprised to find the truck in front of me hadn't moved. "That's not true, and you know it. Name one person who can teleport something with that much mass." I angled my head to glare at her, but tucked against my neck as she was, she remained out of my line of vision. "Besides, I don't think teleporting a car would go unnoticed."

"Mysterious gas leak caused by construction. Lots of hallucinations, very strange."

I snorted, but she was right. Finally—*finally*—the semitruck moved. I gave up on getting to Suite Dreams and pulled into the nearest gas station. If I was dancing a little by the time I opened the bathroom stall, I had no one to blame but myself.

"That was a close one," Peasblossom observed on our way back to the car.

I pulled my black fleece wrap tighter around me. It was warm for February, almost sixty degrees, but the wind remembered it was winter. "You didn't have to come into the restroom with me, you know."

"You say that like you gave me time to get off before you bolted from the car. It was all I could do to hold on and not be left behind to get stepped on!"

"You *fly*," I pointed out, exasperation thick in my tone. "I don't understand why you have to hitch a ride on me all the time anyway."

Peasblossom sniffed. "Downright ungrateful is what you are.

Here I am serving as your familiar, and all I get is guff. Guff, guff, guff."

"And free food, and free lodging," I added.

Another sniff. "If you can call it food and lodging. When was the last time I had a pot of honey?"

"Tuesday, December twenty-first. You opened the pot I gave you for winter solstice and you spilled it all over the recliner."

"Still not over that, I see."

I sat down in the driver's seat, staring out the windshield as I remember my ruined furniture. "I loved that chair."

"You don't pay for lodging either." Peasblossom tugged at a length of my hair, running the dark strands through her fingers. "Mrs. Potter lets you live there free 'cause you're a witch."

"And don't think for a second she doesn't claim that house as a religious site for a tax write-off. Not that she needs the money."

I started the car, waiting for my GPS to reacclimate itself before I ventured back into traffic. With my bladder blessedly empty, I was able to concentrate more on my surroundings.

Cities fascinated me. Mother Hazel had always been of the opinion that witches belong in villages and rural areas. "Leave the cities to the wizards," that was what she said. Which was probably why I'd spent any free time I had immersed in cities like this.

Cleveland was a favorite of mine. In the 1950s, a music store owner named Leo Mintz had successfully talked a local DJ by the name of Alan Freed to play "race music" on his radio station, WJW, in Cleveland. To slide under the disapproving radar of older generations and reach the more open-minded youth of the time, they'd repurposed an old blues term to describe said music: rock 'n' roll. I'd come here a lot over the years, using the enchanted door in my mentor's home to get into concerts and bear witness to the burgeoning careers of such artists as Elvis Presley, David Bowie, and Bruce Springsteen. Treasured memories all.

Everywhere around me, skyscrapers lived up to their name,

stretching into the gray February clouds like sentinels, dark windows like wide-open eyes surveying the endless parade of traffic. In a place like this, when there weren't just hundreds of people around you, but hundreds of people *above* you, it was hard not to feel like your every movement was being watched. I glanced at a pair of security cameras over an ATM, and another scattering of electronic eyes surreptitiously guarding the entrance of an upscale restaurant. Humans watched, recorded, and uploaded everything that happened every minute of every day.

And they still didn't see anything.

I held up a hand to stop Peasblossom from launching herself into the air the second I opened my car door. "A few ground rules."

The pixie hopped onto my finger, clinging to it like a spider monkey. "I don't like ground rules."

"Yes, I know. Ground rule number one, you will not stay out all night. You will return to me within the hour."

She sniffed. "It's cold. I don't want to stay out all night anyway."

"Good. Ground rule number two, you will not steal anything."

An indignant huff. "I would *never*."

I didn't argue. Pointing out that I was well aware that one room in the dollhouse she lived in back home was packed full of things she'd "found" would only lead to a series of outraged explanations on why she deserved that quarter, or why that button was payment for some imagined blessing.

"Ground rule number three…" I looked at her, holding my hand a little closer to my face. "Be safe," I said softly.

Peasblossom's face relaxed, then she gave my finger a ferocious hug. "You too. I don't want you getting into trouble just because I'm not there to watch your back."

"I'll be fine," I promised.

Peasblossom snorted. "Tell that to that second *eurypterid*."

She flew off before I could respond. It was my turn to huff.

"I killed it eventually," I muttered.

Shaking off the pixie's reminder of my brief lapse in vigilance, I marched into the hotel. Lavender enveloped me in a puff of perfume as soon as the door to Suite Dreams swished closed behind me. Tension slid from my shoulders. I inhaled more of the soft scent as I swept a lazy glance over the lobby, taking in the high ceiling painted like the night sky, complete with tiny twinkling lights to mimic the stars. Overstuffed chairs formed two lines down the center of the room, leading to a double staircase framing a glass elevator. The chairs whispered promises of comfortable cushions and a nap that would revitalize me for the day's demands. It was only two o'clock, but suddenly I was very tired.

Focus. Dead woman. Murder. Find clues. I forced myself to abandon the decadent furniture, and lurched toward the long marble counter that traced the wall on the right. The petite blonde behind the counter gave me a bright smile as I approached, and I smiled in return.

"Hi"—I read her nametag—"Katie. May I speak with the manager, please?"

Katie bobbed her head, her pixie cut teasing her ears as she did so. "May I tell him what this is about?"

"Yes, my name is Shade Renard, and I'd like to talk to him about Helen Miller."

She wrote, "Shade Renard is here to speak with you about Helen Miller" on a pale blue Post-it, then disappeared around a corner, into the back of the hotel.

I drummed my fingers against the counter while I waited, unable to resist admiring my surroundings. Soft purples and blues dominated the hotel furnishings. Silver accents glittered from chandeliers and squat lamps centered on side tables pressed between the chairs that still begged me to come have a seat.

Gentle music played in the background, and for a moment I closed my eyes.

The counter cooled my arm as I propped my chin up in my hand, drawing lazy circles over the sleek surface with my finger. I opened my eyes. The counter looked like marble, done in pale purples, pinks, and whites. Like carved amethyst.

I blinked and realized I'd slid down, rested my head on my arm, and practically fallen asleep while standing there. Alarm bells went off in my mind, screaming at me that something was wrong. I didn't question my instinct, just straightened my spine and faced the room, this time without consideration to its beauty and comfort. Magic crackled in my fingertips as I waved a hand out over the room.

"Revelare."

A silver net arced from my fingertips, and as it landed, bursts of light glittered all around me like a sea of diamonds.

Magic. There was magic everywhere, and under the influence of my spell, I saw it as a glowing violet luminescence. The longer I stood there, the clearer the magic became. Individual spells unraveled before my eyes.

"Dream magic," I murmured.

"Shade Renard?"

I whirled around and found a woman standing beside me, much closer than she should have gotten without me noticing. Perfect pale brown skin suggested Middle Eastern descent, and glittering maroon eyeshadow set off dark brown eyes. Her black hair fell over her shoulder like a raven's wing, hiding the skin bared by the scarlet dress falling artfully off one shoulder. The dress appeared soft and supple, as if it doubled as a nightgown. After what my spell had shown me, I suspected that impression was intentional.

"I am Arianne Monet, the owner of this hotel. Please, come with me to my office."

She led me around the counter into the back. I followed her, instantly and without thought. It was ten steps before I realized I'd moved. A chill ran down my spine. Dream magic. Hypnosis. Arianne was a sorceress—I would bet my life on it.

Might have already bet my life on it.

I tried to stop myself from following her, but confusion muddled my thoughts. Why wouldn't I follow her? I wanted to talk to her, didn't I? That was why I came here.

"Who are you and why are you here asking about Helen Miller?"

I blinked, disoriented to find myself sitting on a couch before an enormous wooden desk. The cushions of my seat held me in a supple grip, coaxing me to relax, take a nap. The same magic that soaked the lobby enchanted this furniture. I clenched my jaw and closed my hand into a fist once again, feeling the ring on my finger. A flex of my will and the ring sent a trickle of energy over my skin in a thin layer of protection.

Minor protection.

"Someone from this hotel called Helen Miller several times in the weeks preceding her disappearance. A woman." I forced myself to my feet, putting a little more distance between me and the sorceress, for what little good it would do me. "Her husband said she wouldn't talk about what went on here, acted confused when he brought it up."

"And?" Arianne asked coolly.

"And she's missing."

"The FBI has already been here, and I spoke with them, made myself available for any questions they might have. They found I had nothing to do with Mrs. Miller's disappearance."

"The FBI would have no way of knowing you're a sorceress." I crossed my arms. "A sorceress expending a lot of magic on her clientele."

Arianne's posture stiffened. "You are accusing me of something?"

I called up my temper, used it to fight back the urge to sleep that was stroking my brain like a master petting a cat. "I'm not accusing you of anything. I'm asking for information. What was Helen doing here?"

The anger in her eyes died as suddenly as it had appeared. Arianne folded herself into the chair behind the desk and drew one finger down the arm in a lazy line as she held my gaze.

"Helen Miller is the most accomplished architect in the Eastern United States when it comes to creative design. I hired her to build some extra features in my hotel." She shrugged. "There is nothing suspicious here, Ms. Renard. I will admit, I used hypnosis on Mrs. Miller to protect my privacy. A little suggestion planted in her mind, so she would only remember her projects here when she was wearing the security badge I provided. Nothing serious, nothing untoward. Simply an extra assurance that my secrets would be kept."

Her hostility had made me suspicious. Her cooperation made me paranoid. I debated probing the door for magic that might prevent my escape, but discarded the idea. Arianne had spelled this entire hotel—this was a place of power for her. I had no chance of leaving if she didn't want me to.

She slid her hands down the arms of the chair and stood in a motion so graceful that I feared she'd fogged my mind again. She murmured something and traced a finger on the arm of her chair before stepping away. Before I could react, she was standing in front of me.

"Thank you so much for coming by, Mother Renard. I feel so much better knowing you've inspected my wards. I do hope you'll accept my invitation to come stay with me some time."

I nodded and smiled back as I rose from the chair and shook her hand. "I will, yes. And you're very welcome for the wards. I was only too happy to help."

She beamed at me, opened the door to her office, and led me down the muted corridor toward the lobby. I inhaled lavender perfume as we walked to the gleaming glass doors that led out of the hotel. It had always been one of my favorite scents. So calming. I really should come back here for an extended stay. I could use the relaxation.

"Goodbye, Mother Renard."

"Wait! I missed the whole thing?"

Peasblossom almost fell down the back of my shirt as she crash-landed on my shoulder, tiny feet scrabbling to keep from sliding down the soft fleece of my wrap. I scowled and rolled my shoulder.

"Stop that. Yes, I'm done. The wards are fine."

"Wards?" Peasblossom poked her head out of my collar. "What wards?"

"The wards she was here to inspect." Arianne's voice was a little strained, but her smile remained in place. "And she's all finished, so you can both leave now." She fluttered her fingers at the door as she spoke, then cleared her throat.

"Why are you pointing at me? And did you just say something? I—" Peasblossom squeaked. Without warning, she grabbed my ear, pulled it to her, and bit down—hard.

I shrieked and slapped a hand over my earlobe, narrowly avoiding the little fey. "Why would you do that?"

"She's trying to hypnotize me!" Peasblossom snapped. "And she obviously already got you."

The pain lancing out from my ear drilled into my head, piercing the lavender-infused haze. Suddenly I was aware of two things. Number one, there were at least ten humans in the lobby, and they were all staring at us. And number two, Arianne Monet had tried to mind-roll me. I tilted my body to keep Peasblossom out of her line of sight as I met her eyes.

Arianne frowned and crossed her arms. "Get out."

I took a step closer, my temper burning hot enough to melt away the last of her hypnotic suggestion. "Tell me the truth," I said under my breath, "or I will make an unholy scene. You strike me as a good businesswoman." I gave the enchanted lobby a pointed glance. "If not a moral one. I'm sure you weren't lying when you said you wanted to keep your secrets. So unless you want me to put in a great deal of time and effort exposing those secrets, you'd better talk."

Arianne's eyes darkened, the brown irises sinking into pits as black as tar. "You do not want me for an enemy, *Mother* Renard."

She was right. "You want me for a friend," I countered.

She arched an eyebrow at that. It didn't seem to convince her, but at least it broke the tension somewhat. After a long minute, she gestured for me to step to the side and I followed her to a more private area behind some glossy-leaved plants.

"I told you what you wanted to know," she said. "I simply planted the suggestion that you would not remember it when you left."

It was on the tip of my tongue to ask why she'd bothered to answer my questions at all if she'd intended to wipe the information away anyway. But then I saw the genius of it. Simple hypnotic suggestions worked best when the subconscious didn't work very hard to break them. It was easier to convince someone to forget information they had than to make them forget that they wanted information.

"Then you told me the truth about Helen Miller," I said. "She built your secret rooms and that's it?"

"I never said secret rooms, but yes. And she finished before her disappearance. I had no reason to contact her after that." Arianne shrugged. "I'm sorry she's missing. I had plans to use her services again. She really is the best."

I bit my lip. She was using the present tense. Either she didn't know Helen was dead or she was smart enough to fake it. "Do you know of anyone else who wanted to use her services? Anyone from the Otherworld who might have…valued their secrecy, even more than you?"

"You mean do I know someone who might have used her services and then killed her? No."

"All right." I drummed my fingers against my waist pouch. "Let's say I believe you."

Arianne narrowed her eyes. "I have told you the truth."

"So you say." I held her gaze, gauging the truth of her next response. "Would the hypnotism you used on Mrs. Miller have harmed her in any way?"

"No. As I said, it is a simple, gentle spell. Harmless."

"So it's not possible that your spell damaged her mind in any way?"

"How do you mean?"

I debated telling her about Helen's ghost, but only for a second. If Arianne was lying, I didn't want her to know the victim's ghost had no chance of helping find her murderer. "Nothing. Just one more question. Where were you the night of January twentieth?"

"Here in my hotel, where I am every night."

"Can anyone corroborate that? Anyone not susceptible to your hypnosis?"

She lifted her chin. "No."

I nodded. "Thank you for your time."

Her stare bored into the back of my head as I left, promising that our talk wasn't over, no matter what I might think. The magic of the hotel trailed over my body like sticky cobwebs as I left. It wasn't so peaceful and comforting now, and I swiped at my arms to rid myself of the sensation.

Peasblossom tsked in my ear. "You'll have a tough time appeasing that one. Some people are so easily offended."

"I must devise a subtler way to ask people if they're murderers who lie to the FBI," I agreed, opening my car door.

"So that's a thank you that you owe me, and an apology gift you owe the sorceress."

I groaned and slumped into the driver's seat. It had been a while since I'd offended someone, and I'd forgotten what came after that. If there was one thing my mentor was adamant about, beyond the insistence that everything was a witch's business, it was her warning that someone who lived as long as a witch owed it to herself not to make enemies unless it was unavoidable. To that end, when I offended someone, I was required to send them a gift to attempt reparations.

"She won't be easy to shop for," I muttered, staring at the hotel looming like a sentinel above me. The tower rising behind the main building gave the hotel a medieval appearance, and all that white stone screamed money. Arianne Monet was wealthy and powerful. Exactly the sort of person Mother Hazel had warned me to avoid irritating.

"Don't forget the thank you," Peasblossom reminded me. "I'm important too."

I smiled at her, raising a finger to pat her little pink head. "Thank you. If you hadn't shown up when you did, I'd be on my way home with her hypnotic suggestion still hugging my memories." I shuddered, unable to keep from remembering poor Mrs. Miller. "Do you believe what she said about her hypnotic suggestions being harmless? Could she have caused the damage to Mrs. Miller's ghost?"

Peasblossom sat on my shoulder and kicked her feet. "The hypnosis she used on you wouldn't have caused that kind of damage, but she has other magic. All that amethyst..."

I nodded. "She's using dream magic, and lots of it."

"Dreams can be powerful. If she somehow got into Mrs. Miller's head through her dreams, then she could have done a lot of damage, even without intending to."

"So she's not off the suspect list."

"No. Though I don't see what she'd get out of killing her. Helen was human, there's no reason Arianne's hypnosis wouldn't have sufficed to protect her precious secrets." Peasblossom paced over the dashboard. "Then again, I suppose it depends on what those secrets are."

There was a lilt in the pixie's voice that I recognized all too well. "I don't suppose you learned anything of that nature on your little trip?"

Peasblossom preened, slowly fanning her wings as she twirled a fingertip through a lock of pink hair. "As a matter of fact, I did. And I'd be delighted to share my information with you over a nice cup of tea—and honey."

I pressed my lips together, but didn't argue. Experience had taught me that when Peasblossom had information that would get her honey, she wouldn't give up said information without said honey.

I arched an eyebrow as she huffed and puffed to drag the GPS off the center console.

"Where are we going?" I asked.

"One of the sprites I talked to said there's a fey pub near here. Goodfellows." She punched the name into the search menu.

I halted the key halfway to the ignition. "And what did he say about it?"

Peasblossom snuggled back against the cushion, the GPS propped in her lap so she could watch the search bar spiral through its colors. "He said I could order for myself. They're very respectful to the wee folk."

"And who owns it?"

"Laurie."

My head drooped with the urge to bang my forehead on the steering wheel. "And Laurie is a...?"

Peasblossom furrowed her brow, sparing me a glance. "Pub owner?"

"What is she, Peasblossom? Human, fey...?"

"Why would a human own a fey pub?" Peasblossom shook her head and returned her attention to the GPS. "Sometimes I don't think you think things through."

My eye twitched. The mechanical voice from the GPS told me to head west. I kept my hand on the keys, slowly starting the car, but making no move to leave the parking lot. A fey pub could be a boon or a danger, depending on who owned it. One of the lesser fey might do it to have a place for others from beyond the veil to gather, a way to make money while simultaneously providing a service. But there were some creatures that might do it for less pleasant reasons. Creatures who fed off fey energy, or who spied on the customers for information that might be worth a penny or two.

"*Head west.*"

I jumped as the mechanical voice shouted at me, the volume all the way up. I whipped my head around to see Peasblossom hefting the device in my direction, her little face pinched with irritation. As soon as I made eye contact, she dropped the GPS and tapped rapidly on the screen.

"Go *west*, it said." She pointed out my window. "That's west."

I gritted my teeth and pulled out of my parking spot, heading west as instructed. "You'll need to do a bit of spying when we get there. It'd be nice to know if the owner is evil before we place our order."

"I'll snoop around, but not before I order my honey," Peasblossom countered. "I'm hungry. You know how cranky I get when I'm hungry."

I thumped my head back against my seat.

"Not as cranky as *you* get," Peasblossom continued. "But still. It's in both our best interests that I get my honey first."

The ten-minute drive might as well have been ten hours. Peasblossom hefted the GPS like John Cusack in Say Anything any time I was too slow making a turn, or if I stopped for a yellow light. Add to that the fact that the GPS told me to turn too late and I had to circle the block to get back to the entrance to the small parking lot, and my hands were shaking with a bad case of nerves by the time I parked.

"You should stock up on gatestones," Peasblossom complained, climbing my shirt to tuck herself into the loose fabric of the mock turtleneck. "You're rubbish at driving."

"You should learn to fly yourself, and then you wouldn't have to drive with me."

"I know how to fly."

I resisted the urge to pull the neck of my shirt down to let her spill into thin air. She'd probably just snag my shirt with those pointy little fingers of hers, and I didn't need any more mending to do.

Goodfellows smelled like any other tavern. Polished wood, the mixed aroma of past meals, and that strange wood-metal combination of silverware wrapped in cheap napkins. A sign said, *Seat yourself* so I chose a booth along the right wall. Peasblossom leapt off my shirt and landed too hard on the table. The honey-colored wood offered no traction, and her feet shot out from under her. She landed with a grunt on her bottom, glaring at me as though I'd had something to do with it.

"Don't look at me like that," I said. "If you'd fly more often, you'd be better at landings."

"I am an *expert* at landings, thank you very much. Someone obviously used an insensible amount of polish."

A waitress across the room paused in the middle of straightening one of the picture frames mounted to the red brick wall. Her long blonde hair parted when she moved, revealing the pointed tip of one ear. As soon as she saw Peasblossom, she smiled and headed for our table.

"Hi, I'm Alexandra. Can I start you off with something to drink?"

"No," Peasblossom said immediately. "I want honey. Lots of it."

Alexandra nodded, then turned her attention to me. "And you?"

"Tea," I said tiredly. "With lemon and honey, please."

"Bring her her own honey," Peasblossom added. "I'm not sharing."

"I would never ask you to share," Alexandra assured her seriously.

I waited for Alexandra to leave, then fixed Peasblossom with a stern look. "Snoop."

She heaved a sigh and made a big show of dragging herself to her feet before throwing herself into the air. I ignored the drama and opened the pouch at my waist to search for a notepad and pen. The enchanted pouch didn't make such a simple task easy, and I found a book, a watch, and a handful of keys before my questing fingers touched the clicky end of a pen. The search for the notebook unearthed a sewing kit and three combs, but eventually gave up a spiral-bound notepad.

Peasblossom coincidentally arrived back at the table at the same time Alexandra brought her honey. I narrowed my eyes and set the pen and notebook on the table. "Well?"

"Owner is a witch."

I blinked. "A witch?"

"Mmbpht."

I sighed and rubbed my temples as Peasblossom attempted to answer me with a mouthful of honey. "Anyone we know?"

"Mmph—"

"Oh, swallow the honey before you answer!"

Peasblossom narrowed her pink eyes. She swallowed hard, making an audible gulping sound as she forced the honey down. "No. Just a minor witch, nothing very powerful. Everyone says she's a good one. There's a picture of her with Mother Hazel in the kitchen."

Tension bled from my shoulders and I relaxed against the padded seat. "Good. All right, so tell me what you found. Something about Arianne?"

Peasblossom swallowed the glob of honey she'd just sucked off her hand and gave me a sticky smirk. "Arianne Monet is a sorceress."

I stirred lemon into my tea and waited.

"She specializes in dream magic. Specifically, she uses dream magic to invade her clients' dreams and harvest secrets."

"What kind of secrets?"

"All kinds. Stock tips, personal shames for blackmailing purposes. You name it, she steals it. That's why she's so rich. It's also the reason she's so well connected." Peasblossom dipped her hand into the honey, swirling her arm around the way a carnival worker used a paper stick to gather cotton candy. "You shouldn't have made her mad."

I ignored that, along with the sinking suspicion that she was right. "Anything connecting her to the murder?"

Peasblossom shook her head and shoved most of her hand in her mouth, sucking off the honey. "No proof she's ever killed anyone. She prefers to get rid of her enemies by manipulating their thoughts, making them forget all about her. The sprite in the planter outside said that every few months, a big group of people goes into the hotel through the back door late at night."

"Is that strange?"

She shrugged, dripping honey into her lap in a tacky puddle. "Maybe not. But he also said men in uniforms visit a lot. Arianne doesn't like it when they do."

"Men in uniforms?" I drew a finger around the rim of my coffee mug. "That's not terribly specific. For all we know, they might be health inspectors. Or cops."

"Perhaps."

I took a long sip of my tea, hoping the warm liquid would make up for the sudden weight of my spirit.

Peasblossom looked up at my face then patted my arm with her sticky fingers. "I can ask around some more? When I'm done with my honey?"

"No." I stirred more honey into my tea, staring into the aromatic liquid as if it held the answers I needed. "We need to get back home. I promised Amy I would make her a potion for Shilo's eczema."

"You also promised Mrs. Harvesty that you'd see to her cat first this afternoon," Peasblossom pointed out, wiping a hand along her jaw and smearing more honey up to her ear. "What's one more promise broken?"

"Oh, no," I moaned, slumping back on the seat. "I forgot!"

"That won't go well for you. Mother Hazel was already against our private investigation service. This is just going to convince her you can't handle both being a detective and—Hey!"

I ignored her shout of indignation as I scooped her up in a napkin and downed the rest of my tea in one gulp. I left a handful of bills on the table to cover the tea and a generous tip, then marched to my car with the sticky ball of honeyed pixie in my palm.

"I wasn't done!" Peasblossom wailed.

"I'll give you more honey when we get home."

"Fat lot your word means now," Peasblossom grumbled. "Two broken promises and you want to make it three."

"I haven't broken any promises. I'm just late for my appointment with Mrs. Harvesty. I can still get to Amy's on time and I can still get you your honey."

"Show me the honey, then we'll talk."

As soon as we climbed into the car, I dug around in my pouch for the wand of prestidigitation.

"It's out of charges," Peasblossom said sulkily.

"Of course it is." I sighed and retrieved the empty bowl and bottle of water I kept in the glove box. It said something about Peasblossom and her honey obsession that I carried a makeshift bath for her, but after dealing with a pixie covered in dried, tacky honey a few times, I'd learned my lesson. Wands were fine and good, but backup was crucial.

I pulled out my cell phone and, after a moment of meditation to brace myself, dialed Mrs. Harvesty's number.

"Hello?"

"Mrs. Harvesty, it's Shade Renard. Listen, I'm so sorry I wasn't there this morning."

"Oh, dear, didn't you get my message?"

I pulled my phone away from my ear enough to check the bar at the top. No missed calls, no text messages. I put the phone back to my ear. "No, I didn't."

"How strange. I called you this morning and left you a message. Majesty is doing much better. I think he just needed a little extra attention."

I raised my eyebrows. The last thing that kitten needed was more attention.

"Anyway, everything is all right. And don't worry about forgetting your promise. I'm sure you meant well."

Peasblossom looked up from her bath and shook her head. Mrs. Harvesty was obviously under the impression she'd called off our appointment, but now that I'd let slip that I'd forgot, it was a sure thing she'd remember I'd forgotten. This would come back on me.

I let my head fall back against my seat. "Thank you, Mrs. Harvesty. I'm glad your cat is all right."

"Majesty," she said evenly.

I squeezed my eyes shut tighter. "I'm glad Majesty is all right."

She made a satisfied sound and then we said our goodbyes and hung up. Two hours and what had to be five million orange traffic cones later, I passed into Dresden and guided the car to Amy's house. She wasn't home—a small favor, since I wasn't in the mood to stay and socialize. I left the cream I'd made for her on the porch and drove home.

My instincts flared as I pulled into my driveway. The sun had set and it was dark, but the automatic light on my garage didn't come on. I frowned.

"Did you disconnect the automatic light?"

Peasblossom curled against my neck, her wet dress adding to a sudden chill in the air inside the car. "No."

Unease rolled down my spine. I murmured a spell, drawing a few circles in the air. *"Lumen."* Three glowing balls of reddish light bloomed to life and hovered before me. I kept one over my head and sent the other two forward, illuminating my path to the front door. I didn't open the garage door and pull in, but got out while I was still in the driveway, already preparing another spell as I climbed out of the driver's seat.

"Revelare." My power flowed in a wash of silver toward the house, probing for any foreign magic.

Nothing.

"Stay here," I told Peasblossom. "If I don't call for you, go to Mother Hazel and tell her everything that happened today."

"But I won't have anything to tell her unless I stay to see what happens," Peasblossom hissed. "I'm not leaving you."

"This might be nothing." I kept my voice as low as possible. "The bulb may have burned out. Don't be silly."

"I'm not silly and I'm not stupid. You think there's something bad inside. And a witch never ignores her gut."

A lump rose in my throat, and I fought to swallow around it. "Please stay out here. I can't bear the idea of anything happening to you."

Peasblossom gave my ear a ferocious hug. "I'll stay out here, but only as backup. I will never leave you."

I waited for her to fly up and off my shoulder before straightening my spine. This was my house. My village. Whatever was here, whatever had violated my home, would be sorry. Power rose in my throat, feeding the spell I'd readied.

"Shade, look out!"

I whirled around and spat behind me. The spell hurtled through the air, and I had a split second to see a dark figure separate itself from the maple tree beside my driveway. The spell landed in the grass, the viscous blue fluid of the entanglement spell pooling in the tree's shadow.

"Such attacks will not be necessary."

A man spoke from beside me, smooth and masculine, voice heavy with an accent I hadn't heard in a long time.

A very, very long time.

I turned, knowing I'd never call up another spell fast enough. I raised my hand anyway, needing to try, to go down fighting. A hand closed around my wrist, tight enough that I swore I heard my bones creak. I gritted my teeth and stared into the face of my visitor.

He was dressed in a suit that probably cost more than my car. Long white-blond hair brushed his shoulders and framed a pale face with sharp, graceful features. I couldn't see what color his eyes were in this light, but it didn't matter. I remembered his face.

He went by the name Anton Winters, majority shareholder of the Winters Group, a company that made the Forbes 500 list look like a gathering of struggling start-ups. There were whispers he had criminal connections, that he was former KGB. I knew the truth. And it was scarier.

Anton Winters had once been known by a different name.

Prince Kirill of Dacia.

A vampire.

CHAPTER 5

Humans had their history wrong. This world hadn't started with a bang, big or otherwise. It had started with blood. Royal blood from five princes, smeared on the enchanted trunk of the World Tree. They'd intended to build the perfect kingdom.

It hadn't quite worked out that way.

Reality as humans knew it today was the result of the contamination of the princes' vision. An example of what happens when rumor of a new land spreads to every branch of the World Tree. Creatures poured in from every kingdom imaginable, all of them wanting to claim a piece of the new world for themselves. All that travel through the veils that separated the worlds had left jagged holes in the fabric of time and space and created the chaotic timeline the humans of this time called their own.

I had to give the vampire credit. He'd rolled with the punches, sliding seamlessly from Prince Kirill of Dacia to Anton Winters, billionaire businessman with suspected but never proven connections to crime all over the world.

And he's standing in my driveway.

"I believe it is traditional in situations such as this for me to assure you I mean you no harm."

Anton didn't attempt a reassuring smile, which I appreciated, since I wasn't mentally prepared to see his fangs. Especially not when I was this close.

"You'll forgive me if my concerns are not completely assuaged." I kept my free hand out of sight beside my body, already drawing a new spell.

He inclined his head in acknowledgment. "I understand. Since it seems there is very little I can do to convince you of my innocent intentions, perhaps it would be best if we cut to the chase, as they say?"

"As long as the cutting is completely figurative."

It was a personal failing of mine that humor was my first line of defense when I was nervous. Thankfully, the vampire didn't seem bothered. He released my wrist and flowed backward, putting a few feet of space between us. I held my breath, keeping the fire spell coiled in my palm, ready to release it if he tried to grab me again. I had little hope that I could really hurt him, at least, not without burning down the entire village, but hopefully I could distract him long enough to get away.

"It is my understanding that you are a detective," he began.

I blinked, my hand drooping at my side. "It is?"

Anton arched an eyebrow. "Your surprise is somewhat disheartening. Am I misinformed?"

"No, no, I just—" I stopped and shook my head. "I'm sorry, are you saying you're here to...hire me?"

He plucked at an invisible loose thread near the button hole closest to his belt. "Mother Renard, I'm certain you can appreciate that matters which require a detective are often quite sensitive. I would be most appreciative if you could see your way to moving our conversation someplace more private than your... charming driveway."

I almost laughed, but swallowed it just in time. I was not going to invite a vampire into my house. I was not going to invite *this* vampire into my house. "I'm afraid I'm not set up for company. If you wouldn't mind coming back tomorrow night, I could make other arrangements…?"

"I understand your situation, but I'm afraid I must insist we proceed now. If you will get into your car, I will take you to my office. I promise you, you will be well compensated for your inconvenience."

"Where is your office?" I asked.

"Cleveland."

If I hadn't already intended to say no, that would have cinched it. I'd only just got home, I wasn't turning around and driving straight back. As it was, those orange cones would haunt my nightmares.

Then again, refusing to acquiesce to a vampire's request wasn't high on the list of smart things to do either. Perhaps I should agree to go, make a show of it. I could call Mother Hazel on the way, then pretend I'd changed my mind, backup firmly in place.

Liking my new plan, I smiled at Anton. "All right. I'll follow you."

Anton swept an arm toward my car. "After you."

It took every ounce of self-control in my possession to give the vampire my back so I could search for Peasblossom without giving her away. He must have heard her shout a warning to me, and I didn't like the thought of what the vampire might do if he thought the tiny fey would report on what she'd witnessed. And Peasblossom would never leave as I'd told her to, now that she knew who'd been waiting for me. I needed her on my shoulder, close enough to protect her.

I closed my eyes as I slid behind the wheel, concentrating on the bond between witch and familiar. A flicker at the end of the connection made my heart skip a beat. Peasblossom. She was there, close by. And she was afraid.

Then nothing. One second I could practically feel Peasblossom's heartbeat through the bond, and the next it was gone, and I was alone.

My eyes shot open and I drew in the breath to shout for her, discretion be damned.

I was not sitting behind the wheel of my car.

Shock turned my spine to steel. My car was gone. My house was gone. My driveway, my yard—*Dresden* was gone. In its place stood a massive black lacquered desk. Directly behind the desk, two heavy bookcases flanked a small bar with glass shelves lined with expensive liquor and crystal glasses. The mirrored wall behind the bar offered whoever made the drinks a good view of the room—though the fact that the mirror ended six inches above the counter meant the rest of the room had a less advantaged view of what was going into the drinks.

Gauzy white curtains covered the two windows to my right, but a heavy electric shade at the top of the windows could be lowered to block the light completely. I guessed the employees here were under strict instructions to ensure that the shade was always lowered during daylight hours. I wanted to look behind me at the rest of the office just to ground myself in my new surroundings, but instinct wouldn't let me turn my head from the vampire sitting behind the desk.

Anton sat with his hands close together but not folded on the desk, waiting for me to get my bearings.

I didn't speak until I was sure I could do so without either shouting or betraying the waver I was sure would be in my voice. "What did you do?"

"I did what I said I would do. I brought you to my office."

I tightened my grip on the padded arms of my chair. "So I deduced. But *how* did you bring me here?"

"The how is not important. What is important is that we establish here and now the details of our professional relationship."

He put his fingers on a sheet of paper to his right and slid it in front of me. "This is a confidentiality agreement. It stipulates that you will not share the information I provide you without my express written consent."

I stared at the paper, but made no move to touch it. "You want me to sign a contract?"

"A confidentiality agreement." He laid a pen down beside the document. "Very standard, I assure you."

My doubt must have shown on my face, because he gave me a condescending smile.

"Mother Renard, signing this document represents your dedication to keeping any secrets I may share with you. It does not bind you to my service, nor does it obligate you to take my case." He pulled another sheet of paper to sit beside the first one. "This is the one you will sign if you take my case."

"Still big on signatures, I see." The words escaped before I could stop them. I looked up at Anton, but his expression didn't change.

"I find it's best to be clear."

There'd been another time, another world, when this vampire's contracts had been famous. Or, perhaps, infamous. Back then he'd been a vampire prince determined to be a vampire king, and he'd collected alliances the way some men today collected stamps. Only his methods had been less...civilized.

Never had I thought for a second that I would find myself being offered such a contract.

"So I'll sign the confidentiality agreement," I said slowly, "then you'll tell me what you want to hire me for. And if I take the case, I'll sign the second one."

"Exactly."

Curiosity, monster that it was, grew stronger with every passing second. There couldn't be any harm in just hearing him out...right? I took the offered pen and scrawled my name on the dotted line before my more rational voice could talk me out of it.

Something pricked my finger and I hissed. Blood flowed from a tiny cut on my fingertip, following the lines of ink until my signature shone red in the dim office lights. Anton pulled the paper toward him, blowing on it to help it dry. Maybe it was my imagination, but I could have sworn I saw his nostrils flare, a spark of crimson lighting his eyes.

Before I could say anything, he put the paper in his desk drawer, locked it, and returned his attention to me.

"On January twentieth, someone came into this building and broke into my vault. They killed three guards and stole a book. I want you to find the thief and recover the book." He pulled a file from the top left drawer of his desk and put it in front of me.

The fact that he referred to the culprit as a thief and not a murderer spoke volumes for his priorities. I stared at the three-inch-thick file. Colored tabs stuck out from the top and sides, each one labeled.

"In addition to crime scene reports, I've included the employee records of everyone I believe could have known of the book's existence. You will also find a dossier on everyone with a connection to the stolen item. Those are summaries only, I have more detailed files in boxes that can be delivered to your office at your convenience. Would you like me to go over the summaries with you now, or do you prefer to do your own research first to avoid prejudice?"

It wasn't a thin file, summaries or no, and I didn't relish the idea of being in the vampire's office all night. I pulled the file closer and leafed through the pages. There were photographs too, and I pulled one of the glossy prints out to get a better look.

It was a photograph of one of the victims, a guard, Anton had said. He'd been decapitated. The corpse remained cradled in the desk chair, slumped back, but still posed as if it would continue working any minute.

"It doesn't look like he put up much of a fight."

"No," Anton agreed.

I squinted, noting that the man's head lay on the floor beside the chair. Dark hair, cut short. He'd been a slender man, leanly muscled and as pale as the belly of a snake. On the wall in front of the body, six monitors glowed brightly, depicting what I assumed were different parts of the building housing the vault. The victim should have seen his attacker coming.

"He was looking at a lot of monitors when he died," I said. "Do any of these show the entrance to this room?"

"Yes. But the recordings have been erased, and obviously, Aaron is not available to tell us what he saw."

"But he could have set off an alarm if it'd been someone who shouldn't be there, yes?"

"Yes. But no such alarm was triggered."

"So either it was someone who had a right to be there..."

Anton narrowed his eyes. "No one has a right to be there but the guards on duty, myself, and my wife."

"Then someone hid from the cameras." I tapped a finger on the photograph. "There are ways, of course. It's too bad we can't recover the footage. It would help if we knew whether the culprit used mundane or magical means to get past the camera." I looked down at the photo as I continued tapping. "There's something off about this picture," I murmured. Then it hit me, and it was so obvious, I almost smacked myself. "There's no blood. The wound's been cauterized." I looked at Anton. "Cauterized as it was cut?"

Anton nodded. "The coroner believes the blade was magic. Swords that cauterize as they cut are not difficult to find, if you have the funds to purchase one."

I stared at the victim's neck—the flesh and blood was mottled, looking like some sort of macabre candle. "So someone snuck up on him and cut his head off with a magic sword."

"Look at the other photos."

I thumbed through the photographs, pulling out those that depicted the other victims. Another man, and a woman. Both killed the same way, their wounds cauterized. I frowned. "That's not possible. He couldn't have snuck up on all of them." I pointed to the cup of pens on the shelf behind the long counter, the stool that remained upright. "It doesn't look like there was a struggle."

"And your deduction?"

I stared at the photograph without really seeing it. "No bonds, so they weren't tied up. They couldn't have been gassed or drugged, because they were obviously still upright when they were beheaded." I pointed at the tiled floor, the lack of slashes that would have indicated the killer had removed the heads while the bodies lay on the floor. I looked up at Anton. "Magic again. Someone had to use a spell to keep them frozen in place."

My stomach rolled. There were spells to hold creatures immobile, but they didn't numb the creature affected. The victims would have known what was happening to them. They would have stood there, watching their killer approach, but unable to move to defend themselves or run. Helpless to do anything but watched their death come closer.

And they would have felt it.

"It was probably a quick death," I said, mostly to comfort myself. I tried not to think of what the third victim would have felt, watching the killer decapitate the first two, knowing the same fate awaited them.

"Magic to hold them, a magic sword to kill them." I looked at Anton. "Whoever did this is powerful. The sword can be bought, but the spell to hold them would present a challenge. The killer would only have needed to hold them a short time," I murmured, half to myself. "Just long enough to behead them. It's not that easy to decapitate someone, though."

"If the sword was enchanted, it would have taken significantly less effort. I have a cauterizing sword myself, and I've found it slides through even the most monstrous neck with great ease. My wife could do it with one hand."

I very firmly put that mental image aside. I didn't need the reminder that the vampire trying to hire me spoke of using a sword to decapitate someone the way I talked about what an excellent job my new carrot peeler did.

"Even so, the spell alone tells me we're dealing with someone experienced. Whoever did this isn't squeamish about death, has no empathy…" I looked up. "And isn't afraid of you."

Anton's eyes glittered with that same sparkle of crimson I'd seen earlier. "A small list."

A question that had been plaguing me since the vampire had first shown up leapt onto my tongue. I spoke before I could think better of it. "Why aren't you having one of your own people do this?"

"I'm sorry?"

"You're the vampire mastermind of Dacia. You've been building a spy network for centuries—maybe longer. You've been here since this world started—well, before the timeline changed, but still. You must have someone who could investigate this for you?"

Anton straightened the contract in front of him, settling it directly across from me. "I do. But if this was an inside job, then it is prudent to hire outside people to look into it to avoid inadvertently hiring the fox to watch the henhouse, so to speak. Don't you agree?"

"But why me?" I gave up any pretense of pride. "I'm just starting. Wouldn't you rather have someone with more experience?"

The sparks of red vanished from his eyes, leaving them icy rings of pale blue. In that moment, I felt as if the vampire could see my every weakness, read all my secrets. He leaned forward, and I stiffened my spine, pressing my feet into the floor as I resisted the urge to shove my chair farther back.

"You are investigating the disappearance of one Helen Miller," he said. "An architect from Cleveland who specialized in building secret chambers?"

The vein in my temple pulsed a little harder. "Yes."

"Helen Miller was the architect who designed the security measures for the compromised vault."

I jerked back before I could stop myself, my fingers twitching with the urge to draw a spell. "Did you…?"

Anton held up a hand. "No, Mother Renard. I am not responsible for the young woman's disappearance. However, if you search her records, you will not find any evidence of the work she did for me. Nor will she herself share any such detail with you should you find her." He paused. "Unless she is dead, as I strongly suspect is the case. Upon her completion of the work I hired her for, she destroyed all records of our dealings—in my presence. Before she left, I assured that her memory was equally clean of our history."

He'd used vampiric powers to wipe her memory. I swallowed hard and busied my hands by flipping through the file again to hide their trembling. "When you…cleaned out her memory. Would there have been any lasting effects?"

"Such as?"

Again, I hesitated before revealing Mrs. Miller's state of mind. The fewer people who knew about it, the more I would be able to bluff later, to pretend Mrs. Miller had told me something. That was leverage I couldn't get back once it was gone.

"Could she have recovered those memories?" I asked instead.

Anton didn't blink. Again I had the unsettling feeling he was reading my mind. "No."

I looked down at the file again. "Before I agree to take this case, why don't you tell me a little more about what was stolen?"

"It was a book, leather-bound, black, the size of a small journal."

"And what was in it?"

"Notes."

I waited. He didn't say more.

I sighed and propped an elbow on the desk, vaguely gesturing toward the drawer where he'd locked up the document I'd signed.

"I signed a confidentiality agreement. I assume the bloodletting means something horrific will happen to me if I violate it?"

Anton's eyes flashed red, more than a dusting of embers—a hot glow of burning coals. "Oh, yes."

"Then this isn't the time to be coy, is it? What's in the book?"

The corner of his mouth twitched. "The book contained notes I've taken over the years about various individuals whom I have entered negotiations with, or, in some cases, individuals with whom I am planning to enter negotiations with. A sort of…leverage."

"So, blackmail."

He shrugged. "If you wish. The book is also enchanted. In addition to my personal notes, each page holds a small…pocket, if you will. Evidence to support my notes is contained within."

"So not only could someone you're blackmailing want it to take away your leverage," I said slowly, "but anyone who wanted to become a blackmailer themselves might see this as a one-stop shop." I put my hand on the file. "Shouldn't this be thicker?"

"Very astute. I will admit the list of individuals who would like to get their hands on that book is longer than the list of suspects I've provided you. However, that book is one of many. The vault is one of many. Few individuals could locate any book, let alone the specific book that pertains to them."

I thought of Arianne and what Peasblossom had said about her penchant for blackmail. She could have known about the books. If one of Anton's victims or guards had slept at her hotel, she could have known. I frowned. For that matter, she was a dream sorceress. If she wanted to, she could get into anyone's dreams. I stared at Anton. Did vampires dream?

"So it's more likely that someone wanted any book, not a specific book," I said.

"Perhaps."

I shook my head. The list of people who wouldn't want that

book would be shorter than my current list of suspects. "You said Helen Miller designed the traps that protect your vault?"

"The mundane ones, yes. Mrs. Miller is wonderfully skilled in this area. Her creativity delighted me, and I assure you, bypassing her handiwork was no small feat. In fact, I daresay whoever managed it must have gotten their hands on Mrs. Miller herself."

"Or gotten hold of her plans."

Anton shook his head. "There are no plans. I saw to that personally."

I almost pointed out that many creative types doodled or sketched their ideas before drawing up anything official, but decided not to. No sense riling up the secret-hoarding vampire. "You said the mundane traps. There are magical traps as well?"

"There are wards. Wards designed and implemented by my personal wizard."

"And I assume your wizard is very skilled as well?"

Anton steepled his fingers in front of him. "Isai is one of the most powerful wizards from the Old Kingdom. I also consider him a strong suspect."

"You suspect your own wizard?"

"I suspect everyone."

I flipped through the file he'd given me, thumbing through the pages until I found Isai's dossier. "Why would your wizard want the book?"

Anton lifted the pen I'd used to sign the contract, studying it as he spoke. "In recent years, Isai has begun to voice...frustration with how I handle my affairs in this world. It is his belief that humans have far too much control, and he would like to see the Otherworld take a more...active role. Isai has always been hotheaded and power-hungry, and his arrogance is largely what led to his current predicament as my servant—a role he does not always accept with grace. It is my belief that Isai had finally built up the necessary courage for a coup, and getting that book was the first step. With it, he would have been able to simultaneously gain powerful allies and undermine my position with those same allies."

"Since he laid the wards, he would have been able to get through those," I noted. "I assume he has no alibi?"

"None. Also, he was found at the scene."

I stared at the file, quickly reading through the crime scene description. "The guards reported they found him unconscious in front of the vault. A wound on the back of his skull suggests he was struck from behind."

"Indeed. But I don't have to tell you how easy it would be for him to inflict that injury on himself."

"He didn't have your book on him."

"No. But again, it would have been simple for him to hide it. He could have teleported the book away if he chose to do so."

I tapped a finger on the page. "If he stole it, why hasn't he used it?"

"The book is locked with blood. Even with his spellbook, Isai would need time to force it open. And then, of course, it would take time to contact those within the book, make arrangements to solidify his position."

"What do you mean, 'even with his spellbook?'" My jaw dropped and the file sagged in my hand. "Wait a minute. You... You have his spellbook?"

"Yes."

I shook my head. "No wizard would willingly part with his spellbook. Especially not one as old and power-hungry as you claim Isai is."

"He had no choice. He is bound to obey my direct orders."

"Bound how?" Anton watched me for a moment. I sighed. "Confidentiality contract signed in blood. Horrible death. Complete candor?"

He nodded. "My family was turned in the Old Kingdom. At the time, I was a prince, soon to be king, but after our transformation, my father... Well, let us say, he did not foresee ever stepping down from the throne. I realized if I were ever going to get the throne—and keep it—I would need powerful allies. An ally at the time helped me with my first step—securing the services of the most powerful wizard known to our kingdom. The details are not important, but suffice it to say, I acquired his spellbook and offered him a trade. He would agree to serve me until I became king, and I would return his spellbook. He agreed."

I was more than certain his agreement hadn't been that simple, but I held my tongue.

"I assume Mother Hazel has educated you on how this world came to be?" he said, gesturing toward the window.

"You and the other four princes from the five kingdoms managed to grow a new limb on the World Tree. You started building your own kingdom, but eventually other races and figures found out about it and created their own portals to your realm. Eventually those portals wore holes in the veil between worlds, and everything mixed together. This world was the example she used when she explained retro-causal quantum theory, the idea that the future can affect the past."

Anton sighed. "How nice that the contamination of my creation provided educational value during your studies." He shrugged. "Still, one must make do. When I made the decision to stay here instead of remaining in the Old Kingdom, I renegotiated with Isai. I offered him a choice. He could continue serving as my wizard under the old arrangement, which might continue indefinitely, or he could agree to obey any direct order I gave him and there would be a time limit on his servitude. He opted for the latter."

"How many years?"

"One thousand."

I blinked. "How… How many years does he have left?"

"Five hundred. He is halfway to his freedom."

"And you ordered him to give you his spellbook?"

"After the vault was robbed, yes."

Without his spellbook, Isai was limited to the spells he'd committed to memory. Even a wizard with a really good memory would have a hard time recalling every nuance of a spell. And if Isai was as powerful as Anton claimed, his spellbook would be priceless, compiled over centuries. If the vampire refused to return it...

Anton didn't flinch, just held my gaze.

"If you don't mind my asking," I said slowly, "what makes you think Isai won't kill you to get his spellbook back? He must have memorized some nasty spells."

"I have...safeguards in place."

"Safeguards?"

"If something were to happen to me, Isai would find himself the target of several very powerful individuals. He would not live to enjoy his freedom. And he would never see his spellbook again."

I toyed with the zipper on the pouch around my waist. "Wait, if you have these safeguards in place, then why would he risk betraying you? Wouldn't the same safeguards apply?"

"A century or so ago, he would never have considered it. But as I said before, arrogance was always Isai's greatest weakness." Anton leaned back in his seat. "Isai sees enough of my business that he understands how much power and influence I have. But he is not privy to enough detail to fully understand or appreciate how much work goes into it." He paused and tilted his head. "Consider for a moment an amateur painter envying a master's reputation and success. There are those amateurs who think, *If only I had that person's time, and resources, and money, I could be just as successful.* They don't appreciate what truly goes into those masterpieces, the creativity, the thought, the painstaking planning."

"You think Isai believes that if he had your book, he would have instant success comparable to yours. From one book?"

Anton put the pen down and held it to the desk with the tip of one pale finger. "He is wrong. The book is an invaluable resource, yes, but giving someone a set of paints and a canvas does not mean they can give you a masterpiece. Isai never truly understood that because he cannot imagine anyone being smarter than he is. He cannot imagine that I am able to do things because my intellect is superior." He leaned back in his seat, staring into the distance for a moment. "It is this new world, I'm afraid. It's not like the Old Kingdom. Everything is easier. There was a time that death and blood were much more real to Isai. But now...I'm afraid being rich is all it takes to feel invincible in this world."

I studied the file some more, this time reading through the summary of the suspects. "You have this one marked with an asterisk. Flint Valencia. A fey?"

"*Leannan sidhe*, to be precise. Flint is the most recent entry in the book that was stolen. I had given him until the spring equinox to make his choice on whether to sign. He was...reluctant."

"What did you have on him?"

Anton leaned back in his chair. "Flint's people, the *leannan sidhe*, are a very political people. To survive, one must constantly make connections with others, simultaneously building goodwill and gathering blackmail. Seduction has nothing to do with love and everything to do with power, and marriages are contracts no different from a business arrangement. Not everyone has the taste or the energy for such consistent vigilance and ambition."

He wasn't telling me anything I didn't already know, but he seemed to be building to a point. "I take it Flint was such a person?" I asked.

"It would seem so. Flint has little desire to engage in societal politics, but he does desire the power and protection such engagement provides. And unlike some who merely complain about their circumstances, Flint discovered a way to get what he wanted on his terms. A way to have all the knowledge he needed to force alliances and fend off attacks, without any of the effort that comes from building the trust that gathering such information usually requires."

"And how did he manage that?"

"He used a forbidden ritual to bind the soul of one of his own people. He trapped the man's soul in ink, and used it to tattoo his victim's name on his flesh. The binding allows Flint access to his victim's knowledge and memories, in essence, giving Flint precious information it took a lifetime to gather in mere hours."

Ice slid into my blood, and I pressed my hands flat against my thighs, physically centering myself. "That is an evil spell."

"It is."

"What proof do you have?"

"I have the gun he used to shoot his victim, with his fingerprints on it. I also have the bullet with his victim's blood."

I frowned and crossed my arms. "He didn't take the gun with him? And he left the bullet? That seems...careless." I wanted to add it also sounded suspicious that Anton just happened to be on hand to gather the damning evidence, but I held my tongue.

Anton guessed what I was thinking. "Flint did not perform this ritual only once. He wears the names of three victims that I know of. My spies heard rumors of the first victim, and when I learned what he was doing, I made it a point to keep an eye on him. It took time, but when he performed the ritual again, I had someone nearby to interrupt. They disarmed him, then allowed him to leave with his tattoo."

"But not with the evidence."

"Precisely."

The chill in my blood spread down my arms, and I shivered. "I'm not familiar with all the details of such a spell. But it is my understanding that Flint would get the information he wanted by speaking telepathically with the souls trapped in the tattoos." I tried to swallow past the sudden lump in my throat. "His victims are aware they're trapped."

"That is Isai's theory as well," Anton agreed.

"If his people found out what he was doing, they'd kill him. There are few sins greater among the fey than trapping someone's soul, or their essence."

Something passed through Anton's eyes, and for just as second, he looked at me with a little too much intensity, a little too much...expectation. The look was gone before I could call him on it.

"Yes, they would kill him immediately, I would think," he said. "With the evidence I possess, there would be no need for a trial."

That thought made my skin crawl. Everyone deserved a trial. "You said it would be almost impossible for someone to locate a specific book. Why do you think Flint might have done so?"

Anton tapped a few keys on the laptop sitting in the corner of his desk, then turned it to face me.

The quality of the screen was so clear that I had to squint to make sure I wasn't looking out a window. Anton pointed to a man near the elevator. He had one hand braced on the wall, his body bent over a slim brunette dressed in a pair of black dress pants and a red silk shirt. His muscles bunched as he leaned over, straining his black button-down shirt. When he turned his head, I caught a good look at his smiling face, the strong line of his jaw, aquiline nose, and dark eyes shining with mischief. The blue jeans he wore clung in all the right places, but weren't so tight that you missed how incredibly soft they seemed. Even watching the video, I found myself wanting to feel the denim, trace my fingers up the leg...

"That is Flint Valencia. And the woman he is with was one of my guards."

I leaned closer to the screen. Flint was not what I'd expected. He wasn't a long, lean man, and his ears were blunt and rounded. He looked too...rough to be *sidhe*. Too thick. The man on the screen oozed masculinity, the careless, brutish kind of masculinity that made women—and probably some men—think of being snatched off their feet, dragged down to the ground, and taken like an animal in a fit of mindless passion that was more sweat and grunting than silk sheets and pretty words.

My hand brushed the keyboard. Startled, I blinked, realized that at some point I'd risen from my seat and leaned over the desk to stare harder at the *leannan sidhe*. My breathing was labored, and sweat coated my palms. Anton studied me, and though I saw no judgment on his face, it was clear he knew exactly where my thoughts had gone.

I sat abruptly, not bothering to even attempt a recovery of my pride.

"His power is greater than any *leannan sidhe* I have ever known," Anton said calmly. "Concentrate on the effects you're experiencing now. Imagine how much more powerful they will be should you speak to him in person. Take precautions."

I nodded halfway through the sentence, still trying to force my heart rate to slow down to normal. "Good idea." I grabbed the file, needing a distraction to get my chaotic thoughts back in order. "If one of these people stole your book, wouldn't they have tried to use the information against you by now?"

"I believe they have not attempted to use it yet because they have not figured out how to open it."

"How do you open it?"

Anton tapped the slick screen of a smart phone lying on the left side of his desk. "You have three days. Find the book and the thief before then."

So he's not going to tell me how to open it. I lifted the file, drawing a finger over one of the neatly labeled tabs. A murdered woman. Three murdered guards. A missing book. A list of suspects long enough to choke a dragon. Three days to find the thief. My first case.

Excitement bubbled inside me, urging me to accept, to sign the contract. This was it, my chance to follow my own path, and damn what Mother Hazel said. I pressed my lips together, smothering the hasty response. Despite my desire to live my dream, I was not a fool. This was more than I'd bargained for, more than I'd expected for my first case. This...this was politics. Old Kingdom politics. *Vampire* politics.

"Mother Renard, it is my understanding you live off the respect of your village and a small allowance from your mentor."

I bristled. "You make me sound like a teenager. I receive a stipend from Mother Hazel, as is my due as her apprentice until I've found my professional path."

Anton's lips parted, but it wasn't his voice that answered me. A different male voice interrupted, cutting him off.

"You say that so calmly. But we both know how much those 'stipends' from our mentors grate, don't we? They lord them over us, control us by threatening to reduce it or take it away. A stipend is a leash fashioned of coins, chains that weigh us down, drag in our wake and announce to our would-be peers that we are servants instead of our own masters."

I pivoted in my seat, seeking the voice's source. Tension curled my nerve endings at the thought that the vampire's office was not as secure as he'd claimed. Someone had listened as I made a deal with the devil.

"Dimitri, I have asked you countless times not to eavesdrop on my business dealings." Anton rubbed the bridge of his nose. "This is unacceptable."

"What's unacceptable is your security. Aren't you always telling me that security must be rigorously and *routinely* tested? Better I'm the one to find these weaknesses than one of your enemies."

"Debatable," Anton muttered.

"I'm sorry, who is that?" I asked.

Anton sighed. "Mother Renard, meet Dimitri Winters. My son."

"Call me Dimitri, please."

I slumped in my seat, grateful the chair's high back and padded arms kept me from pitching over. "Your...son?"

"Yes. Say goodbye. He was just leaving."

"I'm not going anywhere," Dimitri said. "I want to chat with Mother Renard."

"Please call me Shade." *The vampire prince has a son. Dear Goddess, he has a son.* I gripped the arms of my chair, grounding myself in the present. Now was not the time to reflect on what the vampire's progeny meant for the world. For all I knew, Dimitri wouldn't even take after his father. I'd heard only good things about Anton's wife, Vera. Maybe the boy had her genes. "Um, I feel rude not knowing what direction to face when I speak with you?"

"It's just a mic, no camera, so it doesn't really matter," Dimitri said.

I glanced at Anton. "When you told me who has a right to be down in the guard room before the vault, you didn't mention your son."

"That's because he is not supposed to be down there." Anton pressed a button on the intercom. "Kevin?"

"Sir?" came a voice from the speaker.

"Schedule another sweep."

"Yes, sir." There was a slight pause. "Dimitri?"

"Yes."

Kevin sighed. "All right. I'll get all three teams in."

There was a snicker over the other speaker. "You'll never find it," Dimitri said, sounding smug.

"I'm sorry, you said you wanted to chat with me?" As much as part of me wanted to watch this odd father-son interaction play out, another part of me refused to forget that I was in the office of a man who was a prince and a vampire. Anton had spilled enough blood to wash away most of his enemies. And he'd drunk a good portion of it.

"Forgive my rudeness," Dimitri apologized. "Yes, I'd like to speak with you. You see, I understand. I know who your mentor is. Being Baba Yaga's apprentice cannot have been easy."

I shivered despite myself. Baba Yaga. One of Mother Hazel's oldest names, and the name mortals feared the most to speak. Hearing it spoken out loud filled my mind with images of headless horsemen, human skulls mounted on fence posts with fire in their eyes and mouths. Meat cooking in the oven, filling the house with the scent of a fool who had dared demand aid from the old crone in the forest.

"Let me guess," Dimitri continued. "She made you train for decades, but always avoided the lessons you were most desperate to learn. She designed every task to make you realize how unprepared you were to live on your own, how much you needed her teaching. You fought every day to learn enough to prove yourself, prove you didn't need her parenting anymore, prove you could survive—could *thrive*—on your own. And now you've succeeded, but that stipend… That allowance is the final chain."

Everything he said reverberated in my head. He understood. He really understood. I glanced at Anton. I suppose if anyone would understand what it had been like to study under Baba Yaga, it would be the son of the vampire prince.

Dimitri spoke the next words with the soft, awed voice of someone sharing a great secret. "There is a way to escape. Financial freedom. That is the last step toward independence."

I strained to listen over the roar of my own pulse in my ears. The way he spoke of financial independence… I wanted it.

"Take my case, and I will pay you handsomely," Anton said, riding the coattails of the promise in his son's voice. "You will have the money you need to start your detective agency. And you will not need another penny from your mentor."

The words "I'll take the case!" tingled on the tip of my tongue as soon as the last syllable left his lips, but I bit them back. I wanted to be free from any dependence on Mother Hazel, Goddess knew I did. But something about his tone made me look a little harder at him. He smiled.

"This is not a manipulation, Mother Renard. And let me tell

you, contrary to what my son seems to believe, I too understand. My father was a vampire as well. King of Dacia. I know what it is like to live off someone else's fortune. And I know what it is like when you finally escape it." He pushed the contract toward me. "It is a feeling I highly recommend."

This time, when the pen bit me, I was ready for it.

CHAPTER 6

"Hi, Mr. Valencia, my name is Shade Renard. I'd like to speak with you, so if you would call me back at your earliest convenience, I would appreciate it."

I left my phone number and jabbed the end call button before collapsing into the deep cushions of my couch. The nervous energy buzzing like a disturbed beehive inside me didn't calm right away, the anxiety that had begun with the first syllable of Flint's voicemail message still gripping my insides. Goddess, he had the very definition of a bedroom voice. Whiskey smooth, but rough enough to make you imagine calloused hands squeezing soft flesh. Never had the words "leave me a message and I'll get back to you" held so much promise.

"This is embarrassing." I curled my hands into fists and heaved myself off the couch, marching straight for the refrigerator. At least I'd had the good sense to contact Flint by phone instead of questioning him in person. I grabbed a can of Coke and glared at it for a second. If his voice discombobulated me over the phone, I could only imagine the effect it would have in the flesh. I popped the tab and took a swig.

With carbonation burning its way to my stomach, I faced my

desk with the stiff posture of a solider preparing for battle. "Peasblossom, would you read our to-do list, please?"

"Sure. Wouldn't want you to have to put down your soda—your *second* soda."

"I've been up since six a.m. and it is now three o'clock in the afternoon. I have spent the last nine hours studying three boxes of files that Anton messengered over. Hundreds of people, employees, enemies. Do you know how to make a *sylph* bard angry?" I snorted. "Anton does."

"Oh, fine, if you're going to whine about it." Peasblossom put down the piece of chocolate she'd been consuming, reconsidered, and picked it back up. The square of Hershey's dwarfed her head, and she grunted as she lugged it across the desk and resumed eating as she read off the list. "Call the *leannan sidhe*."

"Done."

"Identify rash on young Michael's back and advise mother as to treatment."

"Rug burn. Tell Michael's brothers to stop dragging him around the carpet when they play capture the supervillain."

"Figure out how baby Eloise is getting out of her crib and advise mother as to preventative methods."

"She's two. She's hefting herself out with her Goddess-given strength. I took her mother a basket of chocolates and helped her transform the crib to a toddler bed." I paused and looked at Peasblossom still munching on the piece of chocolate. "Where did you get that?"

The pixie froze, then narrowed her eyes at me. "What, she'll miss one lousy piece?"

I kept staring at her. Waiting.

Her little chin jutted out in defiance. "One measly bar?"

"She's about to learn she has a climber, Peasblossom. Have a heart. She needs all the chocolate she can get."

"Meet with possibly evil vampire prince turned probably evil businessman about his book of definitely evil blackmail?" Peasblossom read loudly.

I looked at the clock on my phone. If I left now, I'd arrive at Anton's office by sunset. "Get in the car."

"I don't like driving," Peasblossom complained, rolling onto her back and holding the half-eaten piece of chocolate over her head. "Can't we ask Mother Hazel for a gatestone?"

"No."

Peasblossom let out the exasperated sigh of a put-upon teenager and hugged the chocolate to her chest. After dragging her feet the entire trek to the side of the desk, she hurled herself into the air with the attitude of someone being horribly inconvenienced and dropped onto my shoulder like a wet towel. "She'd give you one, you know. She practically said she doesn't mind you being an investigator."

I closed the door without locking it and got into the Focus. "She did not. She paused longer than usual between admonitions that I'm wasting my skills."

"Same difference."

"I'm not asking for a gatestone. Besides, I made this." I held up a small bag of herbs and crystals and hung it from the rearview mirror. "It's a luck charm. If I'm right, it should bless us with green lights and thin traffic."

"But it won't do anything about construction, will it?" Peasblossom pointed out.

No, it wouldn't. There was no magic strong enough to overcome the necessary inconvenience that was construction.

I pulled out of the driveway, careful not to run over the possum meandering along as if he owned the property, and headed toward the highway. "Why don't we use this drive time to our advantage? Read the files out loud and we'll discuss points as they come up. You'll see, this will be productive."

It wasn't productive. What it was, in fact, was two and a half hours of hearing all the different ways Peasblossom could annoy me with her voice. Reading too slow, reading too fast, pausing too long between words, putting the accent on the wrong syllable. Then there was her attempt to make boring parts "sound exciting" and her insistence on providing a running commentary that had more to do with how Flint might have seduced someone than any evidentiary value.

By the time we arrived at Anton's office, my finger was cramped from hovering over the button that would have rolled Peasblossom's window down and sent her flying out of the car. With near-Herculean strength, I pried my hand away and opened the door to escape. That Peasblossom flew behind me instead of perching on my shoulder told me she'd tormented me on purpose and was more than aware of how close I was to snapping.

The Winters Group building sat in the central business district of Cleveland. An imposing tower of row after row of dark windows, it gave the impression of staring down at you, as if the master of the building himself watched from behind every black, reflective surface. The uppermost floor boasted windows four times the size of those below, and didn't reflect any light. I guessed those windows marked the floor of the building inhabited exclusively by the vampire.

I paused before entering the building to straighten my red trench coat, a stiff breeze making me wish it reached all the way down to my ankle instead of cutting off at mid-thigh. Peasblossom landed on the back of my neck and grabbed two handfuls of my hair to wrap around her.

"Hurry up, I'm freezing!"

"All right, I'm going!"

My fingers had just brushed the silver handle of the door when it flew open, cracking against my knuckles. I hissed as a woman barreled straight into me. She must have been heavier than she looked, because all I got was a fleeting look at blonde hair and a slim black leather coat, and then I was toppling backward. I hit the ground with an undignified grunt, wincing as my hip impacted against the cold cement.

"Oh, I'm so sorry! I didn't see you."

"It's all right," I said, forcing a smile as I looked up into wide blue eyes. I wanted to point out that the doors were heavy, solid glass and it was hard to believe she could have missed me in my vibrant red coat, but she looked genuinely distressed. "No harm done."

"Oh, look at your beautiful coat." She helped me up and brushed the dirt from my arms and back. "I'm so sorry."

"Really, it's all right." I smoothed my hair down, discreetly feeling for Peasblossom to make sure she was okay. A reassuring pat against my neck assured me she was. I exhaled a sigh of relief.

The woman kept brushing off my coat, as if getting every speck off the material was necessary to excuse her faux pas. She stopped a split second before it got awkward.

"You're sure you're okay?" she asked, waving a hand at me and wiggling her fingers at each body part in turn as if to specify she meant all of me.

I held on to the smile despite the throbbing in my hip. I had the stray thought that if I'd torn my leggings, I was going to be really upset. "Absolutely."

She smiled back. "Oh, good. Again, I'm so sorry."

As soon as she left, Peasblossom poked her head out from behind my hair just enough to speak into my ear. "What a weirdo. Was she brushing you off or checking for loose valuables?"

"We're not in Kansas anymore," I muttered. "At least she didn't ask me if I wanted to buy a watch."

Even with the security badges Anton had left at the door for us, it took several minutes to pass the security checkpoints posted at every level. By the time I got to the top floor, I was just grateful there hadn't been a body cavity search.

The lounge area outside Anton's office door was nicer than

my house. Stark, perfect white walls contrasted with the black leather chairs that looked so soft my hand twitched to touch them. The small table in front of the chairs was painted black wood, the top marked with a checkered pattern of different textures. My hip throbbed, stressing how very, very comfortable the chairs looked. Before I could sit down and experience the joy for myself, a door swished behind me.

Peasblossom squeaked, a sound somewhere between a gasp and a scream. Her reaction killed the readied greeting before it left my lips, adrenaline spinning me around in time to see a man with thick orange-blond hair and a long matching beard barreling toward me. He wore an expensive suit like Anton, but unlike the vampire, this man wore a ridiculous amount of jewelry. Chains hung around his neck, a heavy watch circled his wrist, and a ring squeezed every finger. He jingled when he walked, and the furious pace he'd set made quite a racket. I recognized him from the file. Isai, Anton's personal wizard.

"You," he snarled. He slashed a few sharp gestures in the air.

Instinct jerked my hands up. *"Armatura!"* My shields snapped into place, the ring on my finger humming as blue energy spilled over my entire body.

"Apstergeo!" He tore through the layer of protective blue energy like a child through a stubborn candy wrapper, raking a spell down my body. Vibrant gold light lit up my mind's eye, claws slicing my spell to ribbons. I stumbled from the force of it even as some faraway part of my brain registered the lack of pain.

The spell didn't hurt me, not beyond destroying my shields.

It did, however, piss me off.

I gritted my teeth and called another spell. Fire tickled my palm, a comforting warmth begging to sail through the air and bite into my attacker. I doubted I could stop him, not without destroying a good bit of the building in the process. But I could hurt him. I stopped myself before I could give in to the petty urge.

"You fool," Isai bit out. "You incompetent wretch. How could you miss such an obvious spell? How could you not *expect* it?"

My temper notched higher, and the spell flickered. "How silly of me not to expect an attack from the personal wizard of the man who hired me—outside the office I was to meet him in, no less."

The wizard sneered. "I did not attack you, you simple-minded female. I removed the spell someone else put on you. The spell someone else was using to spy on you. The spell you brought *here.*"

My blood ran cold and the fire spell dissipated with a faint hiss. "What?"

"You didn't feel it, did you? You had no idea." His nose wrinkled with disgust. "You have been hired by one of the most powerful men in the world—in two worlds. Do you really think no one is watching? Do you think no one will attempt to spy on you, follow your 'investigation?'"

I ignored the insinuated quotes around "investigation," as my mind raced over recent events, trying to figure out what he was talking about. I'd come straight from home. Who could have—

I froze. The woman who'd run into me. All the time she'd spent brushing me off, the way she'd waved her hand in my direction. I gave myself a vicious mental kick. *Fool!*

I wanted to defend myself, Goddess knew I wanted to defend myself. But I couldn't. He was right.

But he was still an ass.

"You're right. I should have expected something like that. It was a mistake, one I won't repeat." I wrenched my spine a little straighter, bracing myself. "Now I understand how humiliated you must have felt. Standing outside a vault that had just been robbed, and still caught unaware. A powerful wizard, taken out by a blow to the head. Like swatting a fly."

Isai's eyes widened. "Your insolence will be the death of you." The rings on his fingers clinked together as he grasped at empty air, probably imagining my throat in his grip.

"Seems like your job was to know if someone messed with your wards, and if they did, get there to stop them before they made off with anything," I continued, my heart lodged in my throat. "Maybe if you'd been half as good at your job as you want me to be at mine, your boss wouldn't need to hire a 'simple-minded female.'"

He raised a hand, and my stomach rolled on a violent wave of nerves. I unfastened my coat and groped for the notebook in the side pocket of my waist pouch, grateful I hadn't put it in the bottomless main pocket. My hand shook as I slid the little pen from the plastic spiral that held the pages together and opened the notebook with trembling fingers.

"I have some questions for you, if you don't mind? Anton says you're the one who warded the hallway. Is it possible you made a mistake?"

"My wards were perfect!"

I nodded, making a note on the first clean page of the notebook. "Well then, perhaps *you* dropped the wards? I heard Flint's voicemail today, and I have to say, even in a recording, he sounds *very* persuasive. Perhaps he talked you into dropping your...wards?"

Too late, I realized I'd gone too far. A roar ripped from Isai's throat, and a spell exploded from his fingertips. I dove out of the way, feeling the tingle of magic hurtle through the air so close it burned. My notebook fell from my hand in a flutter of paper as I rolled, coming up with a defensive spell already rolling over me.

Isai made a strange choking sound, and a second later, a familiar Dacian accent cut through the cloying press of magic in the air.

"Enough."

Anton's voice froze me in place. I stared with my lips parted in shock. Isai knelt on the floor, pressing his hand to his side. His face remained a mottled red, his eyes burning with hatred as he continued to glare at me even as blood seeped from between his fingers, staining his rings with a red shine.

Penetrating abdominal trauma, right lumbar region. He'll have to heal soon. Hope that Anton didn't puncture a kidney.

I shook off the semi-hysterical diagnosis and held my breath as Isai wrenched his glare from me to Anton. So much hatred. It was a wonder the vampire didn't spontaneously combust. Adrenaline coursed through my system, demanding fight or flight. I clenched my hands into fists and forced myself to hold still and wait.

Anton drew a handkerchief out of his pocket and wiped the blade of his dagger. "Heal yourself and join us when you've recovered your sense of decorum," he said to Isai without turning. "Mother Renard and I will review the crime scene as planned."

He never looked back, never gave the wizard a second glance. Instead, he picked up my notebook and handed it to me, the picture of gentlemanly consideration, then took my arm and led me out a door to a staircase. I followed without a word, but had to stop at the bottom of the first set of stairs when my legs threatened to give out from under me.

Anton's gaze weighed on me with near-tangible force. I leaned on the wall, giving myself a firm mental lecture on picking fights with magically superior bullies and trying to talk my legs into supporting me a little longer.

"You are either much more powerful than I suspected," Anton said after a moment, "or you are unaware of the change in your circumstances."

"What?"

I'd resisted the urge to sit on the steps—barely—but I still wasn't ready to risk continuing down the stairs. My legs were as stable as those inflatable waving tube people that businesses were so fond of using for advertising, and my back itched with the anticipation of an attack still to come.

"As I understand it, you only recently completed your initial training as a witch, expanding your knowledge base and learning the rudimentaries of magic. Your actual repertoire of spells and your control over them is still in the early stages, is it not?"

He wasn't wrong. Mother Hazel had been adamant that knowledge was more important than magic. She'd spent the majority of my apprenticeship making me an expert on "everything." Sure, she'd taught me the basics of spellcasting, but I had a lot to learn. Or, rather, a lot to practice.

How a vampire knew about a witch's training I didn't know. The only people in a position to have told him such things would be me, Peasblossom, and Mother Hazel herself. I hadn't told him. I didn't see Peasblossom flying all the way here without me to have a chat. I narrowed my eyes. "Have you—"

"As I understand it," he continued, "magical ability for a witch is much like a body of water created by an outside force—I believe you call them patrons, or gods. Some witches are puddles, some lakes, and some great oceans. But regardless of how much water a witch holds, what matters is her control, her ability to focus it to accomplish her goals. After all, if one wishes to put out a candle, unleashing an entire ocean on it and destroying the city that contained said candle wouldn't do, would it?"

I blinked. "I... I think that's the best analogy for magic I've ever heard."

He tilted his head, studying me a little closer. "Tell me, Mother Renard. Are you a puddle or an ocean?"

Alarm bells went off in my brain, filling me with a sudden and complete conviction that it was best if Anton didn't know the full extent of my power. After ignoring the little voice during my interaction with the wizard, I was now prepared to listen. "Isai is an ocean, isn't he?"

Anton's facial expression didn't change. "In terms of magic,

Mother Renard, Isai is the seven seas." He shrugged. "Or he was, before I confiscated his book."

I wilted against the wall. "I should probably start thinking of what to get him as an apology gift, then." *That's two in as many days. Wonderful.*

The vampire's eyebrows rose as I resumed walking down the stairs. "Apology gift?"

"My mentor is adamant about them. She said when you live as long as a witch does, it doesn't behoove you to make enemies, so when you think you've made an enemy, you should attempt to make recompense. Mend bridges, so to speak."

"Interesting." He glanced at me. "I do not think you will mend the bridge with Isai. He's rather…emotional."

"Most wizards would be, when their spellbooks are being held hostage."

"It's been very motivational."

"I suppose." A grimace tugged at the corners of my mouth as I recalled something he'd said before. "What did you mean, a 'change in my circumstances?'"

"I refer only to the fact you prodded Isai into attacking you. Logic dictates either you felt you could best him in a duel, or you believed he wouldn't kill you."

My mouth went dry. *Well, when you put it like that.* "I… He started it."

"And he would have finished it." Anton stopped then, turning to face me with a stern, almost parental expression on his sharp features. "I must make something clear, something that perhaps I should have emphasized when I hired you. Isai would kill you, Mother Renard. In cold blood or hot blood, he would kill you, and he would not lose a wink of sleep over it."

"Yes, I get that n—"

"Flint is a *leannan sidhe*, and it is not unheard of for their lovers to die by accident because the *sidhe* lost himself in pleasure and didn't care to notice. That list I gave you, those boxes full of files. Anyone on that list could, and would, kill you, given the opportunity and the slightest motivation."

A chill ran over my skin, and I shivered. I'd been the sole guardian of my village for three years, but now that I stopped to consider it, I'd never faced a threat of the level Anton described. I'd taken care of creatures hunting humans for food out of instinct, haunting a human out of hate. But no one had come after me personally. My death had never been a powerful person's goal.

In that moment, I felt weak, vulnerable.

I hated that feeling.

Anger rose to my defense. I jutted my chin out at the vampire, holding my temper like a shield. "Why are you trying to scare me? I thought you wanted me on this case?"

The skin between his eyebrows pinched. "I am not trying to scare you. I want to prepare you. If you are to be of any use to me, then you must understand you are not in Dresden anymore. What you have taken on is not one of your witch's duties, not a parenting club, or a healer's oath. You are not exterminating a minor monster." He took a step closer, and I fell back a step before I could stop myself. "Someone stole from me, Mother Renard. A person willing to risk the consequences of such a theft would not think twice about ending your life. Make no mistake, you may well die before you see the next full moon."

And on that cheerful note, he continued down the stairs, neat as you please. It wasn't until that moment, that moment when I could have used a word of reassurance, of support, that I noticed Peasblossom's absence.

Oh, dear Goddess, no.

My heart shot into my throat. Slowly, so as not to draw the vampire's attention, I rolled my shoulder, wriggling my body to feel for the pixie, make sure she wasn't clinging to me and had just moved out of her usual position. Nothing.

"So tell me about security," I said a little too loudly, trying very hard not to think about what the nosy pixie could get into in the super-secretive vampire's super-secret headquarters. I had to keep talking, keep him occupied until she came back, and pray he didn't notice her absence. "What sort of—"

I choked on the end of the sentence, halting so fast on the stairs that I nearly pitched forward and fell the rest of the way. Cold sweat dampened my temples as I stared in horror at the next landing.

The first five steps were fine, perfectly normal. But below that, dark water filled the stairwell, licking the walls as the churning surface betrayed movement. I caught a flash of something gray and huge moving under the water before the creature sank deeper.

Anton stepped into the water without hesitation, not even pausing as I grabbed the railing in a death grip and clung for dear life.

"Illusions play a large part," he said.

He continued to descend into the water—past the water. A tiny part of my brain noted his disregard, and I realized the water, and the monster within, were illusions. The rest of my brain controlled my body and refused to let go of the railing, lest the tiny, reasonable part hurled us into a watery, toothy death.

"Mother Renard, I hate to rush you, but if you don't mind…?"

I closed my eyes, took three, seven, thirteen deep breaths, then charged down the stairs.

And collided with the vampire.

The impact of running into the preternaturally strong undead was akin to colliding with that bar in the center of a large double doorway, the one where the two doors met to lock. Not that I spoke from experience…

He arched an eyebrow at me as I regained my balance and tried to ignore the heat in my face. "Would you like me to hold your hand?"

I cleared my throat, too embarrassed to consider if he was

serious or cracking a joke. "That won't be necessary. You were saying something about illusions?"

He continued his descent without further comment. "Yes. This staircase is the only one that leads to this level, and there is no elevator past the floor above us." He opened a door and led me out of the stairwell. We stepped into an area the size of my living room. Straight ahead of me was an L-shaped desk. The bottom of the L pointed toward the left-hand wall, and the chair posted there faced a wall with at least six different monitors. The man sitting in the viewing chair scanned the screens in long sweeps, his hands poised at the edge of the keyboard. The pale tone of his flesh and the eerie stillness that consumed him any time he paused made me think vampire, but I didn't bother using magic to confirm the suspicion. I made a brief mental note that he was sitting in the same chair the last guard with that assignment had died in.

The woman sitting at the desk looked at Anton, meeting his eyes without a hint of hesitation. She was tall, at least six foot six. She had pale blonde hair and blue eyes that reminded me of sunlight reflecting off a frozen lake. There was an analytical quality to her gaze whenever she looked at someone. Valkyrie—I would have bet my last bar of chocolate on it. A second woman stood in front of the door in the far-right corner of the room, only her upper half visible above the desk. Like the Valkyrie, she was stunning. Dark hair and flawless cinnamon skin. She watched me with large, dark eyes, but like the others, remained silent.

I waited for Anton to introduce us, but he paused in front of the desk and looked at me, keeping the room's other occupants in his peripheral vision.

"This is where the guards were found." He gestured to the ground behind the desk where tape marked the bodies' positions.

"Were they human?"

"No. The woman was half-goblin. The two men were fey and werewolf."

"I assume the variety was intentional?"

"Yes. Varying the guards' strengths and weaknesses makes it harder to disable them simultaneously."

I stared down at the body outlines, my heart aching for a moment at the loss of life. "Didn't work out that way. So the murderer came down those stairs. Someone would have heard them coming. Unless he or she teleported in?"

"Impossible. The wards prevent teleportation to this level."

"So they had to hide their approach from the senses of a fey and a werewolf. Not a minor invisibility spell then, but something that would keep them from being heard or smelled." I drew my hand through the air, spreading a thin net of silver energy over the room. *"Revelare."*

Purple mist hung in the air, so faint I wouldn't have noticed if not for the stark white of the walls. I stared harder, ignoring the way the Valkyrie watched me with a little too much interest.

"It's a holding spell," I murmured. "A strong one. It's hard enough to hold one person, but to hold three non-humans…"

"Can you trace it to the person who cast it?" Anton asked.

I shook my head. "There are some spells that can be traced, but usually those are spells created by the caster. This is a generic spell, there's no way to discern the caster just by what I can see here."

I pressed out with my magic, feeling for the remains of the broken wards. If I could see how they were broken, I might—

Only there weren't any.

I frowned and concentrated harder.

"The wards weren't broken," I murmured. "They were dropped."

"Yes. Another reason Isai is so high on the list."

I remembered my earlier accusation. I'd said it to upset Isai, but now... "Could Flint have seduced Isai into dropping the wards for him?"

Anton considered the question. "It is not impossible. But it is very unlikely. Isai does not enjoy the company of men. Flint could have seduced him against his will, yes, but doing so would have brought negative consequences to Isai that would have made it imprudent."

"What do you mean?"

"Flint does not seduce by physical force. To be taken against one's will through violence is traumatizing enough. Flint's power seduces the mind. By the time he takes a lover, they want him to take them. To use that influence on Isai would violate not just his body, but his mind. Given Isai's...strong distaste for men, the damage to his mind would be considerable."

I thought of Helen Miller's ghost, the empty stare. My pulse skipped a beat and I fought to keep my voice calm. "What if he tried to seduce a woman who liked men, but was happily married and rejected his advances? Would that result in 'considerable' mental damage?"

Anton looked at me more closely now, interest in his icy blue eyes. "If she were a strong-willed woman determined to remain loyal to her husband, the damage could range from headaches and vivid flashbacks to severe brain damage. Why?"

I hesitated. The fewer people who knew of Helen's death and the damage to her mental state, the stronger my position if I needed to bluff. But Anton had hired me. He had a vested interest in helping me find out the truth about what happened to Helen, who'd stolen his precious book. Unless he'd killed her. Unless he'd lied about the mental manipulation, and had killed her to keep his secrets.

I couldn't get the image of Helen's ghost out of my mind. I kept seeing those empty eyes, flickering with brief moments of frustration, pain, then going blank again. I could hear that skin-crawling moan. What if the vampire had killed her? Anton stepped closer. I looked up, still thinking of Helen, still seeing Helen. And in that moment of distraction, I forgot the cardinal rule of dealing with vampires.

I fell into Anton's gaze the way one might fall out an open window. I looked into his eyes, and I could see frost, smell it as if a winter breeze blew here in this small, underground room. My world narrowed down to that scent and those cold blue eyes. Tiny specks of red in his irises flared, burning to life like dry leaves kissed by flame.

"You work for me, Mother Renard." Anton leaned a little closer, his eyes swallowing more of my world. The cold blue vanished under hot red, left me gazing into a glowing crimson stare. "You will not withhold information from me. Tell me why you asked about the damage Flint can do with his power. Whose mind did he damage?"

"Helen...Miller's." My voice sounded dull, and too far away. "Her ghost is mute, unresponsive. Someone...destroyed her mind."

Anton's nostrils flared. "Why did you keep this from me?"

"I don't trust you."

My mouth refused to obey my commands to close, to remain shut.

"Tell me everything you know about her death," he said. "Everything you know about Helen Miller."

His voice pulled me deeper under his thrall. Power stabbed at my thoughts, probing for the information like a thief caressing a jewel case, selecting the most promising trinkets. I curled my hands into fists and tried to think of something else, anything that would break the trance. My vision blurred and I swayed, pain throbbing in the back of my eyes.

Peasblossom chose that moment to fall through the air and land with a thud on the vampire's head.

CHAPTER 7

Anton snarled and snatched up Peasblossom before she could make a sound, curled fingers raking her off his head then closing around her in an iron grip. The trance broke as soon as he looked away from me, and I staggered, my stomach rolling from the abrupt release.

A high-pitched squeal of fear from Peasblossom sent a rush of panic over me, pouring adrenaline into my veins, and I threw out a hand. "You'll crush her wings!"

The vampire's stare drilled into me, and I dug my nails into my palms to keep from looking into his eyes again out of morbid curiosity. It had been foolish to forget how dangerous he was, to assume he wasn't a threat because he'd hired me. I'd let my guard down. *Fool me once...*

"Where did you come from?" The edge in Anton's voice belied the calm of his expression.

"The ceiling!" Peasblossom grunted. "This stuff made my wings stick together so I couldn't fly."

Relief weakened my knees. Peasblossom sounded normal, if a little winded. I checked her wings to make sure the delicate limbs hadn't torn, and noticed something odd.

A sticky blue substance covered the pixie. It looked sort of like that Silly String small children went wild with before they were old enough to appreciate how hard it was to clean up. Thin strands of it covered her from wing to toe. Anton held her by the back of her dress with two fingers, trying to avoid getting any more of the blue gunk on him than necessary. I almost giggled at the sight of the residue clinging to his long hair where she'd landed on him, pulled into strings still attached to the pixie. Then I noticed his grip also put his finger on Peasblossom's wings. He could rip them off with a flick of his hand if he wanted to. Tension strangled the urge to laugh, and I swallowed hard.

"Thank you for helping, Peasblossom," I said with forced brightness. "Anything to help solve this case faster."

Anton looked up at the ceiling. I followed his gaze, my eyebrows rising at the trail of blue goop that moved from the door all the way across the ceiling to just above his head.

I thought I saw the Valkyrie smirk out of the corner of my eye, but her expression took on complete neutrality when Anton glared at her.

"She has a security badge," the woman pointed out, gesturing at the tiny badge Peasblossom wore. "You said the witch was bringing her familiar."

Anton's jaw clenched as he raised Peasblossom to eye level. "You were to remain with your witch. That blue substance means you tried to enter one of the vents. What. Were. You. Doing?"

"I was *helping*." Peasblossom squirmed, then seemed to realize, as I had, the dangerous position her wings were in. She went still. "I was checking to see…if someone my size could get in." She nodded, a little too fast. "Yeah. You bigjobs are always thinking everyone has to be your size, but what if it was someone my size?" She scowled and picked at the blue stuff on one arm. "I could have made it in through that vent, but this stuff smells funny. Still, that doesn't mean someone who really wanted your stupid treasure wouldn't have pressed on."

"Had you made it more than three feet into the vents over the corridor, this substance"— he rubbed a little of the blue webbing between his fingers—"would have caught fire. Despite the alarms, help would not have arrived in time to save you from becoming a pile of ashes."

"Oh." Peasblossom seemed to give that a lot of thought. At least two seconds. "I don't think anyone came in that way."

Neither of the two remaining guards said a word, or even moved a muscle, but Peasblossom's announcement seemed to further amuse the Valkyrie. At least, I thought the twitch of her mouth was amusement. Or she saw an impending death. A little creepy how that always seemed to perk up a Valkyrie.

"Do not think I invited you into my place of business on a whim," Anton said, trying to catch my eye. "It is not a decision I made lightly."

I'd intended to stare between his eyes, or maybe at his nose, but he seemed agitated, so to be on the safe side, I gave up all pretense of pride and stared at the floor. "I understand."

"No, I don't think you do." He flexed his hand, and Peasblossom shrieked. "Tell me what you were doing in the vents."

"All right!" Peasblossom wailed. "Fine!" She crossed her arms, settling into a firm sulk. "I spit on Isai."

Anton blinked. I closed my eyes and rubbed the bridge of my nose.

"You…spit on him?" Anton asked.

"Yes. He tried to hurt Shade. He can't do that!"

"So…you spit on him."

Peasblossom giggled, oblivious to her precarious situation. "A couple times. Got him in his stupid beard, too."

"You could check into that if you wanted to," I pointed out.

A thin line appeared between Anton's brows as he glanced back and forth between us. "I don't believe I'll call in the analysts to comb through a wizard's beard for…pixie saliva, just yet."

I didn't breathe easy until he held Peasblossom out, letting me

DEADLINE

accept her into my cupped hands. Peasblossom hugged me as soon as she was close enough to my shoulder, getting plenty of sticky blue residue on my black shirt.

"I want more honey for this," she mumbled.

"A great big pot, as soon as we get home," I whispered. Louder, I said, "We know it would take a powerful magic user to get through Isai's wards. There's no trace of them left, so either Isai took them down himself, on his own initiative, or because someone else blackmailed or bribed him to do it, or someone more powerful than Isai obliterated them."

"Obliterating them would be a next-to-impossible task," Anton mused. "A magic ward as complicated as Isai's is much like a network of spider webs. It is one thing to break through them —that is difficult enough—but I do not believe whoever did it would have taken the time and painstaking care to clean up and erase all signs of the broken wards. Even if someone were strong enough, it would be a waste of power."

"What about the other traps, the ones they would need to pass after getting past the ward?" I asked. "Helen Miller built them for you, so I assume they aren't magic?"

Anton gestured for me to follow him to the door beside the long desk. The new vantage point granted me my first unrestricted view of the guard stationed at the door—and the thick serpentine tail that formed her lower half.

I'd already thought her beautiful, but the tail gave her an exotic edge that made her stunning. She wore a chainmail shirt that moved with her and was so fine I wouldn't have known it was chainmail if its movement hadn't betrayed its weight. I studied her tail, admiring the emerald green of her scales, the patches where they bled to gold. One section of her tail seemed duller. I frowned, trying to look at it more closely without being too obvious.

"There are two traps that are magic," Anton continued. "Both of them powered by objects I acquired, as opposed to a spell."

"Because you couldn't trust Isai to do it, since they're meant to stop him as well," I said.

"Yes. Opening this door triggers the first trap, a spell designed to rob someone of magical ability for five minutes."

"So they can't use magic to pass the traps," I guessed.

"Exactly."

"What if they just stand here for five minutes?"

Anton strode forward to open the door, and the *naga* slid out of the way, her scales making a faint hiss on the floor. I tore my eyes from that strange cloudy spot on her tail to follow Anton's hand when he gestured to the first square of the hallway's paneled floor, a rough section that looked like a sheet of metallic pebbles. "That is a pressure plate. If you stand on it for over thirty seconds, the magnetic field holding it together releases and it falls apart, simultaneously releasing a net of braided iron, silver, and gold to ensnare the intruder and hold them until security can arrive."

"Effective."

"It should have been." Anton's voice was emotionless, but the red flecks in his eyes spoke of his temper.

"You should put a humidifier down here," I blurted out.

Anton paused. "I'm sorry?"

"A humidifier." I gestured at the *naga's* tail, the section of scales that looked different from the rest. "She needs more moisture in her environment or she'll retain patches of old scales after she sheds her skin. It's uncomfortable at best, and could lead to more serious problems." I considered my audience and added, "And discomfort can be a dangerous distraction for a guard."

The *naga* stared at me. It wasn't an unfriendly expression, more like surprise. Anton shared his attention between the two of us, then nodded. "I will make arrangements."

"What about introductions?" I glanced pointedly at the guards, then to myself.

"I do not allow visitors to fraternize with my guards. You

don't need to know them or their names to do your job, and they don't need to know you to do theirs." The corner of his mouth tilted down. "You saw the tape from the hotel. I trust you understand why I wish for the guards to remain anonymous?"

"I suppose." I stopped talking before I continued to say how rude it seemed to act as though a living person didn't exist when they were standing three feet away from you. I'm smart like that. So smart, I even remembered to cover Peasblossom's mouth before she said it for me.

Anton crossed the threshold into the hall. "I will show you the rest. The second magic trap is at the end, near the vault. Its purpose is to prevent teleportation."

"Just in case Isai took down the wards, he still wouldn't be able to teleport in."

"Yes."

I scanned the walls, looking for signs of coming traps. "You really don't trust him. You make him work so closely with you, but you still take precautions as if he'll betray you any day."

"Mother Renard, I may have manipulated Isai into my employ, but make no mistake, he has benefited from our relationship. Especially since settling in this world, he has not always been unhappy. It has only been in recent decades that his ambition has grown in opposition to mine, and he has begun to believe he could make a better life for himself than he has as my wizard."

"So you've been expecting a betrayal. And yet you keep him."

"I have taken precautions."

Mother Hazel had spoken at length about the five princes who'd created this world. I'd asked her once if the vampire was a bad man, and she'd tilted her head, thought for over ten minutes, and, finally, she'd said he was very "practical."

Anton pressed his hand to a panel on the wall. A small panel opened, revealing a large red button.

"You have a kill switch," I said.

"It is necessary." Anton pressed the button.

"Who can access it?"

"Myself, my wife, and any combination of all three guards on duty."

I noticed a drop of blood on the scanner Anton had pressed his hand to. Anton removed a foil packet from his jacket and tore it open. The scent of alcohol filled the air as he cleaned the scanner.

"So if the three guards conspired against you, they could access the kill switch?" I asked.

"Yes. But the guard assignments are random, it would be difficult for them to plan a conspiracy. In addition, the scanner injects whoever presses a hand to it with a poison that changes from time to time. Without the antidote, the would-be thief would die an unpleasant death."

Not a concern for a vampire, I noted. I followed Anton into the hallway. The corridor had at least five turns. At least three traps lined each stretch. By the time we reached the vault itself, I'd seen traps that fired arrows tipped in poison, traps that sprayed a fountain of acid, traps that crushed the unsuspecting with falling rocks, traps that dropped people through the floor into pits of slime, and traps that shocked trespassers with enough electricity to make an elemental twitch.

And that was only a sampling.

Perhaps one of the most interesting things about them was that, despite their barbaric and timeless nature, they were all high tech in terms of what triggered them. Electronic sensors and magnetic pressure plates, etc.

We arrived at the vault and I looked back down the corridor. Just as the report had stated, none of the traps had been triggered, barring the first one that would have prevented the use of magic.

"So someone had to know about that first trap," I said, "and then they would have needed to bypass all these traps."

"Isai believes the thief used a spell. *Tergora inpenetrabiles*, or something like it."

My eyes widened. "I only know a handful of magic users that could manage that spell."

"Isai is one of them. He also claims there are magic objects that could give the possessor that ability."

I nodded. "The Eye of Argus would do it."

"I have people looking into the objects Isai mentioned, trying to track down who possesses them. I will keep you informed."

The corridor opened up, ending in a large room with a vault at the far end. I looked at the ground where an X had been marked out in black tape. "So this is where they found Isai?"

"Yes. As per protocol, when the guards failed to check in, a team was sent down to investigate. One remained in the room with the dead guards, while the rest of the team came down the corridors, one remaining at each turn. It was the final three guards who found Isai."

"Let's say Isai did rob the vault. He didn't have the book on him, so he would have had to teleport it away."

"It would have been simple for him to disable the teleportation dampener once he made it this far, given the proper amount of time."

"All right, but if he was able to teleport the book away, why not teleport himself away with it? He'd have gotten away clean."

Anton inclined his head. "Isai himself made the same argument. However, let me put forth an alternative narrative. Perhaps Isai did teleport the book away, considering that his ace in the hole. Once it is gone and 'safe,' his greed gets the better of him and he returns to the vault to steal something else. The guards are equipped with magic-negating orbs, the size of marbles. They are trained to move silently, and to throw those orbs down this corridor before rounding it. Isai could have been caught off guard. He would not have been able to use magic to escape, or to hide. He would have known the guards were nearly upon him and been forced to use drastic, and mundane, means."

"So he hit himself over the head and pretended to be just regaining consciousness when the guards arrived on the scene."

Anton nodded. "It is possible. The guards inform me that Isai was in quite a rage when they found him struggling to his feet. He promised vengeance on whomever had struck him, demanded they summon me immediately."

"If he had the book as insurance, why would he bother pretending?"

"Isai could not have opened the book the day of the theft. He needed to pretend his innocence until such time as he could avail himself of the information within the book."

I considered that. After a minute, another thought occurred to me. "Why didn't you lock him up if you suspected him? Why give him the opportunity to return to the book?"

"Truthfully, I would have preferred to lock him up, at least for a time. However, our agreement stipulates that I will not imprison him without direct evidence that he has violated our working arrangement. He is to be permitted his unimpeded freedom during his employment. It was one of two stipulations he held fast to."

"What was the second?"

Anton arched an eyebrow. "That I would not kill him. An odd request, since there are fates much worse than death."

I thought I knew the answer already, but I asked anyway. "That first trap, the one that inhibits magic. It's triggered by the door?"

"Yes."

"So if a magic user knew about it, he could use magic to open the door, trigger the trap, wait five minutes, and then enter safely?"

Anton's jaw tightened. "Yes."

Isai's voice halted whatever response I might have offered.

"Do you require my help, or has the brilliant Mother Renard already solved the crime?"

I spun around, startled by the wizard's voice right behind me. Anton didn't react at all, so I was betting he'd heard him approach. Isai was dressed exactly as he'd been before. There were no tears in his jacket, no blood on his rings. Not surprising, the wizard could probably cast a prestidigitation and mending spell with the ease most people blinked.

I bristled at the egomaniac's insulting tone, but consoled myself by concentrating on his beard and the pixie spit I knew was there. The thought made me cuddle Peasblossom a little closer, and she paused her attempts to disentangle herself from the sticky blue webbing long enough to snicker.

"I can't detect any traces of your extremely powerful wards," I said lightly. "Can you?"

Isai clenched his hands into fists, rings clinking together. "No."

"Strange, isn't it? No trace of them left behind?"

A strained smile wrenched his mouth up at the corners. "Not at all. When I found them broken on my arrival, I dismissed the rest of them so as not to inhibit His Majesty from arriving post haste."

Damn his eyes. I bit the inside of my cheek, thinking furiously. Yes, he could be telling the truth. Or he could be the culprit, and I'd just prodded him into providing the perfect defense. *Blood and bone, I should have asked him to describe what he did on his arrival first. Open-ended questions, Shade, open-ended questions.*

"I know you want to blame me for this crime," Isai said in a low voice. "I am a convenient target. But I. Do. Not. Have. That. Book. I am a victim—a victim of the real culprit and a victim of that vampire."

My eyebrows rose as Isai pointed a shaking finger at Anton.

"Someone else stole your precious book. Threatening to burn

pages of my book will not give me the ability to return an object I do not possess."

"So you say." Anton shrugged. "The fact remains, your wards failed. You failed. And you will pay the price until that book is returned to me."

Isai choked, his face mottled with red blotches. "I am no use to you without my spellbook. You'll have to give it back eventually."

Anton met his eyes. "What's left of it."

A howl of rage poured from Isai's mouth and magic broke over the corridor with the sizzling snap of burning oil. I closed my eyes, bowing my body around Peasblossom to protect her. Every nerve in my body braced for impact, for an explosion, for something horribly magical and terribly violent. A second later, the power vanished.

I raised my head and opened my eyes. Isai was gone.

"So dramatic." Anton brushed an invisible speck of lint from his suit. "Do you need to see anything else?"

I straightened with the caution of a tall person standing up in a low-ceilinged room, my heart in my throat. So much anger. So much fury. So much *hatred.* "What kind of precautions have you taken?" I whispered, unable to help myself. "Should you be... taunting him like that?"

"You think I should treat him with kid gloves? Tiptoe around the man who may have betrayed me? No. Whether he stole the book or not, he failed, and I speak to him with the respect he deserves."

I cleared my throat and looked at the vault just for an excuse not to meet his eyes. It was closed, the entire wall nothing but an enormous cast iron door with a lock bigger than my entire body. "Is anything else missing from the vault? Has anything been added?"

"No. My wife and I performed a complete inventory, and the

book is the only difference." He approached the vault and set about entering the combination.

"Was there any damage to the vault door during the theft?" I asked.

"No. Isai tells me the thief likely used a spell. Can you confirm his suspicion?"

I shook my head. "That's not a very powerful spell. There wouldn't be traces of it left after this much time."

Anton pulled open the vault door as if it were a kitchen cupboard and not three feet of steel. "You may enter as part of due diligence for your investigation. You will touch nothing without telling me first and receiving my express verbal permission."

"Hurry up!" Peasblossom said in what I was sure she thought was a whisper. "I want to see!"

"The pixie cannot enter." Anton held out his hand. "I will hold the fey."

I opened my mouth to argue, make some case for needing my familiar with me. Peasblossom had an eye for detail that only the incredibly nosy possessed, a skill that almost made up for her somewhat kleptomaniac tendencies. If I kept an eye on her...

Before I could get a word out, something tugged at my gut. A feeling, an instinct. I was looking at the vault before I realized I'd turned my head, and for some reason I didn't understand, I wanted to go inside.

Now.

Peasblossom hollered in protest as I dropped her into the vampire's hand, still staring at the vault. Tunnel vision blacked out my surroundings, blinding me to everything by the entrance to the vault and my own pounding heart. A cage door waited at the end of the short hallway, and the clink of metal tickled my ears as Anton pulled a key from his breast pocket and unlocked it without a word. I had barely enough presence of mind to check on Peasblossom and make sure the iron wasn't making her sick.

Most fey didn't do well near the heavy metal, ranging from a vague feeling of nausea to downright poisoning. Peasblossom's tolerance was higher than most, a result of how much time we'd spent in the city over the years. Her little pink eyes shone with curiosity, and if she felt sick, she hadn't realized it yet.

Anton swung the cage open and I stepped inside.

My nostrils flared, picking up the familiar scent of ancient texts, the burning scent of strong magic, and the sharp bite of metal. Inky darkness surrounded me, hiding the vampire's hoard. I swallowed hard, shoulders taut with the weight of the vampire's stare. I took a slow breath and drew my magic.

"Lumen." I fluttered my hand into the air, drawing my finger in small spiraling circles. Three balls of soft red light spun from my fingertips and grew to the size of grapefruits. I blew on them until they turned to a pale yellow, then used a nudge of my will to send them up to the ceiling.

The vault was large, bigger than all the rooms in my modest home put together. Glass shelves lined the walls to the right and left, each one loaded down with objects that ranged from gleaming statues to dusty jugs full of murky liquid. Something rubbery pressed against the side of one jar, and I firmly pushed all thoughts of what might be floating in that innocuous container from my mind. I bit my lip. The room was full of magical artifacts. I didn't need a spell to tell me that, I could feel it. My senses swam with enchantments and evocations, like a thousand whispers calling to me. Strong magic. I braced myself for the coming barrage of imagery and centered myself as best I could.

"Revelare."

The silver net flowed out from me, washing over the vault and lighting up the magical objects like Christmas lights. I closed my eyes and kept my breathing even. Very slowly, I opened them. "You said you and your wife did a thorough inventory. You went through every object?"

"Every one," Anton replied. "The only thing missing is the book, and there was nothing here that wasn't here before the theft."

That helped narrow it down. If someone had left something behind, some means of spying or some means of allowing them to return easily, then they would have needed to hide it with magic. I was looking for an illusion spell. I focused on each object with a purple aura, studying them all in turn.

I didn't realize how long I'd been at it until my knees trembled and I swayed on my feet.

"You're pushing it!" Peasblossom yelled. "Take a break!"

I blinked, then shook my head and squinted at the shining silver bracelet on the shelf to my left. "Just two more." I stepped closer, examining the spell. No. Not invisibility. Just a beauty illusion. Greek. Probably a gift from Aphrodite. The final purple light was just a dreamcatcher. Not something sold at a tourist trap, but the genuine object. And old.

I closed my eyes, barely resisting the urge to sink to my knees. My head ached from holding the spell for so long, analyzing so much magic in one sitting. It was worse than caffeine withdrawal.

"You are exhausted," Anton said. "Can you continue, or do you need to rest?"

I gritted my teeth. Anton's voice remained perfectly polite, but the question pricked my pride. I straightened my spine and lifted my chin. "I'm fine."

I caught his nod out of the corner of my eye, but turned my attention away from the vault's entrance to examine the rows of safe deposit boxes on the opposite wall. The smallest ones would have been a tight fit for Peasblossom, and the largest could have held a full-sized griffin. One drawer was open.

"Is that where the book was?" I asked.

"Yes."

I took a step forward, then froze. Slowly, I glanced over my shoulder. Anton was standing outside the vault, still holding Peasblossom. But if he was out there...why did I feel like someone was breathing on my neck?

My skin itched, every nerve hyperalert. With as much calm as I could muster, I looked around the vault, this time without the detection spell blinding me with magical auras. Something—or someone—was watching me.

A section of the far-left wall drew me closer, instinct pushing me to see what was there. Energy tickled the edge of my consciousness as I studied the books before me. The writing was ancient Gaelic, but faded and hard to make out. Some of the books looked like they'd disintegrate if you touched them. I followed the shelf to a section covered in statues so real they could have been living creatures frozen in time. A large feline carved from shadow, a horse of pure jade, and a dragon that glittered with jewel-like scales, all of them etched with such detail I could almost imagine I saw them breathing.

I was reaching for one of the statues before I realized it. I needed to touch it, make sure it was just a statue.

"Do not touch anything."

I jerked my hand back and spun around. Anton had adjusted his position to keep me in his line of sight. His posture hadn't changed, though I could have sworn his shoulders held a rigidity that hadn't been there before. A faint red shine flashed across his eyes when he moved, then vanished. He looked like he wanted to say more. Like he was waiting for something to happen.

I marched back to the drawer that had held the book, unwilling to look at him and that strange expression a second longer. With my back to the vampire, I reached into my pouch.

It took me five minutes to find the fingerprint kit I needed, one of the downsides to having a bag that was bigger on the inside. Before finding it, I found more twisty ties and a phone book I'd been meaning to recycle for the last four months.

"Only you and your family have access to these drawers?" I asked.

"Yes."

I dusted the Bi-Chromatic powder over the drawer, twirling the brush that looked like something you'd find in a makeup kit. "Never Isai?"

I could practically hear his interest crackling behind me. "No. Why?"

"So these drawers weren't warded? They were locked with mundane means?"

"Yes."

I sighed, replacing the brush and powder. The surfaces on and around the drawers revealed no prints, not even a smudge. The vampire had been right. There was nothing. "Are there any traps in this room?"

"A handful of the drawers will trigger a trap. Something simple, since I was forced to build them myself, but suitably...effective."

I stepped away from the drawers. "Well, I think I'm done in here."

"And did you learn anything?"

Again, I felt something watching me. Before I could think better of it, I blurted out, "Is there anything alive in there?"

Anton was silent again, studying me. "Why?"

"Please answer the question." I could barely breathe. Adrenaline poured through my system, my nerves singing with that same awareness, the sensation that I was still being watched. I backed toward the vault entrance.

"It is not relevant to the case," Anton said finally. "Everything in there is as it was before the theft."

Then there was something alive in here.

"I've seen enough, I think," I said.

Anton watched me closely as I half ran out of the vault. Again, he had the look of someone who wanted to say something, ask something.

"Why are you looking at me like that?" I demanded.

My voice was louder than I'd intended. Peasblossom stared at me. For a second, she had the same look as Anton. That excited, expectant look. Then it was gone and her face pinched with impatience.

"She's out of the vault—now let me go!" she told Anton.

Anton eyed the blue patch on his suit jacket and extended the pixie to me. "I'm not sure what you mean. But if I'm looking at you in a way that makes you uncomfortable, I apologize."

My jaw tightened. Something was going on, something he wasn't telling me. "You're hiding something from me. That's fine, it's your prerogative. But I think I have a right to know if whatever you're hiding from me is going to get me killed."

"It would be a grave inconvenience for me if you died," Anton replied.

"Well I wouldn't want to inconvenience you," I muttered, then shrugged. "I thought that contract guaranteed us a relationship of open communication and honestly. If that's not the case—"

Suddenly he was standing right in front of me, gripping my chin, forcing my head up. Instinct screamed at me, but it was too late. For the second time that night, I pitched forward into a winter sky, lost to the hypnotic pull of his vampiric power.

"You work for me," he whispered. "I will share information with you when I feel it is relevant. You will share information with me if there is even the slightest chance it pertains to the task I have hired you to complete. I will be the first to know of any clues you detect, no matter how inconsequential they may seem. You withheld information from me once. You will not do it again."

My brain floated on a warm river, flowing in a lazy zigzag pattern, pulled along by the vampire's voice. I was a fool to have hidden anything from him. He needed to know. He needed to know everything.

Something pulsed inside the vault. I didn't know if Anton felt it too or not, but suddenly his stare was broken, and I'd taken a step back. My senses tingled as cold reality swallowed the last of the trance's effects, leaving me clearheaded and coherent. His eyes widened—a small reaction, but enough to tell me I'd surprised him by breaking away.

That's bad. Don't surprise the vampire. Don't be interesting in any way. A fine trembling began in my legs and climbed up my body until it was all I could do to keep my voice steady.

"Of course, you'll be the first to know of anything I find," I said. "You are, after all, my boss. Temporarily."

Peasblossom clung to my fingers, and even I was shocked at my audacity. It was one thing to crack jokes out of nervousness, but there was a point at which that became downright perilous.

Anton gritted his teeth. "Listen to me, Mother Renard. This is not just a missing book. This is a turning point. Fail this, and I promise you, people will die."

CHAPTER 8

"Who's going to die?" I gave myself Brownie points for keeping my voice steady. Knowing the vampire threatened people on a daily basis, probably killed on a regular schedule, didn't rob his threat of any weight. It rather added to it, in fact. "I don't appreciate threats," I added.

"That was not a threat," he corrected me. "That was my attempt to educate you on the seriousness of the situation. The information in that book could be catastrophic in the wrong hands. There are creatures out there who share Isai's desire for human enslavement. Creatures who yearn for the days when humans feared us, served us at our leisure."

Blue eyes glinted in the muted light as he drew himself up and looked at me from under a fall of white-blond hair. "You say you fear me, but as a wise man once said, 'Better the devil you know.'" His hand drifted over his belt near his right hip as if seeking the comfort of a weapon. "I have spent a great deal of time gathering information. Information on people, events, species. To you, that information is merely fuel for blackmail. But the blackmail you are so disdainful of does not merely fill my coffers. It also keeps creatures who hunger for war from banging their drums and flowing over the land like a dark tide."

"That's very poetic," I said, keeping my voice calm and even. It took effort not to meet someone's eyes when you spoke to them, especially when the conversation involved people dying, but he'd already tranced me twice. If I had to ask my questions to the space between his eyebrows, so be it. "Can I assume you don't intend to give a specific example?"

Blue eyes paled, becoming colder. "There is a reason I lock that information in a vault. You must trust me that the danger is real."

"Real, but hypothetical," I pointed out. "You don't know why the thief took the book. It could have been to keep you from using it against them personally. You admit you were blackmailing Flint, and Isai. I won't waste my breath asking how many others would like to sponge their name from those pages."

"Do not let the current hypothetical nature of the danger lull you into a false sense of security. Do not assume this must be personal, the danger limited to an individual level. That has led to the fall of more than one ruler, more than one civilization. We must hope for the best and prepare for the worst. It is the key to survival."

Dimitri's voice filled the hallway from the vicinity of the ceiling. "Actually, Father, I'm afraid the danger isn't so hypothetical anymore."

Anton glared up at the grate above the space we occupied outside the vault. "We will discuss this later tonight. My office is bad enough, but you go too far putting your little devices outside the vault."

"You never appreciate my efforts to help you improve security." Dimitri sighed. "Security is a key to survival too, Father."

I shared a look with Peasblossom. Her pink eyes were wide and shining with unabashed amusement. I had to admit, it was tempting to let the conversation play out. I couldn't deny a certain fascination with the idea of Prince Kirill of Dacia, vampire feared throughout the five kingdoms, criminal mastermind of the new world, having a son. But the seriousness of the vampire's warning echoed in my ears, and I couldn't let idle curiosity derail the conversation.

"Dimitri, you said the danger isn't hypothetical. What did you mean?" I asked.

"Lovely to speak with you again, Shade," Dimitri responded. "I regret to inform you that the danger has grown somewhat more real. I've been picking up chatter about an auction."

Anton froze. "Auction?"

"An auction," Dimitri confirmed. "There's been no mention of a formal date, but I've heard from multiple sources that your book will be offered up at an exclusive gathering of the most powerful and influential the Otherworld has to offer."

"Who?" Anton demanded between gritted teeth.

"Unsurprisingly, not all who qualify for such an invitation have learned to use the internet, and bugging areas where such things are discussed takes a great deal of time and effort—something you never appreciate. I tracked down one or two shady sorts claiming to be selling tickets to the auction, but they turned out to be scams. I've overheard four conversations that seem to involve people with a legitimate knowledge of the affair, and they all mention having heard of it from someone else." A hint of admiration crept into Dimitri's voice. "Whoever started the rumors was clever. Everyone is talking about the auction, but no one knows the location or who's hosting. All that secrecy gives it unquestionable legitimacy, and everyone wants—no *needs*—to be invited."

"I know the auction's location," a feminine voice said.

The Dacian accent told me who it was before I saw her. It was as thick as her husband's, and much thicker than her son's. Peasblossom perked up, planting her sticky hands on the edge of my palm so she could lean down the hallway toward the visitor.

"It's Irina," she whispered.

In the five kingdoms, the vampire's bonded *rusalka* mate had been Irina Shevchenko, but here in the new world, she was Vera Winters. She flowed down the hallway with all the sensuality of her fey heritage, wearing an above-the-knee black dress with a white fleece dress coat that flared at the hips. A beret sat on her coal-black hair, a splash of red to bring out the rich color of her lips. Warm brown eyes met mine and she held out a hand.

"Mother Renard, I'm so pleased to meet you. My husband told me he'd hired you, and you must forgive me for not arranging a meeting sooner. I've heard of you, of course. What an interesting life you must have led as the apprentice of Baba Yaga."

I smiled back and took her hand. "Interesting is one word for it. And please, call me Shade. May I say, it's such a pleasure to meet you as well. I've heard of all the wonderful work you've done. Even the goblin women speak your name with a smile."

Vera beamed. "I helped them out a bit with child-rearing. It can be so difficult to get those sharp-toothed little ones to sleep, and nursing them to dreamland can be a painful process. A lullaby does wonders."

"Hello, Mother."

Dmitri's voice drew Vera's attention up, and her eyes sparkled as she clasped her hands together in front of her. "Hello, my angel. You've managed to get to the vault. How talented you are!"

Anton pinched the bridge of his nose. "My love, please do not encourage this."

"Oh, you know you're impressed, don't pretend you're not. He's so clever, our son."

The vampire dropped his arm, a look of defeat on his face. "He gets it from you, I'm certain."

I blinked as Anton slid an arm around his wife and then laid a gentle kiss on her lips as she folded against his chest. I knew he loved her—everyone knew he loved her—but it was still something to see it in person. Such a tender moment for a vampire of his...reputation.

"I'm clever too!" Peasblossom piped up, straining to make herself as tall as possible. Her wings twitched as if she would fly over to the *rusalka*, but the sticky blue string kept her glued to my hand. She grunted and tugged harder.

Vera smiled at Peasblossom, turning so her whole body faced the pixie in a silent show of respect and attention. "I'm certain you are." She leaned down until her eyes were level with Peasblossom's. "I'll bet you're very sneaky. Why, you probably know all sorts of things people would rather you didn't."

Peasblossom gave an excited hop, opened her mouth, then froze. Her pink eyes flicked to Anton. The vampire watched her with significantly more interest than a moment ago. "Not really," she squeaked.

"I could stand here all night and talk about the miracles you've accomplished and the wonder that is our offspring, but that may need to wait." Anton leaned closer to his wife. "You say you've heard of the auction and know where it's to be held?"

Vera brushed at a lock of Anton's blond hair, patting his cheek before nodding. "The details aren't written in stone, but I was speaking with Arianne about using her hotel this spring for the children's charity event—you remember?"

"The benefit for immigrant children. Yes, I recall."

"That's the one. You know how strongly Arianne feels about this cause, and she always insists on providing her hotel for these events—free of charge. Anyway, I was speaking with Arianne about this year's event, and I remembered what Dimitri had said about this auction everyone is whispering about."

"You told your mother first?" Anton demanded.

"Please, don't interrupt, darling. Anyway, you know there's no one in the area who even comes close to Arianne's skill with wards. And it occurred to me that if I were planning to have an auction and invite all manner of creatures..."

"Then they would need a place that promises the most safety one can expect," I jumped in. "Somewhere that could contain the damage if a fight broke out so as not to draw the Vanguard's attention."

Anton smiled wide enough that I caught a hint of fang, then took one of Vera's hands in his and laid a kiss on her knuckles. "You are brilliant, my love."

"I know," she told him. "So I asked Arianne about her hall's availability for the coming weeks, and she said that the next three days are booked, but it is otherwise open." Her brown eyes darkened. "That cannot be a coincidence."

"I agree," Anton said. "Did she provide you any more information?"

"No, and I was my most charming self. I could have questioned her more directly, but I did not want to seem too interested. Arianne takes secrets very seriously, and her suspicions are easily roused."

"And she takes the safety of her hotel even more seriously," Dimitri added. "If she's willing to entertain the idea of hosting this auction, then whoever stole the book must have made it worth her while."

"Is Arianne in the book?" I asked.

I hadn't expected an answer, so I was surprised when Anton shook his head. "Arianne is a reasonable woman with her own agenda. She keeps to herself and her own business and does not like to be disturbed."

"Yes, I picked up on that." I bit my lip. "Did you know Helen Miller worked for her the week before she disappeared?"

Anton straightened. "No. That was not in the public record, and Mrs. Miller completed her work for me years ago. I did not keep her under surveillance for more than a year after she completed the project."

Butterflies swarmed my stomach at the thought I'd found a clue Anton had missed. I couldn't be sure if it was pride or nerves. "So if you'd known, then you might have included her in your list of suspects?"

The vampire's cold blue eyes went hazy, like disturbed snow globes. "You are suggesting that Arianne hired Mrs. Miller because she somehow discovered that Mrs. Miller had a hand in my security system."

"I'm not saying she did," I said quickly. "But in the interest of considering every angle, perhaps we should ask ourselves if it's possible. I spoke to Mr. Miller, and he said there was something strange about his wife's behavior after Arianne hired her. He said they called daily for a week, as if she were being hired multiple times. I spoke to Arianne, and she confirmed that she used hypnosis on Mrs. Miller, so she only remembered her work at Suite Dreams when she wore the security badge provided by Arianne herself."

"Did you see the work Mrs. Miller did for Arianne?" Anton asked.

"No."

"So you think it's possible she didn't do any work for Arianne, that Arianne only had her there so she could question her under hypnosis?" Vera asked.

"I don't know," I replied. "But Arianne is secretive, and she hypnotized me just for asking a few questions about Helen. She knew I was a witch, she knew I was investigating Helen's disappearance. I'm not sure why she felt the need to hypnotize me."

Anton brushed away my concern with a wave of his hand. "Arianne's desire for secrecy is well known. It would not surprise me if she used hypnosis on everyone who performed work of any kind on her property." He rubbed his chin. "Perhaps it's time I found out why she's so protective of her precious hotel."

"Good luck with that," Dimitri spoke up. "Her wards are insane. No one takes security as seriously as she does. I'll bet she tests them all the time—probably has hackers try to break in on a regular basis just to make sure they're foolproof."

Anton bristled at the last jab, but Vera blinked and looked up.

"Dimitri, sweetheart, I had completely forgotten you were here. An interactive hesitation spell. Well done, my love, well done."

"It's a gift," Dimitri said modestly.

"And a curse," Anton muttered. "I never should have let you study with the wizard."

"You have so many gifts, Dimitri," Vera added in the voice only a doting mother could pull off.

"Why don't you talk to me like that?" Peasblossom demanded.

I arched an eyebrow at the blue and pink fey. "You're not my child?"

She flopped down on my palm, crossing her arms as best she could with the sticky strands of Anton's security system still bound around her. "I have many gifts too."

I met Vera's eyes, and she put a hand over her mouth to hide a smile. Anton stared at me with a blank expression, though I thought I caught a flicker of empathy in his eyes.

"You do have many gifts," I said, patting Peasblossom on the back between her wings. "You know I would be lost without you."

"Yes, you would." She sniffed. "What are some of my gifts?"

Anton abandoned the conversation in favor of pulling his phone out of his breast pocket and swiping his fingers over the screen, probably starting his research on Arianne and her hotel. Vera pulled her own phone from the pocket of her coat and pretended to fuss with it.

"Well, you keep me organized with Post-its, don't you?" I pointed out. "You make sure I use different colors so it doesn't get boring. And you're brilliant at hide and seek."

Peasblossom grinned. "And hide the egg."

I scowled. "Hide the egg is not a game. It's something naughty pixies do when they want to be grounded." I glanced at Vera, then back at Peasblossom. "It took me forever to get the smell out of that closet."

"It wouldn't have smelled bad at all if it hadn't taken you two months to find it."

Vera chuckled, and I shook my head in defeat. "Well, I should be going. It's getting late, and we have a long drive home."

"I'll walk you out," Vera offered. "I have errands to run."

"Thank you," I said sincerely. I'd been afraid Anton would escort me out. He'd acted strangely about the vault, and I couldn't shake the memory of that expectation in his eyes.

Anton stepped closer and made a not-so-subtle attempt to catch my eye. I looked at his shoes.

"You will call me if you learn anything. I am trusting you to find that book."

Why? I wanted to ask. *Why me?*

I didn't ask. I wasn't sure I wanted to know.

CHAPTER 9

By the time I walked out of Anton's office building, it was almost eight o'clock. The flesh between my shoulder blades twitched the entire walk to my car, an unnerving feeling that someone was watching me from behind that cold, dark glass. I turned up the collar of my coat. It didn't help.

"Isai hates Anton," Peasblossom said, breaking the silence.

I opened my car door and slid inside, closing it with unnecessary force. After a second of hesitation, I locked the doors. "Yes, I noticed that."

"I'll bet he hates a lot of people."

"I noticed that too." I stared at the building, the tinted windows that would hide anyone who might be standing there. Lights on in the offices of the middle floors painted soft orange ribbons around the forbidding black tower, but the farther the building reached into the night sky, the darker it grew.

Peasblossom struggled to sit on my shoulder, the blue threads still sticking to her catching on a few stray strands of my hair. "Do you think he stole it?"

"I don't know." I winced and brushed my hair back, trying to keep it from the sticky pixie. "But I have a hard time believing he'd hold on to it with Anton threatening to burn his spellbook."

"Maybe he realizes that Anton will probably kill him as soon as he returns it."

"Anton can't kill him, it's part of their accord. However, as the vampire said, there are fates much worse than death. Perhaps Isai understands that better now." I drummed my fingers on the steering wheel. "But he could arrange for it to be found. There's no physical evidence tying him to the theft, no direct evidence. If he planted it on someone, he could get away with it."

"But instead, he's auctioning it off."

I flopped back against my seat, wincing when my hand struck the seatbelt buckle. "And that doesn't make sense either. If Isai went to all that trouble to get the book, then why not keep it? All that blackmail is exactly what he needs if he's going to—"

"Take over the world?"

I stopped rubbing my knuckles and arched an eyebrow at Peasblossom. "Sort of."

Peasblossom half climbed, half fell down my arm to land in my lap. After prying her wings free of my jacket, she fell to her knees on top of the pouch around my waist and tugged at the zipper. "What are you doing?" I asked.

"I'm hungry. You have cookies in here somewhere." She grunted and tugged harder.

I put a hand over the zipper. "You aren't getting any cookies until you have dinner."

Pink eyes widened and she flopped back to land on the seat by my thigh, pasting herself to the fabric in a seal of blue goo. "But that's two hours away!"

"We'll stop somewhere on the drive home."

"I want a cookie."

"Well, you're not getting—"

"You have a hole in your leggings."

I glared down at my leg. "Damn. I forgot—"

"I did not attack you, you simple-minded female. I removed the spell that someone else put on you. The spell someone else was using to spy on you."

The wizard's barrage of insults came crashing back. Suddenly, I remembered the blonde woman, remembered what she'd done. I jerked back in the seat, simultaneously drawing a spell to check myself and Peasblossom for any such magic. *Stupid, stupid. If I fell for the same trick twice...*

"Revelare." The silver net of my spell spread over my body, bowing out to encompass Peasblossom and the rest of the car. No answering spark met the glittering strands. Either there was no such scrying spell, or there was, but someone with a lot of skill had hidden it from my magic. I put my fingers to my temples, soothing the sudden headache forming there.

My kingdom for some physical evidence.

Peasblossom peeled herself off the car seat and climbed up my coat, leaving an interesting blue design as the remnants of the sticky substance clung to the fabric. It was a testament to my disturbance that I didn't care, even though the coat's tag demanded I hand-wash the stupid thing. I could use a spell to clean it, but I knew Mother Hazel would find out. She'd sense it somehow, and then I'd get a lecture on using magic for my personal convenience.

I picked up my phone. "There are cameras all over this city. I wonder if any of them caught that woman who tried to spy on me."

"I'll bet Anton's cameras caught her."

I glanced up at the building, then quickly down at my phone. "I'll ask Bryan first."

"You don't want Anton to see you getting tricked by blondie," Peasblossom guessed.

My cheeks heated. "Quiet, I'm on the phone."

Bryan picked up on the first ring.

"Hello?"

"Bryan, it's Shade."

"Mot— Shade, good evening. Hold on just a moment."

He put his hand over the phone and I heard the murmur of a brief conversation, followed by footsteps on tiled floor and then a door closing.

"All right, sorry about that." A chair creaked as he lowered his weight into a seat. "Have you found something?"

"Yes. I'm sorry, Bryan. Mrs. Miller is dead. You were right— her ghost is haunting her house."

Bryan sighed. "I was afraid of that. Do you know how she died? Who killed her?"

"She was in pretty bad shape, so I couldn't speak with her. But I might have something. Is there any way you can access the security camera footage of stores in the area around 1300 East Ninth Street?"

"Without a warrant I can't demand it, but I can ask. What are you looking for?"

"A blonde woman ran into me outside the building, and I need to talk with her. She was wearing a purple coat, black leggings, and huge silver earrings."

"I'll do my best. There's a Chase Bank right across the street. The manager has a soft spot for law enforcement since we stopped a robbery last year, so I can ask him. He's usually there by seven thirty in the morning. I'll swing in on my way to work."

"Thank you, Bryan."

"Thank you." There was a pause, then he sighed. "So she's really dead."

I propped an elbow on my car door and laid my head in my hand. "I'm sorry, Bryan. I was hoping for a different outcome."

"Yeah, me too. I don't know how I'm gonna tell Andy."

"Well, if you think it would help, I can be there when you do."

Another pause, this one longer. When he still hadn't said anything after a full minute, I took a guess. "Bryan, if Andy's there and you'd like me to have a word with him, I'm in Cleveland. I could come over right now."

"Could you?" Bryan exhaled, his relief palpable. "I can't stand the thought of keeping this from him when he's in his office trying to find this woman."

"I'm on my way," I promised, sitting up.

"I'll meet you at the front door. The address is 1501 Lakeside Avenue East."

I started the car and grabbed my GPS, typing in the address before I could forget it. "It's no problem at all, Bryan, I'm happy to help. See you in…" I blinked. "Five minutes. You're only half a mile away."

"Big city, small world," Byran agreed.

I looked at Peasblossom. It was a little disturbing how close the vampire was to the federal agency. On a paranoid day, I might wonder if it was intentional…

I got off the phone and tucked Peasblossom securely into the passenger seat—after retrieving a napkin from the glove box to protect the fabric from the blue goo. I had enough pixie-prints to scrub as it was. The short drive was a blessing, since it limited how long I had to listen to her complain about the cookie I'd denied her.

The FBI Cleveland field office was a wide three-story building of beige brick with white trim. Even at night, with only the illumination of the security lights, the building looked new and polished, as if it were an agent itself, treating its duty to represent the Federal Bureau of Investigation with the utmost seriousness. The landscaping spoke of similar care, and even the wrought iron gate had the decency not to rust—except a little at the very bottom and very top. As I got out of my car, I couldn't help but look over my shoulder toward the Winters Group. Anton's building towered over the cityscape, looking for all the world like it was spying on the government headquarters. If I closed my eyes, I could picture Anton on the top floor, looking out his penthouse window. Watching…

"Isn't there a rule about vampires living this close to a government building?" Peasblossom asked, following my gaze.

"He doesn't live there, he works there," I said absent-mindedly. "But if there isn't, there should be."

Peasblossom snorted and huddled in my coat pocket, tacky blue residue taking care of the pesky lint that had gathered there. Bryan met us at the door, and we made polite, mundane small talk as he walked me through the security checkpoint. He nodded to his coworkers, then escorted me to an elevator across the lobby.

As soon as the elevator doors closed, Peasblossom hauled herself out of my pocket and climbed up the arm of my coat. "Are we going to see Andy so we can tell him about the ghost?" she asked.

Bryan blinked, but recovered quickly, inclining his head at the pixie in a small bow of respect. "He said it was all right to come up. I didn't tell him what it was about. He's in a meeting right now, but he said to wait in his office."

Peasblossom hid again as the elevator doors opened. We walked down a plain white hallway that ran by a room full of cubicles, then rounded a corner where a row of offices took up the left-hand side. Bryan led us to an office with *Andrew Bradford* written on a gold plate on the door. It was the corner office.

Bryan let us in, and we both took a seat in front of Andy's desk to wait. He rubbed his hands together and faced me. "So how is this going to work? Am I just supposed to say you saw her ghost? Is there any way to prove it to him, any sort of…evidence?"

"Well, that depends. Do you want to tell him about the Otherworld, or do you just want him to know she's dead so he stops treating this as a missing person case and starts treating it as a murder?"

"He's not just a coworker," Bryan said, his voice tight with frustration. He shoved a hand through his hair. "He's my friend. I can't be half honest with him. If I'm going to talk to him about Helen Miller's ghost, then I need to tell him about everything."

"I think you're right," I said, trying to sound encouraging. "If you want, you can introduce me. Tell him I'm a witch. I'll tell him about Helen's ghost, and then I can answer any questions he might have about me, her ghost, or the Otherworld."

"Easy peasy," Peasblossom said sarcastically.

I gave her a warning look, then turned back to Bryan. "It'll be all right. Honestly, of all the Otherworldly beings we could be dealing with, at least ghosts are fairly mainstream. For all you know, Andy might already believe in ghosts."

"No, he doesn't," a new voice deadpanned.

I spun around in my chair and found the door to the office wide open. A man stood there staring at Bryan with an expression that was not entirely happy. He wore a navy-blue suit with a sky-blue shirt. His tie hung straight despite the late hour, and his brown hair had been combed back from his face.

"Andy," Bryan said, standing.

"Is that why you needed to talk to me right away, Bryan?" Andy asked, his voice even. "You want to tell me about a ghost?"

Bryan froze. It wasn't a deer-in-the-headlights expression, though, more the stillness of a parent who'd stepped on a creaky spot on the floor and wasn't sure if he'd woken the baby.

Andy crossed his arms and refocused his attention on me. "What are you selling him?"

I raised my eyebrows. "Selling him?"

"I caught what you said about wanting him to introduce you so you could tell me about a ghost. You're a psychic, right? Trying to 'help?'"

I didn't appreciate his tone, or the insinuated quotes around "help." I crossed my arms, mirroring him. "No, I'm not a psychic." I pressed my lips together, smothering the urge to give him the rest of my thoughts on his initial impression of me. This wasn't about me, or my pride. It was about Bryan, and his desire to help his friend. Drawing out this argument, this little conflict, would only complicate matters, drag out the conversation in a way that might damage Bryan and Andy's relationship. I needed to cut through Andy's denial quickly, before he said something he'd regret.

Fixing my attention on the pen sticking out of Andy's pocket, I focused on my magic and snapped my fingers. *"Ignesco."*

Andy's pen flared to life, glowing with a soft but strong yellow light. Like a torch with no heat.

"What the—?" Andy blinked down at his pocket. There was a moment of panic as his instincts told him he was on fire, but to his credit, he realized that there was no pain, no smoke. He grasped the pen between two fingers, holding it as if it might explode, and drew it out to hold it in the air between us.

Seconds ticked by, the silence growing heavier. His eyes met mine. "How did you do that?"

"I'm a witch."

Bryan shifted uneasily beside me, but I kept my attention on Andy. He stared at me for another long minute, and I could almost hear the gears turning in his brain.

"A witch," he repeated.

"Yes."

He gestured with the pen. "This was a spell."

"Yes."

He nodded. Then he put the pen back in his pocket and buttoned his jacket, hiding the light. "Excuse me a moment."

I watched him with renewed interest. It was an intriguing reaction. Most people either passed straight to denial, or—if they had been predisposed to believe in the Otherworld—they got excited. Andy seemed stuck in the middle.

I doubted he'd stay that way. He obviously had an analytical mind. That didn't bode well for a state of not knowing, so eventually, he'd have to decide. Bryan watched Andy leave without another word.

For a moment, silence reigned.

"I think that went well," Peasblossom offered.

I winced as she walked down my arm, ripping out a few hairs that had stuck to her when she'd crouched behind my neck. "Bryan, if you could give me a small dish and some very warm water?" I said.

Bryan stared out into the hallway after Andy, but he nodded and went to fetch the requested items. He returned after a minute with two coffee mugs. Steam curled up from one of them. After setting them on the desk, he poured a little water from the non-steaming cup into the steaming one.

"Tell me when the temperature is to your liking," he said to Peasblossom.

Peasblossom half fell off my arm, then lurched toward the mug. After about ten minutes and two more trips for hot water, they had her bath ready. Peasblossom climbed in and relaxed against the side of the mug with a happy sigh, and Bryan collapsed into his chair.

"Andy's going to be fine," I told him. "Trust me."

Bryan rubbed a hand over his face. "I trust you. And it'll be better this way." He dropped his hand and leaned forward. "To be honest, he needed to know. There's always been strange things that happen and we can't explain them, but lately, they seem like they're happening more often." He shook his head. "I don't want to be the only one who notices anymore, the only one who sees the possibilities."

"Strange things?" I asked.

Bryan nodded. "Little things. Like interviewing applicants and seeing their eyes change color. Or a guy without a trace of drugs in his system scale a fence in a leap a mountain lion couldn't manage." He leaned forward. "I do background checks on people who apply for jobs here. That means a lot of digging, a lot of research. I've seen these things on tape. Showed them to agents. They still don't see it. They don't see what's right in front of them."

I nodded sympathetically. "That's how the human brain works. It's impressive, really. Most people aren't ready to see the Otherworld, and their minds avoid or reinterpret the evidence to reaffirm the normalcy of the world." I smiled. "We can't all be bitten by a *kobold* when we're young. Your belief is a little more… substantiated. Even some of the people in Dresden don't believe I'm really a witch and only call me for help because they think I'm a doctor."

The reminder of his childhood introduction to the Otherworld drew Bryan's attention to his arm, and he rubbed it even though you couldn't see the scar beneath his shirt. "I guess."

"Bryan, where—"

We both froze as the door opened and Andy walked back into the office. He came to a screeching halt, his gaze locking on the pixie bathing in the coffee mug. Peasblossom didn't stop scrubbing the blue stuff from her skin, but she looked up when he entered.

"Do you have any soap?" She scowled and tugged at a thick blue strand stuck to her elbow. "I'll take dish soap if that's all you have."

Bryan rose halfway out of his seat, but Andy stopped him with a look.

"No," he said. "No, don't move. Don't. Move. Just sit there. I'm going to…" He shook his head and pointed at Bryan and me in turn. "Don't move."

He left. I looked at Bryan and couldn't help the smile that came over my face. "I suspect you won't be the only believer for much longer."

Five minutes later, Andy returned. He had a steaming cup of coffee in one hand, a notepad under one arm, and a bottle of Dawn dish soap in the other hand. He paused in front of the table as if centering himself, then leaned forward and added a drop of dish soap to Peasblossom's cup.

Peasblossom beamed at him. "Thank you, Andy."

"You're welcome…"

"Peasblossom."

He pressed his lips together then nodded. "Peasblossom. And you are a…?"

"Pixie."

"A pixie." He nodded a little faster this time. "All right."

He took a big sip of his coffee, and if the hiss that followed was any indication, he'd either forgotten it was hot, or had thought the temperature mattered less than it did.

Been there.

Then he collapsed into his seat, planted the coffee on the desk with a determined thud, slapped the notebook down, and reached into his pocket.

"All right," he said, not making eye contact as he drew a pen from his pocket. "Tell me—"

The sentence died as he realized he'd grabbed the pen I'd spelled. He studied the glowing plastic for a long moment. Without a word, Bryan picked up a pen from the cup on the desk and offered it. Andy took the new pen and let Bryan have the glowing one.

"You're a witch," Andy said. "Name?"

"Shade Renard."

I watched in amusement as he wrote on his notepad, *Shade Renard - witch* then *Peasblossom - pixie.*

"And the ghost you mentioned."

"Mrs. Miller. Helen Miller, your missing person." I paused. "Only she's not missing. She's dead."

"And you know she's dead…because you saw her ghost." He pressed the pen to the paper, as if trying to force it to write something it didn't want to. Then he put it down. "Perhaps you should start from the beginning."

I assumed he meant the beginning of my involvement with the case, so I started with Bryan approaching me with his concerns. I told him about Mrs. Miller's ghost, how she couldn't speak. After only a brief hesitation, I told him I'd looked into her clients and found one that wasn't human. I thought Helen may have been murdered because someone wanted information on a secret project she'd worked on. By the time I finished, Andy had regained some of his calm.

"I trust Bryan." He took a sip of his coffee. "He's a good worker, and a good man."

Bryan remained silent.

"I've been to Dresden a few times," Andy continued. "And I'll admit, I noticed people there have a shared...openness for... things. I passed it off as a quirk of a small village." He drained the rest of his coffee in three large gulps, then met my eyes. "Let's say I believe in this...other world."

He said it like it was two words, but out of kindness, I didn't correct him. His eyeballs twitched with the effort not to look at Peasblossom singing under her breath as she twisted her hair into sudsy towers of bubbles. The man teetered on edge of sanity —the grammar could wait.

"If I'm going to take you seriously, you need to be honest with me." He pointed to the card. "You need to tell me what the 'secret project' was. And you need to tell me exactly what you think happened. Who this non-human client of Mrs. Miller's is."

I put my hand on the desk. "You just found out about the Otherworld. It's good you're willing to believe, but this is only the first step. You don't understand it yet, and it will take time for me to explain it to you—if you want me to explain it to you." I took a deep breath. "So for now, you must trust me—"

I held up a hand when he opened his mouth to argue. "I'm sorry to ask for your faith so early in our relationship. I know it's hard to trust a stranger, but I promise you I will earn that trust. For now, understand that even though I want to tell you everything, I can't. Not because it would put you in danger—and it would—but because I swore a blood oath to protect confidentiality."

"The way you say 'blood oath' makes me think it means more than a pinkie promise."

"It means if I answer all your questions now, I'll wish I was dead a long time before I die."

I watched him chew that over for a minute. He leaned back in his chair, holding on to the arms as if concerned he would fall out of it if he let go. Then he gripped his knees, hauled himself forward, and folded his hands, bracing them on his legs. "If I accept your help, will you tell me who did this?"

I frowned. "I don't have that answer yet."

"But when you find out—if you find out—are you going to tell me? Or will this super-secret other world culprit disappear, never to see trial?"

That made me squirm a little. I hadn't thought about it, but he was right. Somehow I didn't think Anton would be satisfied with whoever stole his book sitting in a human prison.

"A human prison won't hold whoever did this."

Andy nodded as if that had been the answer he was expecting. Then he stood. "Keep in touch."

He left without another word. I stared at Bryan, who hadn't uttered a single syllable the entire time. "That's it?" I asked.

Bryan shrugged. "Let him process everything. He'll probably call you before the end of the week."

He didn't look happy, but he did relax a little more now that I'd formally introduced Andy to the Otherworld.

"I hope so. For me and for you." I glanced at Peasblossom and noted that she'd rinsed the soap from her hair and looked about finished with her impromptu bath. "Well, I should get home. I have a new mothers meeting tomorrow morning, and this weather brings on the sniffles that put new mums in mind of the plague."

Bryan laughed. "My cousin was like that with her first baby. He woke up with that gunk in his eyes and she swore he had pneumonia."

"All normal," I promised. "When you spend that much time and effort bringing a new life into the world, it doesn't take much to scare you into thinking you might lose it."

The last of the tension faded away under a steady stream of comfortable chatter. I retrieved my wet and somewhat less-sticky pixie, and Bryan escorted us to my car. When he left, Peasblossom perched on the hood.

"I'm going spying," she declared. "When I'm done, I'll use someone's phone to find you with that tracking app on your phone."

I pressed my fingers to my temples, my good mood strained. "You're all wet. You'll freeze. Please just get in the car. I need sleep. Besides, I don't like you using random strangers' phones."

She crossed her arms. "No. I'm going spying. I want to know what the wizard is up to. And no one minds if I use their phone. Last time I used someone's phone, I leveled her up in Candy Crush. And it was a magic mixer level, so if anything, I think she owes me a favor now."

I had a spell I could've used to stop her, but Peasblossom flew off before I could argue further, and way before I could raise my hand to draw the spell. I groaned and heaved myself into the car. She'd be fine, I knew she'd be fine. But Peasblossom was my first familiar, hopefully the only familiar I'd ever have or need. I felt like a new mum.

"I should have packed her extra clothes," I murmured.

My cell phone rang then, and I had to tear my thoughts away from my wandering pixie. "Hello?"

"Hello, Ms. Renard. This is Flint Valencia. I am returning your call."

I was glad I was sitting down. He hadn't needed to tell me his name. Every word out of his mouth slid down my back like a soft caress, the whisper of clothing being removed. I had to tighten my hand on the steering wheel to ground myself in reality, convince myself I wasn't lying in bed nestled in silk sheets. *Goddess, how does he do that with his voice?*

"Hi," I managed, congratulating myself when I sounded almost-normal. "Um, please, call me Shade." And already I'd messed up. If there was anyone who needed a reminder of my status, it was the *leannan sidhe*.

"Shade." He said my name as though it were a promise, a mental note to put me on his social calendar. "What can I do for you?"

"Um, I was wondering if you could tell me where you were the afternoon of January twentieth?"

There was a pause, then a soft chuckle. "Have we met? Forgive me, but your name is not familiar. Did I perhaps call you something else?"

My brain wasn't at optimum working condition, so it took me a full minute to realize what he was insinuating. A flare of temper helped chase the haze away from my thoughts, and I scowled. "I'm not a jealous lover. I'm asking for your alibi."

"My alibi? For what?"

Some of the teasing bled from his tone. *Good.* "I'll ask the questions, please. If you'll be so kind as to tell me where you were?"

"Well, let me think. I believe I was with a young *rusalka*. A charming young lady whose name escapes me at the moment."

I had a feeling a lot of names escaped him. "And she can vouch for your whereabouts? Or will your name escape her as well?"

"She will remember me."

I squirmed in my seat. His words brought an image with them, a vision of shadows and bare skin, soft moans echoing in his voice. I narrowed my eyes and dug my fingernails into my palms. *He's doing that on purpose.*

"If you could give me some information that would let me track her down so I can verify?" I prompted.

"She is a model with the Hemington Agency. I believe that night she'd just come from a photo shoot, something to do with lingerie."

"What kind of lingerie?"

"I don't know. She didn't wear it long."

I heard the smile in his voice and my blood heated a few degrees at the seduction underlying his tone. I *knew* he'd done that on purpose. *"Armatura,"* I said under my breath, and threw up my shields, responding to his push with one of my own.

"What is it you think I've done that you are so interested in my alibi?"

"I'm not at liberty to discuss it. Suffice it to say, it would behoove you to give me your alibi, as well as a means to verify said alibi."

There was a brief pause. When he spoke again, I felt every word ping off my shield, a more obvious attempt to influence me.

"Why don't we meet in person? I'm certain I could remember more details, given the time."

"I'm afraid tonight is not feasible. Why don't you think about it and call me back?"

"I dislike phone conversations. So impersonal. When can I meet with you tomorrow?"

"Call me. Tomorrow."

I hung up before he could respond, then dropped my head to the steering wheel and sighed. He was stronger than I'd expected, even over the phone. If I was going to speak with him again, possibly meet him, then I was going to need protection. So much for getting to sleep at a reasonable hour.

It was potion-brewing time.

CHAPTER 10

"This is it."

Peasblossom looked up from where she was seated on my shoulder, her cookie trailing crumbs down my jacket as she leaned forward to look at the twenty-three-story hotel stretching over our heads. The Westin's glass exterior caught the robin's egg blue of the noon sky and held it like an artist's palette, providing a beautiful backdrop for the hotel's name to shine in neat white letters just over the front door. It sat in the center of Cleveland's prime real estate, boasting convenient access to the Rock and Roll Hall of Fame and less than a mile of distance between its front stoop and Progressive Stadium, home to the Cleveland Indians, may they win a World Series.

"That's where spy girl is staying?" Peasblossom asked.

I picked up my phone and looked at the video I'd paused. Bryan's friend had come through and let him have the video from the ATM. I'd reviewed it before leaving the house, and the video was cued up to the pertinent time.

"I don't know if she's staying here, but this is the next building to the ATM she passed, so maybe we'll get lucky," I said. "If she isn't staying here, then maybe they have a security camera that will give us another clue."

Peasblossom took another bite of her cookie, sending a fresh cascade of crumbs down my chest and into my lap. "You want me to have a fly around?"

"No, stay with me until we know if she's here or not."

"All right."

I waited for her to finish her cookie. I was already hyped up on two cups of coffee, I didn't need the added agitation of cookie crumbs falling down my back because she decided to finish her messy treat while hiding in the neckline of my shirt.

"What are we waiting for?" More crumbs fell as she shoved the remaining cookie into her mouth.

I sighed. "Nothing. Let's go."

The Westin lobby made me pause. It wasn't the gold and blue couches facing one another, or the graffiti-ish style of painting on the back wall that surprised me. It was the vertical herb garden.

"Ooooh," Peasblossom said.

I put a hand on my neck, holding her in place before she could zip over to poke around in the leafy greens sunning themselves in the artificial lights that curled in a line from the top of the wall. "Later," I promised.

She sulked as I made my way to the front desk. I couldn't be sure, but I thought I felt a cookie crumb bounce down my spine.

The man at the desk smiled as I approached. "Hello, welcome to the Westin. What can I do for you today?"

I smiled back, reaching inside for my magic and threading it through my voice. "Hi, I'm trying to find this woman." I lifted my phone so he could see the paused video. "Have you seen her?"

The man frowned. "I'm sorry, I…" He blinked and put a hand to his temple.

"It's *really* important I speak with her." I poured a little more magic into my voice, filling the air with a cloud of pale lavender.

I'd expected resistance—five-star hotels didn't get that rating by giving out information on their guests willy-nilly.

"I… Yes. Yes, she's here. I believe that's Ms. Violet."

Ms. Violet of the purple coat. I'd bet my last can of soda that was an alias. "Lovely. And what room is she in?"

"Room 204."

"Thank you, so much." I started to turn, then pivoted back with an apologetic smile. "Oh, I'm so sorry, I almost forgot. I need the room key."

His frown returned, but fainter than the last one. "Room key?"

"Yes, don't you remember? You said my sister is staying in room 204 and she left a key for me?"

"I… Yes, that's right." He smiled. "One moment."

"Nice job," Peasblossom whispered into my ear.

"Thanks. It was spur-of-the-moment bluff."

Peasblossom snorted. "I know."

With the room key in hand, I turned and left while the spell still muddled his thoughts. With any luck, I'd be out of sight before he realized what happened and the magical haze around our conversation would push all memory of me from his mind.

It was a short elevator ride to the second floor. Part of me half expected the doors to open and reveal the mysterious blonde standing in the hallway, ready to blast me with a spell that would catapult me through the wall and out of the building. I had that kind of luck sometimes. The doors slid open, and my heart pounded.

No one.

I let out a breath.

"You have an overactive imagination," Peasblossom commented.

"*Armatura*," I whispered, squeezing the hand with the blue ring I'd charged this morning. The gem glowed with cerulean flame, flaring over my arms and legs, across my chest.

"Better hope she doesn't have a gun," Peasblossom said. A

trace of concern crept into her voice. "Maybe we should wait. I'm sure if you gave him enough time, Dimitri could get you all the information you need on this woman, right down to her favorite ice cream. Why don't we go ask? We could just speak into a planter in Anton's lobby. I'm sure he'll hear us."

"We are in a public place," I reminded her. "We'll be fine. I'm just going to talk to her." I paused. "But just to be safe, I want you to hide on the floor beside the doorway. When she comes to the door, you sneak in while her focus is on me. Hide until it's time to leave. If something goes wrong, you go and get help."

"All right. If you're sure we can't just go talk to Dimitri..."

In response, I strode up to room 204 and knocked on the door. The room key was Plan B, in case she didn't open it. As it turned out, I didn't need it.

The same blonde who'd knocked me down outside the Winters building yesterday answered. Her blue eyes widened slightly as she realized who I was.

"Oh." She blinked. "It's you. Um, are you all right?" She knitted her brows together, the perfect picture of concern.

"I'm fine," I assured her. "I was just hoping I could ask you a few questions."

"Um, I'm a little busy," she said carefully. "What's this about?"

I leaned in. "I'd like to know why you tried to spy on me."

I had to give her credit. She looked so confused, nervous in the way people were when someone covered in tattoos sat next to them on the subway. For a split second, I worried I'd gotten it wrong. Worried it hadn't been her who laid the spell on me.

I was just about to check for magic when she dropped the arm braced on the doorframe. Her posture remained guarded, but she waved me inside with a tight smile.

"Come in."

My nerves danced with anxiety as I followed her across brown carpet painted with bright yellow swirls, to a light blue couch. She was the one who'd spelled me. I needed to be careful. I closed my fist, feeling the ring on my finger. It hummed against my skin, reassuring me the protection spell was still firmly in place. My hostess gestured for me to be seated, then sat on the other end.

"Can I offer you a drink? Coffee? Tea? We could call room service if you like?"

"No, no thank you." I fought not to look around for Peasblossom. This wasn't the first time she'd acted as my backup. She knew what she was doing.

Ms. Violet smiled. "Very well. Shall we get right to it, then?"

"I think that would be best." I gestured at her modest blue pantsuit and white sweater. "Perhaps a real introduction?"

"Alice," she said amicably. "And you are?"

"Shade."

"Lovely to meet you, Shade."

I laid my hands in my lap, but didn't fold them, just in case I needed a quick spell. "Tell me, Alice, is your name as fake as your appearance?"

Her smile didn't falter. "I'm sorry?"

I shrugged, not taking my gaze from her blue eyes. There was something there, something behind those baby blues, that polite amusement. "If you want to continue pretending, that's fine. I can wait." I leaned back against the couch, making a show of getting comfortable.

She studied me for a long minute. "Shade," she said slowly, as if testing my name. "What is your last name?"

"Renard." A lot of people believed knowing someone's full name gave you power over that person in some way. They were right. But Shade Renard was the name I'd given myself. My real name was buried with the rest of my past.

"What were you doing at the Winters building, Shade Renard?"

"Let me look you in the eye—really look you in the eye—and we'll talk," I said evenly.

For a second, I thought she'd refuse. There were ways to force her to drop the glamour, but I wasn't sure it would be the smartest move. Without knowing who she was, I couldn't truly protect myself. Peasblossom could go for help, but if this woman decided to kill me quickly, that wouldn't do me any good.

"Oh, very well," she said finally. "I suppose there's no harm. Certainly no reason to start our friendship off on the wrong foot."

The magic fell away like a severed Broadway curtain, revealing a creamy complexion contrasted by dark slashes of blood-red lipstick and thick purple eyeshadow. Pale lilac hair curled in a pile on top of her head in a complicated mess of curls, and a black cape fastened at her throat boasted a high neckline that rose like a fan of feathers almost as high as her hair. Her long black dress flowed down her legs to pool on the floor.

"And your name?" I prodded.

"Alice is fine," she said evenly, staring at me with eyes that were no longer blue, but a dark brown that reminded me of burnt wood.

I slipped my hand into my jacket and plucked my cell phone from the side pocket of my waist pouch. Before Alice could react, I snapped her picture. A few swipes later, I'd sent it to my own email address. "Have it your way. I'll just show this picture to Mr. Winters, and we'll—"

"Dabria," the woman said, rubbing her temples as though I were annoying her. "My name is Dabria."

I frowned. That name sounded familiar. "Dabria... I've heard of you."

She lifted one pale shoulder in a shrug. "Have you?"

I blinked. "Wait a minute. You stole the Eye of Isis from that sorcerer, the one in Egypt who kept crocodiles as pets."

Dabria didn't answer, but she didn't have to. I knew who she was now. A thief. And not just any thief. She was one of the Old Kingdom's most infamous thieves.

"I thought you lived in the Old Kingdom. You're from Dacia, aren't you?"

Dabria inclined her head. "I am. And I do."

"Then what are you doing here? What were you doing at the Winters building?"

My mind was spinning so fast I could scarcely keep up with my own thoughts. I certainly wasn't holding my tongue the way I should. A master thief had walked out of the Winters building, had cast a scrying spell on me. It couldn't be a coincidence. She had to be the one. *She has means.*

"I was there to see Isai."

"Isai?" I paused, my whirling thoughts stuttering at the mention of the irate wizard.

"Yes. On a personal matter."

"Personal?" I tried and failed to imagine Isai having a personal life. Or, more specifically, I tried and failed to imagine anyone wanting to be part of Isai's personal life.

"Yes."

"What kind of personal matter?"

She wagged a finger at me. "You are a nosy little witch, aren't you? I told you, it's private."

I raised my eyebrows. "I'm sorry, but it's a bit odd to be called nosy by someone who only yesterday tried to use magic to spy on me."

Dabria shrugged. "Force of habit. You'd be surprised how many of my heists have started from information gleaned in just such a way. Don't take it personally."

"Oh, I won't. But you'll understand if I have to bring this up to Anton Winters? I'm not sure he'll like hearing that your 'force of habit' led you to spy on his property, even if you weren't spying on him." I paused. "Or were you?"

The sorceress laughed, her head falling back and one hand fluttering fingers at me as though I'd said something silly. "Oh, my, you do have an active imagination, Mother Renard. No, I was not trying to spy on Mr. Winters." She sighed and leaned back against the arm of the couch. "If you must know, I was there to talk with Isai about an inheritance issue."

"Inheritance?"

Dabria nodded. "Yes. You see, my sister passed away, quite a long time ago, in fact. As her only living relative—her only living *blood* relative—I believe I'm entitled to her property. I'm trying to convince Isai to see it the same way."

"What does Isai have to do with it?" I asked, confused.

"My sister was Serafina Schevchenko. A powerful sorceress who...courted Mr. Winters for a short time. Of course, at that time he was Prince Kirill of Dacia." She rolled her eyes. "My sister had grand ideas of being queen one day. She helped Kirill often, building an alliance here and there. She was the one who helped him get Isai's spellbook, you know."

So that's how he got it. "You said your sister passed away...?"

"Betrayed by the vampire for the sake of that seductress he married. My beloved step-niece." Dabria shrugged. "Serves her right, I say. Only a fool lets her future rest on the affections of a corpse."

"Kirill—Anton—killed your sister?"

"Yes."

And that's motive. "I see."

Dabria snorted. "I rather doubt you do. My sister had no use for me when she was alive. She claimed my magic was too inferior, that it rendered me useless." She sat forward on the couch, her eyes flashing with sudden anger. "She got what was coming to her, but I didn't get what was coming to me. She has an entire castle full of scrolls, items of power, and all manner of desirable artifacts. They're mine now—by all rights, they're mine." She curled her hands into fists in her lap. "That vampire is keeping it from me. He had his pet wizard ward her castle, and no matter how I try, I have not been able to find a way in."

"You went to see Isai to bribe him to lower the wards so you can get into your sister's castle."

"Bribe, seduce, blackmail—I'm not picky. I don't care what it takes, I just want what's mine. *All* of what's mine."

"If you were just in this world to speak with Isai, then why get the hotel room?" I asked.

She grinned. "My presence upsets Kirill—Anton. I like to visit Cleveland periodically and stay nearby just to watch him squirm." She leaned back. "Besides, Isai is quite stubborn. I'm not going to convince him to do what I want in one meeting, so I'm here for a few days."

"He won't betray Anton," I pointed out. "I'm sure the vampire has given very specific instructions that he not allow you into that castle."

"Yes, I'm familiar with Isai's vow. The old fool." She scoffed. "He should have let the spellbook go. Yes, it would have taken time to rebuild, but at least he would have been free. Instead he bartered away his life for the sake of a few spells."

I didn't think Isai would consider a lifetime of power-grabbing "a few spells," but I didn't say anything. Dabria had a reputation for being successful despite a lack of strong personal magic, so I doubted she'd understand Isai's reliance on his spellbook regardless.

"I daresay he sees the error of his ways now," Dabria continued, a malicious grin lifting the corners of her blood-red mouth. "He hates Anton, despises him with a fiery passion. He will betray the vampire in any way he can. And there is *always* a way."

"He signed a contract with Anton. And Anton strikes me as very thorough."

"True. But Anton's contracts have power for two reasons. The first being, of course, the natural consequences of breaking one's word. The gods don't like it, and few magic users are willing to risk the harm to their magic if they're forsworn. And the second is the magic of the contract itself. As to the first, that is a personal choice. It isn't that Isai *can't* betray his master, so much as whether he's willing to accept the consequences of such a betrayal. As to the second… Well, who do you think creates those enchanted contracts? Anton is many things, but he is no wizard."

I remembered what Anton had said about Isai, how he'd grown careless, less fearful in this new world with all its conveniences. Perhaps the wizard was now willing to do what he wouldn't before. Perhaps being forsworn was no longer a fate worse than being the vampire's servant? *More motive for Isai.*

"If Isai has turned you down already—and from what you say, it sounds like he's been turning you down for some time—then what makes you think you'll convince him now?"

"Everyone has a price," Dabria said evenly. "I have acquired some new pieces. I'm hoping one of them will persuade him."

"Pieces?"

She nodded and reached for a box on the table in front of her. I hadn't seen it behind the planter. She put her hand flat against it and there was a clicking sound. The lid rose slightly, but not enough for me to catch a look at what was inside. I held my breath, wondering if I need to move, or run. I tightened my fist until the ring dug into my flesh, pouring more magic into the band.

"Relax, Mother Renard. It's only a stone."

Dabria opened the box and lifted a jewel from its black velvet interior. It was the size of my fist, and glowed with a muted red light. She set it on the table, and I thought she might have scooted back, so that I was closer to the stone than she was.

Before I could move, the stone glowed brighter. There was something about it that made it hard to look away. I sat, transfixed by the dancing flames under the multifaceted surface. It was beautiful. So beautiful, that it almost distracted me from the look on Dabria's face, the wilting of her smile at the corners. I looked up, and for a split second, I would have sworn I saw fear in her eyes. Or maybe not fear, but something similar. Dread? Whatever reaction she'd expected from the stone, this hadn't been it. I called my magic and raised a hand to the gem, ready to find out exactly what it was.

Dabria snatched it up, threw it back into the box, and slammed the lid shut. "Sorry, you just get a peek. Though if Isai does turn me down again and you think you might be interested in a purchase, we can certainly discuss it then."

I gaped after her as she hauled the box across the room and set it on a desk tucked into the corner. "What was that?"

Nervous tension held her shoulders, but when she turned back to me, she had her hostess smile back in place. "As I said, we can discuss it later if my negotiations fail. Now enough about me and my wares." She leaned back against the desk, visibly trying to relax. "You haven't told me anything about yourself."

"Such as?"

Dabria gripped the back of the desk. "Why were you in the Winters building?"

I had a split second to make my decision. I wasn't the best liar, but between having Mother Hazel as a mentor, and a pixie as a familiar, I'd learned how to be vague. "Let's just say I'm opportunistic as well."

The sorceress didn't move. "How do you mean?"

"Well, I don't want to bore you with details. Suffice it to say, I'd heard a little rumor about one of the vampire's more recent acquisitions, and, like you, I was there attempting to negotiate."

"And?"

I sighed and rolled my eyes. "And I was as successful with the vampire as you were with his wizard."

"Pity."

I shrugged, toying with the zipper of my waist pouch. Dabria's stare intensified, bearing down on me until I fought not to squirm in my seat. "If only I had your skill. I'm not trying to convince Anton to do something for me, as you are with Isai, so it's not even a matter of needing his cooperation. If I had the necessary skills, I could...acquire what I wanted without the tediousness of negotiating with the vampire."

A sudden stillness filled the room. I picked at a loose thread on my coat, desperately avoiding looking at Dabria. I didn't want to be too forward. Let her lead. Let her take the bait.

Dabria's eyes glittered. "Is that so?"

I nodded. "Indeed. Perhaps I should try to find someone with the necessary skills to collect it for me. I could even arrange a trade of services. Perhaps you could recommend someone?" There, that was as bold as I could get.

Silence dragged out between us. I met Dabria's eyes, giving up the pretense of fussing with my coat. The sorceress watched me the way Mother Hazel had when I'd first agreed to let her mentor me. When I'd taken that first step down the path to redemption and she was deciding if I had it in me to go the rest of the way.

"I'm sorry, Mother Renard." Dabria pushed herself off the desk and folded her hands in front of her. "I cannot help you. All I can do for you is promise I will not tell the vampire what you're planning—despite how handsomely he would reward me for such a warning." She smoothed the skirt of her black dress, drawing my attention to how out of place the fancy gown was in this stark hotel room. "I must insist you leave now. You are no longer safe for me to associate with."

I hid my surprise behind a polite smile. "Pity. And I thought we were getting on."

"It is nothing personal. I like you. And I do understand your frustration." Her tone hardened, her eyes growing cold. "But I will not end up like my sister. The vampire has had all the blood he'll get from this family. If you know what's good for you, you'll walk away too." She shook her head slowly. "My sister thought she could best the prince of Dacia. Don't make her mistake."

I stood and let her escort me to the door. After I opened it, I turned back to her. "One more question?"

"If you must."

"Where were you Friday, January twentieth, around noon?"

Dabria arched an eyebrow. "That was a couple weeks ago. Let me see..." She tilted her head, then nodded. "Oh, yes, I remember. I was in Dacia...picking up some inventory." The corner of her mouth quirked up. "You'll understand if I can't give you specifics?"

I nodded. Peasblossom should have had time to sneak out, so I left and let the sorceress close the door behind me. My heart pounded and I looked down, praying my familiar was there. Peasblossom beamed up at me, then held her arms up.

I smiled back and scooped her into my hand, putting her on my shoulder before retreating down the hall toward the elevator.

"You think you're clever, don't you?" she said, settling underneath my hair. "Trying to bait her into offering to rob Anton."

"It was worth a shot. I've heard of her. She's got a reputation as one of the greatest thieves the Otherworld has ever seen. And she obviously hates Anton."

"It takes more than greed and hate to make someone go up against the vampire prince of Dacia," Peasblossom declared. "No one wants to mess with him. Especially the sister of someone he killed."

"But someone did go against him. Someone broke into his vault."

"Well, Dabria didn't seem so inclined."

I pressed the button for the ground floor. "She can't give me a solid alibi. Sure, she hinted she was robbing someone else, but that's rather convenient. An alibi I have no way of checking up on. And she was at Anton's yesterday, she put a scrying spell on me. It can't be a coincidence." I shook my head. "I need to find out if she could have known about the book. She has magic and she's good with traps, that much we already know. If she knew the book was there, then she's a viable suspect."

"I could spy some more, look around the hotel. You know

there's got to be a brownie here somewhere, sneaking around at night and cleaning. Maybe someone saw something."

"It's worth a try. You can do that while I talk to Flint." I exited the elevator and, per my promise, took Peasblossom over to the vertical herb garden.

"Whoa, no, meet with Flint by yourself?" Peasblossom protested. "I don't think so."

"I can talk to Flint on my own. You don't need to be there."

"Yeah, right." Peasblossom hopped off my shoulder to land on a sprig of mint. "If I'm not there, you'll end up getting mind-rolled again like you did with Arianne. Only this time when you come to your senses, you'll be in his bed wearing a goofy smile and promising to do whatever your loverboy wants."

An image of the *leannan sidhe* rose in my mind, his dark eyes and sinfully soft mouth. I remembered the way his jeans had clung to his hips, outlined every swell of muscle. *Sidhe* were naturally fit and beautiful, but you didn't get bulk like that without working out.

I shoved those thoughts away, giving myself a mental splash of ice water. The pixie had a point. It might not be smart to meet him alone.

Though part of me liked the idea.

Really liked the idea.

"I'll call him on the phone."

"And say what?" Peasblossom plucked a leaf from the mint plant and curled the stem around like a pretend phone. "'Hi, Flint, I heard Anton is going to expose your murderous rise to power if you don't ally yourself with him by the spring solstice. Did you by any chance steal his little black book?'"

I took the mint leaf from her and pulled her out of the herb garden. "Let's assume Flint could charm any information out of anyone. The question remains, did he know *who* to charm? Obviously he got to the security guard, so he could have gained access to the building. The guard could have seen Anton put the book in the vault. Did he know Helen Miller built the traps? And does he know someone powerful enough to break Isai's wards?" People were staring at me now, and I realized I probably looked like a crazy woman talking to herself. I cleared my throat and made a beeline for the front door.

A cold wind hit me in the face as I left the hotel, and I instinctively put a hand on the back of my hair, making sure Peasblossom didn't get swept away. "Exactly how connected is Flint?" I continued.

"Why don't you ask him yourself?" Peasblossom asked.

I swiveled my head to see where Peasblossom was pointing, and my jaw dropped.

A motorcycle had just pulled up in front of the hotel. Sultry eyes made him look as though he'd just woken up, just rolled over in the sheets to wish me good morning. Brown hair cut short, but long enough on top to comb back. A light beard shaded his jaw, outlining his mouth as if calling attention to how soft his lips were. The simple black T-shirt and blue jeans hugged the swells of muscle that graced his body from head to toe, making it clear he had nothing in his denim pockets.

He wore no helmet, but then, he didn't have to. When it came to motorcycle accidents, *leannan sidhe* could survive anything short of total decapitation or complete immolation. And a helmet wouldn't save him from that. A tiny voice in my head added that surely the gods themselves would protect him, if only to preserve that face. It wasn't right that a man could look so shy and still give the impression that he'd have you in his bed within the hour. Something to do with the half-smile and bedroom eyes…

"Hello. You must be Shade."

I jerked back, realizing that at some point I'd closed the distance between us. He was close enough that it seemed like the most natural thing in the world for him to curl an arm around my hips and pull me closer. Heat from his body soaked through the leather jacket, though it paled in comparison to the heat of his body as he dragged me closer. To any passerby, we'd have looked like a couple meeting up for a date. What did my face look like right now? Shocked? Smiling?

I opened my mouth to say something, but no words came out. He was smiling at me, brown eyes shining. And he smelled... I leaned in and drew a deep breath. Leather and just a hint of after-shave. Dizziness made me sway on my feet, and I put a hand on his shoulder to steady myself. His grin widened.

"Climb on," he said, his voice low, suggestive. "Let's go for a ride."

His arm tugged at my waist, urging me to climb onto the back of the bike. I hated motorcycles. If I wanted to tear through the air like a rocket with no protection around me to speak of, I'd ride a broomstick. I slid a leg over the bike and settled into the seat behind him. His back was so warm. I curled against him, letting his body heat chase back the February cold.

It wasn't until he started the bike that the roar of the engine cut through the haze over my thoughts. I hesitated, frowning down at the bike. Wait a minute. Where was I going? Hadn't I driven here? My car... Why was Flint here?

"What are you doing here?" I asked. The words took a monu-mental effort to form in my brain, let alone speak them with any coherency.

"I'm here for you," he said in the same resistance-melting tone. "You called me, so here I am."

That's right. I had called him. I wanted to talk to him. How nice that he came so quickly.

An instinct deep inside told me something was wrong. I needed to run, needed to get off this bike. But I couldn't for the life of me think of why.

Flint pulled my arms around his waist, revved the engine, and took off.

CHAPTER 11

"Let her go!"

Flint let out a grunt of surprise as Peasblossom punched him in the nose, using her tiny body as a battering ram. Despite her size, the pixie knew how to make momentum work for her, and Flint's head snapped back. She darted out of the way immediately, instinctively dodging his swing. The bike veered sharply to the right, and my heart leapt into my throat. I clung harder to Flint even while the warm fuzziness coating my thoughts froze and shattered as reality crashed down on me. The street looked harder than it had a second ago, panic making me aware of every rock, every stone, every facet of the city that had the potential to bring a great deal of pain to my body if the fey didn't keep control of the motorcycle.

"Shade, get off the bike!"

Peasblossom dove again, but this time, she hit me in right temple—hard.

"Ouch!" I yelped.

"Get off, get off, get off!"

Flint cursed and pulled over to the side of the road. As soon as he'd come to a complete stop, he waved a hand in the air, no longer batting at Peasblossom, but this time trying to snatch her out of the air. The pixie dove into the turned-up collar of my coat, and I felt her brace her back against my spine and start kicking me with her tiny feet as hard as she could. The dull thuds against my vertebrae pushed the rest of Flint's influence from my mind, and I stumbled off the bike.

"Run," Peasblossom spat. "Run to the car now!"

I ran. My hands closed into fists, and the ring on my finger dug into my skin. I jerked the ring through the air over my chest, marking out the same equal-armed cross I'd used before and refreshing the original spell. Blue light flared over me, closing me in enchanted armor.

"That would have been a good idea *before* having a chat with the fey," Peasblossom pointed out crossly.

"I didn't know he was out here," I protested, breathing a little harder. I spotted my car in the parking lot ahead and ran faster.

"I told you he was there!"

"You told me a split second before he made eye contact!" I fumbled for my keys, stabbing at the button on the key fob that would unlock the doors. "He's *strong*."

"No kidding."

I tumbled into the car. Peasblossom leapt out of my coat and landed on the GPS. "Start the car. I'll put in the address."

I didn't argue with her. I didn't think Flint was giving chase, but I wasn't going to stop and check. I needed space between us, space to gather my thoughts and figure out what a sane person would do in this situation.

Three minutes later, the GPS interrupted my chaotic thoughts. *"You have arrived."*

I blinked. "Goodfellows?"

"Yes. I have earned some honey, and I'll collect now, if you don't mind."

I sighed and pulled into the parking lot. "You realize it probably would have been smarter to run away somewhere more than half a mile from the attack."

"Let him follow you here. Didn't you see the sign behind the bar? This is a safe haven. Otherworldly fights will result in the calling of the Vanguard—all parties will be arrested."

No, I hadn't seen that sign. But then, Peasblossom had the better eye for detail. It was what made her a great spy. I paused before closing the car door. "Wait a minute. Did you learn anything last night?" In all the excitement of finding Dabria, I hadn't taken the time to get Peasblossom's report.

She flew up to my shoulder and crossed her arms. "Honey first."

I bit my tongue and locked the car. Arguing would be pointless.

I waited until we were settled at a table, me with tea and honey—my own honey—and Peasblossom with her bowl of honey.

"All right, you have your treat. Now what did you find out?"

Peasblossom raised her hand toward her mouth, greedy eyes glittering as the honey oozed from her palm to the bowl. "I'm a good spy."

I waited. Not so patiently.

"There wasn't anyone at the hotel that had anything worth hearing, so I decided to broaden the search. Nose about the neighborhood a bit." She waggled her eyebrows at me. "Isai has been quite the social butterfly."

"What do you mean a social butterfly?"

"He's been visiting a bunch of wizards, and a few sorcerers. Including Arianne." Peasblossom sucked on her fingers, making loud smacking sounds that drew the attention of several other patrons.

A dryad near the window gave me a sympathetic smile, but the two trolls at the other table touched the weapons at their belts, a warning to mind the pixie. I put my hand up to hide my face.

"Stop being so loud," I hissed.

Peasblossom looked me in the eye and sucked some more honey off her hand. Louder this time.

The vein in my temple pulsed.

I groped for my tea. "What does he want?"

"Don't know. He's very sensitive about spying, keeps casting detection spells—even goes invisible every once in a while." She snorted, almost choked on her honey, then swallowed. "Paranoid, that's what he is. Thinks he's always being watched."

"So none of the wee ones you talked to knew why he was making all these visits?"

"No, but they're always watching him, so they know where he goes. Spitbeard is powerful and cranky, and we like to keep an eye on those types."

I stopped myself from taking a sip of tea just in time to avoid having it shoot up my nose as I laughed at the Spitbeard nickname. "We'll call him that from now on. It will make him less scary." I leaned back against the bench seat's cushion, drumming my fingernails against my mug. "What are you up to, Spitbeard?"

"Maybe he has the book, and he's trying to figure out how to open it."

"Possibly. Or he could be trying to build his own alliances."

"What do you mean?"

I took a sip of tea. "Well, let's say Isai was ready to violate his agreement with Anton and he did steal the book. He figures he'll eat whatever consequences come down on his magic for being forsworn and he'll be fine because he'll have all that blackmail to force other people to work for him."

"No wizard is going to risk his power like that."

"But remember what Anton said. Isai's been watching him all this time. Think about how much power and control Anton has —all with no magic of his own. Isai is arrogant, so I can believe he'd think there was nothing to it, that he could be just as successful as Anton if he had the vampire's resources."

Peasblossom slurped up another handful of honey. "All right," she said in a sticky voice. "So Isai decides to break his word and use the book to build a rival empire."

"Or take over Anton's."

"Or that. He steals the book, but it's locked."

I nodded. "Anton said he had Serafina's castle double-warded so Isai couldn't let himself in. What if he did the same to the book? Maybe Isai is looking for the other wizard who warded the book?"

"Sounds possible," Peasblossom agreed.

"Too bad I can't ask Arianne what Isai came to talk to her about."

"Don't even think about it. She'll just hypnotize you again—or worse. She doesn't like you."

I dropped my head against the backrest of the booth. "I still owe her a present, don't I? Bloody hell."

Peasblossom snorted. "Gonna have to be a big present."

She wasn't wrong. I sighed and unzipped the pouch at my waist. I needed to organize my thoughts.

"Oh, brother," Peasblossom muttered five minutes later, watching me over her bowl of honey. "You need to organize that thing."

My fingers met something sticky, and a small lump attached itself to my skin. I wrinkled my nose and grasped the rubbery tidbit, not wanting to know what it was, but needing to get it out of my bag. A half-eaten red gummy bear. I pressed my lips together and held it out to Peasblossom.

"I was looking for that!" she accused.

"You say that like I took it from you," I said, exasperated. "How many times do I have to tell you to carry your own stuff and stop tucking things into my pack? *Especially* half-eaten food." I used a napkin to pry the candy from my hand, then resumed my search, this time keeping an eye out for a wet wipe as well. "You keep telling me to get organized, but I'd like to know how that's possible when you keep adding to the mess."

"You're so cranky today." Peasblossom sniffed. "I think I'll spend another night here."

"No you won't." I glared at a wadded-up ball of tissues I'd just pulled from the pack, some of which were now glued to the tacky residue on my fingertips. "You're coming home. I might need to make more potions."

"You don't need me for that," she protested. "If you can't do it yourself, like a proper witch, ask Mother Hazel."

The triumph I'd felt when my hand closed around a notebook died at the notion of going to my mentor for help. I imagined the look on her face at the very suggestion she help me down the path of private investigator—the path she seemed to think led away from being a true witch. "I am not going to ask her for potions. Blood and bone, are you trying to make my life miserable?"

"Guff, guff, guff."

I found a wet wipe and cleaned my hands before resettling myself in the seat and pulling a slim pen from the spiral binding of the notepad. The pen made a tiny blue dot as I pressed it to the paper.

"All right, I need to talk with Arianne, but first I need to make myself less vulnerable to her spells. I'm not meeting her at the hotel again—Goddess only knows what fortifying measures she has there. Perhaps if I met her someplace public?"

"You think she'll nip out to have coffee with you because you asked nicely?"

Good point. "Or I can borrow something from Mother Hazel to help."

Peasblossom chortled. "You're going to steal an item of power from your mentor?"

The pen groaned in my grip. "Borrow."

"Are you going to ask first?"

"Next, I have to check on Flint's alibi."

Peasblossom's hand slipped from the edge of the bowl, and only the mad fluttering of her wings saved her from submerging in her sticky breakfast. "Check his alibi?" she demanded, rising into the air. "You got his alibi? That didn't happen today. You met with Flint without me?"

"No. I talked to him on the phone."

"Without me."

I gave her a satisfied smirk over the notepad. "If I recall, you decided to have an impromptu sleepover."

She scowled and made a fist that forced honey through her fingers in oozing golden lines. "You didn't make staying home a tempting alternative."

I chuckled and shook my head. "All right, I'm going to see if I can't coax Arianne to meet with me here. You find this Hemington Agency and snoop around to see who knows Flint. He says he was with one of their models, but of course he doesn't remember her name. Still, shouldn't be too hard to find her if you recruit some help."

Peasblossom crossed her arms and flew into the air to hover an inch away from my nose. "No. I want to stay with you."

I had a flash of brilliance and shoved my hand into my bag. After three minutes of finding nothing but junk that didn't belong there in the first place, I crowed in triumph and raised a handful of honey packets. "Take these. Use them to reward those of your spy network who do properly impressive reconnaissance."

Peasblossom's eyes widened and she dipped, attention locked on the condiment samples. "A spy network?"

She took the honey packets with humorous reverence, and I allowed myself a moment of self-congratulation. I'd known that would appeal to her. Ordering some of her kin about would be a real power trip, something all the wee ones were susceptible to.

And honey would buy her a lot of authority.

"I'll check back here before I go home," I said. "If you want to stay longer, text me. Remember, adults' texts are less likely to be reviewed by worried parents, so don't use a teenager's phone."

Peasblossom hugged the honey packets to her chest, her eyes a little glazed, as if she were already thinking ahead and was no longer paying attention to me. "Okay."

It said a lot about Peasblossom's pride that she let a thin layer of honey remain behind in the bowl and left to start building her network. I smiled, affection for my familiar warming my chest. She'd probably give herself a title and everything. At least today's technology meant she could find me again when she needed to. What had I ever done before—

I froze.

The phone.

I could *call* Arianne. Her hypnosis spell wouldn't work over the phone. My brow furrowed and I tapped a finger on the table-top. At least, I didn't think it would work. Definitely not if I distorted her voice somehow. It was so obvious that I almost smacked my head with my hand. Why hadn't I thought of this sooner? With the phone and a lucky bluff...

I opened the app store and, after a quick search, found what I needed. A distorter that would filter the voice I heard instead of filtering my voice should be enough to break any charm Arianne might try. I looked up the number for Suite Dreams.

Even with the extra precaution, my nerves were still a little raw when I dialed her number. I signaled the waitress for a refill on my tea.

"Hello?"

I snorted, then clapped a hand over my mouth. The app had chosen a voice that sounded like a cartoon chipmunk. "Um, hi," I managed. "May I speak with Arianne?"

"May I ask who is calling?"

I looked down at the app, frantically trying to change the voice selection. "Yes, this is Shade Renard."

"One moment, please."

I chose a different voice and put the phone back to my ear.

"Mother Renard. I did not expect to hear from you again."

I froze, horrified. The new voice made her sound like Mother Hazel.

"I, uh…" I stared down at the phone, scanning the list for a safer voice.

"I had nothing to do with Helen Miller's disappearance. If you call me again, the next time you hear from me will be in your dreams, *Mother* Renard. Or perhaps I should say your nightmares."

"No, no, wait, don't hang up!"

I gave up choosing a new voice and put the phone to my ear. "This isn't about Helen Miller. In fact, I apologize for that. I realize now how insulting I was."

"If that's all, I am rather busy."

She didn't sound inclined to accept my apology. "There is one more thing."

"Another missing person you'd like to lay at my doorstep?"

"No!" I forced myself to calm down, curling my fingers around the mug's smooth handle. Goddess, she sounded like my mentor. Why did she have to sound like my mentor? "No, actually, it's about a wizard."

"A wizard?"

Interest lightened her tone, a definite improvement over the suspicion of a moment ago. I took a fortifying sip of tea. "Yes, a very powerful wizard. I've been contacted by several people—magic users—claiming he's been threatening them. One of them mentioned seeing him entering your hotel and thought he might have visited you too, and I wanted to see what your impression was."

"Who is this powerful wizard?"

"His name is Isai."

Arianne scoffed, disdain thick in the sound. "I am not threatened by Isai. He is the vampire's pet now, and everyone knows it."

"So he didn't threaten you?"

"He would not dare. I suppose he insulted me, offering me money and thinking I would be stupid enough not to see the danger in what he asked of me." She paused. "Is this about what happened to Tybor Aegis? Do you believe Isai killed him?"

Tybor Aegis? Killed? I thought fast. "Well, you can see why people are concerned. And the task Isai was asking for help with…it's dangerous, isn't it?" *Stay calm, stay calm.* "He must realize you would guess what he's up to."

"Any ward strong enough that Isai needs help to break it is protecting something powerful or something dangerous. If Tybor didn't realize that, then that's his fault. Personally, I have no desire to involve myself in something guaranteed to bring trouble. Which is why I will say goodbye to you now, Mother Renard. I trust this will be the last time we speak."

I nodded, then realized she couldn't see me. My brain whirred, trying to incorporate what I'd just learned into what I already knew. "Of course. Thank you for your time. And if something changes and he does threaten you, don't hesitate to call."

"Excuse me?"

Her voice turned to ice, those two words sharp enough to cut through the din of a kindergarten classroom. The fact that she still sounded like my mentor made it exponentially more disturbing. My stomach twisted and I tightened my grip on the phone, holding on for dear life.

"And why would I call you, witchling? Are you suggesting that I would need your help? Need you to save me?"

I bristled at that, despite the unease snapping along my nerve endings. Witchling was a word for a young witch, an *inexperienced* witch. I had started my studies later than most, and that made me a joke in some circles. I didn't appreciate it.

Before I could think of a response, let alone say it, my phone beeped, alerting me that Arianne had hung up. And she'd been angry.

I set my phone on the table and slumped back against the booth. That was two apology gifts I owed her.

I shoved that thought from my mind and focused on the blank notebook in front of me. A dead wizard. A possibly murdered wizard.

"It might be completely unrelated," I muttered.

After staring at the notebook long enough for the waitress to bring me a fresh pot of hot water for my tea, I pressed the pen to the paper and began to write. *Start with the facts, then move on to supposition.*

Isai. He was the perfect suspect. He'd created the wards, he could've dismissed them with a thought. And though Anton had noted that Isai had never met Helen, he'd admitted in the file that it was possible the wizard had seen her coming and going during the actual work. After a second of hesitation, I added, *possibly killed another wizard to steal his power.* There was no doubt about it, Isai had the means, motive, and opportunity.

But Anton was burning his spellbook. A spellbook that Isai prized enough to give up his freedom, serve someone he despised. If he had the stolen book, he must know by now that it was spelled shut. How long would he attempt to open the book before he gave up and returned it to save what remained of his spellbook? Anton would never trade for it, but if Isai framed someone else for the theft, he might at least stop the vampire from burning any more pages. Who would he frame?

Dabria. A professional rogue, weak in her own magic, but unrivaled when it came to stealing from others. She had the skill to best the traps. Anton had no doubt customized the wards in Serafina's castle against her specifically, but I doubted he'd have had her in mind when designing the wards to his vault. But she wasn't in the book. How could she have known the book existed, to say nothing of where to find it?

Flint. He knew about the book better than anyone, had his name written in it. He'd seduced a guard, had known where to find the book. He claimed to have an alibi. To kill the guards, to break the wards, to pass the traps...he would have needed someone else for all of that. Would have needed to seduce someone much more powerful. Possibly even one of my other suspects? And he had tried to kidnap me today. Why do that if he wasn't worried?

I dropped the pen and slouched back in the seat. I needed proof, physical evidence. And I didn't have any.

"You're going to regret that."

I looked away from my notes to the table beside my booth. A man sat there, a glass of whiskey on the table in front of him. He turned in his seat, speaking to a man standing at the to-go counter trying to balance two travel cups of coffee one on top of the other to free up his other hand for the bag of food. The man paused in the middle of settling his chin on the top cup for added stability to stare at the speaker.

"I'm sorry?"

The man next to me gestured at the coffee with his whiskey. "You're going to regret that."

"I'll be fine."

He shrugged and continued staring into his glass.

Curiosity made me watch the man with the carry-out order. He made it to the door with impressive balance, giving the man at the table an I-told-you-so look. As he pressed his back to the door to push it open, someone else opened it from behind him. I caught a flash of a man in a business suit with his phone glued to his ear, and then all my attention was on the carry-out man hissing as hot coffee spilled over his shirt.

The man with the whiskey didn't glance up at the disaster

happening in the doorway, but he seemed to feel my gaze on him. He met my eyes without reacting.

"Precog," he said.

I tilted my head. "Witch."

He nodded. "First time here?"

"Second."

His eyes clouded. "Won't be the last."

His precognitive observation comforted me. Perhaps that meant I wasn't going to die solving this case. Or it might mean that Peasblossom would drag me back here for more honey before I closed it.

I took a breath, ready to introduce myself, but the clouds in the precog's eyes grew thicker. He turned back to his table, staring into the golden whiskey as if he were looking straight through it to another future. Precogs had notoriously short attention spans. Hard to blame them, considering how many futures vied with the present for attention.

My tea was cold, but I drank it anyway. I needed the caffeine to fortify me against the barrage of orange construction cones waiting for me on the long drive home.

I gathered my notebook and pen as a woman at the table on the other side of the precog burst into a fit of giggles. She rose from the table, fanning her cheeks with her hand.

"Of course I'll go to your sister's wedding with you!" she told the skinny teenager still sitting. "Oh, Landon, this will be so much fun!"

The teenager grinned, but before he could speak, the girl backed up a few steps, taking her cell phone from her pale pink jacket. "I'm going to call my sister. She's going to be so jealous!"

I stood. As I left, I heard the precog's voice and turned to see him lock gazes with the teenager, gesturing toward the retreating giggler with his head.

"You're going to regret that."

CHAPTER 12

Finding a wizard wasn't as easy as looking him up in the phone book. It took seven calls to other witches I knew before I found someone who'd heard of him. It took three more calls to find someone who knew where he lived. It was almost four thirty before my GPS led me to a nondescript house in a cozy suburb in Olmstead Falls. I gazed out the windshield at the small ranch-style house with its red brick and white trim. It didn't look like a wizard's house.

Most wizards were prone to shows of power and affluence. They didn't all go to the extremes Isai did, with gold rings bedecking every finger and matching chains hanging like champions of capitalism around their necks, but more often than not, they were the peacocks of the magic world. Not so for Tybor Aegis.

"What's your game, Tybor?" I said to myself. "You don't live in an upscale building. You don't distinguish your house from the outside with magical or non-magical decoration." I frowned and extended my senses, reaching out with my power the way one might extend a hand, feeling for a wall. "You don't even put wards around the property to warn trespassers they've stumbled onto the territory of a mighty wizard." I tapped a finger against the steering wheel. "Either you are an anomaly, or you aren't a very powerful wizard. Or you are powerful...and you are in hiding. *Were* in hiding."

After a few minutes sitting in the car, I acknowledged that I wouldn't learn anything that way and I needed to go inside. The only problem with that was the rather large man sitting on the porch. He watched me sitting in my car, the sharp look in his eyes belying his relaxed position. To any human, he was just an average Joe hanging out on his porch, enjoying the few hours of the day that didn't threaten to freeze your eyeballs in their sockets. The black T-shirt and jeans made him look human enough. But if I concentrated, I picked up a greenish tint to his skin. He had ogre in his bloodline somewhere. I'd bet my broomstick on it.

I was also willing to bet he was a member of the Vanguard, here to protect the crime scene.

"Mother Renard."

I whipped around in my seat, my heart leaping into my throat. My eyes widened when I saw who stood on the other side of my car.

Vera raised a hand. "It's all right, it's only me." The red and black checkered skirt she wore flared around her legs, swaying as she stepped back from where she'd bent toward my passenger window. Her black peacoat parted to reveal a formfitting red shirt the shade of crushed strawberries. She nodded toward the door. "You heard, then?"

I forced myself to relax and quickly rolled down the window. "I spoke with Arianne earlier. She mentioned it."

Vera's lips pressed into a thin line. "Arianne again. I don't like the way her name keeps coming up."

"I don't think she had anything to do with it." I hesitated, toying with the black zipper on the pouch at my waist. "Peasblossom heard rumors that Isai has been going around trying to get help breaking a ward."

The *rusalka's* eyes narrowed. "Oh? What ward?"

"I don't know yet. I considered the possibility he might have the book and be trying to get into it." I ran the pad of my finger over the nylon of my pouch, drawing absent-minded designs. "I was at Goodfellows, and I got to thinking. You said Arianne is the best at wards. If Isai has the book, maybe that's why he's looking for help. The book is warded, right? Would Arianne be able to open it?"

"Not yet," Vera murmured. "But eventually, yes." The soft peacoat shifted as she slid her hand into the pocket. "And did he ask her to do such a thing?"

My nerves tightened as my focus narrowed down to her hand where it disappeared in black fabric. I tried not to hold my breath, tried not to think too hard on what sort of weapon the vampire's wife might carry in that pocket. *Don't be stupid. Why would she want to hurt you?*

I cleared my throat. "Yes. Well, maybe. I called her and made up the story that several magic users had contacted me claiming Isai visited them, and they felt threatened. I asked if he'd been to see her, and she admitted he had, but she claims she turned him down."

"She didn't mention what he wanted help with specifically?"

Her hand was still in her pocket. I resisted the urge to throw the car into drive and speed away. My, wasn't I feeling paranoid. "No. She just said any ward strong enough that Isai needed help to break it means trouble, and she has no interest in anything that will bring trouble."

"Sounds like Arianne." Vera pulled a tube of ChapStick from her pocket and popped the cap off to spread it over her lips. A soft breeze carried the scent of cherry into my car. "She is reclusive. But I've never gotten the impression she's a bad person. And I'm a very good judge of character."

I didn't raise the question of how someone who was a good judge of character ended up marrying the Otherworld's equivalent to a mob boss. I gave myself a mental pat on the back for the show of tact.

Now that her hand was out of her pocket, and the would-be weapon was revealed to have been a harmless tube of ChapStick, some of the tension bled from my shoulders. I unzipped my pouch and dug around for a mint. "Anyway, it was when I mentioned people felt threatened that she dropped Tybor's name. She thought his murder was the reason the other magic users felt threatened. She said she had no need for my protection and hung up."

Vera's eyes widened and her cherry-scented lips parted. "You…offered her protection?"

My cheeks grew warm. I put a handful of tissues and a thermometer on the passenger seat and continued digging for the mints. "Not in so many words. I simply said she could call on me if she had need to. I offended her earlier, I was hoping to smooth things over."

"But you offended her again instead."

I sighed. "She's so touchy."

Vera gave me a rueful smile. "I'd say I'd put in a good word for you, but Arianne can be stubborn once she's formed an impression of someone. I'm sorry to say you should consider a charm against nightmares, at least for a few weeks."

A chill ran down my spine, but I pushed it away. I found the mints and pried open the circular tin. "I'll think of something." I popped a mint into my mouth, then held them out for Vera. "Well, relevant to the case or not, something about Tybor's death brought the Vanguard. So either there's evidence that his murderer was another species…"

"Or it was sensational enough it was guaranteed to make a huge splash in the human news," Vera finished. She waved off the mints.

"I hope it's the former." I put the mints back in my pouch, then paused as something occurred to me. I looked at Vera. "Wait a minute. I'm here because I talked to Arianne. Why are you here?"

"Tybor used to work for Anton," Vera explained. "When his death was reported, Dimitri's system flagged it—just as it did when Helen Miller disappeared. I know Anton will want details, so I thought I'd come out and see what happened so I would have more information for him when he wakes up." She leaned in. "Between you and me, he can be quite cranky if he has too many questions and not enough answers."

I'd noticed that. "So Tybor worked for him. Something to do with wards?"

Vera nodded. "Yes. Tybor warded my stepmother's castle for Anton, back in the Old Kingdom. When it came to wards, he was second only to Arianne, that I know of." She looked toward the house. "When I heard of his murder, I thought perhaps the thief may have come to him to open the book."

I held up a hand. "Wait. Tybor warded your stepmother's castle? Serafina's castle?"

Vera's mouth tightened at the mention of her stepmother, her dark pupils swallowing the brown of her irises until she looked at me with an almost-avian stare. "Yes. Did you know my stepmother?"

"No," I said, resisting the urge to lean back. "It's just...I thought Isai warded that castle?"

"He did. But Anton worried that Isai would try to help himself to some of that wretched woman's property, and so he had it warded a second time."

There was something unnerving about her eyes. I stayed where I was, but closed my hand into a fist, feeling the comforting weight of the ring on my finger. "I'm surprised Anton didn't help himself to what was in there."

"That's because you know nothing about my stepmother, or

what went on in that castle," Vera said coldly. "*I* asked Anton to seal it. As far as I'm concerned, it no longer exists. No one will ever set foot on that cursed ground again."

I hesitated, but only for a second. "Serafina's sister doesn't appear to share your idea of closure."

Vera's eyes sharpened. "You spoke to Dabria?"

I nodded and filled Vera in on my morning. "I was going to call Anton with an update, but obviously he's not awake yet," I added quickly.

If Vera noticed my nervousness, she didn't show it. "So that's why Dabria has been making her little visits to Cleveland. She's been tempting Isai." She narrowed her eyes. "And I thought she was just tormenting Anton."

I didn't point out that tormenting the vampire had indeed been a secondary reason. "She seems to think it will work eventually," I said instead.

"She would," Vera muttered. She looked at the house. "So perhaps Dabria finally figured out that Isai does not have the power to let her in on his own. He would need Tybor to drop the wards he built as well." She thumped her hand on the passenger door a couple times. "Let's go have a look, shall we?"

I stared at her. "You realize the Vanguard left someone behind to keep people out? One guard means they've finished their initial assessment, and when they get the results in, they'll send the second team." Part of the Vanguard's purpose was to assure that no species could take advantage of another. Hence, when a crime occurred, it was protocol to have two teams analyze the scene separately, each one made up of different species.

Vera waved a hand as she skirted the front of my car. "I've been a consultant for the Vanguard, and an ambassador for numerous races, countless times. I promise you, they will not mind if I bring you along for a little peek."

I paused with my hand still on the door handle. "You... You're a member of the Vanguard?"

"Consultant," she corrected me, waiting by my door as I rolled up the windows before getting out of the car. "We thought it was best not to make anything official out of concern that some might view me as...impartial."

Well, yes. She was the wife of the prince of Dacia. There wasn't a race from this world or the Old Kingdom that didn't view him and any who associated with him with...caution.

Something of my thoughts must have shown on my face, because Vera smiled. "I promise you, Mother Renard, I am very capable of impartiality—much to my husband's consternation."

I let that go. As solid as Vera's reputation was, and as much as I believed she was a good woman at heart, I also knew she loved her husband. If push came to shove, I had no doubt whose side she would take. I was sure the Vanguard understood the same.

The large man stood as we marched up the driveway, his full attention on Vera. He was large, close to seven feet. "Mrs. Winters, how nice to see you." He paused, the hard planes of his face pinching with confusion. "Though I'm not sure to what I owe the pleasure?"

Vera beamed at him as if they were old friends. "Chad, how wonderful to see you again. How is your mother?"

"Still undefeated."

"Fantastic. You tell her I wish her the best." She took my arm and tugged me closer, almost pulling me off balance, since I hadn't been expecting it. "Now, Chad, it has come to my attention that Tybor met with foul play. I believe what happened to him may relate to a personal situation, and I'd like to see for myself. You will be a dear and let us in, won't you?"

Rusalki were a very convincing race to begin with. Even when they weren't actively seducing someone, there was just something about them that fascinated people, humans and Otherworld alike. Add to that Vera's genuine reputation as a friend to all, and the power behind her in the form of her husband, and I doubted she heard the word no often. If at all.

186

Chad didn't hesitate. As if Vera had flipped a switch, he fell back a step, simultaneously picking up a clipboard from a small iron and glass table by his chair. That one moment told me that even with all I'd known about the vampire and his wife, I had still severely underestimated their reach.

"You remember the rules?" he asked.

"I will touch nothing," Vera promised.

"I'll have to mark down your visit?"

"As well you should—protocol is important." Vera took the clipboard and scrawled out a truly gorgeous signature as if she were granting an autograph. "And, Chad, this is my good friend Mother Renard. Baba Yaga's apprentice."

Chad blinked and looked me up and down. I tried not to squirm as he took in my purple and black leggings.

"Hello." I accepted the clipboard from Vera and wrote my name in significantly less sophisticated script.

"Mother Hazel's apprentice?" Chad asked, his voice rising with surprise.

Vera pulled me into the house. "Yes, that's her. Well, we'd best get inside. We won't be long."

The inside of Tybor's house was as unimposing as the outside. A faded blue sectional couch took up most of the left-hand wall, and a laughably old television sat opposite, rabbit ears akimbo. The paintings hanging over the ancient television set and the back of the couch were a little rich for most people in this neighborhood—I recognized at least two of the names as fey painters. Other than that, the house looked perfectly mundane.

It wasn't until I walked to the back of the living room that I could see through the open entryway to the kitchen-dining room, and the bedroom beyond. Yellow police tape crisscrossed the door.

"It's strange, isn't it?" Vera asked. "The Vanguard is made up of some of the most intimidating investigators the Otherworld has to offer, but they still use the same simple crime scene tape as the humans."

"It almost makes you believe that what's behind that door is a simple gunshot," I said, my voice a little thick.

"Or a stabbing," Vera offered.

We stood there for another minute.

"Arianne didn't mention any specifics." I cleared my throat. "Did you hear anything?"

Vera shook her head and reached for her ChapStick again. "My contact in the Vanguard said it was unpleasant, but we didn't discuss it over the phone."

Another minute ticked by.

"Can you feel it?" I asked quietly.

Vera took a deep breath, then nodded. "Magic and death. Sadly, a feeling I became familiar with early in life." She glanced at me. "My stepmother, not my husband." She ran a hand over her hair, smoothing it down. "I promised myself it would never get easier, though. That feeling should be just as awful every time I feel it."

"Mother Hazel always said something similar. Death shouldn't be feared, but it should be respected. And a loss of life is always a tragedy. You should always feel something when it's taken too soon."

We were both stalling now. I straightened my spine, and we shared one more look before marching through the house to that yellow-striped door. I carefully removed enough tape to open it, then turned the knob.

The scent of blood struck me in the face like a physical blow, flowing up my nose and into my open mouth until I gagged. I staggered back, clapping a hand over my face even though it was too late. Bitter bile washed up the back of my throat, and I closed my eyes, all my concentration going into not vomiting. *Must not throw up on the crime scene.*

"Oh, Goddess."

I opened my eyes to find Vera standing just inside the room, a black handkerchief held over her mouth and nose. I didn't want to know what she saw. I didn't want to go in that room.

But I did.

The bed had been turned into a macabre altar. Tybor Aegis' body lay with his feet toward the pillows and his upper torso dangling off the foot of the bed. A single bullet hole in his forehead acted as a grisly tap, allowing his blood to drain down his forehead and drip into a small pot on the floor. The bowl was beaten gold, imperfect and obviously hand-crafted. Dark flecks of dried blood dotted the sides, and the inner rim glistened with a velvety black liquid.

Wizards were not like the fey. Not like vampires. They died much the same as humans did. Which was not to say they died as easily as humans. A wizard would live for centuries, left unmolested—which they nearly never were. And a powerful wizard could heal himself of just about anything. But for the most part, things that killed humans also killed wizards.

Being completely drained of blood, for example.

"It's a pity the preservation spell doesn't help with the smell," Vera said lightly.

I nodded, turning up the collar of my coat to cover my mouth. The Vanguard's preservation spell would keep the evidence—including the body—from deteriorating while they conducted their investigation, but it didn't help the scent of blood and brain matter that thickened the air of the room in a nauseating cloud. Vera and I both stayed back, neither of us willing to disturb the spell.

"How old was Tybor?" I asked. I studied his brown hair with just a scattering of gray, the muscles that retained definition despite the softening of a sedentary lifestyle.

"Hardly middle-aged," Vera said, sadness in her voice. "Only one hundred and fifty."

"Such a waste." I took a shallow breath, taking in as little of the blood-scented air as possible, and pointed to his forehead. "A single gunshot wound. And I recognize some of those symbols etched into the pot."

"Alchemy?" Vera guessed, her voice quiet.

I called my magic, waving an arm toward the battered gold. "It's transmutation of some kind," I murmured. The silver net fell over the altar, and green light flickered like emerald flame over the pot. I took a step closer, focusing on those green flames. My stomach sank. "Ink. The blood was turned to ink."

Vera sucked in a breath. "Flint?"

Anton's words from two days ago echoed in my head, filling my mind with images of Flint performing his soul-ensnaring ritual. "It would appear so. This is how his other victims died, right? One gunshot to the head, drained of their blood so it could be turned to ink?" I spoke slowly and calmly, trying to treat this as clinically as possible. If I concentrated on the facts, only the facts, then perhaps I could ignore the part of my brain that had started screaming, the part that wanted to run from the room and find the nearest receptacle to vomit into. If Flint had tattooed Tybor's name on his skin, then the wizard would be trapped with the *leannan sidhe*. He would know what had happened to him. He would understand his fate. Denied an after-life. Robbed of his next turn of the wheel.

"Do you think you could get me a copy of the autopsy report?" I asked Vera, when I was sure I could speak without vomiting.

"I believe so." She stared into my eyes, the look a little too intense, as if she needed to look at me, as if I was her reason for not looking at the body. "I think we're done here?"

"I doubt the Vanguard would appreciate me taking any samples, or poking around for more clues." I didn't take my eyes off her, accepting the safety that having something else to concentrate on offered. "If you can get me the crime scene reports, I'm sure that would be all I need." I swallowed hard and asked the next question before I could talk myself out of it. "If you could get any reports from Flint's previous victims, that would also be helpful. It looks the same, but I don't want to jump to any conclusions."

"All right."

Something about her voice sounded off, and her brown eyes held a haunted expression that hadn't been there before.

"Vera, what's wrong?"

She stared at me even harder, then her gaze bounced from the floor back to me, as if she had trouble meeting my eyes.

"Vera, what's wrong?" I repeated.

She rubbed a hand over her face, then looked at me for a long moment. Finally, she sighed. "I just think... Perhaps Anton should have hired someone else."

I jerked back as if she'd punched me. It was on the tip of my tongue to defend myself, to point out that I was doing just fine. I'd found Dabria, hadn't I? I'd found out about Tybor. But there was something about that look in her eyes. Fear. Fear for me. My earlier question to Anton repeated itself in my head. Why me? Why had he hired me?

"Vera," I said carefully. "Am I the first person Anton has hired to find the thief?"

At first, I thought she wouldn't answer. She pressed her lips harder together and started to turn away. Then she stopped, visibly forcing herself to meet my eyes. "No," she whispered.

My heart lodged in my throat. "How many?"

"Two. Both dead within twenty-four hours of taking the case." Vera swiped a hand through her hair, pushing it back off her shoulders. "Shade, I—"

"Why me?" I interrupted. My pulse roared in my ears, so loud that I had to raise my voice just to hear my questions. "Why did he hire me? I assume the first two detectives were more experienced?"

Vera nodded miserably. "Yes."

"Then why hire me? Two experienced detectives are killed twenty-four hours after taking the case, and he decides to hire me next? Did he think he'd try the other end of the spectrum? Try someone the murderer wouldn't think was worth killing?"

Vera met my eyes, but her expression remained as closed as the gates of a dragon's hoard. She wasn't going to tell me either. No one wanted to talk about why the vampire chose me.

"I will speak to Anton if you wish to drop the case. You will have nothing to fear from him, or his contract. Confidentiality is all he will ask."

Irritation rose, fighting back some of the fear. I lifted my chin. "I'm not going anywhere. I've been on this case for more than twenty-four hours, and I'm not dead." Hysteria bubbled just under the surface of my skin, and I threw up my hands. "What makes you think the killer would let me live if I walked away now anyway?"

"Shade—"

"No." I shook my head and turned away from her. "No, I'm done talking. You obviously have no intention of answering my questions, so if you'll excuse me, I have to get home. I need to research that spell—oh, and try not to get killed. Please send me that file as soon as you can."

"I'm sorry, Shade."

"You can update Anton, can't you?" I asked.

She sighed. "Yes, of course."

I had nothing more to say that I wouldn't regret later. I turned my back on Vera, marched past Chad without a word, and made a beeline for my car.

I would find my own answers.

CHAPTER 13

"Mrs. Harvesty, do you think it's possible that perhaps your kitten is just moody?"

I braced my hand on the open grimoire on the desk in front of me, trying to hold on to my temper long enough not to snap at the woman on the phone. My skin itched from the dust of piles of old texts, and I'd drunk enough soda that my hands shook as I turned the pages. Today was the deadline. I had twelve hours left till midnight, twelve hours until the vampire would demand results. I'd been up since dawn researching the stupid ritual, and I probably had hours more ahead of me. I had no time for this.

"Majesty is not *moody*, he's *sick*. I know he's sick. And you promised you would come last time—even though you *forgot.*"

My jaw tightened. "And if I remember correctly, he was fine by the next morning. Perhaps that will happen again, hmmm?"

"I could bring him over right now. It's only noon."

"I'm afraid that won't work. I'm sorry, but I have a lot to do today." I scowled and stared down a page depicting a *kapala*, a cup made from a human skull used to catch sacrificial blood. Decorated in gold, but not made from gold. I slammed the book shut and added it to the discarded pile of texts.

"Tomorrow, then? First thing in the morning. The very first thing?"

I swallowed a growl. "Why don't you *call* me tomorrow morning if he's not feeling better, all right? We'll chat more then."

"I will call you because I'm sure he'll still need help."

"I'll talk to you tomorrow, then." The last part came out too sharp, almost a yell. I closed my eyes and took a deep breath. I was angry, yes. I was scared, yes. But that was no reason to take it out on a woman worried about her cat. "I know how scary it can be when someone you love is sick," I said, my voice softer this time. I said a silent apology to the kitten, then added, "Make sure you give him lots of love. A mummy's love is always best."

"Oh, I will," she promised.

I could almost hear her hugging the poor creature. Perhaps his bones were brittle and cracking from all the loving embraces from his mummy.

When I got off the phone, I grabbed another book from the stack on my desk and flipped it open. I needed to know more about Flint's ritual. I had to know everything that ritual would give him. Did he get Tybor's knowledge? His magic? His life force? If it granted the murderer access to Tybor's magic, then Flint would have a spellcaster's ability. He could have done the magic himself, taken down the wards himself. It would make him a much, much stronger suspect. But if it only granted him access to Tybor's knowledge, he would still need help. He could tell someone how to take down the wards, but he couldn't do it himself.

I dropped my head. Why hadn't I had these transcribed? If these were digital text, a simple search would be all I needed. Minutes of research instead of hours.

The thought was all it took to send me to the fridge, trampling my dietary restrictions on the way. The light that shone on me when I opened the door was practically ethereal.

"You don't need this. You've had enough. Just put it down."

I stared at the soda, the bright red comfort of the Coke promising to make this day all better. A little caffeine, a little carbonation. No judgmental pixie hanging about to count how many I had. What was the harm?

The knock at the door wasn't harsh or violent, but it startled me all the same, thanks in no small part to the amount of caffeine burning through my system. I jumped and lost my grip on the soda. The can fell in what seemed like slow motion, giving me plenty of time to flail about like a blind cat who'd heard a mouse, trying to catch my beverage before it hit the floor.

I didn't.

I scowled down at the dented can. "Well, I can't open that one."

Another knock. Louder this time.

"This is a sign," I said reluctantly. "A sign I'm not meant to have another soda."

Dejected, I put the can back in the fridge, my mood somewhat mollified by the row of potions in the door. Liquid armor against charms, a little *oomph* for my shields. I would need those as soon as I figured out which delightful suspect to chat with next. And if someone was out there intending to kill me, I might need to start popping defensive potions like vitamins...

I shuffled to the door, feeling foolish for letting my temper get the better of me earlier. I needed to call Vera. I needed to know how the previous investigators had died. Maybe visit those crime scenes too. I reached the door and pulled it open. "Hell—"

The compulsion hit me like an orb of honey, smacking into my mind and oozing down to coat it completely in warm fuzziness. The stress of researching the grisly ritual, the fear over learning that there very well might be someone out there planning to kill me—it all melted away, leaving a dopey smile in its wake.

"Hello, Mother Renard."

I slumped against the doorframe, grinning at my visitor. "Hello, Mr. Valencia."

A wolfish grin spread over his handsome features and he stepped closer, filling my senses with the scent of his aftershave. The bite of February's winter breeze gave the aftershave a sharper edge, like an erotic slap to the face.

"I wanted to apologize for our little misunderstanding earlier. I'm afraid the wee one thought I had ungentlemanly intentions when I invited you for a ride."

My brow furrowed as I tried to remember what he was referring to. "Oh, yes. Well, Peasblossom is very excitable. Most of the wee ones are."

"Let me come inside, and I'll explain everything. It was all really very innocent."

The word innocent did not belong on that mouth. "Of course. Please, come in."

His grin widened as he stepped over my threshold, moving with the grace one usually associated with a large cat. He winked at me and I giggled.

"Can I offer you a drink?" I asked.

"I would love one, thank you."

Still smiling, I sauntered to the refrigerator, kneeling down to reach for two Cokes. My ring caught the shelf above the soda with a loud clink and I scowled. Irritated, I pulled the ring off. It wouldn't do me any good anyway until I recharged it, and it was only getting in the way. I glanced at the row of potions in the fridge. Besides, I had plenty of potions. I should probably put a few of them in my pouch now…

Alarm bells went off in my head, somewhat muted by the gooey persuasion coating my brain. Potions. Yes, I'd made more potions while I studied Anton's files. I'd made more potions because I was dealing with an angry wizard…and a seductive fey.

The fey who had likely killed a wizard sometime last night.

The fey who was now standing in my living room.

I popped the cork on one of the potions and drank it in one long gulp. It tasted like strawberry soda and burned my nose the way carbonation did sometimes. Magic washed over me, invigorating my senses, straightening my spine. Cold reality pushed back the cloud Flint had laid over my mind, stealing that hazy, dreamlike euphoria. Fury rose on a wave of bad temper, and I let it come, let it destroy the last of the fey's influence. I stayed still while it filled me up, swelling until the magic glittered over my skin in a thin blue shield. I grabbed two Cokes and gritted my teeth. He'd pushed me. It was time to push back.

By the time I stood, Flint was no longer standing in the living room, admiring my bare walls. Now, he stood behind me in the dining room—at my desk.

Reading Anton's files.

My heart seized, and I almost dropped the sodas. "Mr. Valencia, that is private, and I'll thank you to step away from my desk."

My voice lashed across the room. It wasn't power, per se, not a spell. More like ultimate authority. A witch who served her people, used her power to help others, earned a right to be heard. That right bestowed on them a certain tone that froze people in their tracks.

All mothers had it too.

Flint didn't recoil, but he stepped back from the desk. He moved like a shifter, all rolling muscle and careless grace. If he was surprised I'd shaken off his influence, he didn't show it. "You aren't working for a jealous husband."

I frowned. "What?"

He tilted his head, considering. "When you contacted me the other day, asked for my alibi, I thought you were working for someone's husband." His attention slid to the file again, my notebook lying beside it. "But you're not. You're working for the vampire." When he looked at me again, there was a glint to his eyes that hadn't been there before. "Someone stole his little black book."

A few decades ago, Mother Hazel had taken me to meet a seafaring medicine man in Florida. While swimming there, I'd had the unfortunate experience of looking toward the shore to find a very large alligator watching me. For what had felt like an eternity, the beast just watched me. Not moving, not baring its teeth. Just watching. Deciding. Flint looked at me now the way that alligator had looked at me then.

I couldn't move. I could barely think, scarcely breathe. If it weren't for the potion, I didn't know how long I would have stood there, unable to fight or speak.

"I'm not at liberty to discuss it." My voice came out a whisper. I wrenched my spine straighter and tried again. "Get away from my desk."

He didn't move. "You have little notations here about the sorceress Dabria. Do you think she has it?"

I tried to think past the pounding of my own heartbeat. Was he toying with me? Pretending not to know who had the book? Or had he really been unaware of the book's missing status? "Do you know Dabria?" I asked.

"Everyone knows Dabria. There is no kingdom she hasn't stolen from, no creature she hasn't robbed of a treasure of one kind or another. She is a master thief."

He knew Dabria was a thief, and a good one. He could have seduced her into stealing the book for him.

"Do you believe Dabria has the book?"

His eyes shared the same quality as his voice. Sensual, and full of wicked promises. The potion flared inside me, reacting to his power and snapping against my skin like a rubber band.

My willpower writhed beneath his magic, keeping the silken net from ensnaring my senses. He was trying to influence me again—and he was good. The seduction wasn't overt this time, wasn't dramatic, over-suggestive. He wasn't trying to seduce me —he was just oozing sensuality in a way designed to make me wish he would. Preparing me for his next attempt. I stalked over to the desk and thrust the can of Coke at him.

A long-fingered hand took the drink before I punched it through his ridiculously muscled chest, an easy smile wiping away the surprise that had widened his eyes.

I needed to get him out of my house, get him away from me so I could think. Interviews with the fey needed to be restricted to phone calls. Always. "Mr. Valencia, I'm sorry, but I am very busy today. I have to ask you to leave. I will call you later, at a time convenient for us both." I gave my voice the lilt I used with small children when I was trying to bribe them with a sucker. "You may take the Coke with you."

He didn't move, and kept gazing at me with a hint of admiration on his face. A silent *touché* for resisting his influence?

"I want to help," he said finally, gesturing at the file. "How can I help?"

"I do not want nor need your help. In fact, you've done considerable harm just reading part of my *private* file."

"I would not have read any of it, had I realized it was private. I was merely occupying myself while you fetched me a drink."

He opened the Coke with a loud crack of aluminum, followed by a carbonated hiss. Brown eyes watched me over the rim as he took a drink. I put my own Coke down on the desk so I could open it with one hand, keeping the other ready to draw a spell if necessary.

"You must be a talented detective if Anton hired you," he continued. He gestured at the file. "Pity about his book. I know how that vampire prizes his…secrets."

"And the secrets of others," I said evenly.

Flint's jaw tightened. "Do you have any leads?"

My shields flared again. I gritted my teeth. "I thank you for your offer of help, but I must decline. I have things well in hand, and, as you might imagine, I have promised to protect my client's privacy. So if you don't mind, I'll say goodbye now."

"I have a gift for getting people to...open up. I could assist you in this investigation."

The words "open up" pinged off my shield like bullets. Not very subtle, that one. My temper spiked, and I narrowed my eyes.

"Tell me, Mr. Valencia, are you an experienced man?"

He paused, genuine surprise shifting his eyebrows up. Supple lips curved in the start of a grin. "Yes."

Cocky bugger didn't even think to ask, "Experienced in what?" I sniffed, channeling Mother Hazel as I summoned the witchy look of all witchy looks. "Then I would think you would have better control over your power. Unless your attempts to influence me—a witch standing in my own home—are deliberate?"

Flint studied me for a moment, running his gaze up and down my body. It tugged at my shield, like a man pulling on the strap of a dress, preparing to pull it off a woman's shoulder.

He gestured with his chin to the file. "He thinks I did it, doesn't he? Thinks I seduced someone into letting me in."

I took a sip of my Coke, still holding the witchy look. "Good-bye, Mr. Valencia."

He didn't back off, but he did look away, hiding the small retreat behind a casual sip of soda, his throat bobbing as he swallowed. "Dabria is ruthless when she sets her sights on something. And there is nothing she wants more than access to her sister's castle."

I tore my eyes from the muscular slope of his throat, concentrating on the magic of the shield potion humming inside of me. "I am not discussing this with you. Please leave."

"She's tried for years to make Isai let her in. Only two people can give her access—the wizard and the vampire."

He didn't know the castle was double-warded, that Isai couldn't get in himself. I didn't share that information. Brownie point for me. And later, a real brownie.

"If Dabria got her hands on one of his little black books, she'd have the means to bargain for access to the castle."

Over Anton's undead body. The thought almost made me smile. Holding on to that brief distraction, I put my Coke down on the desk. "I do not want your help. I will not discuss this case with you. Please, leave, so I can attempt to salvage my *very busy* schedule."

"Anton probably told you Dabria is a failure as a sorceress. He thinks her magic is weak, that she relies on objects of power?"

I didn't answer. There was no reason to point out that Anton hadn't pointed me at Dabria, that I'd found her on my own.

"He's right, of course," Flint continued, "except for one specific magic. Spying. When it comes to spying on others, there is no one who comes close to Dabria's magic. She wasn't always so skilled with traps. In the beginning, she eavesdropped, learned how to trip the traps from the people who set them. And how do you think she finds out about those objects she steals, chooses what to go after next?"

I gritted my teeth. I was familiar with Dabria's gift for spying, as Isai would now attest to.

"She's used spells to spy on wizards who never felt a thing," Flint went on. "For the love of flesh, I've seen sorcerers fail to detect her spying magic even when they were looking for it. She ties it into their aura, makes it part of them. I don't know how she does it, but the magic isn't taking information. It's more like the person she's spelled is offering her the information, giving it up without even knowing it. If you've never seen it before, you won't find it. You can't."

I felt a little better about not knowing she'd put the spell on me now, but I was beyond irritated that Flint ignored my commands for him to leave. He hadn't called me a witchling, as Arianne had, but he may as well have. He was disrespecting me in the same way. I jutted my chin out. "So it works like your power."

Flint had been pacing around me as he talked, like we were

business partners working through the mystery together. Every once in a while he'd gesture with his soda and take a sip. At my words, he paused and stopped a few feet away from me.

"I'm sorry?"

"Your power doesn't drag people into your bed. It just makes you so very tempting. Dresses you up in layer after layer of sensuality, raw sexual appeal, complete and utter masculinity." I was staring at the breadth of his shoulders again, and I rolled my eyes at myself. "You make people *want* you to seduce them. Make people want to seduce you."

Flint's eyes changed. Not a lot, just a subtle shift. His irises darkened to match his pupils and the stare fixed on me now was more sinister, not so easygoing. The alligator was in the water now.

"It's not working on you," he said softly. "But, for what it's worth, I don't think I'm as mercenary as you think I am. I'm offering my help. That's all. If you feel an attraction, then that's—"

"Please do not suggest that what I feel has nothing to do with your deliberate attempts to influence me. You insult us both." I called my magic, drawing a lazy zigzag pattern on my thigh then curling my fingers into my palm. The ghostly touch of flames licked my skin. "If you're being so helpful, then let's talk about you. You seduced one of Anton's guards. You could have known about the book."

"Oh, I knew about the book." Anger tightened his jaw. "The vampire wants to use me as his own personal weapon. He was crystal clear." His jaw twitched. "I will not sign his contract. And yes, I would have loved to get my hands on that book." He took a step toward me. "I would still love to get my hands on it. I'd like you to help me with that, Shade."

"Could you have gotten past the traps?" I asked, my throat dry. The heat of my fire spell grew hotter, and I prepared to force him out of my house by any means necessary.

"Not by myself. But if I located someone with the necessary skills…then yes."

That hungry gaze started at the top of my head and dragged down the length of my body. A strange sensation followed in its wake, more intense then the last time. I had the unnerving sensation of a veil being peeled away from my body, stripped by that look.

His mouth curled into a lazy grin. "My skills are more of the interpersonal sort. They don't work on mechanized traps. Or wards."

"Where were you last night?" I asked, the pulse in my throat throbbing so hard that it was difficult to swallow.

"In bed."

The way he said it told me he hadn't been alone. "Not with Tybor Aegis?"

Flint paused. "Who?"

"Tybor Aegis. The wizard. He's one of the best at wards. Or was."

"Are you telling me he's dead?" Flint took another step toward me. "What does a dead wizard have to do with me?"

I retreated a step. "The ritual you used—the one that got you into Anton's book. What does it do? Does it let you steal someone's talents?"

"Let's not talk about that now. Let's talk about what I can do for you." He took another step, and another. "You have so many questions, Shade. Let me help you find your answers. We can help each other."

Alarm bells went off in my head, but I couldn't concentrate enough to figure out what they meant. My thoughts were sluggish, my body feverish. His power was sinking past my shields. I'd underestimated him. Again. I raised my hand, only to realize my attention had wandered too far, I'd waited too long. The spell had dissipated.

Shake it off, Shade. Concentrate. You need another spell. "You could have seduced someone to get the book for you. That's how you work, isn't it? You seduce people into doing what you want done, getting you what you need?" I put a hand to my forehead. *Goddess, why can't I think?*

His eyes glittered. "Yes."

I never saw him move. One minute, he was a few feet away, pacing as he answered my questions. The next, I was in his arms. Those thick biceps I'd so admired earlier flexed as he wrapped his arms around me, holding me against the solid line of his body. One hand palmed the back of my head, and he swallowed whatever feeble protest I might have offered when he put his mouth over mine.

Heat soaked my body. Everywhere he touched me burned with a delicious sensation that had my head falling back, my hands pressed to his chest. He opened his mouth and coaxed me to open mine. His tongue swept in to taste me, a deep rumble of satisfaction vibrating his chest when I did as he wanted, letting him deepen the kiss. My head swam, thoughts bobbing along like limp flower petals on a swollen river.

Something cool pressed against my back, and I realized he'd backed us up, had me pressed to the wall. I tried to pull away, tried to turn my head to break the kiss, even as I wriggled to press more of my body against him. Goddess, it had been a long time since I'd been kissed, since physical pleasure had been more important than all the other things I needed to get done.

Needs I'd denied for too long worked against me, and when his leg slid between mine, pressing his thigh against the dull ache that had started between my legs, I gasped. For a moment I was lost, drowning under a fresh wave of sensation.

He pressed his mouth to the side of my head, velvety lips caressing the shell of my ear. "Do you want me?"

That question probably worked for him all the time, leading to pleas of "Oh, Goddess, yes!" But we'd just been talking about his power, just been talking about how he twisted a person, made them want to give in. It was enough to give the alarm bells in my head a solid clang, giving me the moment of clarity I needed, a split second when I could think past the pleasure caressing my nerve endings.

If he wanted to force me, he could. He had more power than this, but was holding back because he didn't think he'd need it. I had one shot, and I had to make it good. I prayed I'd opened the garage door earlier when I was getting ready to leave, then slid my hand down Flint's body.

His breath caught in his throat as I curled my fingers around the bulge in his pants. There was a second when I almost lost my train of thought, almost gave in to the less intelligent urges demanding attention. I gritted my teeth and grabbed hold of my magic. I traced a pattern over the hot denim over his zipper and he grunted, pressing harder into my hands. I whispered the spell.

Frost erupted from my fingertips, coated the front of his jeans, and sank through to the swollen flesh beneath. The sound that came from Flint was a combination of pain and pure shock. He didn't move, barely breathed, his eyes wide, mouth working soundlessly.

The anger would come later.

I needed to leave before that happened.

I bolted for the desk and grabbed the file. With panic riding me like a screeching demon, I ripped open the door, not bothering to close it behind me. My hands shook as I threw myself behind the wheel and locked the doors around me. My car had outside entry, so I'd gotten in the habit of leaving my keys in the car for convenience, and I was never more grateful for that than I was now. I started the car and peeled out of the garage.

The explosion took me by surprise.

CHAPTER 14

The explosion threw the front bumper of my car into the air. My heart seized and my knuckles turned white as I clung to the steering wheel, gaping as the world in front of me blurred, filling with fire and black smoke. Every nerve in my body spasmed. I couldn't think, couldn't move, couldn't do anything but stare in horror as the crackling of burning wood scratched my ears. My car slammed back into the gravel driveway with a groan of metal, and I fought to breathe as I stared at the fire eating the edge of my garage roof.

Instinct took over. I waved my hand from my lawn toward the fire. *"Extinguo!"*

The remains of this morning's melted frost coalesced above the ground, forming a sphere of water that shot toward the flames and exploded on the worst of the blaze. Hot wood hissed as the flames sputtered and died. A tiny voice screamed a reminder that the bomb had failed to kill me, but another threat remained inside the house. A very unhappy *leannan sidhe*.

I shot down the driveway, taking a fraction of the time I usually did to check there were no people or animals crossing my path. My car screeched in protest as I raced down the street with the carelessness I judged other people for, my mind a chaos of images that kept adrenaline pouring into my blood.

Fire and smoke, the top of my garage burning. A bomb. A. *Bomb.*

Someone tried to blow me up.

"Two. Both dead within twenty-four hours of taking the case."

This could be a good thing. This could mean I'm on the right track.

But you're not on a track. Not one track. You're on three tracks. You can't travel on three tracks and expect to get anywhere. It's not possible. You need to pick a track, one track. Or maybe two tracks will become one. Or start as one.

Hysteria peeled away rational thoughts faster than they formed. I floated on a cloud of panicked confusion until the sound of my erratic breathing and the warning of metallic clunks under the hood of my car brought me back to reality. In the wake of that hysteria, that blinding fear...came rage.

Magic roiled within me, churning in a red-hot fury that threatened to pour out my mouth in a flood of spells too dangerous to speak. I jerked the car around a corner, ignoring the squeal of rubber that drew the attention of a murder of crows. One of them tilted its head, following my car as I raced by.

Flint Valencia may have stolen Anton's book.

He may have killed Tybor Aegis.

He tried to kidnap me.

And I let him in my home. He mind-rolled me in my home. He ambushed *me in my home.*

My home. My territory.

"Should have set him on fire. Burned his bits to ashes."

His voice whispered in my mind, an echo that made my skin buzz with the memory until I felt the heat of his body pulsing against me. I smacked the steering wheel hard enough to send a bolt of pain down my arm. I'd known who he was, what he was. I'd known he wanted to manipulate me.

And I'd still let him distract me, blather on about inconsequential information, all the while circling like any other predator. I'd let my potion lull me into a false sense of security, forgotten he was fast, forgotten that, with a little charm, he could cloud my mind, blink here to there.

"Never again."

And then there was the bomb.

Someone had planted a bomb at my home, in my driveway. A bomb that, had I been going my normal speed out of the garage, would have gone off underneath me. Would have killed me.

I swerved down the dirt road that led to the clearing where I could always access my mentor's cottage, stomping on the brake just before the car would have careened onto her front porch, nearly putting my foot through the floor. Strange noises came from under the hood, and the car jerked as I slowed down, like a cat getting ready to vomit the world's largest hairball. Great. This car would never make it back to Cleveland. I shoved the gearshift into park and threw the door open with enough force to make it screech in protest before hurling it shut with a satisfying slam. Fury carried me over the porch, and I grabbed the doorknob like I'd strangle it.

As always, there was a period of adjustment after entering my mentor's house. Herbs and enchanted objects took up every inch of space, every breeze filled my nose with the scent of tea, old feathers, and the eye-itching burn of raw magic. I adjusted quickly to the familiar mess, weaving through the clutter to the back of the cottage where the Door to All Places waited.

Mother Hazel was home. She didn't look up when I stomped past her, didn't make a sound. Just stood there stirring her cauldron, her old, lined face cast in an eerie orange. glow from the flames. I kept my chin up, my hands fisted at my sides. I'd been ready for a fight, but apparently, I wouldn't get one. Pity. I was in precisely the mood for it.

The gargoyle perched above the Door to All Places opened its eyes, revealing milky orbs with no pupils. Small, pointed wings framed its stout, rounded body, and gray lips revealed a toothy grin, its obsidian claws digging into the frame as it leaned forward in greeting.

"The Cauldron," I said, fighting to keep my voice polite, if not pleasant. "Please," I added in the same tone.

The gargoyle didn't speak, but a second later, I opened the door and the unmistakable scent of a magic shop greeted me. Silver, iron, and gold fought to be the dominant metallic odor, with copper outshining them all thanks to the blood-bound artifacts in the more expensive section. The earthy odors of herbs and feathers tickled my nose, which made me sneeze. I nodded my thanks to the gargoyle and plunged through.

"We're out of Post-its!"

The announcement was wailed in the sort of cry usually followed by the ringing of an alarm bell. I blinked, momentarily distracted from my rage as I searched for the speaker among the towering shelves laden with ancient artifacts, arcane knick-knacks, and glittering charms. A brownie scuttled across the floor, her stocky body nearly bowling me over as she fired herself from one end of the shop to the other like a possessed pinball.

"We are not out of Post-its. Calm yourself, Muriel. Your husband is unloading them in the back now, a brand-new shipment."

"Different sizes?" Muriel demanded. "I need different sizes. The new inventory includes items from the wee ones, and they will not hold a full-sized Post-it." She crossed her arms over her bosom, tilting her flat face up at Dominique, the owner of the shop. "If you want me to get this place organized, I need different sizes."

"Different sizes and multiple colors," Dominique said, her eyes never leaving the amulet on the counter before her. The enchantress frowned and tapped one long red fingernail on the multifaceted face of the emerald.

The brownie's eyes glazed over and she hurtled herself to the back of the shop, disappearing behind the inventory. There'd been a time that witnessing the office supply panic would have amused me.

Now was not that time.

Dominique glanced up at me as if my temper heated the air in front of me, warning her of my approach before I stepped on a loose floorboard that creaked an announcement of my presence. Dominique Laveau II was a descendant of a powerful voodoo priestess, and an incredibly powerful enchantress in her own right.

I marched up to the counter and gripped the edge with both hands, wishing it was Flint's neck I held. His neck was so thick that I'd never get my hands all the way around it, but by the gods, I would love to try. My fingers dug in tighter, going white as I fought to calm myself enough to speak.

"I am dealing with a *leannan sidhe*, a sorceress, a wizard, and a vampire. I need protection from seduction charms, something against spying, something against force attacks, and something against trances." I paused after that last sentence, a flicker of concern pricking my consciousness. Anton had tranced me, or tried to. What if he'd made me forget something? Something important?

"And I need something that will let me remember something a vampire forced me to forget. Money is no object."

Dominique's expression didn't change. "Trying to get at information a vampire has tranced you to forget is a challenge with more risk than reward. Unless the information is worth losing the entirety of your mental faculties, I suggest you let it go."

I swore, using a few words I hadn't spoken since leaving the Old Kingdom the first time. Dominique didn't flinch.

"Are you similarly unable to help me with the other objects?" I demanded.

I regretted the words as soon as they were out of my mouth. The enchantress' gaze bored into mine, and green eyes as hard as the emerald in her grasp pinned me in place. She didn't raise her power, but she didn't need to. I knew who she was, what she was capable of. And her anger burned the air between us.

"Well," she said, drawing the word out. "Let me see. You said you are dealing with a *leannan sidhe*, a sorceress, a wizard, and a vampire, and you need protection from seduction charms, spying, force attacks, and trances. Is that right?"

I clenched my teeth and nodded.

"If you need an object from my shop to deal with these people, then perhaps you were not ready to join their company?"

My lips parted. "Excuse me?"

She slid the emerald to the side and laid her hands on the desk, palms flat. "If you have no spells of your own, no power of your own to keep yourself safe, then I suggest you avoid these people. Objects can break, they can fail, they can be taken from your, or lost. Some can be used only once. Having the money to spend it carelessly in my shop will not prepare you for what you're dealing with."

I wanted to scream. I wanted to lash out, to throw power around the way some foolish humans brandished guns to prove how invulnerable they were. But it would be pointless. I had power. Dominique would feel that. But she would also know power meant nothing without control. Did I have the power to kill them all? Yes. Yes, I did. Did I have the control to kill *just* them? No innocents, no collateral damage? No. No, I didn't.

The fact that I was here, begging to throw huge amounts of money at magic objects to protect me from all the bad guys I'd let into my life... Well, even if the woman before me wasn't Dominique, they would have guessed I was in over my head.

The anger churned more violently inside me, poisoned by my own doubts, the shopkeeper's admonition. I swallowed the stream of obscenities that rose in my throat, forcing myself to breathe before I said something unfortunate to a woman who could end my existence with a sneeze.

"I want an interrogation scorpion."

Dominique didn't gasp, or anything theatrical like that. But the lines around her mouth tightened, and for her, that was as good as a jaw drop. "That is an evil spell."

"But you have one, don't you?" I didn't search the shop. If she had one, it wouldn't be in plain sight. She was right. It was an evil spell.

An interrogation scorpion looked like a dried-out scorpion husk. But when put on someone's chest and activated with magic, the essence of the scorpion rose from the dead shell like a ghost, glittering to life as a spectral form of the arachnid. It grew larger and larger, wrapping sharp, segmented legs around the victim's chest, and brought its tail down to press the stinger against their forehead. It would hold them like that, helpless and terrified, while the one who'd sparked the magic asked questions. A refusal to answer, or a lie, would make the scorpion press its stinger against the person's forehead a little harder. A stubborn person, or a liar, would die a very slow, very unpleasant death.

Dominique didn't answer. She stared at me. She had a very good stare. So much like Mother Hazel. It was a stare that a mother gave her child when they'd done something horrible, or were thinking about doing something horrible. An expression that said, "I know you're better than this. *You* know you're better than this. You *will* be better than this."

Rage isn't just anger. It's fear, too. Real rage, the kind that drives you mad, is always knotted with fear. That's what keeps the person from thinking too hard on it, keeps them from clearing their head. No one wants to face that kind of fear. But Dominique's stare bored into me. And before I could stop it, my fear poured out, like honey tapped from a hive.

"I have a job to do." I pried my hands off the counter and folded them on top of it, not bothering to hide their shaking. "A job I *want* to do. I finally found the courage to live the life *I* want for myself. I can't let the first person—the first people—I meet on my path scare me away."

The enchantress studied me, not unsympathetically. "Any path can fork. And sometimes, you won't realize your path forked until you've followed the wrong one for too long." She held my eyes, and it was as though she'd grabbed me and hauled me to stand up straight. "Come back tomorrow. If you still want the scorpion, I will sell it to you. But I will not sell it to you one second less than twenty-four hours from now."

I opened my mouth before I knew what I'd say, before I knew if it would be anger, fear, or something else that poured out. Dominique silenced me with a look.

"Are you alone?"

Her tone imbued "alone" with more significance than it needed, but there was no judgment. She wasn't asking if there was anyone here in the shop with me. I started to say yes, I was alone, but then stopped. "No. I have a pixie."

Dominique's eye twitched. "A pixie."

I nodded, thinking of Bryan now. "And...perhaps a human." *Andy.* "Two humans." Mother Hazel's firm countenance roared to the center of my mind's eye. "And a witch."

"All right, then. Go home, or someplace safe. Let the temper pass, let the people you trust help you. I will see you in twenty-four hours. Or not."

Thinking of my allies drained some of the anger away, but not all of it. Part of me still wanted that scorpion now, wanted to press it against Flint's body and watch him suffer as I stood over him, holding all the power and getting the answers I needed—the real answers.

"Twenty-four hours," Dominique repeated.

I whirled around, not trusting myself to linger, to consider a different purchase. There were a hundred, a thousand objects in this store, and I could afford any, probably even most of them, but I couldn't stand in front of that woman any longer. Not when it felt like she'd reached a hand inside me, ripped out my guts, and was studying them at her leisure while I stood bleeding before her.

I ran out the door, shrugging off the sensation of magic as the gargoyle brought me back to Mother Hazel's. My momentum carried me down the short hallway and dumped me to stand before the fireplace and the cauldron hanging within it. My mentor was still stirring, filling the air with something that smelled like potato soup.

"There's bread on the table," she said without turning.

I clenched my jaw, marched to the long, thick wooden table, and half threw myself onto the bench. My eyes burned with tears, and it only made me angrier. I wanted to smash everything in this house. I wanted to scream. I wanted to reach inside me for the swirling pool of power and just hurl it out at the world.

A bowl of potato soup slid in front of me. A second later, she poured the contents of a small cup into it and stirred it a few times. Clams. She'd turned it into clam chowder for me. My favorite.

The tears slid down my face. Mother Hazel sat opposite me with her own bowl of soup, still not saying a word. She ate her lunch and let me cry. I felt like a child. A child who had insisted they'd do it only to find out they'd overestimated themselves. I was hurt, I was frustrated, and dammit, I was *angry.*

I grabbed a hunk of crusty bread from the bowl on the table and dipped it into my clam chowder. My taste buds sang with the familiar flavors, buttery broth, thick cuts of potato, and succulent pieces of clam. It was comfort food, had always been a comfort food. The warmth of the soup, the satisfying crunch and spongy softness of the bread. It healed my soul, warming me from the inside out. My shoulders relaxed, the tension easing into a gentle hum instead of the skin-searing bite it had been.

I was halfway through the bowl and starting to feel normal, when a streak of pink shot across the room, and Peasblossom crash-landed on the table. She hit the bread bowl and sent the bread flying into the air, then bounced off the table and landed in a pile of mismatched buttons.

Mother Hazel caught the pieces of bread one by one, not taking her gaze from her soup. She replaced them in the now-cracked bowl and kept eating.

I stared into my soup, keeping my eyes open wide to prevent any more tears from falling.

"Shade!" Peasblossom gasped. "I'm back!" She paused with a button in her hand. "You're having dinner without me?"

I held out a piece of bread, without looking up. Peasblossom flew to the offering, took it, sat down, and munched away. She lasted twenty seconds. "Aren't you going to ask me what I found out?"

I ate another spoonful of soup. "What did you find out?"

"Well, I can't find the *rusalka* alibi at the Hemington Agency. Apparently, she left to have a swim back to her family. But I found out other stuff…" She swallowed her bite of bread and contemplated me with narrowed eyes. "That is not the attitude I expected. What's wrong with you?"

If I knew what was good for me, I'd fake it. I'd smile at her, flatter her a little, get her to tell me what she'd found out. But the rage was gone, and the tears had taken what energy I had left. I was too tired to pretend. "Flint came to see me."

I must have looked worse than I thought. Peasblossom didn't swoon, didn't complain she'd missed him. She landed in front of me, by my bowl of soup.

"Are you okay?"

"Yes." I clenched my teeth and stared into the chowder while I tried to swallow past the lump in my throat. "I was so stupid. I should have made him leave as soon as he got there. Demons take it, *I* should have left. I knew how powerful he was, knew what he'd try to do. He made me look like an idiot, like an incompetent…witchling."

Peasblossom's pink eyes widened. She looked at Mother Hazel, but my mentor remained silent, eating her soup as if she didn't hear us at all.

"You're not a witchling," the pixie said. "You're a proper witch. And a private investigator. You can do this. And I can help."

"I was unforgivably stupid. He peeled the protection potion off me as easily as though he were slipping off a pair of panties."

Peasblossom's eyes almost bugged out of her head, and I scowled. "Don't look at me like that. My panties remained where they should be. It was just a kiss, but he played me, played me when I should have been too smart for that." I glared at my spoon. "Then there's the bomb. My reputation isn't even strong enough to discourage—"

"A *bomb?*"

I grabbed the spoon, wishing it was a knife. "Someone set a trap right outside the garage. I set it off when I drove over it, and if I'd been going a little slower, it would have gone off with me right on top of it." Images of my three suspects fanned out like playing cards in my head, and I tightened my grip on the spoon. "I don't know who did it."

Peasblossom put her tiny hands on mine and leaned in with excitement bright in her eyes. "Dabria went to see Isai again." Her voice dropped to an excited whisper. "And you won't believe what she did."

I dropped the spoon, and the chowder swallowed it in a creamy hug. "What?"

"She *tortured* Isai."

I fell back in my seat, forgot it was a bench, and tipped backward. Heart pounding, I grabbed the edge of the table and hung on, keeping myself upright. The oak table was heavier than some cars, and remained still despite my tugging. Mother Hazel took another piece of bread from the bowl and continued eating her soup.

"Tell me," I urged Peasblossom, when my breath came back enough for me to speak. "Give me the details."

"I followed Dabria to this event where Isai and Vera were setting up for some charity. She strung him up with magic and screamed at him that he better tell Anton where the book is. Said she wasn't going to die because he's stupid enough to steal from the vampire." Her eyes widened. "She *cut* him. With *swords*. Two of them—she was spinning them like pinwheels!"

"Is he dead?" I asked.

"No. Vera stepped in, made Dabria stop. Got cut for her trouble, too. Anton will be furious."

"Did Isai admit anything?"

Peasblossom leaned forward again, and her hand slipped on part of the rim coated with chowder. She slipped and fell with a squeak, catching herself on the bottom of the bowl. I'd eaten most of it, so the remainder only came to her elbow. I offered her a napkin to clean herself up, but she didn't seem to notice.

"No, he didn't confess anything. He screamed at her, saying he didn't have the book." Peasblossom pulled herself out of the bowl, her arm coated in soup, and looked at me with a new level of severity. "Foxglove says he said *a lot* of really, really, *really* bad words."

My head spun as my brain tried to organize the new information, to process it with what I already knew. "Why would Dabria torture Isai?"

Peasblossom licked the potato soup off her hand, then wrinkled her nose. "Ew. You put clams in it."

"You said she told him she doesn't want to die. Obviously she thinks Anton believes she took the book. But why?" I dangled the napkin in front of her, urging her to clean herself up. "I have no evidence on her. More than anyone, all suspicion against her is circumstantial, based only on what she's capable of. We know she could have known about the book from Isai, and she has the skill to get past the traps. But there's no proof. She wasn't seen anywhere near the building, wasn't caught talking to anyone connected with the vault."

"Maybe Anton found more evidence on her?" Peasblossom offered, wiping her hand on my napkin.

"Then why wouldn't he tell me?"

"Maybe it's a trick."

I glanced down and blinked. She was sitting with her body wrapped around a small cup of honey, the size of a shot glass. I pressed my lips together and narrowed my eyes at Mother Hazel. "She hasn't had dinner yet."

My mentor gave me the look grandmothers give mothers when they've indulged a grandchild the way they never would have indulged their own offspring, then resumed eating her soup as if she'd done nothing.

"Maybe she tortured Isai to make everyone think she didn't do it, that she thought he did it and she wanted him to admit it before she got killed by accident," Peasblossom said.

"If she got killed for it, it wouldn't be an accident," I muttered. "It doesn't make sense she'd be that worried unless Anton knows something I don't." I hesitated, then looked at Mother Hazel. "Is there any way to recover information Anton tranced me to forget?" I'd asked a similar question of Dominique, but though the woman was powerful, there was no comparison to my mentor. I had no idea why Anton might trance me to forget something about Dabria, but then, I didn't pretend to understand how the undead master's mind worked.

Mother Hazel swallowed her soup. "If he tranced you to forget something, a psychic could search your memory for gray spots. Vampires don't erase memories, they blanket them in a very strong sort of hesitation spell."

"So could a psychic help me get those memories back?"

"You'd be hard-pressed to find one who will try. Perhaps with a lesser vampire, but with one such as the prince of Dacia, chances of doing irreparable damage would be too great." She pointed at me with her spoon. "Do you recall last fall when Carter ate his sucker while wearing that cheap, lacy Tinkerbell costume?"

I winced. "Yes. No one noticed the bits of candy stuck to the lace till they'd dried."

"Indeed. And when his mother tried to pull the hard candy off the lace, she tore it to shreds."

"And his sister cut the lace off and used it to make a dead bride costume for the Day of the Dead celebration a few days later."

Mother Hazel smiled at that, then grew serious again. "Think of that Tinkerbell lace as your mind and that piece of sucker as the information you're trying to get."

My stomach rolled. "I see." I looked at Peasblossom. "Did Isai admit anything? Accuse Dabria of anything? Did he say anything?"

Peasblossom licked honey from her lips, smacking them happily. "Yes. A lot of really, really bad—"

"Besides the bad words."

She shook her head. "No. He kept screaming he didn't do it, and calling Dabria a *lot* of—"

"Really bad words." I retrieved the spoon from the bottom of my bowl and absent-mindedly licked it clean. If Dabria wasn't putting on an act, then someone had made her feel like the prime suspect. And she believed Isai was the real thief. Isai had been going around to other wizards, trying to find someone to help him break a ward. Perhaps he did have the book.

It was even possible he'd gone to Dabria for help. She'd been breaking wards to steal from other magic users for centuries. Perhaps he'd promised her entrance to Serafina's if she would help him. If he could open the book, chances were that he could force Anton to have the wards on Serafina's castle lowered. If Dabria refused him, maybe he'd threatened her. He could have said he'd tell Anton that Dabria did it, fabricate evidence.

But if Dabria feared Isai was framing her, couldn't she have gone to Anton and told him Isai had the book, told him Isai had asked for her help opening it? If she didn't know the vampire had sealed the castle at his wife's vehement behest, then she wouldn't know that ratting out Isai wouldn't get her access. Or maybe she was sneakier than that.

"It could have been a stunt to throw off suspicion," I said. "Which would mean there is evidence out there somewhere, something to make her think I'll find out it's her."

"They might have planned it together," Peasblossom offered.

I tapped the spoon on my lip. They could have planned it together, set the scene to make them both appear innocent—Dabria for being frightened, and Isai because if he had the book, surely he would give it up under torture, to save his life?

A headache throbbed at the base of my skull. There were too many possibilities. I needed evidence. Physical evidence.

Like a fresh crime scene.

Mother Hazel arched an eyebrow as I fell off the bench in my haste to get up, but she said nothing as I scrambled to my feet and bolted for the door. Peasblossom shouted as she struggled to take her honey with her, then gave up with a curse and flew after me. She pinned herself to my head like a mangled bobby pin and continued grousing about her abandoned honey as I paused in my old bedroom to retrieve my bike. The contraption was old and rusting in more than one place, and I said a small prayer of thanks that the wheels hadn't gone flat. Mother Hazel watched me push it out the door without a word.

"Stupid, stupid," I murmured, climbing onto the bike as soon as I was off the porch. "A fresh crime scene and I left it."

"You left the *sidhe*," Peasblossom snapped. "He just happened to be at the crime scene."

"True." I bit my lip. I had a scroll in my pouch somewhere, I knew I did. It had a spell for tracking teleportation. And it was beyond my skills. I pedaled faster.

"You ran a stop sign."

"I'm on a bike."

Peasblossom clucked her tongue. "You're still supposed to stop at stop signs."

I ignored the small stab of guilt. Peasblossom was right. But then, the only person I was going to hurt on a bike was myself. And right now, I didn't care.

I lived on a quiet residential street lined with mostly small one-story houses with good-sized yards and almost mandatory gardens. I stared down the street, straining to see my driveway, scanning the sky for any sign of smoke that would suggest the fire had survived my water spell. I wasn't too worried. I couldn't leave my car lights on without someone popping by to let me know, a fire would have been reported long before it became dangerous.

Peasblossom rolled over on my head, propping her chin on her elbow and digging her bony joint into my scalp. "I don't see what the big hurry is. The spell won't work anyway. It's way over your head."

"I appreciate your vote of confidence." My nerves twisted a little tighter, a silent acknowledgment that the pixie was right. Tracing a teleportation spell was not something I'd ever attempted before. The focus it required, the complicated weaving of different energies…

"And the trail will be cold. Even for a properly trained witch, it would be difficult."

"Another vote of priceless encouragement, thank you."

The pixie scooted forward and hung down over my forehead, blocking my vision enough to make me swerve. "Peasblossom!"

"What if Flint is still there?" she demanded.

With my heart lodged in my throat, I righted the bike and turned into my driveway, pulse racing both from that hair-raising moment of driving blindness and Peasblossom's mention of the *leannan sidhe*. "He's not here. He had no reason to stick around, especially since he must have heard the bomb go off." I gritted my teeth. "And if he is here, I've got another handful of frost for him."

"*Another* handful of frost?"

I didn't explain. The last thing I needed was for Peasblossom to know how I'd escaped Flint. It was just the sort of thing she'd find amusing enough to share with others, and nobody spread the word like pixies.

Despite my claim of confidence, I couldn't help but glance at my front door and hope I was right. If Flint was there, he'd be ready for me this time. I didn't think he'd fall for the same trick twice. *Next time, we'll see how he likes fire.*

I got off the bike and left it in the yard before approaching the circle of charred stones in my driveway. Based on the damage, it seemed like the force of the bomb had gone straight up, but it had still blackened a solid circle of the pale gray gravel beneath it. I glanced around, searching for debris, but I didn't look too hard. I knew nothing about bombs. I dug in my pouch for the scroll, shoving aside a pair of gloves, a pillowcase, and a shower curtain ring.

"I have a pretty good idea who did this, and if I'm right, she teleported here." *No sorceress would tolerate those construction cones if she didn't have to.*

"Dabria probably teleports everywhere," Peasblossom agreed. She flew over my head, hovering a few inches below the top edge of my garage, staring at the blackened wood. She dipped, worry pinching her delicate features.

I didn't need telepathy to guess what she was thinking. "I'm fine," I said gently.

She crossed her arms and looked away, hiding whatever emotion was on her face. "I know. Just do your spell."

Affection warmed my chest at the gruffness in her voice, but I let her have her privacy. The scroll felt heavy as I lifted it from the pouch and turned my thoughts to the spell. I took a deep breath and knelt down. The parchment of the scroll weighed against the pads of my fingers like the dry, scaly hide of a lizard, so different than the modern paper I was used to holding now. I used that tactile difference to adjust my frame of mind, imagining I was the condescending old wizard who'd traded it. *Think like an arrogant old coot.*

Just as Mother Hazel had trained me, I read the scroll several times, so I could say the spell out loud without tripping over the words. I spoke clearly and loudly. Sometimes, confidence was the difference between success and failure.

And sometimes, confidence didn't do squat.

CHAPTER 15

The snapping sensation against my tongue warned me something was wrong. The energy of the words fought the restraint of my voice, fought against being forced into the shape I needed them to be. Tiny pricks of pain against my vocal cords made me wince, slurred my syllables. I faltered.

The writing on the scroll caught fire, searing silver light crackling with veins of gold burning an impression on my vision like a brand. The magic flowed from the parchment, up my arms, then bored into my brain with all the delicate care of an electric cattle prod. I choked on a breath, my body seizing as I tried to hold my concentration, keep the image of how I wanted the spell to work in my mind. The picture I had of the magic flowing over the surrounding area, highlighting in brilliant mercury any spot where someone teleported to or from, erupted with blinding white cracks. It shattered like a scene viewed in a mirror, the energy snapping the bonds of my control, exploding outward.

Gravel launched into the air like popcorn. Only instead of a fluffy snack, it rained down small stones. Small, heavy stones.

Boulders if you were a pixie.

"Aaahhh!" Peasblossom shouted. She dove into the garage,

gossamer wings a blur as she rushed to escape being crushed by the hail of rocks.

I swore in Old Sanguenayan and covered my head and neck. Rocks pelted my back and arms, pain sparking everywhere they landed, an occasional hit against bone drawing hisses and more bad language. By the time it finished, I felt like one huge bruise. As did my pride.

"I told you it wouldn't work. But did you listen? Noooo…"

Peasblossom glared at me from her perch on the garage door opener. As I forced myself to my feet, she slid down the manual release cord and planted her feet on the plastic handle. Her movements set the cord to swinging, making it more difficult to keep glowering at me, but she did her best.

"You almost crushed me!"

I fished a rock out of the mock turtleneck of my shirt where it protruded from my jacket and threw it over my shoulder. "I'm so sorry. You could have been hurt and it's my fault. I should have protected you first. Are you all right?"

Peasblossom's wings drooped, the fire of her tirade stolen by my premature capitulation. "Yes," she grumbled. She stuck her chin out. "You'll listen next time, won't you?"

The door to my house was still ajar from my mad escape earlier. Peasblossom's voice faded into the background as the memory of what had chased me from my home took center stage in my thoughts. Flint's eyes stared at me from the memory, his grin still turning my knees to rubber. If I closed my eyes, I could feel the press of his charm, the warm caress of his power as he peeled the shield from my psyche…

"You still have that potion from the druid that will let you talk to animals," Peasblossom suggested. "Why not try that?" She pointed at the maple tree in my front yard. "That squirrel is always here. Bet he saw something."

My cheeks warmed and I refused to look back at the rodent in question. I'd already used the potion Peasblossom was talking about. I had, in fact, used it to talk to that squirrel. There'd been trouble with a stubborn dryad, and I'd wanted to know if she'd been hanging around my house. The squirrel had been unhelpful, having little to say besides a few snarky observations about how many Reese's Peanut Butter Eggs I'd eaten last spring.

"I'll stick to talking to people," I muttered.

After a second of hesitation, I got out my cell phone and texted Vera, telling her about the bomb. There was no sense hiding it from Anton. If I was suddenly worth killing, maybe it meant I was getting close. And if I was getting close, she should know it just in case…

I tapped send, then put my phone into my coat pocket. "Let's go inside. I need to look through those books again."

Peasblossom landed on my head. "Books? What books?"

I paused. "I forgot to tell you, didn't I?"

Peasblossom stomped on my head, sending a shooting pain over my scalp. "Tell me what?" she demanded. "I told you about Dabria, and now you're saying you had information you didn't share? This is what I get for spying for you? Do you know how *far* I flew today?"

That made me stop walking. "Wait a minute. Cleveland is over a hundred miles away."

"I know!"

"You can't fly more than forty miles an hour."

"I can so!"

"Not for long distances!" I stopped and took a deep breath. "Peasblossom, how did you get home so fast?"

She hesitated.

"How?" I barked.

"I went to Goodfellows and asked the witch to send me home."

I grabbed Peasblossom off my head, barely remembering to be careful of her wings. "You what?"

"I needed to get home fast!" Peasblossom complained. "She's a friend of Mother Hazel's. It's fine."

Frustration tightened my voice, but I forced myself to remain calm. "I thought you didn't take favors from strangers?"

Peasblossom sniffed. "Don't insult me. I traded favors. She said she'd ordered too much honey, and said if I ate the excess, then she'd send me home. Said I had to tell Mother Hazel 'hi' from Granny."

I blinked. "Granny?"

"That's what she said."

I relaxed and almost sank to my knees. "You didn't tell me the owner was Granny."

"And you didn't tell me you got more files!"

"All right, all right," I said, putting her on my shoulder. "Tybor Aegis was murdered last night. It looks like the same ritual Flint used."

"Really?" Peasblossom kicked her feet as I walked through the garage and let myself back into the house. "So Flint killed a wizard?"

"I don't think so. Something just doesn't feel right. I was hoping if I could find the ritual he used, I might be able to figure out who else could have done it, but I can't find it."

I opened the file on Tybor's case. Peasblossom hissed, and I cursed and put a hand over her eyes. "Don't look at those pictures."

"I'm older than you," she said crossly, trying to climb over my hand. "Let me see!"

It was incredibly human of me to think of Peasblossom as a child. She was so tiny, and so excitable. It was hard to remember that she was, as she'd said, older than me. Still.

"Why don't you go get a cookie?" I suggested.

Peasblossom perked up. "Really?" She hesitated, then gave me a sly look. "How many?"

I narrowed my eyes. "One. You didn't have any dinner, and

you've already had honey." I wagged a finger at her. "A lot of honey, apparently."

"Maybe these pictures are better than just one cookie?"

"Maybe the offer of a cookie pre-supper is good for the next five seconds. Five, four…"

Peasblossom scowled and flew for the pantry. There was a good chance she'd eat as many cookies as she could while I was distracted by the files, but I had to take that chance. Priorities.

Reading the files was better than standing at the murder scene, but it was still awful. My brain was all too willing to provide sensory memories of what that blood had smelled like, what that lingering death had felt like. I read the autopsy report and frowned.

"No defensive wounds," I murmured. "Who just stands there and lets someone put a gun to their head?"

"Are you all right?" Vera asked from behind me.

I spun around, my heart in my throat. Magic crackled against my skin, my nerves spasming as my brain reminded me of the last time I'd let my guard down in this room. "Blood and bones, please don't sneak up on me like that!" Sweat beaded at my temples and I put a hand to my chest, willing my heart to slow.

Vera winced where she stood just over the boundary where beige Berber carpet ended and kitchen linoleum began. "I'm sorry. That was horrible. You were just nearly killed, I should have known better than to sneak up on you."

I frowned and looked from her to the living room. "How did you get in?"

Vera pointed at the floor. A small gargoyle sat on the line between the living room and the dining room. The creature had an almost feline head with thick paws and sharp teeth, like a jungle cat, only smaller and with the ribbed wings of a bat.

"A gateway gargoyle?" I asked.

Vera nodded. "Yes. He's been with Anton since before this world came to be."

I nodded a greeting at the small creature. "Hello."

"Hello, Shade Renard."

The gargoyle's voice held the echo of stone grating against stone. There was something about the way it said my name that unnerved me. As if it knew me. I shrugged the feeling off and returned my attention to Vera. "What are you doing here?"

"I came as soon as I got your text." Vera wrung her hands. "You said someone tried to kill you. With a bomb?"

I nodded, then paused. "I don't suppose that's how the first two people your husband hired were killed?"

She bit the inside of her cheek, then nodded. "Yes," she whispered.

"Well, that might have been good to know before." I sounded pissed, and I was. I pointed to the computer screen. "Flint didn't kill Tybor."

"What?"

I pointed at the reports lying on my desk. "Flint's first two victims were shot outside, from a distance of over three hundred yards. They were expert shots." I lifted Tybor's file. "In this case, the coroner found particles of soot and unburned powder in the wound track. Which means Tybor's killer pressed the muzzle of the gun to his head and fired."

"That doesn't rule Flint out," Vera objected.

I shook my head. "I don't think he did it. Tybor had no defensive wounds, nothing to suggest there was a struggle. I don't think Flint walked in and pressed the gun to his forehead and Tybor just stood there."

Vera's eyebrows rose. "You think someone used magic to restrain him."

"Just like someone used magic to restrain the guards," I said, nodding.

Vera's eyes darkened. "Isai could do that spell even without his book. It was one of his more frequently used tricks." She clenched her hands into fists. "And Isai was the one to research the spell when Anton first discovered what Flint had done. That ritual wasn't in his spellbook, it was in one of his texts. He would still have access to it."

I stared at Vera. "If Isai performed that ritual, he would have access to all of Tybor's knowledge."

"And thus, all of his spells," Vera finished. She nodded. "I think you may have just solved the case, Shade Renard."

I waved a hand, my pulse pounding hard enough that it was difficult to swallow. "Wait, wait. We don't have any proof. Flint could have an object of power that would let him restrain someone the same way Isai does—that is not a complicated spell. And if Dabria found out Tybor played a part in warding Serafina's castle, then she would have the perfect motive for stealing his knowledge. We don't know it was Isai."

"I will share your concerns with Anton when he wakes."

She turned and I stumbled forward. "Vera, wait."

Vera looked over her shoulder, and I clenched my jaw. "You and I both know what Anton will do to Isai if he believes he's the one who stole that book. I have to be one hundred percent certain."

"I assure you, Anton shares your desire for one hundred percent certainty. I am certain he will refrain from any permanent action until after he hears back from you."

I waited until the gargoyle transported her away, the air between my living room and dining room shimmering as she stepped through it, followed by the gargoyle. As soon as they were gone, my shoulders slumped.

"I have less than twenty-four hours left. I don't think the vampire likes waiting until the last moment. I need proof."

"He doesn't like waiting, and he's probably going to like waiting even less when he finds out Vera was hurt," Peasblossom pointed out. "He loves her, you know."

I stared at the pixie. "What did you just say?"

"I said—"

I held up a hand. "Wait." An idea hit me and I dug in my pocket for my phone.

"What?" Peasblossom demanded. "What are you up to?"

"The blood."

"What blood? There's blood all over this case."

"Vera's blood." I looked up at Peasblossom, my heart pounding. "Listen. What if Dabria stole the book? It was locked with blood."

"Anton's blood?" Peasblossom guessed.

I tapped the side of my nose. "And like you said, he loves his wife. And he doesn't just love her—he's bonded to her."

Peasblossom's eyes widened. "Vera's blood. You think that's what the confrontation with Isai was about. You think Dabria put on that whole show because she knew Vera would try to stop her and she'd be able to get her blood."

"Exactly."

Peasblossom gave me a sly look. "Then you owe me a thank you."

"Why?"

"I took it." She took another bite of cookie, her eyes shining.

I tightened my grip on my phone. "You took what?"

"The handkerchief."

I paused, took a deep breath, and counted to ten. "What handkerchief?"

"The one Dabria used to clean her blades. The one with Vera's blood on it. She tried to be sneaky, tried to wipe it while Vera was getting Isai down, but I saw her. I saw her wipe Vera's blood onto a handkerchief, and she put it in her pocket." She puffed out her chest. "And I stole it."

My jaw dropped. "You have Dabria's handkerchief with Vera's blood on it?"

"Yep."

"Why didn't you say that before?" I demanded.

"You almost got blown up! I was distracted!" Peasblossom

scowled. "Besides, I didn't know it had anything to do with the case. I like Vera, I just didn't want that wench Dabria to have her blood. A lot of nasty things can be done to someone if you have their blood, you know."

I smiled, so wide that I almost couldn't talk. "Peasblossom, you are brilliant. Where is it?"

"I hid it. It's—"

"Wait, wait! Don't tell me. Don't tell me."

She paused before taking another bite of her cookie, looking at me over the crumbling treat. "Why?"

I sat down at my desk, hands dancing over the keyboard. "If you don't tell me, then no one can make me tell them. I have a plan."

"Oh." She licked some of the cream off her cookie. "So do you think Dabria killed Tybor?"

"Probably. I think he was killed to frame Flint."

"Then call Anton. Tell him you solved the case!"

I shook my head. "Not yet. It's just a theory. I need proof."

"I don't like that look. What are you going to do?"

I opened my browser and searched for the phone number to the Westin. "I'm going to confront Dabria."

Peasblossom squeaked and almost fell off the shelf, dropping her cookie as she scrabbled to stay seated. The Oreo landed on the floor with an explosion of crumbs. "What? She'll kill you!"

Pieces of a plan fell into place with beautiful clarity. "Not if she can't use magic against me."

"You're going to bind her?" Peasblossom scoffed. "You don't have that kind of control."

"I'm not going to bind her. I'm going to lure her into a ward."

"Same problem. Your wards are woefully basic—they won't be more than dense fog for her. For the gods' sakes, she got through Anton's wards. You think you can do better?"

"No," I said smugly. "But Arianne can."

Peasblossom growled in frustration. "You're not making any

sense. Arianne won't help you. You'll be lucky if she doesn't kill you just for making a nuisance of yourself."

I shook my head. I didn't have time to explain—I had to start preparations. Dabria's attempt to kill me had failed, but I wasn't sure she knew that yet. I had to act before she put any other plans into motion. More effective plans.

My first call was to Suite Dreams. Only this time, I reserved a room. Peasblossom narrowed her eyes, listening with rapt attention as I made arrangements with the concierge using a fake name. When I finished, I entered the phone number for the Westin. I took a slow, steady breath, staring at the digits on my phone's screen in black and white. *This is it.*

A soft hand on my knee made me pause before hitting send, and I looked down into Peasblossom's worried face.

"Is it scarier than you thought it would be?"

I stared hard at the screen, concentrating on the phone number and not the person said number belonged to. "What are you talking about?"

"Being a detective. You thought about it a lot, but it's not the same as doing it, is it? It's different when people try to kill you."

"I'm not afraid. I'm excited." I tightened my grip on the phone, staring at the number. "I'm about to solve this case."

"You're about to run headlong into an angry sorceress because you're in a hurry for this case to be over. Flint scared you, and Dabria might have tried to kill you. You want it to be over, but challenging two angry sorceresses is not the way to ensure your safety."

"Hence the reservation at Suite Dreams." I looked away from the phone to meet Peasblossom's eyes, my own pounding heart echoing the fear I saw there. "The one thing everyone seems clear on is that Arianne is the best at wards. And your spies told you the police are there a lot, and Arianne is paranoid."

"So?"

I couldn't help but smile. "So, a ward strong enough to protect me from Dabria isn't something I can buy. It's a talent I don't have—yet. So I need to borrow Arianne's."

Peasblossom's eyebrows met her hairline. "You think Arianne will activate her wards to protect you? She doesn't even like you."

"No, she doesn't. But she'd protect an FBI agent."

"Oohhh." Peasblossom frowned. "No, I don't get it. She knows you're not FBI. And your previous attempts at disguises have been nightmares. Remember when you tried to dress up as Catwoman for Halloween?"

I scowled. "That was a good costume."

"You looked like a rat. Everyone said so."

My mouth tightened into a thin line, and I attempted to heave the conversation back on track. "I'm not dressing up like an FBI agent. I won't have to. I'll have a real one."

The wrinkles between Peasblossom's brows didn't go away, her confusion still pressed into her tiny forehead. I took advantage of her silence and called the number before I could lose my nerve. It took very little time for the concierge to connect me to Dabria's room, and the wretchedly inconsiderate woman answered on the first ring.

"Hello?"

"Dabria? This is Shade Renard. Mother Renard."

I imagined I could hear her surprise in the shocked silence that followed. My nerves sent a rush of energy flowing through me, and it swept me away before I could fight it, throwing me into a well of bloated self-confidence.

"I'd imagine you're surprised to hear from me, what with your little deathtrap in my driveway. So sorry to disappoint you."

"Mother Renard," Dabria started, her voice dripping with false sweetness. "How lovely to hear from you. I'm sorry, I don't know what trap you're referring to, but I'm so pleased you're all right."

"Oh, I'm more than all right," I responded, my voice equally saccharine. "I'm enlightened. You're the murderer I've been looking for."

"Murderer?" Frost shattered her sugary tone, leaving her voice ice cold. "Careful, witchling. I haven't killed anyone. I haven't committed any crimes as far as you can prove. And it seems to me I was the one to turn you down when you wanted my help stealing from the vampire."

"Don't like to do the same trick twice?"

The sorceress growled. "You are making a very serious mistake."

"No, you made a very serious mistake. You made a mistake when you killed Helen Miller. You made a mistake when you stole that book. You made a mistake when you tried to blow me up. And you made a mistake when you tortured the wizard."

There was a brief silence filled with the crackling energy of an angry magic wielder. When she spoke again, her voice was the harsh almost-whisper of someone planning violent retribution. "Let us meet in person so you can say these lies to my face—and take the punishment such lies deserve."

My hand holding the phone trembled, and I clapped my other hand over it to make it stop. "I would love to meet in person. Because you also made one more mistake."

"And what is that?"

The satisfaction in her voice made me think she could hear the tremor in mine. It was time to fix that. I sat up straighter and stuck my chin out. "You lost your handkerchief. All that effort to get Vera's blood, and you lost it. And now I have it."

I almost didn't get the words out—my heart pounded so hard that it stole my breath, made it hard to speak. I wished with every fiber of my being I had a can of Coke, something to wet my dry throat, to hold in my trembling hand. Peasblossom held on to my finger in silent support.

"What do you want?" Dabria asked finally, her voice deadly calm.

"I don't agree with the way I suspect Anton deals with thieves," I responded, trying not to collapse with relief. "I'll give you a chance to walk away. Bring the book to the Suite Dreams hotel. Room 706. Eight o'clock. I'll return it to the vampire."

"And you think he won't punish me just because you returned it?"

"I won't tell him who returned it."

She barked out a laugh. "You say that as though he couldn't reach into your mind and pull the information free as easily as plucking a rose."

"Not if I bury the information first. Anton isn't the only one who can repress memories."

"That won't stop him from trying. You'll end up like Helen Miller."

I clutched the phone, fingers turning white. "You know about that. It was you, then."

There was a pause, but this time I couldn't interpret it.

"I will see you at eight o' clock, Mother Renard."

She hung up before I could ask any more questions. I fell back in my chair with a shaky exhale. Peasblossom climbed onto my stomach and crawled until she perched on my chest, staring down at my face.

"I don't like this," she said. "I don't like it at all."

If I were honest, I wasn't feeling so invulnerable anymore either. I had a good plan. And Dabria had as much as admitted her guilt. But something about that last pause, when I'd asked about Helen, felt wrong.

I shook my head, trying to rid myself of the sudden unease rolling over my skin. No time to second-guess now. Cupping Peasblossom in the palm of my hand and giving her a smile filled with confidence I didn't feel anymore, I searched my phone for Andy's number.

He answered on the first ring. "Agent Bradford."

"Hi, Agent Bradford. This is Shade Renard. Bryan's friend?" I considered adding "the witch," but then figured he didn't need the reminder.

There were a few seconds of silence. "Yes, Ms. Renard, what can I do for you?"

He didn't sound like he was having a mental breakdown. A promising sign for someone who'd just learned of the Otherworld. "Please, call me Shade. And I was hoping you could help me with a little...errand."

"What do you need?"

"An escort."

Another long silence. "An...escort?"

It wasn't until he said it that I realized what it sounded like. "Not *that* kind of escort," I mumbled, cursing the heat in my cheeks. "I mean an FBI escort." I huffed out a breath. "Look, I just need you to come to Suite Dreams with me at four o'clock. All you have to do is walk me inside."

"You want me to walk you inside the hotel and just leave you there?"

When he said it like that, it sounded ridiculous. "I need the owner of the hotel to see an FBI agent with me, that's all."

"Why?"

This wasn't supposed to be the hard part of the plan. I bit my lip. "Because she doesn't care what happens to me, but she'll care what happens to you."

I waited for more questions, but to my pleasant surprise, there were none.

"All right. I'll see you there at four o'clock."

"Thank you so much, Agent Bradford. I'll see you then."

Peasblossom watched me tap the end call button, a suspicious look on her face. "He was awfully agreeable for a nosy human who wasn't given any details."

"He's a professional—he doesn't waste time demanding details he doesn't need." I tucked the phone into my pouch and stood up, careful not to dislodge Peasblossom where she perched on my shoulder. "We need to make a short trip to The Cauldron."

"Again? You always said The Cauldron was too expensive. Now you're making the second trip in as many days."

"Because I can afford it," I pointed out.

"The vampire was rather...generous."

I paused in the middle of snagging a celebratory Coke from the fridge. "What's that supposed to mean?"

"The vampire isn't stupid. You would have done this job for a lot less than what he's giving you." She snorted. "You were doing it for free when Bryan asked for help."

"That was a business move," I said. "Prove my worth and then become a paid consultant."

"Wonder how that would appear on his paperwork."

I laughed a little, my good mood returning as my plan moved even more smoothly than I could have hoped. By this time tomorrow, the case would be solved, Helen Miller's ghost would be able to rest in peace, the vampire would have his book, and I'd have my first case under my belt.

I rode my bike back to my mentor's, flying over the road and actually enjoying the wind in my face. Mother Hazel's house shifted on its foundation as I stepped onto the porch, and I halted my march inside to stomp on it.

"Don't even think about it," I warned.

The house paused, like a child considering making a break for it with a stolen cookie. Wood creaked as it shifted on the chicken legs that grew from the foundation, hidden from sight for now, but waiting, always waiting for an opportunity to stretch. Past experience taunted me, reminded me of the house's penchant for straightening its legs suddenly, flinging the house into the air above the trees with enough speed to drop your heart into your stomach. It had done that to me once or twice, and the experience had left a mark. Several marks. And bruises. Apparently, now that I wasn't running in a blind fury, it was considering having a bit of fun.

"Don't. You. *Dare.*"

I felt more than heard the cottage capitulate, the tingle of restrained energy fading as its legs relaxed beneath me. Quiet, peaceful. Sulking.

I rolled my eyes, even as I patted the shingles beside the front door. I didn't have time for this.

I was feeling so good about my plan that I was almost disappointed when I found my mentor wasn't home. My bowl of soup and Peasblossom's honey still sat on the table, and I winced at a stab of guilt. I took a few minutes to wash my dishes and wipe down the sticky traces Peasblossom had left, and only then proceeded to the Door to All Places.

"Back so soon?" the gargoyle asked. Apparently, like the house, the gargoyle was feeling more interactive now that I wasn't stewing in a blind fury.

"The Cauldron, please," I said.

The gargoyle drummed its claws on the shelf above the door. "An expensive shop, The Cauldron. And this is your second trip."

Everyone has an opinion... I counted to ten before answering, careful to keep the irritation from my voice. Rudeness to a gateway gargoyle was never wise. One was apt to find themselves dropped in the middle of the frozen tundra as a subtle reminder of the importance of good manners. "Yes. I hope I'm not being a bother?"

"Oh, not at all. I just find it...interesting."

I held my breath, hoping the beast didn't ask any more questions. The gargoyle didn't have to let me pass, didn't have to take me anywhere. It was an independent creature who stayed here because it pleased it to do so. It also shared Mother Hazel's irritating habit of refusing help if it thought I was getting myself into trouble.

Finally, it smiled. "You may pass."

I didn't let out the breath I'd been holding until I walked through the doorway and into the magic shop. As the relief wore off, I blinked.

The place was in chaos. Brownies scurried back and forth across the floor, their aprons full to bursting with multicolored Post-its, and pens held in their small grasps. Dominique stood in the center of the room arguing with a cat on the highest shelf of a bookcase. Something about a flea. When she saw me, she gave the furry beast one last scowl and marched to the counter, the thick skirts of her red dress swishing madly around her legs.

"It has not been twenty-four hours yet," she snapped. "And we're in the middle of inventory, so I don't have time to argue."

I cleared my throat, resisting the urge to retreat through the door like a child who'd come to ask for a cookie and found Mum in a poor mood. I forced myself to approach the counter. "I'm not here for a scorpion," I managed. "I just need a stone of protection."

"From vampires, wizards, sorcerers, and *leannan sidhe?*"

I flushed. "No. Just something to give my willpower a boost. All I need is an edge, a few seconds of clarity when it matters."

Dominique studied me, those green eyes probing deeper than my skin, seeing more than I wanted to show her. Whatever she saw there softened the lines around her eyes and mouth. "Isn't that what we all want?"

She smiled and I forgot what I was doing. Dominique was gorgeous, but when she smiled…she was radiant.

I relaxed, waiting there as she disappeared into the chaos of her shop. When she returned, she was holding a green stone that looked like a cloudy emerald. She put it on the counter for my perusal. I extended my magic senses, and excitement rose as I felt the sleeping power inside the stone. Touching it with my magic gave me a faint but reassuring sense of calm.

"Do you know how you'll wear it?" Dominique asked.

"Oh! Let me help!"

I blinked as a woman fell off a shelf in a swirling cloud of black taffeta and hot-pink lacy skirts. Arms and legs akimbo, she floundered on the floor for a second before shoving herself to her feet and lurching toward me, brandishing a wand of what looked like melted black metal.

"Where did you come from?" Dominique demanded. She leveled a dark look at the intruder, and the shelf she'd fallen from. "It's Inventory Day."

She said "Inventory Day" in a manner that gave the words a lot more significance than I'd ever heard them have before.

"If you broke anything, I'll have your thumbs in jars," Dominique promised.

The woman—a witch, I gathered—waved a hand. "Charge it to my account. Now, hush, I have work to do."

She heaved herself over the desk, her head bobbing up and down to look me over from head to toe. When her gaze hit my legs, her eyes widened. "Someone's painted your legs?" She paused, squinting. "Oh. No, you're wearing leggings." Her eyes glittered. "Do you want your legs painted? I could fix it so you could go around naked and people would think you were properly dressed. Wicked fun, that."

My cheeks burned at the idea. "Um, no thank you?"

"She's going to see a *leannan sidhe*," Dominique snapped.

The witch blinked bright blue eyes. "Oh, well, then, it doesn't really matter what you wear, does it? Won't be wearing it long in any case."

"She's here for this." Dominique gestured to the green stone, her voice thick with exasperation.

The witch's eyes flicked to the stone. "You plan on resisting? Why?"

"I'm sorry, if I could just take the stone...?" I said.

"Oh, don't be silly. You have to let me do this."

The woman waved her wand, pale brown curls dancing around her face as she trailed her wand in waving lines around my head. A disturbing sensation washed over my scalp, then concentrated in my hair. The dark waves writhed like a nest of snakes, rising in my peripheral vision and tugging here and there as they entwined with one another. The stone floated off the counter toward my head, and was ensconced in a knot of complicated braids.

The witch gazed at me with her chest puffed out with pride. "Damn, I'm good."

"How much do I owe you?" I managed, afraid to move lest I disrupt the hairstyle. I didn't want to know how ridiculous I looked with hair that looked like it'd been done up for prom and a shirt and leggings that could double as pajamas.

"Not a cent. I was happy to do it," the witch assured me.

"She's talking to me, Betsy," Dominique said, rubbing the bridge of her nose the way I did when Peasblossom used one of my bras for a hammock.

I paid for my purchase and left, walking like someone on a tightrope. I didn't get my hair done a lot.

"Dominique, you have to come out with us tonight," Betsy whined behind me. "It's the night of the full moon! Everyone lets their guard down on the full moon."

I froze. The full moon. It was tonight.

"You have three days."

Three days. The full moon. That was it—that was the connection. Anton must have spelled the book so it could only be opened the night of the full moon. Which meant at sundown, the thief would be able to open Anton's book.

CHAPTER 16

Andy could not have looked more like an FBI agent if a wardrobe guru from Hollywood had chosen his clothes for him. Dark blue suit, starched white shirt, black sunglasses. For Pete's sake, there was even just enough of a breeze to blow his jacket open to flash his FBI badge as he walked. I got out of my new rental car and stared at him as he approached, long, even stride screaming authority.

"Good evening." He took off his sunglasses to meet my eyes. "Bryan said witches have a special title. I'm supposed to call you Mother Renard?"

"Please, don't," I said. I gave myself a sharp mental kick. Wasn't this what I'd been regretting before? Abandoning protocol and the safety it offered? The reputation it built?

What reputation? Mother might have been an appropriate title in the Old Kingdom, but here in the modern setting of the Blood Realm—America, specifically—it sounded outdated at best and ridiculous at worst. I curled my hand into a fist. I would make my own reputation. Without the title. "Call me Shade. Please."

If he'd noticed my mental tug of war, he was kind enough not to comment. "All right, Shade. Now, why don't you tell me why we're here?"

I waved a hand to brush off the question and walked toward the hotel. "The details don't matter. I just need you to—"

"I'm sorry, I think there's been some confusion."

His tone stopped me in my tracks. "What?"

He planted his feet on the blacktop of the parking lot, shoulder width apart like a man prepared for battle. "I'm not going anywhere until you tell me what's going on. *Everything* that's going on."

My stomach dropped. "I thought you understood that I can't go into detail. I just needed—"

"An escort, I know. You want me to be a prop that you can discard when it's time to face the real danger because you don't believe I'm capable of facing the threat head-on."

The first stirring of anger started in my gut. "When we spoke earlier, you seemed all right with that."

"And I gave you that impression for a reason." He stepped forward, a ferocity in his eyes that didn't match the polite expression or the dry business suit. "This is *my* case. I'm the one who's been searching for a body for two months just so I can tell Helen Miller's husband he can mourn her. I'm the one who had to tell a grieving husband that it was possible his wife just left him and didn't care enough to tell him. I'm the one questioning scum day after day, trying to figure out if my missing person was a victim or if I might have to tell her husband his wife wasn't the woman he thought she was. I haven't worked my ass off on this case just to bow out when answers are in reach. Especially when we both know you may not share any answers you get."

I started to speak, to tell him I would get him those answers, but the muscle in his jaw tightened, and he continued before I could open my mouth.

"You gave me a glimpse into something strange. It's insane, and mostly I know it can't be real. But I have worked too long and too hard to hone my senses, my reasoning, to doubt them now, to doubt the…impossible things they're telling me now. So I believe you that there's…magic. Witches." His eye twitched. "Pixies. I believe those things exist. And somehow, they're involved in my case."

He took a step toward me and I almost fell back. Almost. I readied my witchy look, reminded myself who I was—*what* I was.

"I'm not a chess piece," he said evenly. "I'm here to help, and I can't do that if you keep me in the dark. So unless you can devise an alternative plan in what can't be very much time, you'd better start talking."

I let the witchy look fly. The force of it straightened my spine and made the well of power inside me roil like a leviathan-churned sea. I had studied for years. Decades. Blood and bone, for all I knew, it could have been centuries. Hard to tell in a multidimensional house. I was a greenhorn when it came to investigating, and even spellcasting. But I was still a witch. An educated witch. I could deliver a baby, set a compound fracture, and send a demon running back to its mother. I would not be cowed.

Andy tensed, but to his credit, he resisted taking a step back. Some of the ferocity bled from his eyes, and he relaxed his stance, no longer using his size to bully me. He didn't back down, though. His jaw lifted in stubborn defiance. A gesture I knew all too well.

Frustration pulled my skin taut. A charm would fix this. And I could do it. It would be nothing to pour a little power into my voice, sweet-talk him into following me inside like a sheep. Heck, I could daze him and just drag him along the way a designated driver might lead an inebriated comrade. I didn't need him to talk. Arianne or her people just needed to see him with me.

But I admired his resolve. He'd had a peek at the Otherworld, and like Bryan had said, he'd gone home, he'd thought about it, and he'd faced it. If I wanted to start a detective business, be a proper private investigator, then having another FBI contact would come in handy. Having another FBI contact who knew about the Otherworld would be priceless.

"All right," I said. "So be it."

I told him everything, the condensed version that left out any mention of Anton, or any specifics that would violate the confidentiality agreement. Someone killed Helen Miller because they needed information from her to steal an object. I was hired to recover said object. Said thief was inside waiting for me. I needed Arianne to see Andy with me so she'd use her magic to keep the thief from using hers.

It was hard to explain why I didn't want him to come with me into the room without making it sound like a Harry Potter movie, and I floundered for a good way to put it.

"I'm going to confront her, and if Arianne doesn't put up the wards, I could end up having an impromptu...duel."

"Like a wizard's duel," he said.

I opened my mouth to head off what I *knew* was coming, but I wasn't fast enough.

"Sounds like Harry Potter."

My shoulders sagged in defeat. "Yes, just like Harry Potter," I grumbled. "If I die, do be kind enough not to use that comparison in my eulogy."

"You will not die. How can I help?"

I rubbed a hand over my face, but froze before I could touch my hair and disturb the complicated style. "Don't you see? That's what I'm trying to tell you. You can't help. You're human, and what's more, you're new to all of this. I don't even have any armor for you."

"I'm wearing my vest."

I snorted. "Bullets are the last thing I'm worried about."

Andy set his shoulders, straightening his spine. He wasn't backing down. My stomach twisted into a sharp knot. I couldn't be responsible for his death.

I tried to keep my intentions off my face, hide them behind a bright smile. "If you insist on getting yourself killed, you can come to the room with me. If she points at me, shoot her. Maybe it will distract her long enough for you to run."

And with that, I marched toward the hotel.

If I wasn't so short, it would have taken him more than two seconds to catch up with me.

"Where's the"—he took a silent running start—"pixie?"

"She's inside. It's her job to make sure Arianne is standing where she'll see you, and, if necessary, lead her to activate the wards."

"Is there a reason you couldn't just ask this woman to use her wards to help you?"

I cleared my throat. "We aren't on the best of terms."

We entered the hotel then, cutting off any further questions Andy might have had. This time, I was ready for the magic that washed over me, that false, lavender-scented calm that filled me with the desire to find a comfortable bed, let reality fade away as I slipped into a dream world that would be so much less work than reality.

I resisted the magic and raised a hand, ready to grab Andy's shoulder and shake him out of the enchantment. My lips parted when I found him scanning the lobby as if expecting armed men to rush him at any second, muscles tensed and ready for action. The magic hadn't fazed him. My respect for him ratcheted up a notch.

Peasblossom was around somewhere, but I didn't search for her. She was good at hiding, and that was what I'd told her to do. If she'd done her job well, Arianne should be on the lookout for me...

And there she is.

I swallowed the shout of joy I wanted to let out as I caught sight of the dream sorceress out of the corner of my eye. Violet silk wrapped her body like the cocoon of some exotic butterfly, hugging the graceful lines of her legs and torso. Sapphires glittered around her neck on a silver chain, and her makeup was so expertly done that it seemed she wasn't wearing any at all. She stood behind the main counter next to a concierge, staring at me with murder in her eyes.

"Stay here," I whispered to Andy. "Flash your badge to the woman in the purple dress if you can. Be subtle."

Andy didn't acknowledge what I'd said, but I knew he'd heard me. It was almost scary just how alert he was. Probably had high blood pressure. I hoped he limited his sodium intake—too much salt could wreak havoc on high blood pressure.

"Mother Renard," Arianne said, her voice as welcoming as a cold fireplace. "I didn't expect to see you again."

I gave her a bright smile. "You have such a lovely establishment that I couldn't resist. I have business in town, and it's such a long drive home." I looked to the concierge. "May I have the room key for the reservation under Andy Bradford?"

"A long drive home," Arianne said. "Yes, I suppose Dresden is a bit far."

A tinge of fear twanged against my spine, and I dropped the pen I'd just used to sign the register as Andrea Bradford. Had I mentioned I was from Dresden? I didn't think I had.

A lump swelled in my throat.

No. No, Dabria cut Vera. She took her blood. Why take her blood except to unlock the book?

Dabria is one of the most renowned thieves in the Otherworld. She's the perfect patsy.

But then why did Dabria agree to meet you?

An image of Isai being strung up and tortured fluttered through my mind like a swarm of bats. Peasblossom's report of what Dabria had said to the bloody wizard. Her fury, her panic over the thought of suffering Anton's wrath for something she hadn't done.

My knees turned to jelly and I clung to the counter to avoid collapsing to the floor. Had I made a horrible, horrible mistake?

"Ms. Renard? Are you all right?"

I groped for my room key, only vaguely aware that Arianne had disappeared. A strong hand on my waist dragged me back to reality, out of the spiraling chaos of my panicked thoughts.

"She's fine, thank you. Shade, let's get you to your room so you can rest."

Andy's deep voice reverberated against my bones, and I let him guide me away from the counter, my room card digging into my hand.

Get it together, Shade. You're just doubting yourself because you're almost there. Dabria did this. Arianne wasn't even on Anton's list.

By the time we got to the elevator, I'd gotten my legs under control. Andy was watching me, but to his credit, he didn't comment.

"So what room number are you?" he asked.

I avoided his eyes, waiting for the elevator doors to open. As soon as they did, I darted inside, knowing he'd follow, assuming I was trying to lose him. He flowed after me, planting a hand on the wall opposite, crowding me close enough I couldn't get away, but with enough distance he'd be able to block any funny business I tried. Smart man.

"I'm room 314," I said calmly.

His jaw hardened and his eyes bored into mine. "Don't lie to me."

That intense stare did half my work for me. I called my power and let it flow upward, filling my eyes with a purple light visible only to magical senses. The energy was reflected in Andy's eyes, holding him still as the charm oozed into my voice. "Wait here."

I ducked under his arm and checked the lights above the elevator door. Number three lit up and a soft electronic ping preceded the opening of the door. I punched the button for the ground floor and darted out of the elevator.

Andy stared at me, confusion dulling his brown eyes, robbing him of his earlier clarity. Guilt bit me, hard, but I ignored it and ran for the stairs. Andy wouldn't stay dazed for long. He was sharper than I'd given him credit for, and something told me he wasn't the type to be manipulated easily. There was no time to wonder if his resistance came from FBI training or if there was something in his family tree to explain it. I had to get to the room before he realized what I'd done.

Four flights of stairs later, I was out of breath and regretting my choice to take the stairs rather than wait for another elevator. Room 706 loomed before me, the little silver numbers much more imposing than they should have been. I scanned the empty hallway as I stood in front of the door to the stairs, my chest rising and falling too rapidly.

I hovered outside the door to my room, the key card in my grip. Of course Dabria couldn't be in there making a great deal of noise, assuring me that she was here and waiting. No, she would be silent, would force me to consider the possibility she hadn't done as I'd expected, perhaps had arrived early to ambush me. The potion I'd gulped down gurgled in my stomach.

A spell struck me from behind, slamming into my brain with the muted force of a pillow stuffed with apples. Not quite the violence of a sock full of quarters, but it'd do. I didn't have enough breath to shout as I slammed into the door, hard.

My head bounced off the unforgiving surface and I blinked to clear my double vision as I raised a hand. I drew power on my next deep breath, then spit toward whoever had struck me. Tar so dark a blue it was almost black shot from my mouth to splatter my attacker. A muffled curse preceded a feminine voice.

"Peasant," she spat. "That's disgusting."

Dabria held still, trying to keep from further entangling herself in my spell. She swirled one finger around and bit out a counter-curse, dispelling the adhesive resin holding her in a sticky web. I reached for another spell as I shoved myself to my feet, but she held up a hand.

"Enough!" She smoothed her hands down her black dress, fluffing out the purple feathers decorating the neckline. "Let us not squabble like grubby street urchins." She lifted her chin and looked down her nose at me. "We are here for a civil trade, are we not?"

"There is nothing civil about striking someone from behind," I said. "That was not nice."

Dabria waved a hand as if I'd accused her of not saying my name correctly. "Whatever. Shall we proceed?"

I almost argued with her on principle. Dabria was like a child trying to reason their way out of using good manners, and the witch in me needed to set her straight, to point out how rude she'd been and correct the bad behavior. A more logical part of my brain told me I was standing in an un-warded hallway, and if I wanted to enjoy the protection I'd gone to such trouble to attain, I needed to move this conversation into my room. Besides which, I had a horrible headache, and the sooner I got through this, the sooner I could lie down and die.

"Fine." I put my card in the lock without turning my back on the rude sorceress. An electronic mechanism buzzed and the lock snapped open. I pushed the door with one hand, backing into the room.

Dabria followed me with a condescending smirk. "Don't trust me?"

"I don't trust thieving murderers."

The sorceress gave me nothing. Instead she folded her hands, neat as you please, in front of her and met my eyes like a mother preparing to give her child a firm but loving lecture. "There is no reason for that sort of language. We can be friends, you and I."

I shook my head, then regretted it as the headache screamed in protest. "You tried to kill me. I'm afraid that puts a damper on the future of our relationship. The only offering I have for you is as I said on the phone. Give me the book, and I won't say a word about who stole it."

Her expression hardened, the line of her jaw going taut. "Last chance, witchling. We can be friends, or you can be dead."

"Kill me and your name goes straight to the vampire." I smirked. "You think I'm the only one who worked it out?"

She lowered her hand from her hair and there was something small and blue in her palm. She threw it at me, and a cloud of cerulean dust flowed outward like a rolling fog. Her eyes flashed. "Who? Give me a name."

I put a hand over my nose, squeezed my eyes shut, and prayed I hadn't misjudged Arianne, prayed that Peasblossom had been properly panicked.

Nothing happened. I opened my eyes and glanced down at my body. A few seconds passed and shock spread over Dabria's face. I lowered my hand from my nose with a grin. "Well," I said, dusting the harmless blue dust from my clothes, "that was pretty. Now, hand over the book."

"You aren't strong enough to shed my spells," Dabria snarled. "What's going on?"

I'd been working on a clever line in anticipation of that very question. I opened my mouth, eyebrow quirking in an appropriately mocking manner…

Pain exploded in the back of my head and everything went black.

CHAPTER 17

I woke up with a headache that only monumental stupidity deserved. Every hair on my head seemed to be trying to escape, tugging at its root like a cat fleeing a bubble bath.

"I'll shave it all off," I mumbled. "Wear a wig. Maybe red. Or purple." I frowned. "No, not purple."

"What is she talking about?" demanded a masculine voice.

"She's not talking about anything, you old fool, she's delirious. I told you, you hit her too hard. You're lucky she's not dead already."

"*You're* lucky she's not dead," the man snarled back.

All my concentration was going to not letting my head fall off my shoulders, but I recognized that voice. That arrogant, insulting voice, couched in what had to be a gallon's worth of cologne.

"Shut up, Spitbeard," I said. "There's no need to shout."

Silence. I wrinkled my nose. Speaking had let some of that noxious odor into my mouth, and now I tasted wizard. *Ew.*

"What did she call you?" Dabria asked.

"I have no idea. She's delirious."

My brain finished processing the bad smell and taste from

Isai, and the full realization of my situation struck me like a sledgehammer between the eyes. Someone had hit me from behind, knocking me unconscious. Not someone. A wizard. Isai, who was now standing over me talking to the woman who'd stolen his employer's book. The woman who'd tortured him and accused him of stealing said book. My head throbbed and I groaned.

"This is ridiculous. She's no good to us like this," Isai muttered.

There was the smack of skin against skin and Dabria's sharp voice. "Don't heal her, you idiot. That's not how this works."

"Why not?" I forced my eyes open. Light speared into my eyes, stabbing into my brain. I whimpered and squeezed them shut again. "Gods, it's bright in here."

"Turn the lights off," Dabria commanded.

Isai scoffed. "I am not your servant. You're the one who wants the woman in pain. If you want the lights off to spare the witch's delicate eyes, turn them off yourself."

"I think you're forgetting who you're talking to. I said turn them off. *Now.*"

I opened my eyes, too interested in my surroundings to be bothered by exploding eyeballs. Isai's face darkened with rage, his cheeks mottled red. He moved with all the grace of a remote-controlled robot, but he stormed over to the light switch all the same. In a childish show of temper, he slammed his staff down on the light switch, cracking the plastic base as he "turned off" the lights. I eyed the cracked setting as my head throbbed. I sympathized.

With the beams of light no longer stabbing into my brain like a fork into an undercooked roast, my hands took their turn to tell me something was wrong. My fingers felt funny, swollen and tight. A quick flexing told me they'd tied me to the bed. They'd only secured my wrists, though, my legs moved freely. Small favors.

The hotel room I'd rented was smaller than some, larger than most. The headboard of the bed pressed against the wall, so I had a view of the entire space. To my left, a short hallway led to the main door and the bathroom. A dresser sat against the wall opposite the bed, and a closet lay to the right. Windows covered the wall on the right, but my captors had drawn the shades.

Isai stood at the wall to my left, his back to the short hallway. He wore his expensive suit, his twisted staff squeezed in a ham-fisted grip. The reddish orange of his beard caught the light as his jaw moved, his teeth clenching and unclenching. Not a happy man, that wizard.

Dabria sat in a chair beside the bed, looking for all the world like a doting family member visiting an ill relative. It would have been a more convincing picture if she weren't dressed like a woman ready to go to a Gothic-themed ball.

I was the prisoner of a sorceress and a wizard, both of whom were rather annoyed with me. And, I suspected, both of whom had a vested interest in making sure my investigative career came to a sudden and bloody end.

Panic sharpened my nerves into needle-fine points to stab at my skin in an unpleasant prickling sensation. My chest rose and fell a little faster as my breathing quickened, and for a chaotic second, I thought I would hyperventilate.

"Spitbeard!"

Without conscious thought, I shouted the nickname Peasblossom had given the wizard. Saying it out loud reminded me of how he'd gotten that nickname, and some of my building hysteria leaked out in a high-pitched laugh. Isai blinked at me as if I'd grown a second head. His bewilderment made me laugh again, and I threw myself into the funny side of hysterics. So much better than blind panic.

"I would say I'm surprised you're letting Dabria boss you around," I managed, my voice a little too breathless. "But then, maybe I shouldn't be. How long has it been since you controlled your own life?"

Dabria chuckled and lifted something from the small bedside table. "He does seem very fitted to the role of servant, doesn't he?"

"The vampire thinks so," I agreed. I stared at the delicate cup in her hand, the fine saucer in the other. She was having tea? My dry throat tightened, a sudden thirst twisting my gut.

Dabria laughed again at my little joke and I tried to join her, hoping a little camaraderie might get me a cup of tea. The sorceress' eyes glittered with sadistic pleasure as she took an extra-long sip, holding my gaze the entire time. *No tea for me.*

An irrational surge of anger swept over me, diluting my fear, soothing my pain. They were going to kill me. I understood that—perhaps, on some level, I'd accepted it. But I would not lie here and be mocked, manipulated into spending my last hours of this life suffering.

Denied tea.

When I regained the capacity to process full, coherent thought without risking permanent brain damage, I looked from Isai to Dabria. The wizard stewed in his own fury, a state of mind I assumed he was used to by now. Dabria remained the epitome of cool confidence—arrogance, even. She thought she'd won.

Isai was following her orders, though he raged against the idea, obviously hated her. Just like his relationship with Anton. Which meant... My head throbbed, and I closed my eyes, focused only on breathing for a moment. Which meant...

Memories peeked into my mind, hesitant, cautious. When I didn't suffer an aneurysm, they grew stronger, became clearer.

"You incompetent wretch. How could you miss such an obvious spell? The spell someone else was using to spy on you."

"She's used spells to spy on wizards who never noticed a thing. The only way to even sense the spell is to use a potion or a wand, something physically bonded to the magic that will touch the energy of her spell."

I stared at Isai, then Dabria, then back. An epiphany pressed against my mind. I just—

My eyes flew open wide, my lips parting in sudden realization. "You figured out she was spying on me."

Isai's mouth never lost its perpetual sneer, but there was a flicker in his eyes, a moment when he looked away, refusing to meet my gaze. Dabria paused with her lips on the edge of her teacup, dark eyes peering at me over the rim.

"Is she still delirious?" Dabria asked.

Isai's jaw tightened. "No."

"But that's not possible." My head throbbed and I winced, leaning back into the pillow. "She's too good. You couldn't have known just by looking at me, *seconds* after looking at me." I tried to force my pain-addled brain to work faster. "In fact…you knew before you saw me. You were already mad when you opened the door."

Pressure built behind my eyelids, rolling to the back of my head like a tide thick with heavy-bodied sharks, threatening to pop the top of my skull off like a champagne cork. I clenched my teeth. I needed the pain to stop and let me think. My fingers felt ten times as thick as they should have, barely twitching when I tried to move them and trace out a healing spell. Before I gathered the will to push through the discomfort, force them to obey me, I remembered the wards.

Dabria's blue dust hadn't worked, the spell as harmless as a summer breeze. Arianne had activated the wards. My plan had worked—sort of.

I abandoned the healing spell and flailed for the end of my train of thought. "You knew about the spell before you saw me, so you had to find out about it from someone else." I looked at the sorceress. "You."

A smile curled Dabria's mouth. "Very good, witchling. Yes, I called Isai."

"Shut up," he growled.

She ignored him, and I didn't think any other reaction would have infuriated him more. "He called me after Anton hired you. So frightened, so scared we would get caught. He's hired a PI, she's going to figure out what we've done." Dabria snorted. "Of course, I knew seconds after meeting you that it was a joke. You're just a witchling." She rolled her eyes. "I called him from the parking lot. Told him he was worrying for nothing and to keep his head. Or else."

Solving that one small mystery did miraculous things for my head. The pressure eased, and my thoughts flowed more freely, though I was far from pain-free. "You guessed she'd try to spy on me."

Dabria snorted again. "Well, I would hope he could put that together. It was the same spell I worked on him. Fool me once," she added.

I lifted my head to gape at Isai. "You shouted at me and called me incompetent...when you fell for the *same thing?*"

Dabria laughed, a sound of pure joy. "He yelled at you?"

I scowled, anger chasing back more of the pain. "Yes, he did. Ranted on and on and on, in fact, called me names, said I was incompetent. I thought he would strike me, he was so angry."

The sorceress laughed, shaking her head at Isai. "Shame on you for being so hypocritical."

More puzzle pieces fell into place, each mystery solved giving me a vital piece to the next one. "Blood and bone, I know how you did it." I shut my eyes and flopped back on the bed. "What an idiot I am."

I sighed and opened my eyes to look at Isai. "You did it. You did it all. You forced your way into Helen Miller's mind. That's what killed her. Then you killed the guards, dropped the wards."

Isai ground his teeth, but said nothing. His face did erupt with a few more red blotches.

"But you didn't know she was spying on you." I glanced at Dabria. "Hit the jackpot, didn't you?"

"Oh, my, yes," she breathed. She set her empty teacup on the table and let out a sigh of pure contentment. "I'd been trying to get this old goat to let me into my sister's castle for years, but he was so stubborn." She rolled her eyes. "I had no idea he was so mistrusted by the vampire that the castle had been warded twice. That's why I failed to break them, failed to get inside."

She sniffed. "I resorted to spying on him, hoping I'd catch him going into the castle himself so I could figure out how to get in. Then to see him break into the vault, steal that book..." She clapped her hands, a little girl's glee lighting her face. "And he took down all the wards. All those pesky wards that prevented me teleporting in."

"You teleported in, knocked him out, and took the book," I finished. "Left him lying there in front of the vault, knowing Anton would think it was him."

"Because it was him," she finished, an evil, satisfied glint in her eye.

"But you couldn't open the book," I said.

She shrugged. "It took longer than I would have liked, yes. But I figured it out. I have a sample of Vera's blood, and now all I need is the light of the full moon and Anton's secrets will be mine."

"Mine, you mean," Isai snapped, striding forward.

Dabria glared at him and rose from her seat. "No. *Mine*. Until you get me into my sister's castle, the book is mine, and only mine."

"Or whoever wins the auction," I pointed out. I gave Isai the most innocent look I could manage with my nerves threatening mutiny if they didn't get a healing potion soon. "You did know about the auction, right?"

Isai's eyes widened and he stared at Dabria.

She shrugged. "Just in case you fail. Again."

"We had a deal," he said, his voice hoarse, his hand shaking where it gripped his staff.

"Our deal was the book for entrance to the castle. If you do not fulfill your end of our bargain by the full moon, I will auction it off to the highest bidder who can get me past those wards. I will have my sister's legacy!"

"That's why you've been going around begging for help with wards," I said to Isai, pricking at his pride, urging him to get even angrier. Angry wizards made mistakes. It would likely make him even angrier if he realized he'd killed the other wizard who'd warded the castle, so in fact he could now access Serafina's castle any time he wanted. He could finish his deal with Dabria now and be done with it.

I kept that to myself.

"In his subtle way," Dabria agreed, annoyance thick in her tone. "I've met pixies with more tact."

There was still one thing bothering me. I furrowed my brow. "But it was the perfect crime. Anton only suspected you because of your reputation, and your visits to Isai. Why set the bomb at my house? You were in no danger from me."

"But Isai was," she pointed out. "He tried to put suspicion on Flint with his little ritualistic killing of that oaf Tybor, but, of course, that was a complete failure. Then I spoke to Arianne myself when I arrived in town. She mentioned you, said you had offered her protection against Isai." She quirked an eyebrow, eyeing me with new consideration. "You insulted her. I daresay you have made a rather powerful enemy without meaning to." She shrugged. "I needed you gone before you found evidence to accuse him."

She met my eyes then, and there was a cold finality there. "In twenty-four hours, it won't matter what Anton knows. But until then, I'm afraid I'm going to need to hold on to you. And I'll need the name of who else knows. You seem like the stubborn sort, so..."

I barely saw her hand move. Pain erupted over my body, burrowing trails of agony clawing down my body as if an eight-headed dragon had breathed fire in multiple streams down my entire form. My vision went white, my brain halting all processes, trying to dump me into shock to avoid the coming torment.

I didn't know how long I lay there, how long my body remained taut, arched off the bed as every one of my muscles contracted and froze, helpless against the spell. I regained my senses to find myself lying in what felt like a pool of blood. Tears slid down my face, pouring from my eyes with no permission from me. It was another eternity before I could move.

Dabria waited, once again seated in her chair, letting me come back to myself in my own time. She lifted her teacup, and steam wafted from the fragrant liquid inside. I'd been unconscious long enough for her to get a fresh pot.

"Tell me," she whispered. "Tell me the name of this person. There's no reason to keep it from me. I won't hurt anyone. I just need to keep an eye on them, make sure they don't speak out of turn to the vampire."

"No."

Dabria's face darkened with rage, a red flush filling her pale cheeks like an old thermometer about to burst. "You little fool," she snarled. "I'll make you wish you were dead."

"I already wish I was dead," I mumbled. "Anything to escape you and that awful shade of purple. You look like you fell ass over teakettle into a tainted cotton candy machine."

Her eyes widened and Isai let out a loud guffaw, slamming his staff on the floor to punctuate the sound.

Dabria's attention swiveled to him, and something brushed my ear.

"Shade!" Peasblossom whispered.

My eyes widened, and I quickly wiped all expression from my face and held perfectly still. I couldn't speak, couldn't risk giving away Peasblossom's presence.

"Arianne found Andy," she said, speaking under her breath

directly into my ear. "She figured out what you were up to, and she was *angry*. She dropped the wards in this room. Says she's going to let you suffer the consequences. She has people in the rooms on either side holding up wards to limit the collateral damage. She's going to punish Isai and Dabria when they leave, but...but..."

But that wouldn't save me. Dabria was now free to torture me with magic as much as she pleased. I closed my eyes.

"I'll fix it!" Peasblossom promised. "Hang in there!"

I opened my mouth then, needing to tell her to save herself, but the pressure on my ear vanished, and I knew she'd gone. I collapsed against the sheets. Peasblossom. If anything happened to her...

Don't think about it. Think about something else. Like the torture that's coming your way. It was little consolation that Dabria could have tortured me without magic too. I didn't have a high pain tolerance, never had. Too sensitive. Hysteria seeped into my brain, the only protection I had left against blind panic.

"I could never get a tattoo," I murmured.

The voices stopped, then Isai growled. "Now who's the fool? You hurt her too badly—she's nonsensical! How will you get the information?"

"Can't you take it out of her mind like you did with Helen?" Dabria snapped.

"No! She's lived between planes for most of her life. It would be hard enough to erase a swath of her memory. Finding something that specific would be impossible!"

"Would it be hard for a vampire to erase my memories?" I asked, realizing with a start that my eyes were closed.

Isai muttered something, and heavy footsteps paced the floor.

"I will get the information," Dabria said, irritation thick in her tone.

A cool hand touched my leg, chilling my skin through my leggings. The pain faded away. It was like being placed in a cool stream on a raging hot summer day, water flowing over me, washing away the heat and grime and sweat. I felt clean, calm, and pain-free.

With the physical comfort came clarity. Dabria had just used a healing spell on me. After a pain spell. She could keep the pain going…forever.

My realization must have shown on my face, along with my new clarity. Dabria smiled down at me. "Now, where were we?"

"You'll never find them." Fear washed up the back of my throat on a splash of bile, my thoughts threatening to scatter like so many mice before a hungry owl. Dabria was sitting too close. She looked like an angry, feathered chess piece, but that comparison didn't make me feel any better about being tortured by her, didn't make my imagination less creative in thinking of everything she could do to me. "If you don't let me go, they'll go straight to Anton. You think I came here without taking precautions?"

Isai's long legs ate up the distance between the wall and the bed in two strides. The bored expression he'd worn while Dabria tortured me melted under a sudden fury. "You little wretch. What have you done?"

"Calm yourself, old man," Dabria said. "She's bluffing."

"And what if she's not?" He glared at her, pools of melted gold illuminating his eyes as his power responded to his emotions. "If someone goes to the vampire now, then your grand scheme is finished—then we are both finished!"

My heart rose a little higher in my throat, threatening to cut off my air. "I'm not bluffing."

Dabria rolled her eyes. "Yes, you are." Isai opened his mouth, but she held up a hand to silence him. "Regardless of what I think, we will soon know the truth of it."

Sometimes the gods get bored and decide to have a joke at we mortals' expense. I had one of those moments now as Dabria reached down to take something beyond my field of vision.

When she sat up straight again, she held something in her hand—a dried-up scorpion. She held it up to the light, a dull glow glinting on the dead arachnid's brittle exoskeleton.

A semi-hysterical voice in my head wondered if she'd gotten it from The Cauldron.

Cruel pleasure twisted her features as she leaned closer, making sure the scorpion stayed in my line of vision. I couldn't look away, couldn't drag my eyes from the evil coming toward me. My brain, cleared from the haze of pain by Dabria's considerate healing spell, was now all too equipped to provide me with frightening images of what was coming. What that scorpion would do to me.

"Cease the theatrics and just do it already!" Isai said. "It is already dark. The vampire might summon me at any moment."

"And if that happens, you will run home like a good lap dog and serve him," Dabria said, apparently annoyed at having her dramatic moment ruined. "I can handle things here."

"Why did you do it?" I blurted out.

Dabria and Isai both stared at me.

"Do what?" Isai asked.

"Break your word. You gave Kirill your word that you would serve him for another five hundred years, but you betrayed him. How could you do that, knowing what it might mean for you?"

Isai curled his lip. "You mean the old wives' tale that I'll lose my magic? That my spells won't work if I'm forsworn?"

Dabria quieted, as if she too were interested in the answer.

"It's real," I insisted.

Isai scoffed. "In the Old kingdom, perhaps. But not now." He gestured toward the window. "Look around you, witchling. The gods don't care about honor anymore."

"Yes, they do. But even if they didn't, there are other consequences."

"You refer to demons and the fey." Isai shrugged. "It is true, most of them will not do business with a wizard who is forsworn. But then again, once I have Kirill's empire, I will not need them, will I?" He stared at me. "Wizards are not like witches or sorceresses. We are not gifted magic by some mysterious patron." He glared at Dabria. "We are not born with it. Wizards get magic because they want it, because they want it bad enough to go out and find it. We learn magic through study, and it takes ambition for someone to become a truly great wizard. You have no idea what I had to do to get where I am."

"A vampire's pet?" Dabria suggested.

Isai's face turned red. "I am the most powerful wizard the Old Kingdom—indeed, *any* kingdom—has ever seen! That bloodsucking corpse is no more than a petty thief who rode to greatness on my shoulders!"

"That's not even a little bit true, and the fact that you don't realize it is what makes you a servant, not some contract," I said.

"You—"

I spoke over him. "You have no idea what goes into running Kirill's empire, what went into building it. He doesn't trust you enough to let you see those details. Having his book won't get you anything but a list of names. It's nothing more than a box full of car parts, and you're no mechanic."

The analogy went over his head.

"The vampire is weak. He is always more interested in the future, always chasing the next prophecy, instead of seizing the opportunities before him now." He sneered at me. "Like you. The vampire is more interested in the future, in what you will be, rather than what you are now."

My heart skipped a beat and I strained against my bonds. "What? What do you mean, he's interested in my future? What will I be?"

Isai's eyes glittered with malice. "You will be nothing." He raised his hand. "Save your parlor tricks, Dabria. *I* will make her talk."

I squeezed my eyes shut. It was that instinct that made me miss what happened next.

A loud popping sound peeled back my eyelids with all the suddenness of a loose Venetian blind. Fear and confusion made me slow on the uptake, and it wasn't until I saw the room's newest occupant that I realized what that sound had been.

A gunshot.

CHAPTER 18

Flint held a gun in his hand, his arm extended toward the spot where Isai had just been. His grip remained casual, as if he were used to the weight and shape. He wore black jeans and another black T-shirt just tight enough to accent every line of muscle, but loose enough to appear casual, almost careless. His clothes matched the gun, but I had the semi-hysterical thought that was probably a coincidence. At least, I didn't think he accessorized to that level.

Blood and thicker things coated the wall behind the spot where Isai had been standing a moment ago. The light made the blood glisten, and as I watched, a piece of brain matter slid down the wall like a particularly energetic slug. I looked down and could just make out the fan of Isai's orange-red hair. More brain matter leaked from the top of his ruined skull.

I gaped at Flint, staring in shock at the *sidhe* who'd just killed one of the most powerful wizards to ever live. With one bullet. It didn't seem a fitting end.

Flint lowered his gun as he turned to the bed, and I caught a glimpse of a barrel that looked too long. My knowledge of guns was limited, but not nonexistent. It was a pistol with a suppressor.

I wasn't the only one Flint had surprised. Dabria was still holding the scorpion, the shock on her face reflected in the still tension in her body, her immobility in the face of the *leannan sidhe's* approach. She twitched, survival instinct trying to push her out of shock, make her flee, fight.

I knew what was coming.

I didn't warn her.

"You won't hurt anyone," Flint murmured, his voice a deep, honeyed tone thick with power. "I don't want you to hurt anyone."

I couldn't avert my eyes. I had an idea of what Dabria must be feeling, but I couldn't imagine what it would be like to bear the full force of the *leannan sidhe's* charm. This was no slow seduction, no subtle influence. He hit her with everything he had, pouring it all into his voice. All for her.

The sorceress never stood a chance. For all her cleverness and planning, her personal magic was no match for the *sidhe's* power. Dabria's face went slack, her fingers releasing the scorpion, her arms falling limp to her sides. The arachnid disappeared from my field of vision, and some irrational part of me recoiled at the thought of the creature scuttling around unsupervised.

It's dead, I reminded myself. *It's a spell, not a living thing.*

"Stay in that chair, lover. Don't move until I ask you to."

The push in his voice was velvet on my skin, a soft, decadent caress. He wasn't even talking to me and I felt his power, the desire to do what he said—whatever he said. I pressed my head deeper into the pillow until the gem hidden beneath the complicated folds of my hair dug into the back of my scalp. The hum of magic was reassuring, a reminder that I had some protection against Flint's influence.

Some protection.

Whoever had tied my hands to the bed had done their best to

make them tight enough to cut off circulation—a deliberate attempt to hinder any spell I might attempt. Moving my fingers took an inordinate amount of effort, and for a few panicked seconds, I worried I'd need telekinesis just to raise my hands. I swallowed hard and flexed my fingers, almost fainting in relief when a bit of blood trickled back into them, the sensation of needles stabbing at my hands a painful but welcome experience.

Before I attempted escape in earnest, the weight of Flint's power slid over me. It wasn't unlike being covered in a heavy blanket. A soft, downy blanket that promised the best night's sleep I'd ever had—after the best night I'd ever had. My body grew heavier, more liquid, and I squirmed in the sweat-soaked sheets.

No.

I held an image of the green jewel in my head, and concentrated on its weight, its magic. Dominique did not sell weak items of power. It would protect me. It *had* to protect me.

"So nice to see you again, Shade."

That voice. It was a gentle caress on my cheek, the stroke of fingers down my jaw. A lover's greeting. I cleared my throat. "Really? And I worried you might see me differently after our misunderstanding."

Something flickered in his eyes, but I couldn't tell if it was amusement or anger. That the two blurred together for the *sidhe* was concerning.

"I'm sure you'll be pleased to know I've *fully* recovered."

The suggestion in his voice plucked at things low in my body, and I clenched my jaw against the urge to writhe in pleasure. His eyes darkened and he took another step toward the bed. He'd tucked the gun into his waistband, and a tiny part of me wished he'd kept it out. A gunshot seemed less threatening than his voice, those eyes.

"How did you find me?" I asked, tugging at the ropes around my wrists.

"You ran from me rather suddenly and you seemed... distressed." His brow furrowed. "Also, there was an explosion. Seems someone tried to kill you." He shrugged. "It was not difficult to deduce that you would go to your mentor's. One of your neighbors was kind enough to loan me her car."

Loan you her car. Yeah, I'll bet.

"I went to Mother Hazel's, and I waited there. When you left, I followed you."

He was too close now, his legs brushing the sheets. My heart leapt into my throat and my voice rose an octave. "How did you get into the closet?"

"You were speaking with a man in the parking lot. I came inside and asked the lovely young lady at the counter for help. She figured out what room you'd reserved and let me in to wait for you. I heard the commotion outside the door and hid until I... understood the situation." He shook his head. "You've made quite a mess for yourself, haven't you?"

I cleared my throat. "Just a minor hiccup in negotiations. Nothing we can't move past."

I would never get out of the ropes with only my pathetic physical strength. My head felt like it would fall off, still throbbing from where Isai had struck me, and my hands were weak from the blood deprivation. I'd need a spell to escape this. There was only one that might work. *This is going to hurt.*

Flint arched an eyebrow. "You joke when you're nervous." A smile slowly spread over his mouth. "It's cute."

My body tightened in response to the compliment, and the resulting embarrassment was what I needed to clear my head. Flint was in full charm mode, but he wasn't focusing it all on me —some of his attention was still bleeding onto Dabria, keeping her entranced. And the gem in my hair offered some protection. With the embarrassment burning my cheeks, I had just enough irritation to start a logical train of thought.

"I can't help but notice you've removed the two people who

were threatening my life a moment ago, but you've yet to untie me," I said. "Not exactly a white knight riding in on his valiant steed, are you?"

His head fell to the side, his gaze a physical weight as he slid it up and down my body. "I rather like you tied to the bed."

The gem pulsed, growing hot enough that I raised my head, trying to keep it from burning the back of my scalp. There'd been more of a push in those words, a heavy-handed attempt to grab hold of my hormones and lead me around by them like an errant dog on a leash. I pressed my fingers to the bed, drawing the spell I needed. I hoped my body hid that hand from his sight long enough to activate the spell before he noticed what I was doing.

"Dabria has the book," I reminded him, my voice a little too breathy for my taste. "If you ask her for it, she'll give it to you. You don't need me."

Flint considered me, head still tilted to the side. "Yes," he said. "And she will give me the book soon."

I had to keep pausing in the middle of the spell, fighting to hold on to it, keep the energy together while I waited for the pain to subside enough to continue. My hands throbbed.

"So what are you waiting for?" I snapped, my voice sharp with frustration.

"Have you ever met a *leannan sidhe*?" Flint asked.

"Never had the pleasure," I muttered. "Before your charming introduction, of course."

"We are a very political race. Brute strength is a poor man's weapon, and any man or woman who cannot anticipate the future—stay three, five, ten steps ahead of everyone else—is as good as dead."

"A lovely people, I'm sure." I drew out another circle. *One more...*

"Why did the vampire hire you?"

Surprise almost killed my spell. I closed my eyes and said the words in my head as I traced the final circle. I blocked out his voice as much as possible and forced myself not to think of what he'd said, not to think of how he'd asked the very question I'd been asking myself since the vampire had first shown up at my house.

"Anton is as good as one of my people, the way he plots, he plans, and he always looks to the future," Flint said. "He could have solved his case himself, could have hired many more powerful creatures to do it for him, were he so inclined. But he chose you. A witchling with little experience beyond serving as a village witch, and apprenticing for an old crone." He crossed his arms, a gesture I was positive he'd intended to make his muscles swell, to present an even more mouth-watering spectacle. "So why did he come to you? Why did he trust you with his secrets, bring you into his circle?"

He leaned over me, close enough he would see my hand now if he looked away from my face. His power roared forward like a wild animal, raw and primal, determined to tear through whatever defenses I might have, get at what was inside, what he wanted to know.

"Who are you, Shade Renard?" he whispered.

I met his eyes as my finger slid through the final gesture. *"Incendium."*

Fire flowed over my hands, yellow and orange flames that licked over my fingers, my palms. I gritted my teeth and pressed my fingers to the ropes around my wrists. The position hurt, pulling muscles that weren't meant to stretch that far, but a good wave of desperation gave me the strength I needed to do it. The ropes caught, smoke curling into the air.

Flint growled and retreated a few steps, searching for a fire extinguisher. I jerked at my bonds, panic swelling in my chest, making it hard to breathe. The spell protected my hands from the flames, but not my clothes, and not the rest of my body. Not the bed. My sleeves caught fire at the same time as the rope and the sheets, my flesh screaming as it blistered under the heat. I cried out as the ropes broke, then I hurled myself off the pyre the bed was becoming.

"Don't move," Flint snarled, abandoning the search for a fire extinguisher to turn his full focus on me.

I dropped my gaze to the ground, avoiding his eyes, the power that was already rolling toward me. "You can't hold Dabria like that if you put all your focus on me," I shouted. "Look around you. Mortal danger interferes with mind magic!"

The fire swept over the sheets, hungrily biting into the thick comforter bunched at the foot of the bed. I staggered back, still smacking my sleeves to put the rest of the fire out. My skin screamed, the sight of the blistered flesh touching a primal part of my brain that panicked and began a whining screech of "Get out of there!"

Dabria blinked and stirred. Flint whirled to face her, throwing more power over the charm to keep her still. I stared at the door through the flames, wondering if I could leap over the bed and make it out before Flint grabbed me. There was a scuffle of movement, then Flint swung at Dabria. Out of my peripheral vision, I saw the gun connect with the back of her head, and then she crumpled to the floor.

"Stay there," Flint said. "Or so help me, I'll shoot you."

Dabria was on the floor, swaying on all fours as if the blow to her head had stunned her. Her purple hair was mussed, most of it having escaped its complicated 'do, and some of the feathers along her neckline were smoking or burned away.

I focused on the door. It had to be now or never. The bed was turning into a bonfire, the flames reaching for the ceiling. If I didn't jump now, there'd be no bed to jump over, just a wall of heat.

"Move one foot, one finger, and I'll shoot you too, witch."

Flint's voice stopped me cold, ripping my attention from the door and dragging it to the gun in his hand. A loud hiss preceded a sudden shower as the air in the room grew hot enough to set off the fire sprinkler. A fine spray shot over the room, sending tiny droplets into my eyes like miniature projectiles. I blinked, raising a smoking arm to block the worst of it.

The *leannan sidhe* was soaking wet. But whereas I knew I looked like a drowned rat, the *sidhe* looked…incredible. The water glued his clothes to his muscled form, giving the impression he wasn't wearing clothes, that he'd been painted to appear as though he were. Things low in my body tightened at the picture he made, the raw appeal of it, and there was no power there, no magical influence. Just plain physical attraction.

The gun he pointed at me ruined the effect.

"Don't. Move."

I swallowed hard. "Let's all just stay calm."

Flint irritatedly swiped at his face with his free hand. He opened his mouth again, but before he said a word, Dabria launched herself off the floor and made a mad dash for the door. The gun popped again, the sound loud despite the suppressor. I smacked my hands over my ears just as Dabria screamed and hit the ground clutching her leg. Blood seeped from between her fingers, staining her pale skin.

My heart leapt into my throat as Flint glowered at me.

"You are turning out to be a great deal of trouble," he said tightly.

"I really am. Loads of trouble. And not worth it at all." I inched toward the door. "I don't know why he hired me. I swear, I don't."

"You're coming home with me," Flint growled. He looked at Dabria. "Both of you. I will have answers, and I will have them tonight."

"You can't walk us out of here at gunpoint," I said. I gestured at Dabria. "You'll have to carry her. And we're all soaking wet. We're going to draw attention."

Dabria moved a hand, and Flint raised the gun. "Don't. Move. It's not a complicated arrangement, sorceress. You move, you get shot—that's how guns work." He gestured at me. "She gets it."

The sorceress bared her teeth at him, a wild animal cornered and ready to fight to the death. "I need to heal. Let me bleed to death and the book's location dies with me." Her voice shook, but to her credit, she sounded more angry than hurt.

"Then we'd better make our bargain quickly."

The mention of a bargain chased some of the pain from Dabria's face. "Bargain?"

I didn't like where the conversation was headed. I bit my lip and debated making a run for the exit. Or maybe screaming for help.

Flint nodded. The sprinkler chose that moment to shut off, and he smiled and swiped the water from his face as if it had stopped at his personal request. "I know you can teleport us out of here."

Dabria sat up, then hissed as the pain in her leg made her stop. Her fingers twitched, trying again to cast a healing spell, but one glance at Flint's gun made her freeze. A snarl curled her lip. "I will teleport us nowhere until I have your oath, *sidhe*." She paused, taking a moment to smooth back her hair, adjust the feathers she had left, as if her hands weren't coated in blood. "There's no reason we can't both use the book to get what we want. Swear that you will let me go—in full possession of my free will and free of any influence—and I will teleport us out of here. We can ransom the book back to Anton together."

"Your cleverness is well known, but so is your lack of personal power," Flint said. "There's no reason I can't convince you to give me the book without making any such bargain."

"Then do it."

Flint rolled his head, tendons popping as he considered the sorceress. A thought tickled the back of my mind, trying to tell me I'd forgotten something.

He'd charmed Dabria, hit her with enough power she should have been stupefied for hours. But she'd shaken it off, made a break for it not once, but twice. I glanced at the bed, then the sprinkler. Had Arianne activated the wards again?

The gun made that popping sound, a sound that wasn't scary enough to reflect what it was capable of. My chest tightened, my breath freezing as Dabria screamed. There was rage in the sound, rage and pain. More blood stained her skirts, this time pouring from her other leg. She scrambled to keep a hand over each wound, trying to stanch the flow of blood. The whole room smelled of copper, and some hysterical part of my mind was convinced I could smell Isai's brains, could smell decaying flesh, despite the fact he hadn't yet begun to cool.

"You bastard!" Dabria screamed.

"You will give me your oath to teleport us to safety—safety for all of us," Flint said. "And then we will discuss a bargain."

Dabria shook her head, her chest rising and falling too rapidly. Shock would claim her soon if she didn't heal. Already she looked too pale. "No. I will have your oath before any of us leaves this room. I am no fool, *sidhe*. My bargaining position will never be as strong as it is now."

Flint raised the gun again, and Dabria jutted out her chin, the blood she'd smeared over her hair and the feathers of her dress giving her the appearance of a demented, injured harpy.

"Your oath on my freedom," she rasped. "Your oath that if I hand over the book, you will make it a stipulation of return to the vampire that he give me full, unrestricted access to my sister's castle." Madness lit her eyes as she faced me. "And you will kill the witchling."

Seven stories up, jumping out the window would kill me. I couldn't look at Flint, didn't want to see if he was considering her offer.

"I will grant your freedom," he said, "and the stipulation to get you access to your sister's castle." He paused, and I felt his stare on the side of my face. "But the witch is mine."

Dabria's mouth fell open. "What do you want with a witchling?" Her voice rose an octave, riding a rising tide of hysteria. "What does *everyone* want with this witchling?"

I wanted to shout at her to quit calling me that, but since part of me wanted an answer to the question too, I held back. My arms were bloody and blistered, the shreds of my shirt sticking to the oozing wounds. Shock was wearing off, and the pain was eating more and more of my thoughts. I would pass out soon, and I looked forward to it.

Flint studied me, keeping Dabria in his peripheral vision, the gun still aimed in her direction. "That is what I want to know. The vampire does nothing on a whim. If he brought this woman into his life, he has a reason. She is more than she appears."

"Make her tell you," Dabria said, her voice strained, her breathing ragged.

She'd probably never suffered a wound she hadn't been able to heal immediately. I noted idly that she should put pressure on the wounds or she would bleed out. I didn't say it out loud, though.

Bad witch.

Smart witch.

"She seems to have developed a way to resist me," Flint murmured. He smiled. "A little. I'm certain some alone time will allow me to figure out a way around that."

"I don't know why he hired me," I said, frustration and pain tightening my voice. "I swear, I have no idea."

Flint studied me now, that strange glitter in his brown eyes. "We have time to figure it out." He looked back to Dabria. "You have your guarantee for freedom and your sister's legacy. Give me your oath to teleport us somewhere neutral, and I will allow you your spell. Don't try anything. I daresay our witch will know if you're attempting a different spell, and I don't think she's likely to keep your secret."

"Agreed," Dabria growled. She shot me a look of pure hatred that made me pray she'd never find me alone.

Dabria drew the teleportation spell in the air, tracing complicated lines, the furrow between her brow a combination of concentration and pain. I held my breath, watching for the last line. Waiting to have my suspicion—my fervent hopes —confirmed.

"Lanuae magicae."

Nothing happened.

I almost fainted dead away in relief.

"Well?" Flint said, his voice cold.

Dabria stared at her hands. She drew the spell again, faster this time. *"Lanuae magicae!"*

Nothing.

"It's not working," she sputtered.

Flint pointed the gun at her shoulder, his finger tensing to pull the trigger. Dabria cowered back, but rage filled her features.

"I'm trying!" she screamed. "It's not working! I swear."

"Don't lie to me, sorceress."

I didn't realize I was smiling until Flint noticed me. He turned the gun to me.

"What have you done, little witchling?" he asked softly.

A soft mechanical whir preceded the thud of the door hitting the wall as it was thrust open. Time slowed down, moved at a crawl. I had plenty of time to see Andy stride into the room, gun raised, eyes taking in the scene with practiced speed and efficiency. I watched him register Flint's gun, note it was aimed at me. Saw him take in Isai's dead body, Dabria curled up on the floor, the epitome of feminine helplessness as she wailed over her injuries for the benefit of her new audience.

She was pointing at Flint and screaming, but I couldn't hear what she said. All I heard was the pop of Flint's gun. My hand was in the air, fingers moving in a spell that wouldn't work, a shield spell that would never activate under Arianne's wards.

Andy jerked back, and I screamed.

CHAPTER 19

"Andy!"

Pain seared my arms with every brush of tattered sleeves against burned flesh. Even the air hurt, grating over the ruined skin like steel wool. I ignored all of it and scrambled over the soggy remains of the bed to get to Andy where he'd collapsed on the floor, propped up with one arm. He kept his gun trained on Flint, and I was vaguely aware that the *leannan sidhe* was lying on the floor, unmoving.

"Andy," I gasped, reaching for his chest, searching for blood, some clue where he was hit. "Are you—"

"Get out of the way!" He arched his body to keep me from blocking his line of sight.

I glanced back at the fey then at Dabria. Both of them were unconscious. Or...asleep. A heavy presence drew my attention to the doorway, and my chest tightened.

Arianne stood there, her arms stiff at her sides. Rage burned in her eyes, so bright that I flinched and looked away. She'd already taken in the scene, the gun, the dead wizard, the black remains of what had once been a queen-sized bed. She took a step inside, and the carpet squelched under her feet.

Andy grunted, and it was only then I realized I'd grabbed his arm, was clinging to him as if the human could somehow protect me from the furious sorceress. I made a mental note to make sure I left with him.

"He's asleep. I…put a spell on him. And her," I added.

I doubted my feeble attempt to hide Arianne's true nature from the FBI would do anything to repair our…less-than-friendly relationship, but it was the least I could do after bringing my mess to her hotel. Even with Anton's money, I didn't think I could afford a thank-you gift that would head off the feud I could feel blossoming between us.

Andy didn't take his eyes off Flint, just pulled his arm free of my grip so he could stand. He moved as if he were in pain, but still a lot better than I'd have expected after taking a bullet to the chest. He approached Flint with slow, careful steps and kicked the gun away from his limp hand. Only when he'd retrieved the weapon did he speak.

"You spelled him asleep?"

I didn't meet Arianne's eyes. "Yes. Why aren't you dead?"

The last sentence could have been phrased better, but my arms hurt and I didn't have the energy to be polite.

Andy's mouth quirked. "I told you, I'm wearing my vest." He met my eyes. "Bullets are the last thing you're worried about, huh?"

I scowled. "He's an anomaly." I wanted to add that if Arianne's wards hadn't been up, his vest wouldn't have saved him from what Flint could have done. But I was reasonably sure revealing Arianne's true nature would sign my death warrant, so I refrained.

"Check on the woman," Andy said, lowering his weapon.

I leaned over Dabria and felt for her pulse, but I didn't need to. Arianne had erred on the side of caution and cast a sleep spell on both the sorceress and the fey. A teeny part of me hoped that the reason I wasn't asleep as well was because she trusted me to explain things to Andy, to make sure nothing I'd brought her did any permanent or lasting harm to her reputation or her hotel. It wouldn't go well for me if I failed.

I glanced up at the sorceress, letting my question show in my eyes. She nodded, once. I drew a spell over Dabria, sending a pulse of healing to close the worst of her wounds. The magic flared to life, confirming the wards were lowered once again. I wasn't strong enough to completely heal two bullet wounds, but she wouldn't bleed out. I wanted to inspect the injuries more carefully, but I couldn't with Andy in the room. Not unless I wanted to complicate matters.

Another spell mended the bullet holes in her dress, but the bloodstains were still damp. The black material didn't show the blood, but her palms were crimson where she'd touched her legs.

I need a potion, fast. I fumbled in my bag.

After I pulled out a miniature figure of Batman, a handful of mini 3 Musketeers bars, and another ball of twisty ties, Arianne let out a sound of disgust. She stalked close enough to touch Dabria with the toe of her violet shoe. Power flowed over the sleeping sorceress' clothes, and the bloodstains vanished, leaving both Dabria and her clothes as good as new.

"Thank you," I mumbled.

"Witchling," Arianne muttered.

"She's fine," I said, blushing.

Andy finished cuffing Flint and knelt by Isai's body, careful not to put his knee in the thick pool of blood surrounding the dead wizard. "Did he shoot this guy?" he asked, inclining his head from Flint to Isai.

I nodded. Andy scanned the room, that serious stare taking in every detail, seeing more than I would. Then he looked at Arianne. I noticed the sorceress managed a convincing facade of horrified confusion.

"I've got things under control here, Ms. Monet," he said. "Thank you for your help."

Arianne nodded. "Let me know if I can be of further assistance."

As soon as the door closed behind her, Andy fixed me with a severe look. "Start talking."

I cleared my throat. The pain in my arms ate at my attention span, making it difficult to concentrate on anything but the throbbing in my blistered flesh. It was getting hard to breathe, and I realized I was going into shock again.

Andy stared down at my arms as if just noticing them. "Jesus, what happened to you?"

"Fire," I said, trying not to choke on my tongue. I started to cast another healing spell, but my hands shook too badly, and the pain filled my head with cotton. I couldn't concentrate. I choked on a sob and gestured to my pouch. "I have something for the burns…?"

Andy nodded. "Go ahead."

I scooted to sit with my back against the nearest wall, not at all sure I wouldn't pass out if I tried to keep sitting up of my own accord. I bumped into Dabria as I passed, too hurt to be graceful. I wasn't worried about waking her, or Flint. Arianne was power-ful, and I had no doubt that when she spelled someone to sleep, they slept. I'd check to see what spell she'd used in a minute, but for now, I needed that healing potion.

The enchanted pouch felt no such sense of urgency. By the time my hand brushed against the thick glass bottle of the right potion, I was crying, biting my lip to keep from breaking down into those body-racking sobs that only ever seemed to end in a fitful sleep.

Someone took the bottle from my shaking hand, and I watched Andy's strong fingers pull the stopper free. He held it over my arm, and I jerked my head up and down in what I hoped looked like a nod. He poured it over my arms and the tears flowed faster, harder. Cool, sweet relief washed over my ruined flesh, easing the heat, soothing the tortured skin.

I wasn't sure if it was the whole situation being over, or if it was having Andy administer first aid with a potion like I was a child with a skinned knee, but I crumbled. I sobbed, those big, ugly sobs that could turn even the most beautiful woman into a splotchy, red-faced mess. A tissue appeared in front of me, and I accepted it with gratitude if not grace, blowing my nose like a cartoon character.

Andy just let me cry. He didn't say anything, didn't touch me. I thought at one point I heard him on his phone, talking about an ambulance and evidence. It didn't matter. Dabria and Flint weren't human, and the human justice system wasn't equipped to handle them. Even if it was, I didn't think Anton would give up his pound of flesh. And he'd find out soon, somehow. If he didn't already know.

For some reason, that made me cry harder.

Eventually, I ran out of tears. Mentally and physically exhausted, I lay there against the wall. Andy cleared his throat after a few minutes, and I lolled my head to the side so I could meet his eyes.

"It wasn't exactly like Harry Potter," I joked. My voice was squeaky and hoarse from all the crying.

"What happened?" he asked.

"I don't want to talk about it," I murmured, closing my eyes.

"What. Happened?"

I frowned and opened my eyes, surprised by the hard tone in his voice. He was still there, kneeling beside me, but the sympathy I'd thought I'd seen in his face was gone. If not gone, then in the background. Somewhere behind the determination. And the anger.

"I told you." I cleared my throat when my voice came out too thick. "I was hired to find a thief." I pointed to Isai. "He's the orig-inal thief." I moved my finger toward Dabria. "She stole it from him." I jabbed my finger in Flint's direction. "He wanted to take it from her."

"And what did they steal?"

I looked away, leaning harder against the wall. "I can't tell you that."

"And you won't tell me who it was stolen from."

I clenched my jaw. "Not won't. Can't."

The sound of knuckles cracking broke the silence as Andy pressed his fist into the floor.

"All right," he said, his voice tight with forced calm. "Can you tell me what they are? I assume they aren't human."

"Wizard, sorceress, *sidhe*." I gestured at each in turn.

"He's a she? So…a transgender person?"

"Not s-h-e. S-i-d-h-e. It's Gaelic. He's a fey."

A soft scribbling snagged my attention, and I caught Andy writing in a little notebook. It almost made me smile. Almost.

"I'm taking them all in," he said, putting the pen and notebook in his pocket. "What precautions do I need to take?"

I stared at him, shoving myself into a sitting position and regretting it as the room spun around me. I leaned back against the wall, but shook my head with as much vigor as I could manage. "You can't take them in. You said it yourself, they're not human. You can't put them in a human prison."

Andy's jaw hardened. "They broke *human* laws."

I bristled at the insinuation. "Not just human laws. The Otherworld has laws too. And that doesn't change the fact that your justice system isn't equipped to handle them."

"You said he's fey, right? Won't cold iron keep him locked up?"

He'd done his research. I wondered if he'd gone the internet route or actually taken the time to find the proper books. Books were always more reliable.

I hesitated then nodded. "It will make it harder for him to use his abilities, yes. But not impossible. He'll still be a danger to everyone around him."

"Then I'll put him in solitary."

I shook my head again. "Andy—"

"What about her?" He pointed to Dabria.

As if sensing she was being discussed, Dabria moaned and shifted on the floor. I smacked my hands on the wet carpet, shoved myself into a higher sitting position, readying my magic. Dabria's breathing evened out and she remained still. Heart pounding, I glanced at Andy. "Do you know how long it's been since you first came in?"

He frowned. "Not that long."

Not a helpful answer. I extended my senses, feeling for the spell Arianne had laid over the sorceress and the fey. Purple energy shrouded them in a cocoon, but the color was pale, a light lavender. The spell was nearing the end of its duration.

"They'll wake up soon. You need to let them go."

Andy gaped at me as though I'd suggested we change our names to Mickey and Minnie and move to Disneyland. "You have to be kidding me. You told me they're both thieves. He's a murderer."

"Taking her in would be an exercise in futility. She could teleport out of there as soon as she regains consciousness. And him?" I shook my head. "Iron or no iron, you don't want to know what he's capable of."

"I have a dead body in this hotel room," Andy said, his voice rising with his temper. "I've already called it in. A team will be here any minute."

I struggled to my feet, grabbing his hand and trying to pull him with me. "We need to leave now. You can meet the team downstairs, stall them. With any luck, by the time you make it up here, they'll be gone."

Andy pulled away from me, his mouth set in a tight line. "Isn't there any way to keep them from doing magic?"

I stared at him and opened my mouth before I even knew what I'd say. Flint stirred, and my heart skipped a beat. "I'm not that powerful," I told him, my voice strained. "We need to get out."

In response, Andy drew his gun and put his back to the wall so he could keep both sleeping suspects in sight. "Is the wizard really dead?" he asked, his voice calm.

I looked at Isai. His face was pale, his body still. The hole in his forehead was small, a sharp contrast to the puddle of his own blood forming a macabre halo around him. The liquid was so thick and so dark that it was nearly black. He was lying close enough to the bed that most of his suit had burned to ashes.

"Yes, he's really dead." *Whether he stays dead or not is another matter.*

"Yes, he's really dead, but...what?"

I blinked. "What?"

"You sound like there's more. A condition. He's dead, but...?"

Damn him and his perceptiveness. "He is dead. But there have been stories of dead wizards coming back."

Andy's throat worked as he swallowed, but it wasn't fear. It was anger. "How?"

I shrugged. "I don't know. I'm not even sure the stories are real or if it's just something wizards claim to make people more afraid to kill them. There's a theory they can use their death curse to fuel a prepared resurrection spell, or they make pacts with necromancers, or—"

I was babbling now, and Andy cut me off with a sharp jerk of his hand. "Enough. I get it, you don't know."

That hurt. Bad enough to be called a witchling by people powerful enough to kill me with the same effort required to swat a fly, but to have a human say it—a human who was supposed to be my friend... I gritted my teeth. "No one can know. Not for sure."

Andy's phone rang, and he answered it without taking his eyes off the suspects. "Room 706."

"You can't take them in!" I protested. "Haven't you been listening?"

He hung up the phone and put it back in his pocket. "I can and

I am. He killed someone,"—he pointed to Flint—"and he shot me." He glared at Dabria. "I don't know how I'll prove she tortured you and robbed someone you won't name of something you won't describe, but I'll worry about that when I get her in interrogation."

I stared at him. "You can't be serious."

"Why not?"

I hardened my jaw and stared down at my clothes, giving myself a few seconds to think. With a few gestures and a whispered word, I mended my ruined shirt. The sleeves closed over my healed arms, hiding the pink skin that had borne third degree burns a few minutes ago. I looked up at Andy, noting the way his eye twitched.

A knock announced Arianne's arrival with two men and two women, all wearing EMS uniforms. The sorceress didn't make eye contact as she strode farther into the room than I knew she was supposed to. I thought I was the only one who noticed her hands moving, heard her whisper the same sleep spell as before. I didn't need my magic senses to tell me she'd renewed the slumber enchantment on Flint and Dabria.

For what good it would do.

Andy spoke to the medical personnel, probably making up some story about why the two suspects were unconscious. They nodded and loaded Flint and Dabria onto two stretchers, one at a time. The room wasn't very large, and they had to pay attention so they didn't run the gurney over the dead wizard, but they managed with impressive efficiency. I stayed out of the way, standing next to the wall beside the chair Dabria had sat in when she'd questioned me, sipping her tea while her pain spell tried to turn my nerves into origami. When the medics were ready to wheel her body out of the room, Andy stepped out of the way, putting him right beside me.

"This is a mistake," I said under my breath. "I'm sorry this is hard for you. I'm sorry you can't treat this as a normal case. You can't arrest the bad guys and lock them up. But that's the way it is. And if you can't accept that, you will drive yourself mad."

Andy turned to face me so he could speak without being overheard, but he didn't turn his back on the bodies. "You're right —this isn't a normal case. And I can't just do what I usually do. But that doesn't mean I let the people responsible for killing an innocent woman go free."

The accusation in his voice rubbed me the wrong way. I knew he was having a bad day—thanks to me—but, blood and bone, I was having a bad day too. "I'm not saying you need to let them go free."

"No? Then what are you saying? Who's going to punish them?"

I snapped my mouth shut. We did have a justice system, and an organization that enforced it—the Vanguard.

But my contract with Anton had specified that I would turn over the name of the culprit to him.

Fresh tears welled up. Something passed through Andy's eyes. Anger. No, not anger. Fury. I took a step back, startled by the intensity of the emotion.

"Why are you so angry?"

At first, I thought he wouldn't answer. His jaw was too tight to allow speech, his breathing so controlled that it sounded painful. He fixed his gaze on me, and it was hard not to look away.

"You used magic on me."

I winced. "I'm sorry. I was only trying to—"

"I just found out there's a whole other world," he continued, his voice hot despite how quiet he was, how careful not to be overheard. "A world full of dangerous people and creatures capable of crimes straight from a cop's worst nightmare."

I groped for my witchy calm, my empathy. "And I know that's disorienting and—"

"*Disorienting* isn't the word," he growled. "It's *terrifying*. But you know what? I thought I could handle it. I thought I could handle it because a man I trusted brought me you. He brought you to my office and told me I could trust you. I could trust you to guide me in this new world, to answer my questions, to help me protect people from these threats I'm just now learning about."

Guilt bit me, hard. I opened my mouth, but he cut me off again.

"You used me," he said, his voice deadly quiet. "You used me, and then when I was no longer convenient for your plan, you used your magic to drug me, and you left me behind."

"Andy—"

"Agent Bradford."

My throat tightened. "Agent Bradford—"

"How the hell am I supposed to trust you now?" he asked. "How am I supposed to believe anything you tell me?"

My neck ached with the need to look away, but I forced myself to keep meeting his eyes. "You would have been killed. Do you understand that? You would have died."

"I risk dying every day I do my job." His voice was tired now, but still angry. "But I do it anyway. I protect myself as best I can against the threats I know are out there, and I do my job."

"You can't protect yourself against what's out there in my world. You're human."

"You're telling me you can't help me. You can't prepare me for what I'll face if I go after these…people?" He took a step closer, forcing me to look up at him. "Tell me, Mother Renard, how did you see this partnership going?"

"Partnership?"

He met my eyes and held them. "Bryan tells me you're a private investigator. And today you asked for my help. I assume you told me about this other world because you anticipate asking for my help in the future?"

I blinked. He was right. "I—"

"I thought so. And how did you see that working? You come to me when you need me to use my resources to get you information, then I sit with my arms folded while you solve the case?"

"I—"

"And when you find out who the bad guy is, maybe you'll tell me or maybe you won't? I'll just have to trust they're being punished?" He stepped closer until a hard breath would have made us touch. "Did you expect me to make excuses for why the cases are never officially closed? Or did you want me to lie or arrest a human to use as a patsy?"

"No!"

My anger stirred, but it had nowhere to go. Andy wasn't wrong. I hadn't thought this out. I'd kept him safe, yes. But I wouldn't have needed to do that if I hadn't used him, put him in danger in the first place.

He seemed to read my thoughts as easily as if they were tattooed on my face. "It's a complicated situation. I know. But complicated doesn't mean you give up, it means you find a way to make it work." He shook his head. "But not without trust."

"You can trust me," I insisted, but the words were weak even to my own ears. "We'll figure it out."

"I'll trust you when you earn it back. Fool me once, and so on." He straightened as agents appeared at the door, two women and a man, all dressed in dark suits and button-down shirts. Cool, analytical gazes swept the room, then they went to work with silent efficiency. It was like watching an army of ants disassemble a picnic.

"I have to speak to them. Stay here," he said quietly. "You're coming in too. We're not done talking."

I nodded. We did have more talking to do. And Goddess help me, I didn't know what to say.

As he turned away from me, I stopped him with a hand on his arm. He looked back at me, and I reached into my hair and felt for the smooth green gem. I dug it out and slipped it into his breast pocket. He tensed and grabbed my wrist.

His mistrust hurt. "It will help protect you from mind tricks," I whispered. "If Flint regains consciousness, you'll need it. It won't stop him, but you should be able to keep your senses enough to notice when he's trying to manipulate you. It will give you a chance to get out." I straightened my spine. "If you can interview him over the phone instead of in person, that's even better. His influence will be stronger in person. A voice manipulator that changes the voice you hear will help too."

He didn't say anything, but let me slip the gem into his pocket.

"If you talk to Dabria, make her keep her hands flat on the table. If she moves her fingers, make her stop. Tape them together if you have to."

"She can't use magic if she can't move her fingers?" He kept his voice low, so he wouldn't be overheard.

"No, she still has magic. But she's not very strong, so she'll be limited. She relies more on magic objects. Search her, and put anything you find in a circle of salt."

He took out his notebook and scribbled notes. "Anything else?"

"Putting a circle of salt around her when you talk to her would be smart."

"What does it do?"

My teacher voice made it easier to speak. Reciting facts, that was all. Educating. "Salt is a natural barrier against magic. It's not foolproof, but it will slow her down."

He nodded.

"You can't hold them in a prison," I said quietly. "I'm not lying about that."

"You'd better not be lying about any of it."

I closed my hands into fists, frustrated and angry, but helpless to do anything right now.

He took a deep breath, then nodded. "Thank you."

The words were sincere, but cold. The thank you of a professional, not a friend. I waited while he spoke to the other agents and watched him give them orders. I thought of the unconscious *sidhe* and sorceress in the ambulance. What would happen when they woke up?

I retrieved my phone and stared down at the screen. I'd signed the contract. Given my word. I closed my eyes and swallowed past the lump in my throat.

Very slowly, I dialed the vampire's number.

CHAPTER 20

"If you ask me, the interview went rather well, all things considered."

I pulled the pillow down harder over my head, trying to block out both the morning sunlight and the voice of the well-meaning pixie. My circadian clock told me it was past nine o'clock, and I couldn't remember the last time I'd slept so late. My to-do list loomed before me, full of duties I should have crossed off by now. But, somehow, I couldn't get out of bed yet.

Andy had kept me at his office for hours last night. He'd questioned me, quizzed me, demanded to learn as much as I could tell him about not just the theft, the murder, but about the suspects. *What is a wizard? What is a fey? What is a sorceress? What are their strengths, their weaknesses?* He'd been a voracious student, and my brain ached from the constant picking and prodding.

"Isai killed Helen Miller, and now he's dead," Peasblossom continued. "Dabria stole the book and she's in jail. Flint was naughty and he's in jail." She walked over the pillow on top of me and sat with a barely perceptible press of down. "You solved the case! Your first case. Solved!" She crawled over the pillow and wedged herself underneath it, toward my face. "Doesn't that make you happy?"

"Five pots of honey says they're already out."

Peasblossom burrowed farther beneath the pillow, invading the shadowy space that was getting too stuffy. "What do you mean?"

"The vampire's lawyers will have gotten them released by now, probably late last night."

I threw off the pillow and hauled myself into a sitting position, wincing as daylight stabbed me in the eyes as punishment for avoiding it this long. I ran a hand through my hair, then groaned as I found it a tangled mess. I hadn't taken the time to undo what Betsy had done, and now it was a mess of knots. Great.

"Really?" Peasblossom asked.

My phone rang as if in answer to her question. I noted the caller ID and the time. Andy. Nine thirty. He'd have discovered his prisoners' absence by now.

"Agent Bradford," I said, not bothering to hide the tiredness from my voice. "Good—"

"They're gone." His voice was hard, clipped. Angry.

I closed my eyes. "I know."

"You know?"

"I guessed."

I could imagine him seething on the other end, shoving a hand through his hair, pulling at his tie. The random thought came to me that Andy had seemed very put together when I'd met him. Calm, cool, and rational. I remembered how he'd taken learning of the Otherworld, seeing his first pixie—an encounter that even Otherworlders didn't always take in stride. A sharp contrast to the nerves and agitation I sensed now. I wondered how much of that was my fault.

Probably all of it.

"Word is the order came from *very* high up—I'm talking one step down from a goddamn presidential pardon."

"You shouldn't say that," I said.

"What?"

"Goddamn. You shouldn't say it."

"A murderer, a thief, and a kidnapper just got sprung from prison and you're lecturing me on religious sensitivity?"

"It's not religious sensitivity, just caution. Some of them have a sense of humor and they'll hear that as an invitation."

Andy made a sound of frustration. "Some of who?"

"Gods."

He drew a deep breath and rustled some papers. "All right," he said. "Let's start over. My prisoners are gone. Not escaped, but released. Released because someone with a lot of political clout, and a lot of money, made calls to get them out."

I nodded, realized he couldn't see me, and said, "Okay."

"All right. Now, that means that someone from the…Other-world…has political ties. Influence. In my world."

I let the "my world" go. Eventually I'd tell Andy about the Blood Realm and its creation, but not right now.

"I need to know who it is," he said. "I need you to tell me who it is."

For a second, just a second, he sounded like he had when he'd first met me. Open, questioning. Trusting me to tell him the truth. Part of my brain must have considered it, considered telling him everything, just for a moment.

At least, the spell on Anton's contract assumed I was considering it.

My throat itched, and that was the only warning I had. A second later, I had the sensation of razor-fine wire wrapping around my voice box, tightening just enough hold my full attention, to get my imagination working on what would happen if it kept getting tighter. It didn't hurt, but it was uncomfortable. And because I knew what it was, it was terrifying.

When the vampire made a contract, he made a contract.

"I can't tell you," I said, my voice strained.

"Won't," Andy snarled.

"Can't," I insisted. I closed my eyes. "The contract I signed wasn't mundane, Agent Bradford. It was magic. I can't tell you what you want to know. At best, I would lose my voice, be unable to tell you."

"And if you wrote it down?"

The wire hummed, constricting just a little. "My best guess is I would die. In a most unpleasant way."

There was silence for several minutes. It dragged on so long that I wondered if he'd hung up, walked away. I stayed on the phone anyway, unable to hang up. I needed to hear his reaction.

"I don't know if I can believe you or not," Andy said. "I don't know if I can believe anything you say."

"That's not fair," I protested. "I've been honest with you—"

"Except for that one spell?"

I pinched the bridge of my nose, hard. "I was trying to keep you safe."

"But you weren't so interested in my safety that you didn't ask me to be there in the first place."

I wouldn't win this argument. I'd done what I'd done to keep him safe, and I still wasn't convinced I'd been wrong about that. But he was right. I shouldn't have risked his life to begin with.

We'll call it a draw.

"Unless you have information you aren't magically prevented from sharing, then I'll say goodbye now," Andy said coolly. "I'll have to find the answer the old-fashioned way."

My heart skipped a beat, a sudden image of Anton's reaction to a persistent and too-observant FBI agent front and center in my brain. "Andy—Agent Bradford, let it go, please. You don't understand who you're dealing with."

"No, I don't, because you won't tell me. But I have an idea. Did you know they had to drag Dabria out of the jail kicking and screaming?"

Yes, I could imagine Dabria's reaction. Considering she had to have figured out who'd posted her bail. And why. My stomach turned and I closed my eyes. That only made the mental image worse, so I opened them again.

"She was terrified. Begged to stay in jail. Then this lawyer looks at her and she just shut up, completely silent. Magic, right?"

"Probably," I said quietly.

"So that's your idea of justice? What happened to her?"

Anger burned inside me then, hot and bright. This was not what I'd wanted. This wasn't what I'd *expected*, dammit. I was not the bad guy here, and I would not be talked to as if I were.

I gripped my phone harder. "No, Agent Bradford," I said, my voice hard. "No, it isn't my idea of justice. But I learned a long time ago that the world doesn't care what my idea of justice is. Sometimes all you can ask for is closure, and that's it. Sometimes you only get half the answers you want."

"Only if you stop trying, stop asking questions," he said.

"Sometimes if you keep asking, you get more answers," I agreed. "And sometimes, you get dead. Or turned to stone. Or transmutated into something small and furry. Or *dead*."

"Goodbye, Shade."

I squeezed my phone as if I could force Andy to stay on the line. "Wait."

He paused. "What?"

I took a deep breath, trying to fight back the emotions warring in my chest enough to speak in a calm, clear voice. This had not gone as I'd planned, true. But I wasn't giving up. I could make a difference, and I could do it following the path I wanted. To do that, I would need help.

"You have a chance to bring closure to people who never would have gotten it otherwise. To solve cases you wouldn't even have begun to understand four days ago. You may not get all the answers you want, but you have a chance to get a whole lot more than you used to." I swallowed hard. "But you have to decide if those answers, that closure, is worth it if it doesn't come with the justice you want. The justice you're used to. You must decide if being able to tell Mr. Miller his wife is dead, and her killer is dead, is worth not being able to point to the murderer and say, 'He did it, and this is how he died.' I think Mr. Miller would rather have those limited answers than none at all."

He fell silent for a long time again, and I dared to hope that he understood, that we were all right. I hoped we would be all right.

"Stay away from Mr. Miller," he said, though his voice was tired more than angry. "I'll make the notification myself. It's my job."

I didn't bother telling him I'd already been to the Miller's house. I'd gone to make sure Helen had moved on, could rest in peace. She had, and though there was a long road of grieving ahead of him, Mr. Miller would be all right.

There was a hesitation, like Andy wanted to say more, and I held my breath, waiting. But then he hung up, and I was sitting there listening to a dead phone.

I slumped back against my pillows, letting the phone fall from my hand. "Well, that's one thing off my to-do list," I said lightly.

Peasblossom harrumphed as she climbed up my arm. "He's being a grouch. Give a little, get a little, that's my motto."

"Since when?"

"Since now. It works better for humans. And witches. I want some honey." She hauled herself up the rest of the way to sit on my shoulder and patted my neck. "He'll come around."

"Perhaps." I sighed and rubbed a hand over my face. Then I smiled at Peasblossom. "I do owe you some honey. You saved my life last night."

Peasblossom tensed, her little face pinching with concern. "I thought I would be too late. I told Arianne there was about to be a non-human fight in your room, and she set the wards, just like you said she would. She headed up to put a stop to it herself, but then she saw Andy stumble off the elevator. When she realized he didn't know where you were and wasn't going up, she dropped the wards and wouldn't put them back. Said she wasn't going to be used so you could fight battles you couldn't win on your own."

I twitched, remembering Dabria's spell, the pain it had traced over every nerve, every muscle. "She wasn't wrong."

"I told Andy something horrible was happening, and I gave him your room number and told him he should demand to go up there." Peasblossom tilted her head. "He's quick for a human. Intimidating, too, in the right light. That is, if you're not used to things with fangs and enough magic to turn you into a toadstool."

I looked at my phone, my chest tight as our conversation replayed itself in my memory. "He's really angry."

"He's frustrated. And he should be." Peasblossom leaned against my neck and snuggled in. "He wants answers, though. And with what he knows now, he knows you're the only one who can give them to him. He'll be back."

Against all reason, I felt better. Maybe Andy wouldn't agree to work with me again because he wanted to, because he respected me. But Peasblossom was right. He wanted answers. He wanted the truth. He would work with me again. And the longer he worked with me, the more he would understand.

I stopped that train of thought before it could turn into something unpleasant, something along the lines of turning a strong FBI agent into a jaded bounty hunter.

"Flint's out of jail," I told Peasblossom.

The pixie perked up, then scowled. "I don't like him anymore. He was going to hurt you."

I patted her head. "Did you get what I asked for from The Cauldron?"

"Yes." She paused. "I don't think that woman likes me. Her eye kept twitching when I was talking."

"What were you talking about?"

"I don't remember *everything* I was talking about," she said. "But I have a hard time believing a random eye twitch could last for two hours."

My eyebrows rose and I hid my mouth with my hand. "Two hours?"

Peasblossom was already flying toward the bedroom door. "I'm hungry and you promised me honey."

I heaved myself out of bed, my outlook on the day improved despite what I knew the evening would bring. I'd left a message for Flint on his voicemail, and if he was out of jail, it meant he'd gotten it by now, gotten my invitation to meet me here at five o'clock. Butterflies swarmed my stomach, a case of anxiety looming on the horizon. I breathed through it and marched to my dresser. I couldn't have a breakdown yet. I had witch duties to perform.

My resolve not to regress to a basket case lasted until four thirty. At which point, I drank two sodas in twenty minutes, ate half a box of strawberry Frosted Mini-Wheats, and downed an entire potion in one desperate gulp. By the time there was a knock at my door, I felt sick, and I wasn't sure if it was nerves or what I'd done to combat my nerves.

I lurched toward the door, moving with all the grace of the newly risen dead. Flint's image was burned on my memory, so it was less of a punch to the gut when I opened the door and saw him standing there in all his glory than it had been the first time.

Less of a punch.

Pale blue jeans and a white shirt. As always, the jeans were snug, but not tight, and the shirt somehow hugged every swell of muscle without looking strained. I had the semi-hysterical thought his clothing might not be mundane either, that it might be enchanted—or, at the very least, created by something less than human. Betsy, perhaps.

"Good evening," he said, his voice as deep and sexy as I remembered.

"Right on time," I murmured. I stepped back. "Please, come in."

The almost-smile never left his lips, as if the upturned corner was meant to hold my attention, draw my eye. And it did. Not so much that I didn't notice the knowing sparkle in his eyes, the way every movement seemed tailored to my benefit.

"I was surprised to get your invitation." He strode across the room, brazenly standing in the same spot he'd been last time, right before he'd...

I gave myself a firm mental shake, my trembling fingers making me regret the amount of caffeine I'd imbibed in the last hour. "You're looking well. How is Anton?"

Flint's smile didn't falter. "I signed. The details are unimportant." He stared into my eyes, watching me as if searching for some hint to my thoughts. "He told me he did not anticipate needing my services anytime soon."

I blinked. "Really?"

"Yes. Immediately following that statement, he informed me that he would keep an eye on your health and wellbeing—and rather pointedly told me there would be no reason for me to check in on you myself."

The trembling in my hands flowed down to my knees, almost spilling me onto the couch. I forced them to straighten and locked them to keep from falling over. Anton had warned Flint to stay away from me. Why did that sound so ominous?

You can have a nervous breakdown later—first, get through this meeting.

"Why do you suppose the vampire is so interested in you?" Flint asked, giving voice to the same question echoing in my head.

"I don't know."

My honesty must have been clear in my voice, because Flint nodded. He didn't look away, though. "I find it...fascinating." His grin broadened. "Of course, the vampire never said I had to ignore an amicable invite from a…friend. It would have been rude for me to ignore you, I think."

I blinked and he was three steps closer. His scent wrapped around me, not a cologne or anything man-made, but a natural, masculine scent. The scent of warm bodies and sunlight, followed by a crisp night breeze and the promise of soft sheets. I lost my voice for a second and stood there like an idiot.

My befuddlement seemed to please him, the cocky jerk. He leaned forward and put his mouth only an inch away from my ear.

"Next time you want to set the bed on fire…we'll do it together, eh?"

This time, my legs gave out. That was just fine with my plan.

I threw my arms around his neck and used my weight and the fact I'd caught him off guard to drag his face to mine. He made a small sound of surprise, but his strong hands closed over my hips, holding me up with the same effort he might have carried a paper cup.

If he smelled good, he tasted heavenly. I opened my mouth, deepening the kiss, chasing that flavor that was uniquely Flint. The *leannan sidhe* growled his approval and dragged my body against him. Hard muscle against soft curves provided a delicious friction that made me squirm. For one dizzying moment, I forgot my plan, forgot the spell hidden against my palm. Something jerked a hair from my head, and I swallowed a gasp of surprise. Rational thought made a valiant comeback, and I realized what had happened.

Thank you, Peasblossom.

I held the words in my head, concentrating on the pixie to keep myself from drowning in sensation. Without breaking the kiss, I slid one arm from around his neck and stroked the side of his face. Rough stubble tickled my palm, telling me he hadn't shaved before coming here. He banded an arm around me, letting me feel his strength—as if I'd needed the reminder. Desire stabbed low in my body, twisting things in a way that did not bode well for rational thought. Flint was gorgeous, and sexy, and a fantastic kisser.

I had no choice.

I laid my palm flat over his cheek, my heart pounding, sweat beading on my forehead. I shoved away the mental picture of what I was about to do and squeezed my eyes shut. With one desperate pull, I broke the kiss and whispered the word to activate the spell in my hand.

Power pulsed from my palm. Flint felt it a second too late, and some part of me preened to think he'd been caught up in the kiss enough for it to slow his reflexes. He released me and took several quick steps back, staring hard at me, at my hands, trying to figure out what I'd done.

I stared at his face, unable to look away despite the fear rising in anticipation of the final result. The magic bled onto his skin in a line of deep indigo ink. The enchantment swirled and thickened, taking form as if molded by unseen hands. A round body, small fangs, eight spindly legs. The ink swelled and contracted, fading in some places and darkening in others. By the time it finished, the flawless shadows and lines made the tattoo look three-dimensional in a way no human artist could have managed.

"Little witch, what have you done?" he asked, his voice calm for someone who had figured out they'd just been the victim of a powerful enchantment.

"I find you threatening in a very sneaky way," I said, my voice strained—and not from desire. "It seems when you're around, my willpower needs a little...help."

I gestured to the couch and the small mirror I'd put there earlier for exactly this moment. Flint looked from me to the mirror then picked it up.

His eyebrows rose as he saw the tattoo of a spider on his right cheek. A spider that looked very real. Very alive. Shiny black body...bright red hourglass on its abdomen.

"A black widow. It's good," he said slowly, his voice a little higher with surprise. "Very good." He frowned at me over the mirror. "I'm not sure I understand?"

"I hate spiders," I managed. It was getting harder to look at him, so I focused on his opposite shoulder.

Flint took a step toward me, and I almost fell over backing away. I felt the first real touch of his power, the first flexing of his will against mine. The potion I'd taken to give me the resistance to get this far wavered and thinned under the pressure. Power caressed my skin like a body-warmed blanket.

"Shade," he said in that bedroom voice. He took a step closer.

I squeaked and stumbled back, skirting the couch to put it between us. My hands shook with the promise of the compulsion that always followed an encounter with a spider. Soon I would be swiping over and over at my head, trailing my hands down my hair, searching for the spider I knew must have dropped on me from the ceiling. There were probably thousands of them up there, hanging down like creeping vines, waiting for me to pass under them.

I couldn't force myself to look at him, risk seeing that thing on his face. Even without looking, even with my eyes squeezed shut, I knew it was there, and that was enough to fill my blood with shards of ice. He raised a hand to cover his cheek, to hide the tattoo that was turning my spine to solid ice. I turned my head farther away, knowing what would happen and desperate not to see it. Not looking didn't save me. My mind was all too willing to provide an image of the spider tattoo scuttling out from behind his hand, baring itself to the world no matter how he tried to hide it.

When Dominique weaves a spell, she weaves a spell.

"I will get this little enchantment off soon," Flint said finally.

The amusement in his voice irritated me enough to give me my voice back. "Good luck with that."

CHAPTER 21

I didn't hide for the rest of the evening. I conducted research. I conducted research underneath a blanket, curled up in the corner of my couch. If it took me two hours to find an office to rent two blocks away from my house, then so what? That was called being thorough.

"Mr. Grey owns that building," Peasblossom said, staring at the screen. "Bet he's not much fun to have as a landlord."

She wasn't wrong. Mr. Grey was infamous in Dresden as a sort of Grinch-meets-probable-serial-killer. A pale man with greasy black hair, pinched features that always looked disgusted, and a hair-trigger temper that had destroyed more than one Christmas display and traumatized countless raccoons.

"It's reasonably priced and two blocks away," I pointed out. "And this is Dresden. Not a lot of offices for rent."

"Then get an office in Cleveland. You'll probably find more clients there anyway."

I'd thought of that too. And my dismissal of the idea had nothing to do with Andy, or the image of his angry face that I couldn't exorcise from my mind. Though he didn't strike me as a

man who got angry easily, so the fact he'd been that mad at me...
Well, I didn't like thinking I'd scared him. And with fury like that,
I had definitely scared him.

"I have a better idea," I countered. "I—"

A sharp knock on the door cut me off. I let my head fall
against the back of the couch for a moment as I mourned the end
of my quiet time, then closed the laptop with a sigh of resigna-
tion. Peasblossom opted to stay under the blanket, leaving me
alone to shake off the chill that came from leaving a good cocoon.

It was harder to shake off the chill that came from finding a
vampire on my doorstep.

Anton was dressed in a dark gray suit with a black button-
down shirt. A cloak the ashy black of a crow's wing hung down
his back to his ankles. It was the wrong time period for the cloak,
and coupled with the business suit, it should have made him look
ridiculous. It didn't.

Blue eyes so pale they were almost silver glittered at me from
the shadows of my front porch, and if a sudden bolt of lightning
had struck the sky behind him, I wouldn't have been the slightest
bit surprised. The gods loved a dramatic entrance, and they lived
for tradition.

Letting go of any pretense of pride, I picked a spot on his
forehead and stared at that one patch of pale skin. My peripheral
vision caught the corner of his mouth tilting up in an almost-
smile, as if I amused him.

"Good evening, Mother Renard. May I come in?"

No! "Um, why don't we talk outside?" I suggested. "It's such a
nice night."

It was, in fact, raining, but the air was only cool, not cold, and
the covered porch offered some protection. Anton inclined his
head in a gentlemanly fashion and gestured for me to have a seat
on one of the two chairs on my tiny porch.

I shook my head. "I'll stand."

"I am not here to harm you."

I hesitated, debating the wisdom of offending the vampire. I should sit down, not make a big deal out of it. An image of Flint's new tattoo crawled across my memory, the image of the all-too-real spider dragging a whimper from my soul that I only just managed to swallow back. "It's not you," I said, my voice hoarse. "I don't sit on porches."

"Because...?"

Spiders. "Just not comfortable."

Truth be told, I didn't like to stand on porches either. Too many outdoor corners, perfect hiding places for eight-legged nightmares. But I could not let this fear make me invite a vampire into my home. Not this vampire.

It wasn't until Anton cleared his throat that I realized I'd been looking all around me, studying the small roof, the narrow ledge created by the window. Searching for arachnids. I flushed and cleared my throat. "How can I help you?"

He watched me a minute longer, and I would have sworn he was reading my mind as if it were the evening paper. Then he nodded toward the garage.

"It seems your people rushed to repair the damage as quickly as possible. That is a testament to how much they value you as their witch."

I followed the gesture, then blinked in surprise. My garage had been repaired. The blackened wood was gone, new wood fastened in its place. Fresh paint made it look bright and new. How had I missed that?

It was late and you were exhausted.

A smile slid over my mouth, and it felt too good to fight. "I guess so." I paused, risking a brief glance at his eyes. "But that's not why you hired me, is it?"

The vampire smiled, and I thought I caught a hint of fang. "The rest of your fee is in your account, as agreed."

I waited, but he didn't continue. "Thank you, but was it necessary to deliver that news personally?"

He tilted his head, considering me. "I find myself without a wizard. I'm offering the position to you."

Shock rocked my system, hitting me hard enough that I almost lowered myself into one of the plastic chairs. Almost. "You're offering me a job?"

"Another one, yes."

"As your...personal witch?"

"Yes."

I laughed. I couldn't help it. I laughed harder than was polite, longer than was smart. I couldn't shake the image of Mother Hazel's face if she found out I'd been offered such a position, much less considered it. Anton raised an eyebrow, and that just made it funnier.

"No," I said when I'd pulled myself together. "No, thank you. I'm happy here."

"As a village witch and private investigator."

"Yes." I nodded, and realized I was smiling. Yes, I was happy. As a village witch and a private investigator. For all the mess I'd made, I'd started down the path I'd wanted for myself for years, and it felt...good.

"Told you she wouldn't take it."

Anton scowled and looked down at his jacket, patting his pockets. I grinned and leaned closer to the source of the voice.

"Dimitri?"

"Good evening, Shade." Dimitri's voice held the same smug amusement as before. "Well done turning my father down. No more chains for you."

"Or you."

He chuckled. "I haven't worn those chains in a long time."

"You'll wear a different chain altogether if you continue to plant your little bugs on my person."

Anton's voice was stern, but there was a glint in his eyes I'd seen from enough parents to recognize. Pride.

"Father, I only want to press you to be the best you can be," Dimitri said. "You must be more observant, more careful. Security is too important to be treated lightly. As your son, it is my duty to protect you as old age claims your mental faculties, and I shall continue to test—"

There was a spark and a faint metallic crunch, and Dimitri's voice cut off. Anton lifted something from his pocket, a small, coin-shaped object no bigger than the pad of my pinkie finger.

"He's a bold one, isn't he?" I observed.

"His mother dotes on him too much. He does not fear me as he should."

Again, the shine in his eyes betrayed his words. He could pretend outrage all he wanted, but his affection for his son was real. And I would have bet his son's audacity and lack of fear for his father was responsible for a good deal of that pride.

Suddenly, the larger implications of his offer struck me. "Wait. You would offer me a position as your witch. But I've been called a witchling more these past few days than in my entire life. I'm nowhere near as powerful as Isai, nowhere near as powerful as any number of witches you could find a stone's throw from your office door. Why would you want me?"

Anton smoothed a hand down the lapel of his suit jacket underneath the cloak. "You have turned down the job. I'm not sure I see that this is relevant."

"The vampire does nothing on a whim. If he brought this woman into his life, he has a reason. She is more than she appears."

Flint's words came back, twisting something in my stomach until nausea spiraled up my throat. Hiring a less-than-experienced PI was one thing. Offering me a job as his personal witch was another. Flint was right. The vampire had a plan I couldn't see. A plan that involved me.

"Why did you hire me?" I gave myself a mental pat on the back for keeping my voice from cracking.

"I already told you why the first time you asked that question." Anton's voice was calm and patient, a parent explaining something simple to a small child. "When I became aware of Mrs. Miller's absence and likely demise, you were already investigating. It seemed logical to—"

"I'd just started," I countered. "I knew next to nothing. You could have gotten someone much more experienced than me. And with the severity of the consequences..." I straightened my spine, trying to muster all the dignity I could while staring at his forehead. "Mother Hazel says you never do anything without a reason. Why did you hire me to find the thief? Why do you want to hire me as your witch?"

Something flickered behind Anton's eyes, but it vanished before I could get up the nerve to look into his gaze to analyze it.

"If I may," he said, "I will paraphrase an...old friend of mine. I cannot see the future, I do not know for certain what will happen. But let us say I suspect you will do...interesting things. I wouldn't want to miss it."

Frustration pulled my hands into fists, and I almost forgot myself and looked into his eyes. "I think you know a lot more than you're telling me. What is it you think I'll do?"

Anton didn't answer, just stepped to the edge of the porch. "Keep following your path, Mother Renard. We will meet again."

"What was in that vault?" I demanded. My heart pounded faster. "*Who* was in that vault?"

He took one step off the porch and vanished.

I glared up at the roof of my porch, certain that if I'd looked a moment ago, I'd have seen the gateway gargoyle.

I was still glaring when headlights swept over my driveway, gravel crunching as a car pulled up to my garage.

"I'm getting no peace tonight," I muttered. I tried to shake off the unease the vampire's visit had left me with, straining to pull my face into something that might resemble welcome. Then I saw who was behind the wheel and my smile faltered.

Mrs. Harvesty waved frantically at me and threw open the door of her small sedan. She was in her late forties and blessed with smooth peach skin and red hair that looked strawberry blonde instead of grayish red, with no help from a bottle. Her face pinched with concern as she scooped a tiny ball of fluff from the passenger seat and hauled it out with all the urgency of someone air-evacuating a shark attack victim.

"It's Majesty," she cried out. "He's sick!"

The rain had stopped, and I met her halfway, pulling on my confident veterinary face. "Tell me what happened."

"We were watching the kids do sparklers in the garage, and he just curled up into a ball and wouldn't move. He didn't respond to my voice, and when I tried to lift him up, he didn't react. He hasn't made a sound for hours!"

She was cuddling him to her chest, but I didn't touch him yet. I watched him, noting the steady rise and fall of his little body. "He seems to be breathing fine," I said. "Maybe the sparklers scared him?"

Mrs. Harvesty shook her head. "No, no, that's not it. Mr. Jackson set off a load of fireworks last year, complete with a finale. Majesty loved them, chased the colors like he could catch one of the sparks. Sparklers wouldn't scare him."

"I think you're thinking of a different cat," I said gently. Goddess knew she had enough of them. "Majesty's just a kitten—he can't be more than a few months old."

Mrs. Harvesty froze. I reached out to pet Majesty, watching him to see if he reacted with pain.

She jerked him away, the blood draining from her face and leaving her as white as the vampire who'd just left. "You're right," she said. "It was just the sparklers. I'll just get him home. I'm sure he'll be fine."

Suspicion drew my attention to the woman's face, the lines

around her eyes and the sudden anxiety tightening her features. She backed away, her spine tensing as she prepared to turn and run back to her car.

"Mrs. Harvesty."

I used what Mother Hazel called a witchy voice, the tone sharper and more commanding than my usual manner. It was meant to grab attention and arrest movement. And it did. Mrs. Harvesty halted, stood there unmoving, as surely as if I'd thrown a net over her. Fear widened her eyes.

"Let me see Majesty," I said quietly.

"I'm sure he's fine," she whispered.

I held out my hands. Mrs. Harvesty was shaking now, and whatever was going on, I didn't want to upset her. Reaching into the well of power inside me, I poured a little magic into my voice. "It's all right, Mrs. Harvesty. Let me hold him. Everything will be fine."

A tear slid down her cheek as she put the little furball in my hand.

Magic bit my skin, hard. I hissed, but didn't drop the kitten. The energy snapped against my flesh everywhere it touched me, like trying to hold the end of a live wire. I took a deep, steadying breath, and drew a spell over his fur with my free hand, whispering the words to banish some of that excess magic.

The pain receded and the kitten slumped in my hand, not unconscious, but exhausted. The magic was still there, still strong, but it was a soft orb of magic now, not the hissing, sizzling fireball it had been.

I met Mrs. Harvesty's eyes, and it was difficult to keep the anger from my voice. "What have you done?"

The tears were flowing now, and she clapped a hand over her mouth to muffle a sob. "I didn't want him to die. They always die, don't they? I just lost Princess, I couldn't lose her son too. He was the only one that lived."

Mrs. Harvesty was very good with cats, but when you took

care of twenty at a time, you were bound to be surrounded with the unique pain of a pet's death. I knew that last year she'd had a bad run—six cats dying within days of each other. And I'd known it hit her hard, made her stop adopting new cats for a while. But I hadn't realized how deep her pain had gone. What it would drive her to do.

"What did you do?" I asked again, gently this time.

"I...I just wanted him to stay young. To stay healthy. She said it could be done."

I closed my eyes, dread tightening my stomach like the fist of a toddler trying to keep a piece of candy from being taken away. "You took him to a sorceress."

She nodded, too fast. "I asked Mother Hazel, but she wouldn't do it. I thought you were her apprentice, so you wouldn't do it either, so I went to Akron and I... I found someone to do it."

I didn't want to know how she'd found a sorceress. If your mind was open to the Otherworld, it wasn't hard to notice Otherworldly happenings. And it wasn't hard to follow them, to ask the right questions to find someone who could do what you wanted. But it was very, very dangerous.

"Majesty is hurt," I said, keeping tight hold of my temper. "The...spell on him is..." I had to stop and remind myself to breathe. I was so angry. Heat flamed in my cheeks, in my stomach. "It's hurting him."

She broke down into sobs. I didn't have it in me to comfort her though. Not when I could feel the pulse of magic threatening to take over the tiny kitten in my hand.

"I understand why you did this," I said. "But no one—human or animal—lives forever. People die, Mrs. Harvesty. Cats die. It hurts, but that pain is a sign that their life meant something." I held the kitten close to my chest, wincing at the throb of energy inside its downy-soft body. I didn't know what spell had been used on him, but to keep something from dying was no easy feat. And this spell wasn't just making him live forever—it was keeping him young. Keeping him from growing. And all that energy that should have gone into aging, into living, into getting older...it had nowhere to go. Eventually, it would have to go somewhere.

"Mrs. Harvesty, I will keep Majesty. I will do what I can to help him."

"Oh, can't I keep him?" She sobbed. "I'll take care of him. I won't try—"

"No. He's in pain, and I need to help him. And it won't be easy."

I hadn't needed to add that last part, but she had to understand how bad it was. How serious what she'd done was. I needed to know she wouldn't do this again.

She nodded, her brief resistance crumbling as she looked at the still kitten. "All right." Her shoulders sagged and she turned like someone going to their death instead of their car.

"Who did the spell and what did they charge you for it?" I called after her. If I was going to help the kitten, I needed more information. Even if I suspected I wouldn't like the answers.

She stopped and turned. "I don't remember her name...but I have it written down somewhere."

I nodded, a lump rising in my throat as I waited for an answer to the second part of my question. "Find the name and call me. And how did you pay for it?"

She shook her head. "There was no charge."

My blood ran cold, and if I hadn't been so very aware of how important it was for me to stay strong in front of Mrs. Harvesty, I would have crumpled to the ground. There was always a price for magic. Always. Either Mrs. Harvesty was lying—and I didn't think she was—or the person who'd done the spell had an ulterior motive.

I looked down at the gray and black furball snuggled against my chest. What could someone possibly gain from putting a spell that strong on this little feline?

The sound of a car door closing with all the energy of a sloth drew my attention back to Mrs. Harvesty, and I watched her put on her seatbelt and back out of my driveway. She looked like a zombie, the life leached out of her as she left behind one of her furry children. I made a mental note to call her daughter—her human daughter—and ask her to sit with her mum.

A weight landed on my head, and Peasblossom leaned over. "I hate cats," she reminded me.

I looked down at the little kitten curled up in the crook of my arm. "She had him spelled to stay young. The spell is powerful, and it's hurting him. He needs our help."

Peasblossom made a doubtful sound, then crawled down my arm. Inch by inch, she moved a little closer until she was peering into the furry face from a pixie's arm away. Her face softened. "He does look a little weak, doesn't he? Probably couldn't jump onto the bed to reach me even if you let him out of your sight long enough to try."

I nodded and turned to the house. "He'll be fine. We'll figure it out." I paused when I noticed a package by the door. A small brown box sealed with black packing tape, nestled under one of the plastic chairs. "I didn't order anything."

Paranoia was just forming the word "bomb" on my tongue, when Peasblossom zipped for the package in a pink streak of light. "Oh! It's here!"

Relief washed over me, and I followed her to the porch and snagged the package from under the chair—after checking to make sure no spiders had crawled onto it. "What is it?"

"A present for you! Open it."

I did. Inside was a name plaque, the sort that sat on a desk. It read, *Shade Renard, P.I.* My heart swelled. "Oh, Peasblossom. Thank you."

She flew up to stand on my shoulder and gave me a one-armed hug. "I always knew you would do it," she whispered.

We stood like that, looking down at the plaque and thinking

of the case. Wallowing in our success. After a few blissful minutes, Peasblossom spoke again, her voice soft.

"I used your credit card."

*****

Time to meet the local pack… Continue with Blood Trails #2!

ABOUT THE AUTHOR

USA Today bestselling author Jennifer Blackstream is...odd. Putting aside the fact that she writes her own author bio in third person, she also sleeps with a stuffed My Little Pony that her grandmother bought her as a joke for her 23rd birthday, and she enjoys listening to Fraggle Rock soundtracks whether or not her children are in the car.

Jennifer makes it a point to spend at least one night a week with her sibling binge-watching whatever show they're currently plowing through, and she ferociously guards quality time with her son and daughter. She cooks when she has the sanity for it and tries very hard not to let her arachnophobia keep her out of her basement on laundry day.

Jennifer's influences include Terry Pratchett (for wit), Laurell K. Hamilton (for sexual tension), Jim Butcher (for roguish flair), and Kim Harrison (for mythos). She is currently writing the series of her heart and her dreams, the series that has been percolating in her brain for the last decade...Blood Trails. An Urban Fantasy Mystery series that will combine the classic whodunit spirit with a contemporary fantasy setting. Expect mystery, magic, and mayhem, with characters that will make you laugh, cry, and stare at the screen with your jaw hanging down to the floor. Well, that's how they affect Jennifer anyway...

DID YOU FIND A TYPO?

I hate typos. Really, they upset me on a deeply emotional level. If you find a typo in one of my books, please contact me through my website at www.jenniferblackstream.com. I have a monthly drawing in which I pick a name from those who have submitted typos, and I award said winner with a $25 gift certificate.

Death to typos!

JB